Drought Season
Over

Drought Season Over

The Sequel

Keith L. Bell

To order additional copies of this book, contact:
Xlibris
1-888-795-4274
www.Xlibris.com
Orders@Xlibris.com
774982

"If I Could"

If I could do anything in the world once, just one time, I would probably take a trip to Europe to visit Romania or to Italy to check out the old Roman Empire of Rome. Yeah, that sounds like royalty. But there must be something more superior than visiting Europe and Italy right? So…

If I could do anything in the world once, just one time, I would probably kick it with the president of the United States of America or instead of landing on the moon I'll land on the sun. But I couldn't do that because ill burn to death before I got there so ill shoot for the stars and become star struck, literally. Now that's extraordinary! But still, there must be something even more extravagant than that, so…

If I could do anything in the world once, just one time, I would probably climb the highest mountain ever or scuba dive to the deepest part of the sea to see what's really down there or pass through the Bermuda Circle to see what's really on the other side. Now that's adventurous! But still there must be something more promising, so…

If I could do anything in the world once, just one time, I would probably end all poverty and feed every hungry stomach in the world. Or I would probably rewind the hands of time and go back a million years to when God first created the Heavens and Earth and help Him bring the universe into existences. Yeah now that's promising and probably what I'll do!!

But nothing I said in this poem was definite. Everything had "**probably**" in front of it. So if I could "**definitely**" do anything in this world once, just one time, I would bring my mother back. If it was only for a day, an hour, a minute I would bring my mother back. If it was only to hug, hold and kiss her I would bring my mother back. If it was to only say the things that was left unsaid or to do the things that was left undone I would bring my mother back. Yeah that's exactly what I'll do. "If I could" I'll bring my mother back. –

Keith L. Bell

Prologue

After Kilo's eyes adjusted to the lights in the room he seen that he wasn't the only person tied up. Sitting on his left was Quick and on his right was Fresh then Slim. Seeing his niggas tied up Kilo already knew what this was about and the four Puerto Ricans that was standing in front of them clarified it all. *'Pedro.'* Kilo thought. *'He wasn't feeling Slim tryna get out the game.'* Pedro emerged from behind the four Puerto Ricans with a look of depression on his face. Taking a few steps forward Pedro said something in Spanish and his men left the room. Once Pedro seen that his men was gone he knelt down in front of Kilo, Slim, Fresh and Quick and looked them all in the eyes before he spoke. "I'm sure everyone knows what this is about so there's no need in me saying." Pedro said looking off and out the hotel window. Over the years of doing business with Kilo and them Pedro grew to like them on a personal level which made this hard for him. "I talked to my brother about this and he didn't agree with letting Slim walk." Pedro said then stood up and walked over to the window. "He said he told you that the consequences of leaving the Cartel would be death and that there are no other options. So now he wants me to kill not only you but your families as well." Hearing Pedro speak about José wanting to kill their families made Kilo's stomach turn. Sorrow and sadness is what Slim felt knowing that it was his fault that him and his niggas was tied up in the first place. Slim wanted to tell Pedro that it was his life that he should take instead of his niggas since he was the only one trying to get out of the game but the duct tape that covered his mouth stopped him. Quick sat there thinking about all the wrong he done in the streets and figured that he was reaping what he sowed while Fresh was still trying to figure out what was going on. "But I'm not going to do it." Pedro said. "I feel that your families have nothing to do with it this so therefore they shouldn't be killed." Pedro didn't want to keep talking to them like everything was going to be okay knowing that he was about to take their life so he told them that if it was up to him none of this would have happened then kissed them all on the forehead and left the room. Two of Pedro's henchmen came back into the room a few minutes after Pedro left and riddled Kilo, Quick, Slim and Fresh bodies with assault rifles killing them instantly which caused the states to experience "The Longest Drought Ever...."

Chapter 1

Ten Years Later

"Keon!" Kenya yelled banging on Lil Kilo's door. "I know you hear me knocking on this door! Now get up before you're late for school." Kenya kept banging and yelling. Lil Kilo was now 18 years old and a senior in High School and was about to graduate in a couple of months. "Fuck school!" Is the attitude Lil Kilo had after his father was killed which caused him to fell his Freshman year. *"Get your education son..."* Lil Kilo heard his daddy tell him one night while dreaming and that was all the motivation Lil Kilo needed to get back on track and become a straight A student although he was the only 18 year old student in the school. "I'm up ma, dang! You beating on my door like I'm deaf or something. I heard you the first time." Lil Kilo said stretching and yawing at the same time. "Boy I know you not getting smart. I'll come in there and knock some manners into your ass. Keep on." Kenya said dusting some imaginary lent off her uniform. "I ain't getting smart ma. I was just tellin' you that I was up." "Well you need to take some of that bass out your voice and lower your tone.

I'm on my way to work. Breakfast is on the table. I'll see you when I get home, okay." Kenya said. "Aite ma love ya." Lil Kilo said getting out the bed. "I love you to baby. Now get on up." After taking a shower and putting on a fresh pair of 501 Levi jeans and a brand new white Polo collared shirt Lil Kilo grabbed his wheat colored Timberland boots from out his closet and slid them on. "I can't wait 'til it get hot outside!" Lil Kilo said to his self standing in front of the full length mirror he had in his room. Pulling his dreads back into a ponytail Lil Kilo grabbed one of the chains he got from his daddy when he was younger then headed downstairs to see what his momma cooked for breakfast. Not really having an appetite for the pancakes his mother cooked Lil Kilo tossed them in the trashcan. *I'll stop by Micky Dee's on my way to school.* Lil Kilo thought while pulling his hoody over his head hearing his cell phone ring and knew exactly who was calling from the ringtone. "What up nigga?" Lil Kilo answered. "What's up fool, you goin' to school?" "Yeah I'm leavin' out the door now. You got something rolled up?" "Fa show. But stop and get Lil Fresh before you come get me." Lil Slim said breaking some weed down so he could roll a blunt for them to smoke on their way to school. Since Lil Kilo was a little older than Lil Slim and Lil Fresh he was able to drive being that he had his licenses. Lil Kilo was the only person driving to High School in a hundred thousand dollar car. The principal wasn't even driving a car with that kind of price tag on it. "How are you able to afford a Porsche Panamera coupe?" The principal asked Lil Kilo one day after school. "Damn you nosey." Lil Kilo told his principal. When Lil Kilo's daddy got killed the government tried to seize everything that belong to him but couldn't because there was a money trail showing legal revenues of where the money came from for his purchases even though most of his purchases was made with drug money. Kenya was back and forth in court for almost six months fighting for everything that belonged to Lil Kilo's daddy until one day her lawyer which happened to be her best friend found a will that his daddy left behind giving all rights over to his son for everything he owned once he died so Kenya didn't have to fight to hard for Lil Kilo's daddy's possessions. "Aite well call that nigga and tell him I'm bout to pull up." Lil Kilo said leaving out the house locking the door behind him. After picking Lil Fresh up who looked and acted just like his daddy before he was killed the two swung by Lil Slim's house to pick him up then made their way to school smoking the blunt of purple dro Lil Slim had listening to NBA Youngboy new mixtape. School was nothing but a fashion show for Lil Kilo, Lil Slim and Lil Fresh. All the attention was on them when they pulled up and walked the halls. They were the most popular kids at the school which made everybody want to be cool with them but the three kept their circle tight. "Hey Lil Fresh…" Is what you heard 70% of the time a female spoke to them. When it came to running game on a female Lil Fresh had a mouthpiece out of this world. It seemed like every time he approached a girl in the hallway she went for whatever line he tossed at her. Half of the girls in the school knew about him messing around with other girls but that didn't stop them from handing over them digits. Lil Slim was more of the cautious and conservative type when it came to sleeping with the girls that went to school with them mainly because he knew that Lil Fresh was knocking them down with ease. When it came time for Lil Kilo to pick something he liked he always went for the females with the most class or the captain of the cheerleading squad or the pretty girl that seemed to always work in the office. "Man ya'll ain't gone believe who I was jokin' with after class and asked her to let me take her out and show her a good time and she agreed to it." Lil Kilo said walking up on Lil Slim and Lil Fresh after third period. "Who Sarah dooty ass?" Lil Fresh said talking about the prettiest senior in the school. "Nawl not Sarah. I already had her fool. She old news. I played her my sophomore year." Lil Kilo said giving both Lil Fresh and Lil Slim some dap. "Who you talkin' bout then nigga? Cause it ain't too many bitches in here that I ain't hit already." Lil Fresh said trying to think of another pretty girl in the school. "Ms. Brown." Lil Kilo said grinning. "Ms. Brown? You talkin' bout the 12th grade English teacher Ms. Brown?" Lil Slim asked. "Yeah that Ms. Brown. She gave me her number and everything and told me to call her Saturday any time before 7." Lil Kilo said showing them the piece of paper Ms. Brown wrote her number on. "If you fuck Ms. Brown I'll tip my hat to you fool. But Ion think she goin' like that. She too fye and too much of a woman." Lil Fresh said opening his locker throwing his books in there then shutting it back. "Get ready to tip yo hat then nigga cause I'm showl bout to try to hit that thang. It's lunch time tho. What they got in the cafeteria?" Lil Kilo asked. "Nothin' worth eatin'. Let's hit the Chicken Shack right quick." Lil Fresh said. "Nigga ain't you tired of eatin' there every day for lunch? I know I am." Lil Slim said leaning against the lockers pulling his phone out. "Nigga I'm from the hood. I'll never get tired of eatin' chicken." Lil Fresh said back. "Let's swing by Ms. Cook's and grab a plate from there. I gotta taste for some soul food. Besides, yo granny be havin' all type of lil college broads up in there round this time." Lil Kilo told Lil Slim. The three headed outside to the parking lot where half the school was either hanging out or getting into their cars going to get them something to eat for lunch as well. "Hey Keon!" One of the cheerleaders said as Lil Kilo was passing her car. "What's up Kora?" Lil Kilo said giving her the head nod. "Man I think Kora wanna give a nigga some pussy." Lil Kilo said after they passed her car. "Why you say that fool?" Lil Fresh wanted to know. "Cause she always flirtin' and shit givin' me that "I want you look." Lil Kilo said. "Don't she know you fuck with Neka?" Lil Slim asked hopping in the front seat of Lil Kilo's whip. "Who don't know I fuck with Neka?" Lil Kilo said after he got in and started his car. "I thought they were like cuzzins or something." Lil Fresh said. "Nawl they just cool but the way Kora be eyein' a nigga I can tell she don't care bout none of that." Lil Kilo said pulling out the school parking lot. Sitting inside Ms. Cook's restaurant Lil Slim's grandmother owned the three talked shit about who was getting the most pussy in school while they waited on their food. Lil Kilo and Lil Slim didn't want to admit that Lil Fresh was the one getting layed the most so the debate kept going. After eating and going back to school for the reminder of the day the three left school and headed over to Lil Kilo's house where they smoked blunt after blunt playing NBA 2K on Lil Kilo's PS4. "Man ya'll niggas can't fuck with me at this shit!" Lil Slim said beating Lil Fresh with the Warriors. "Nigga you got lucky. I'm tired of playin' anyway." Lil Fresh said setting the controller down and falling back on Lil Kilo's bed. "You just sorry nigga! I would be tired of playin' to if I ain't won a game. Now sit back and watch some pros go at it." Lil Kilo said grabbing the controller. "Man ya'll niggas ain't no pros." Lil Fresh said staring up at the ceiling. "I'm about to walk around Cheri's house because she's the pro." Lil Fresh said then called Cheri to make sure she was home. "Man you gone catch something fuckin' Cheri. Everybody 'round this bitch done hit that." Lil Slim said picking the Warriors again. "That's why I don't fuck her nomo. I just be doggin' her head. She a beast with it!" Lil Fresh said getting up grabbing his jacket. "That ain't gone stop you from catchin' whatever she got tho nigga! You can still catch that shit gettin' head fool." Lil Kilo said. But that didn't stop Lil Fresh he went anyway only because he made Cheri take a test a few weeks ago. "That nigga crazy!" Lil Kilo said after Lil Fresh left. "All that nigga think about is pussy! I don't care how cute a bitch is, ain't no pussy worth diein' for." Lil Slim said. "Speaking of pussy, you think Ms. Brown gone let you hit that?" Lil Slim asked Lil Kilo. "Ion know. I forgot all about Ms. Brown givin' me her number. I'm glad you said something tho cause I need to hit the mall. You wanna go?" Lil Kilo asked Lil Slim pausing the game. "Yeah I'll roll with cha. I need to get me some mo' kicks anyway." On the way to the mall Lil Kilo was thinking about where he was going to take Ms. Brown to eat while Lil Slim sat on the passenger side in a whole nother world. "What you thinkin' bout over there?" Lil Kilo asked already knowing the answer. Anytime Lil Slim was in deep thought like he was Lil Kilo knew that he was either thinking about his daddy or his sister that was killed when they were younger. Almost twelve years ago Lil Kilo and Lil Slim mothers took them to the State Fair and on the way home somebody shot their car up and one of the bullets hit Lil Slim's twin sister in the chest and killed her. Lil Slim didn't know why she was killed until he was old enough to put two and two together from the stories his mother told him and the ones he heard about who his daddy was. "I'm just tryna figure out how come don't nobody know who killed my daddy, yo daddy or Lil Fresh daddy and they ran the city. Somebody 'pose to know something." Lil Slim said. "Ima find out who did this and I don't care what it takes!" After walking around the mall for two and a half hours the two left with more cloths and shoes then they intended on buying then swung through the hood to buy some more weed from Big Ed an old school cat that kept the best weed around who they nick named Ol' Man Ed. "What's up youngstas?" Big Ed said as Lil Slim and Lil Kilo was let into his weed spot. "Nothin' much. What's up with cha Ol' Man?" Lil Kilo said sticking his fist out for some dap. "Same shit, you know hangin' and slangin' tryna stack some change. Don't much change around here." Ol' Man Ed said then gave Lil Slim some dap. "I feel ya. But what you got for us to smoke?" Lil Kilo asked. Big Ed told them that he had some cool lil mid-grade weed right now and that he was waiting on a shipment of Kush to come in. "Some mid? What it smoke like?" Lil Slim asked. "It burn good. I been smokin' on it for the last two days." Big Ed said pulling out a sack to let them see what the weed looked like. "It look and smell aite. What you want for a lil quarter of some of this?" Lil Kilo asked sticking his nose in the sack again. "Twenty five a quarter and a hunnit a zip but I'll fuck with ya'll for eighty." Big Ed said grabbing a ounce of the weed that was already bagged up off the table. "Aite let us get that." Lil Kilo told Big Ed then asked him to split it in half for them. Lil Kilo and Lil Slim left Big Ed's and stopped at the corner store to grab some cigars and bumped into some older cats from their hood that use to sell dope for their daddy. At least that's what they was told. "What's up Cutt?" Lil Kilo said walking into the store. "What's good lil one?" Cutt responded. "Not shit funa get me some gars so I can fill my lungs. What's up Ben?" Lil Kilo spoke to the other nigga that was with Cutt. "Slow motion lil nigga. What ya'll smokin' on?" Ben asked. "Some lil mid Big Ed got 'round there." After hollering at Cutt and Ben Lil Kilo and Lil Slim got their cigars and left the hood headed over to Lil Slim's house to chill for a second. "I think I've found out how to find out who killed our daddy fool." Lil Slim said sitting on the edge of his bed rolling a blunt. "I've been thinking about it for a while now." It wasn't a day that went by that Lil Slim wasn't contemplating on a way to find out who killed his daddy. "How?" Lil Kilo asked sitting in front of Lil Slim's computer on Facebook. Lil Slim finished rolling the blunt and fired it up before he spoke. "I been thinkin' bout sellin' dope." Lil Slim said inhaling a big cloud of smoke. "Sellin' dope? How is sellin' dope gone help us find out who killed our daddy fool?" Lil Kilo asked taking his eyes off the computer screen to look at Lil Slim to make sure he was serious. Lil Slim explained to Lil Kilo how he planned to start at the bottom of the game to learn the ends and outs then after a while take some of the money his daddy left behind to find a connect. "I see where you goin' with this but then again I don't. I mean how is finding a connect gone help us find out who killed our daddy?" Lil Kilo asked grabbing the blunt from Lil Slim. "Think about it." Lil Slim said. "It's not just any connect that can help us. It's the size of the connect that will be able to help." Lil Kilo looked at Lil Slim like he was crazy. "You startin' to lose me now fool. What you talkin' bout not just any connect and the size of the connect and all that?" Lil Kilo said. "If our daddies ran shit like the streets say they did, I mean from state to state then whoever they was gettin' the dope from had to be even bigger than they was. You following me?" Lil Slim asked taking a hit from the blunt that Lil Kilo passed back. Lil Kilo was still confused. "Just break it down for me." Lil Kilo finally said. Lil Slim broke it down and Lil Kilo understood exactly what Lil Slim was trying to do. "Man why you didn't just say that at first! You had me reckin' my brain tryin' to figure out what the hell you was talkin' bout. All you had to say was "We gone start off at the bottom to get the feel of things then use our money to buy a connect and hopefully that connect know something about our daddy gettin' killed since they was the next best thing to the mob." Lil Kilo said. "Exactly! And it ain't no tellin' who a nigga gone meet startin' off at the bottom that knew our daddy. We might be able to find out who did it from the street gossip. What you think?" Lil Slim asked Lil Kilo. Lil Kilo thought about what Lil Slim was saying and even though he didn't totally agree with everything he felt that Lil Slim's idea might work. "I think that might work. But what we gone do just go post up on the block with a bag of dope? Them niggas might not go for that fool. Besides don't neither one of us know how to sell the shit." Lil Kilo said. "I ain't worried bout them niggas and sellin' dope can't be that hard.

We'll catch on eventually." Lil Slim said then told Lil Kilo
that it wasn't all about the money so it was okay to lose a little.
Lil Kilo wanted to find out who killed his daddy just as bad
as Lil Slim did and told him that he would be right there by
his side when they found out. "I'm with you homie. But what
about Lil Fresh, you think he wit it?" Lil Kilo asked. "Yeah I
think Lil Fresh will roll with the punches because his daddy
was killed to." Lil Slim said passing Lil Kilo the blunt back.
"That weed right there ain't strong enuff tho. I need some of
that shit that's gone burn my chest and make a nigga cough."
Lil Slim said talking about the mid they got from Big Ed. "I
was thinkin' the same thing. This that amateur weed." Lil
Kilo said laughing. Lil Kilo and Lil Slim sat and talked about
how they could get in the game and how they was going to
get their hands on some dope until Lil Slim's mother came
home and interrupted them. "Issac!" Lil Slim heard his
mother yell from downstairs. "Mam!" Lil Slim hollered back
down the steps. "I was just checking to see if you was up there.
Have you ate yet?" Lil Slim mother asked walking up the
stairs. "Yes mam. Me and Lil Kilo stopped and got us
something." Lil Slim said. Lil Slim's mother got to the top of
the stairs and stood in his doorway then sniffed the air. "What
did I tell you about smoking that stuff in my house? If you're
going to smoke you need to find you someplace else to do it!"
Lil Slim's mother snapped. "I tried to tell him Ms. Ivonne but
he don't listen. I said Issac you know we not 'pose to be
smokin' in here. He said man you sound like my momma."
Lil Kilo said spinning back around in the computer chair so
that Lil Slim's mother couldn't see the smile on his face. "Boy
stop lying before I come over there and knock you upside your

head." Lil Slim's mother told Lil Kilo. "Where is your momma at anyway? Kenya haven't called me all day." Lil Slim's mother said wanting to laugh at what Lil Kilo just said. "She should be at home. I talked to her a few hours ago and she said that she was leavin' work early for something." Lil Kilo said. "Well I'm about to call and let her know about this." Lil Slim's mother said. "Man momma you always talkin' bout you funa let somebody know something." Lil Slim said knowing that his mother was all talk. "Aw I am." Lil Slim's mother said pulling out her cell phone. "Well you still haven't let me know when you gone take me to get my licenses so I can get me a car." Lil Slim said. "Boy I ain't thinking about you or a car right now. I told you whenever I got time I will take you. Now don't start worrying me." Lil Slim's mother said walking off talking to Lil Kilo's mother on the phone. "Ima have Lil Kilo take me then." Lil Slim said to his mother's back. "Man yo momma cool as hell. She kinda remind me of my momma sometimes." Lil Kilo said. "Yeah they act just alike if you ask me. The only difference is yo momma look better." Lil Slim said knowing that Lil Kilo didn't like when he made comments about how cute his mother was. "Don't let yo mouth get you tied into a knot in here fool! You know I don't play them momma games." Lil Kilo said. Lil Kilo outweighed Lil Slim by fifteen pounds easily and liked to put him in wrestling moves that he couldn't get out of. "You ain't gone do nothin' but try to grab a nigga. You don't wanna see these hands." Lil Slim said knowing that he was quicker than Lil Kilo with his hands and that was proven a few months ago when Lil Slim bought some boxing gloves to prove his point. "Forget all that." Lil Kilo said. "Tomorrow after school we gone holla at

Cutt to get us some dope to post up with." The next day Cutt was nowhere to be found. Feeling like Cutt was their only go to guy to get the dope from since he claim to have done business with their daddies Lil Kilo and Lil Slim decided to wait until they seen him to buy some dope instead of going elsewhere. "Out of all the days to not be in the hood this fool choose today not to be. I bet if we wasn't lookin' for his ass we would've seen that nigga a hunnit times by now." Lil Slim said as Lil Kilo was pulling into the gas station to get some gas. "Ain't no tellin' where that nigga at. Call Big Ed and see if he got his number. He might know it." Lil Kilo said getting out the car. "And see if that nigga got some Kush in. That mid shit ain't nothin'!" After paying for and pumping the gas the two headed over to Big Ed's spot to get them some Kush to smoke and to meet up with Cutt. "So he said he was goin' to meet us there?" Lil Kilo asked pulling off from the gas station. "Yeah. He said he was right around the corner from Big Ed's spot and to just call him when we pulled up." Lil Slim said. Lil Kilo and Lil Slim pulled up at Big Ed's spot 15 minutes later and seen that Cutt was already there. "Go get the weed from Ol' Man Ed while I hop in the car with Cutt to see what this nigga talkin' bout." Lil Kilo told Lil Slim. Hopping in the car with Cutt Lil Kilo didn't waste any time telling Cutt what him and his niggas was trying to do. "What's good lil nigga?" Cutt said giving Lil Kilo some dap after he got in the car. Lil Kilo looked Cutt dead in the eyes. "I'm tryin' to get my hands on something." Lil Kilo told Cutt who was reaching for the blunt that was sitting in the ashtray. Cutt stopped reaching in mid air and looked up at Lil Kilo and said "Something like what? I ain't puttin' no gun in your hand for you to do something stupid with." Cutt said reaching in his pocket for a lighter to fire his blunt up. "Who you havin' problems wit?" Cutt asked wondering what type of trouble Lil Kilo was in. Lil Kilo chuckled. "Ion need a gun. I need some work." Lil Kilo said. "Some work?" Cutt said not really believing what he just heard Lil Kilo say. "What you funa do with some work? I know you don't plan on hittin' the block?" Cutt asked with a little more aggression than he intended. "Ima keep it real Cutt...this shit bigger than me just hittin' the block. I ain't doin' this shit cause I want to." Lil Kilo said looking back over at Cutt who was all ears. "I'm doing this shit because I have to!" Lil Kilo said. "And it ain't about the money either." Cutt thought about what Lil Kilo was saying and read between the lines. *This must have something to do with his daddy.* Cutt thought then took another pull from the blunt, blew the smoke out slowly then chose his words carefully. "I catch yo drift lil homie and see where you goin' with this. But Ima tell you straight up that there ain't no love in these streets and ain't nothin' nice about them either. It's nothin' but hatred and jealousy in these streets. Niggas hate to see another nigga winnin'." Cutt told Lil Kilo passing him the blunt hoping that he was soaking up the game he was giving him. "Yo own partna will be the one to set you up. And keep these bitches...you gotta keep them out yo bizniz they'll pull yo dick just cause you shinin' and turn they brother on to rob you at the same time." Lil Kilo sat there taking everything in that Cutt was saying. "Just let me know what you tryna do and I'll see that it gets done." Cutt said grabbing the blunt back from Lil Kilo. Cutt felt that if he could help find out any information on who was behind killing Lil Kilo's daddy then he was down for the cause because it's been ten years and there's still no word on who killed him. "Aite well I'ma call you in bout a hour to let you know how much work I'm tryin' to get. How much is it for the whole brick?" Lil Kilo asked knowing that money wasn't going to be the problem. "Right now because of this drought that's been the longest one ever the prices are fucked up. Niggas payin' thirty three and thirty four thousand a brick dependin' on where they gettin' it from. I can probably get one for thirty two as long as my people straight." Cutt told Lil Kilo. Lil Kilo told Cutt to call and see if his people was straight before he got out the car. "What he talkin' bout fool?" Lil Slim asked Lil Kilo as he was getting back into the car. "I told him that I would call him in a hour to let him know how much dope we wanted." Lil Kilo said pulling off. Pulling up in front of Lil Kilo's house the two sat and talked about how much dope they would buy while smoking a blunt. "He said he could get us a whole brick for thirty two thousand." Lil Kilo told Lil Slim after Lil Slim asked what Cutt was charging for the dope. "Thirty two thousand for a brick of cocaine is a lot ain't it. What come with it, a life time warranty?" Lil Slim said. "Ion know bout no warranty. He was saying that the prices are fucked up because of a drought that 'pose to be the longest one ever. I'm thinkin' we could get Cutt to teach us the basics of the game as far as cookin' cuttin' and weighin' the dope. I'm sure he wouldn't mind." Lil Kilo said dumping the ashes from the blunt they was smoking out the window. "Where we gone get $32,000 from? You should have asked him to front us a couple of ounces or something." Lil Slim said. "Don't worry bout the money I'ma take care of that." Lil Kilo said then ran in his house and came back out with a zip lock bag full of money and tossed it in Lil Slim's lap. "Where you get this from?" Lil Slim asked holding the zip lock bag full of hundreds in his hands. Lil Kilo winked his eye at Lil Slim then called Cutt back. Meeting back up with Cutt Lil Kilo asked him how much would he charge them to show them how to cut and cook the dope they just bought. "I won't charge you nothing. Just let me keep the overs I bring back." Cutt said. Lil Slim and Lil Kilo looked at him like he was crazy. "Let you keep what?" Lil Slim asked. "The overs." Cutt said then explained to them what overs were. "So you tellin' me that you can cook this and bring some extras back?" Lil Kilo asked still not understanding. "I can show you better than I can tell it to you. Tryin' to explain it will confuse you. Follow me to my spot and I'll show ya'll what Jeezy meant when he said "If you want the real bread dawg it's all about yo whip game."

Chapter 2

After learning how to turn powder cocaine into crack rocks Lil Kilo and Lil Slim made plans to hit the block after school let out the next day. "Have you talked to Lil Fresh yet?" Lil Kilo asked Lil Slim as they were walking towards the gym doors. "I hollered at him last night on the phone." Lil Slim said pushing the gym door open. "What he say?" Lil Kilo asked scanning the gym floor with his eyes looking for no one in particular. "He said that he was wit it. You know how Lil Fresh is fool. He wit everything we wit." Lil Slim said as they were walking out the gym headed to the bathroom so they could smoke. Lil Fresh was leaning against the lockers talking to some girl when they came out the gym. "Okay I'll call you later on to see what you talkin' bout then boo." Lil Fresh told the girl before she walked off. Lil Fresh seen Lil Kilo and Lil Slim coming his way and turned straight up. "I'm tryna tell ya'll niggas that ya'll ain't fuckin' with me when it comes to these broads!" Lil Fresh said smiling as Lil Slim and Lil Kilo got closer. "I peeped ya'll walkin' in the gym and was on my way up there when lil momma stopped me talkin' bout she heard about me and how I put it down. Then said she wanna see for herself. So what that tell ya?" Lil Fresh said putting his phone back in his pocket. "Shid Ion know, she probably done heard about you eatin' booty." Lil Slim said laughing causing Lil Kilo to laugh also. "You got me fucked up nigga I ain't eatin' no ass!" Lil Fresh said. "That ain't what I heard." Lil Slim said driving Lil Fresh. "Yeah I heard the same thing my nigga." Lil Kilo said. "Nawl ya'll ain't heard nothing like that bout me. If a bitch say I ate her booty she lyin'. I can count on one hand how many times I done gave my head away so you know I ain't eatin' no ass. I get to much pussy for that. But that might be something ya'll two niggas want to start doin' cause ain't neither one of ya'll fuckin' yet." Lil Fresh said flipping the script on them causing them to become defensive and Lil Fresh to laugh. "Fuck all that jokin' tho! What's up with this afternoon we still gettin' down?" Lil Fresh asked. "Yeah me and Lil Kilo was just talkin' bout that before we bumped into you. You still down?" Lil Slim asked. "You better know it." Lil Fresh said just as the bell ring signaling that third period was about to start. "Damn! I didn't get to smoke the rest of this blunt fuckin' with ya'll." Lil Kilo said walking towards the steps. After third period was over Lil Kilo was asked to stay after class. "What's up Ms. Brown? You wanted to see me?" Lil Kilo said walking up on the teacher's desk. "Yes I did. Give me one second please." Ms. Brown said flipping through a stack of papers that was on her desk. After the last student left out the classroom Ms. Brown looked up from the stack of papers. "You don't have to be scared to use my number, you know that right?" Ms. Brown said which kind of shocked Lil Kilo. "What you talkin' bout Ms. Brown, you told me to call you Saturday didn't cha?" Lil Kilo asked.

"I gave you my number Tuesday expecting to hear from you before then. I guess you was going to call me whenever you was ready to meet up huh? Is that how you do when you meet one of the girls around the school?" Ms. Brown asked. "You get their number and call them whenever you get ready, is that how you do?" Lil Kilo smirked hearing Ms. Brown talk. *'She musta been waitin' on me to call.'* Lil Kilo thought. "It ain't nothin' like that Ms. Brown I just figured you would be busy grading papers or something and I didn't want to distract you from gettin' your work done that's all." Ms. Brown frowned. "I don't know if that was an excuse or a lie Keon but you're dealing with a grown lady that sees right through the bullshit so save that for the little girls you're use to dealing with." Ms. Brown said then stood up to grab her bag off the file cabinet that was beside her desk. Lil Kilo was stuck staring at her beauty and tripping off the way his English teacher was acting because he haven't called. "Honestly Ms. Brown I didn't want to give the impression of being desperate that's why I didn't call. But had I known that you wanted me to call you, you best believe I would've broke the world record for the most calls in a day callin' you." Lil Kilo said. Ms. Brown smiled knowing that Kilo probably would have blew her phone up for real. "It's lunch time boy where are you eating at? I know you aren't eating the food in the cafeteria." Ms. Brown said. Ms. Brown was one of those school teachers that every student in their right mind wanted to hit on but was too scared to approach her in that way because of her sophisticated look and her maturity level. "Ion know where I'm eatin' at. My niggas probably want to hit the Chicken Shack but I think I got a taste for some fish." Lil Kilo said to see if Ms. Brown would catch on to the hint he was giving. And she did. Ms. Brown told Lil Kilo that she liked her fish scaleless and smooth meaning that she shaved her public hairs. "That's exactly how I like my fish too." Lil Kilo said then winked his eye at Ms. Brown. "Have anybody ever told you that you and Sanaa Lathan look just alike?" Lil Kilo asked Ms. Brown as they was leaving out the class room. "All the time." Ms. Brown said. As Lil Kilo was coming down the stairs Lil Slim and Lil Fresh was coming up the stairs looking for him. "Where you been at fool? We been all over the school lookin' for yo ass." Lil Slim said. "I been up there hollerin' at Ms. Brown fine ass. You know how it is when you dealin' with a real woman. They want that alone time. That's something yo hoes might not know about Lil Fresh." Lil Kilo said picking with Lil Fresh. Lil Fresh just laughed. "You right. And that's something they ass ain't gone get fuckin' with me. Ima pimp. I ain't got time to be spendin' quality time with these hoes. I just feed em' fuck em' and leave em'. I leave all that other shit to ya'll." Lil Fresh said. After school the three swung by Lil Kilo's house where they had the dope stashed and took three ounces out of the 36 ounces they had and left the rest. The plan was for each of them to take an ounce and break it down to dime rocks and twenty rocks and try to make $1,500 dollars off the rocks. "Since this is our first time sellin' dope we probably won't make $1,500 but that's our goal once we get the hang of it." Lil Kilo told Lil Slim and Lil Fresh as they were on their way to the block. Pulling up they noticed the block wasn't as live as it normally be on a Friday afternoon. "Where in the world is everybody?" Lil Slim said as Lil Kilo was parking. "Ion know. Let's hop out and ask Percy and 'em where everybody at." Lil Kilo said getting out his car. "What's up Percy?" Lil Kilo said crossing the street to where Percy was standing with two other dudes. "Same shit. What's good with ya'll lil niggas?" Percy said back. "Why the block so dry?" It look like a ghost town round here." Lil Slim said giving Percy some dap. Percy was a little older than they were and was well known around the hood for selling dope. "Them alphabet boys pulled up and hopped out. And you know when they pull up everybody run." Percy said looking towards the top of the street to where a car was coming down. "The feds been in town all week tryna snatch a nigga ass up." One of the dudes said that was standing with Percy. "I don't know why they round here fuckin' with us anyway when it's hardly any dope out this bitch. They should know about this drought shid they know about everything else." Percy said. Lil Kilo heard that and looked at Lil Slim. "I been hearin' bout this drought. They said the prices been fucked up for a lil minute now." Lil Kilo said. "Yeah they have. Niggas chargin' fourteen and fifteen hunnit a ounce dependin' on who you know." Percy said pulling out a pack of cigarettes and fired one up. Lil Slim thought about what Percy said about how high the prices were and figured that they could afford to sell ounces for twelve and thirteen hundred dollars and still make a profit. "You know me and my niggas be doin' a lil hustlin' on the low. Fuck with us on the work and we'll let you get them thangs twelve fifty all day long." Lil Slim said sounding like he knew what he was talking about. Percy thought that Lil Slim was talking just to be talking because the people he was getting his dope from wasn't even giving it to him for that price. "Shid if ya'll got ounces for $1,250 I ain't got no choice but to fuck with ya'll. I'm paying damn near $1,400 right now. I'll be a damn fool not to shop with ya'll." Percy said. "Ya'll got some work on ya'll now?" Percy asked waiting on one of them to come up with an excuse as to why they didn't have the dope on them. Lil Slim pulled out the ounce of crack he had in his hoodie and showed it to Percy. "How much you tryna get?" Lil Slim asked. "I gotta make sure it's dope first." Percy said. "Because this drought got these niggas sellin' whatever they can get they hands on. What ya'll lil niggas doin' hustlin' anyway?" Percy asked untying the bag of crack Lil Slim handed him. "We just tryin' to get ours like everybody else." Lil Kilo said. After Percy seen that the dope Lil Slim gave him was real he wanted to know where the dope came from. "That ain't what's important. Either you want it or you don't." Lil Slim told him feeling like Percy was being nosey. "I want two of 'em. You got another one on ya?" Percy asked pulling out a wad of money. Lil Kilo handed Percy the once of crack he had on him. "Shid if ya'll lil niggas got it like that I got $1,200 for one." The dude that was standing with Percy said. "We'll fuck with you this time and let you owe us fifty but next time we need everything up front." Lil Slim told him. After Lil Fresh sold dude the ounce he had on him the three hopped in Lil Kilo's whip and smashed off to go get some more dope. "Man we might not have to post up on the block the way we just got rid of that shit. We can just give them niggas our cell phone number and pull up when they call." Lil Kilo said pulling off the block. "All we gotta do is chill until our phone ring." Lil Slim thought about what Lil Kilo said and didn't think sitting around waiting on their phones to ring would help them find out who killed their daddy like being out there in the streets would. "I think posting up on the block will give us a better chance to network. We'll be limitin' who we meet sittin' around waiting on our phones to ring." Lil Slim said from the backseat. Leaving Lil Kilo's house with three more ounces of crack the block was back live when they pulled up. "It didn't take long for these niggas to come out of hidin' did it?" Lil Fresh said wondering where in the hell did everybody run to when the police pulled up. Getting out the car the three walked up the street to where Percy was to let him know they had some more work and was stopped by the dude that owed them fifty dollars. "Here go them fifty I owe ya'll." The dude said then reached in his pocket and pulled out some money. "Ya'll gone have some more of that ain't cha? Cause Ima need anotha one in a minute." "Yeah we straight just holla at us when you ready." Lil Kilo said walking off to go holler at Percy. While talking to Percy a dude named Rachean they went to school with walked up mugging. "What's up P, you got some work?" Rachean asked Percy still mugging Lil Kilo, Lil Slim and Lil Fresh. "Yeah I got some. What you tryna do?" Percy asked wondering why Rachean was looking at Lil Kilo and them like he had beef with them or something. "I got $425 for seven lil bitty ones. Fuck with me one time." Rachean said now looking at Percy because he knew he was twenty five dollars short on the 7 grams he was trying to buy. "I'm funa show you some love." Percy said then told Rachean from now on he was going to charge him four hundred flat for the seven grams. While Percy was bent over weighing up the seven grams of dope for Rachean, Rachean ran his mouth. "What ya'll niggas doin' out here? Shouldn't ya'll be somewhere studyin'?" Percy looked up to see who Rachean was talking to. "Nawl we where we 'pose to be my nigga. You gotta problem with that?" Lil Slim said stepping in front of Lil Kilo so that him and Rachean would be face to face. "My bad homie! I just don't want ya'll momma to roll up and see ya'll out here wit the real niggas and ya'll get a ass whoopin'." Rachean said right before Lil Slim punched him in his mouth and Lil Fresh and Lil Kilo stomped him out. Seeing a fight in the hood was like a rumor being spread that the government was increasing welfare checks, everybody wanted to see the outcome. "Bitch!" Lil Slim spat kicking Rachean in the face. "Don't you ever come out yo mouth sideways at us again!" Lil Slim said then kicked Rachean in the ribs. Lil Slim had a lot of built up angry inside of him that he knew nothing about since his daddy died. "I will fuckin' kill you nigga!" Lil Slim said kicking Rachean in the face with the front of his shoe as hard as he could. Percy seen how furious Lil Slim was and pulled him off of Rachean. "You gone kill that nigga or give him brain trauma you kick him like that again." Percy said holding Lil Slim back. "Fuck that nigga!" Lil Slim said looking back at Lil Kilo and Lil Fresh and noticed the crowd of people that gathered around watching them kick the shit out of Rachean. "Yeah fuck that bitch ass nigga! Let's get outta here." Lil Fresh said. "Nawl we ain't goin' nowhere! Fuck him and whoever's down with him. We ain't runnin' from nobody!" Lil Slim snapped. Lil Kilo pulled Lil Slim down the street to where they parked so he could calm Lil Slim down while Percy and a few other people helped Rachean off the ground. "Listen to 'em. He still talkin' shit like we didn't just whoop the shit outta his ass." Lil Slim said ready to go back up the street and give Rachean another round. Unable to hear Rachean telling them not to be there when he got back Lil Slim stuck his middle finger up at him. "Reach in the glove box and grab that bag of weed and one of them cigarillos Lil Fresh so I can roll one up." Lil Kilo said. Lil Fresh grabbed the weed and a cigarillo and handed it to Lil Kilo then walked around an abandoned house to piss. "Don't be back there playin' with yo self fool then come back 'round here and smoke wit a nigga." Lil Slim joked with Lil Fresh before he walked off to go pee. "Nigga I ain't played with myself since Middle School and that lil bitch you had a crush on helped me do that." Lil Fresh said from behind the house. Lil Kilo finished breaking the cigar down and licked it but before he had the chance to fill it up with weed Rachean appeared from behind another abandoned house on the opposite side of the street holding a gun. "Talk that gangsta shit now ol' bitch ass nigga!" Rachean yelled. Lil Kilo looked up just in time to see Rachean coming out the gate pointing a gun at them. "Ol shit! He gotta gun fool run!" Lil Kilo told Lil Slim dropping the weed and the cigar then took off running behind the same house Lil Fresh went behind to piss. Lil Slim stood there shocked for a split second until he heard the gun go off. "BOOM!" "Don't run now nigga!" Rachean said now walking towards Lil Slim who duck down and tried to run but the second bullet that jumped out of Rachean's .32 ACP handgun hit him square in the back causing him to fall. "BOOM...BOOM...BOOM." Rachean kept shooting. Lil Slim got up and tried to run again and was hit in the shoulder. "BOOM!" Rachean was a few steps away from Lil Slim. "BOOM!" Rachean let off another shot hitting Lil Slim in the thigh. "Agghh fuck!" Lil Slim yelled in pain. "You done fucked wit the wrong one. Now turn over bitch!" Rachean told Lil Slim then kicked him in the side. Lil Slim figured that he was about to die so he turned over and tried to spit on Rachean but missed. "Fuck yo.." Was all Lil Slim got out before Rachean emptied the rest of his clip into his chest. "BOOMBOOMBOOMBOOM...ClickClickClick!" Rachean realized that he was out of bullets and took off running. Everything seemed as if it was moving in slow motion for Lil Kilo and Lil Fresh as they ran from behind the house. "Noooo!" Lil Kilo yelled. Lil Kilo scooped Lil Slim up in his arms. "Don't die on me Lil Slim just hold on. Ima get you to the hospital homie just hold on." Lil Kilo whispered in Lil Slim's ear with tears in his eyes and blood all over him. "Help me get him in the car." Lil Kilo told Lil Fresh.

Chapter 3

Leaving the conference meeting which was a requirement for the High School teachers Ms. Brown was the first one out the building once the meeting was over. Tired and ready to soak in a tub of hot water Ms. Brown made a beeline straight home to her three bedroom house that was where most of the kids that lived in the hood called the white folks part of town or where the rich people lived. "Ain't nothing rich about my house or where I live." Ms. Brown often told the kids in her class that assumed she was rich. "I just carry myself aristocratically." Ms. Brown always told them. Stopping to check the mailbox before pulling into her driveway Ms. Brown pulled out a stack of junk mail which is what she called all the coupons to fast food restaurants and grocery stores the mailman dropped off that she never used. Dropping the coupons in the trash Ms. Brown then checked her voicemails and began undressing as she listened to them. Feeling like none of the messages was important Ms. Brown deleted them and made a mental note to call her girl Maria back. *'She left two messages she had to want something.'* Ms. Brown thought picking her clothes up off the living floor making her way to the bathroom to take a shower. After bathing Ms. Brown slipped on some sweatpants and a tank top then climbed in bed and dozed off almost immediately watching the six o'clock news but the sudden ringing of the house phone that sat beside her bed on the nightstand snapped her out of it. "Hello…" Ms. Brown picked up the phone without checking the caller ID. "Well it's about time you answered the phone. I've been calling you all day Ms. Za'Mya Lee Brown and I've been getting the VM. Explain please!" Hearing the Puerto Rican accent and her whole name being called Ms. Brown already knew who was on the other end of her phone. "I got your voicemails Ms. Maria L. Sanchez. I was going to return your calls. I had a conference meeting after school and was tired afterwards." Ms. Brown said snuggling up under her covers. "So that explains why your cell phone been off. I've been calling and calling thinking something was wrong with you girl." Maria said. "I haven't been thinking about that darn phone. Taking me a hot shower and climbing in this bed was the only thing on my mind." Ms. Brown said. "Well take you a beauty nap in and call me when you get up." Maria told Ms. Brown before she hung up. Ms. Brown met Maria a few years back at a fall festival that was held to help raise money to fight against breast cancer and the two have kept in touch every since. Ms. Brown sometimes wondered how Maria was able to afford the house she lived in and the cars she drove being the head of a law firm but never asked because she knew her girl was making an honest living and that's all that mattered to her. Waking up out of her nap an hour and a half later Ms. Brown got up and fixed her something to eat. "Let me call Maria crazy tale back to see what she's doing tonight." Ms. Brown said to herself sitting down in the living room with her food in hand. Maria told Ms. Brown that she didn't have nothing planned for the night but if she wanted to that they could go out for drinks. "The treats on me." Maria said happy that her friend called her back. "The treats are always on you. I got it tonight. Where are we meeting at?" Ms. Brown asked taking a sip of her drink. "I'm coming to pick you up. I know a bar in Cleveland where the grown and sexy be and we're grown and sexy so that's where we'll be." Maria said. "I'm not ready now. I just woke up 15 minutes ago." Ms. Brown said thinking about what she could put on. "Well you better be getting ready because I'm on my way." Maria said before she hung up and was knocking at Ms. Brown's door 30 minutes later. Ms. Brown opened the door trying to pull her shirt over her head without messing her hair up. "Come in for a second. I'm almost ready." Ms. Brown told Maria. "Girl you pulling that shirt over your head like you just got out the same hair stylist seat that do Beyoncé hair." Maria said walking into the house laughing. "Come here let me help you." Ms. Brown had some long natural straight black hair that she had just finished flat ironing. "Don't hate. Because you know everybody wasn't born with horse hair like ya'll Mexicans. My roots come from Africa where the real nappy heads are. I just keep mine done." Ms. Brown said knowing her girl was about to say something real smart because she hate being called a Mexican. "Hold up now, who you calling a Mexican? I'm not Mexican! I'm Puerto Rican! There's a difference! I can't help it that I don't have to do much to keep my hair straight." Maria said whipping her hair around that fell halfway down her back. Ms. Brown knew calling Maria a Mexican would get her going. "Girl I know you're not no damn Mexican. That's what I call you to get under your skin girl. Now let me go grab my purse so we can get out of here." Ms. Brown said. Sitting at the bar drinking Long Island Ice Teas and Pineapple Martinis Ms. Brown and Maria was enjoying their night and the compliments they were getting. "I need to use the restroom. These drinks done ran through me." Ms. Brown said sitting her glass down on the bar. "Don't think you gone leave me sitting out here by myself to keep hearing these lames ass compliments. I'm coming too." Maria said getting up off the stool. "Girl you know you like hearing these men call you Mami don't front." Ms. Brown said looking around for the bathroom sign and caught eyes with a dude that looked just like Lil Kilo minus the dreads. "I see you got jokes." Maria said watching Ms. Brown stare across the bar. "You see something you like?" "I thought I seen somebody I know but he's just a look alike. Which way is the bathroom?" Ms. Brown asked now thinking about Lil Kilo because of the look alike she just caught eyes with. "It's over there." Maria said pointing in the direction of the look alike. "Follow me." Ms. Brown follow Maria through the crowd that seemed to have grown since they got there. Ms. Brown passed Lil Kilo's look alike and smiled but didn't say a word. Standing in front of the bathroom mirror fixing her mascara Maria asked Ms. Brown did she hear about the student that was gunned down earlier that day. "I haven't heard about that. Did they say who the student was?" Ms. Brown asked from behind the stall. "They didn't release any names at the time just said he was a High School student. I know you teach at the High School that's why I asked." Maria said now fluffing her hair. To be Puerto Rican Maria had the body of a black girl and after giving birth to her daughter her body filled out even more. Ms. Brown was in the stall praying that it wasn't Lil Kilo that was gunned down earlier. "Lil Kilo don't do nothing illegal besides smoke weed so I'm sure it wasn't him." Ms. Brown said to herself coming out the stall to wash her hands. Before leaving out the bathroom Ms. Brown checked her cell phone for any missed calls and was kind of mad when she seen that Lil Kilo still hadn't called. *I don't know why I'm anticipating his call anyway when I know he's not ready for a real woman like me.* Ms. Brown thought putting her phone back in her purse. After sitting at the bar for another hour or so drinking, laughing and telling every guy that tried to hit on them that they were girlfriends Ms. Brown and Maria was ready to go. "Let's get out of here girl before these fools get to drunk and start demanding we talk to them." Ms. Brown said after finishing her third Pineapple Martini. "Yo ass need to talk to some damn body girl cause as long as I've been knowing you I've only heard you *talk* about one dude and that was over a year ago." Maria said putting emphasis on the word talk. "Don't let me find out that you into girls for real." Maria laughed. "Girl please what can a girl do for me that I can't do for myself?" Ms. Brown said. "But I know you not talking. Not when I've never seen or even heard you talking about getting your back dug out!" Ms. Brown was the one laughing now. "So don't let me find out that's it's you that have a girlfriend you been bumping coochies with." Ms. Brown and Maria loved joking with each other about not getting laid. After leaving the bar Maria dropped Ms. Brown off at home and told her that she would call her when she got in. Looking at the clock on the wall that hung above her T.V stand Ms. Brown seen that it was going on one o'clock in the morning. "I guess I'll strip down take another shower and lay my lonely ass down." Ms. Brown said to herself wiggling out of the jeans she had on. Laying back on her bed after showering with nothing but her panties on Ms. Brown pulled the covers over her body and let the T.V watch her as her mind wondered and her fingers found their way down between her legs. Rubbing herself through her panties Ms. Brown felt herself become wet. Still buzzing from the Pineapple Martinis and the Long Islands she drunk at the bar Ms. Brown slid her panties over and slowly ran her middle finger across her pussy lips. "Ummm…" Ms. Brown let out a soft moan as she slid her finger inside her vagina feeling her wetness then slid that same finger out and slowly across her clitoris which caused her to moan again. "Ummm…" Just as Ms. Brown was about to spread her legs open a little wider to stick her finger further inside of herself her phone rung breaking her concentration. "Who in the hell is this calling at one something in the morning?" Thinking that it was Maria calling to let her know that she made it home safely Ms. Brown ignored the ringing of the phone until the caller hung up and called back. "This better be important whoever it is!" Ms. Brown said out loud reaching for her cell phone answering it. "Hello..!"

Chapter 4

Sitting in the waiting area of the hospital waiting on the doctors to come out and tell them what kind of condition Lil Slim was in Lil Kilo was in a state of despair watching his mother console Lil Slim's mother who was crying frantically. "Man I pray Lil Slim aite." Lil Fresh said to Lil Kilo. Lil Kilo and Lil Fresh was at the hospital an hour and forty five minutes before they called Lil Slim's mother to let her know what happened. They was hoping to find out how stable Lil Slim was before they called his mother but the doctor never came back out so after an hour and forty five minutes of waiting Lil Kilo called Lil Slim's mother. "I hope he pull through too man. That nigga Rachean got something comin' tho. He done fucked up big time." Lil Kilo said whispering so that only Lil Fresh could hear him. "I been thinkin' the same thing fool. I know where his momma stay at. We can swing by there and chop that bitch down!" Lil Fresh said. "Shhh...you talkin' to loud. But we ain't shootin' no houses up. We gone catch and wet his ass up. But we been here since 6 and it's going 11:30 and we still haven't heard nothin'. Ion think that's a good sign." Lil Kilo told Lil Fresh. "Here comes the doctor now." Lil Fresh said as the doctor walked into the waiting room and spoke in a very low tone to Lil Slim's mother. Not being able to hear what the doctor was saying but seeing the reaction and the face expression on Lil Slim's mother face sadden, Lil Kilo and Lil Fresh knew things weren't looking to good. Then Lil Slim's mother got up and followed the doctor through the doubled doors so Lil Kilo walked over to his mother who was crying as well to try to figure out what was going on. "Is everything okay ma?" Lil Kilo asked sitting down next to his mother wrapping his arms around her. "I'm afraid not son. The doctor said that the ventilator system that Issac is hooked up to is the only thing keeping him breathing." Lil Kilo's mother said as tears fell freely from her cheeks. Lil Kilo hugged his mother and let her tears fall on his shoulder knowing that his mother looked at Lil Slim like a son. "It's gone be okay ma. He gone pull through." Lil Kilo told his mother to comfort her more than anything because he was doubting his own words as they left his mouth. Hearing that a machine was the only thing keeping Lil Slim breathing and knowing that he was shot seven times Lil Kilo felt that there was a chance that Lil Slim might not make it. "I'm about to take Lil Fresh home before it get to late ma. Tell Ms. Ivonne that I truly apologize for what happened. I know she probably don't want to hear it from me." Leaving the hospital Lil Kilo and Lil Fresh stopped by Big Ed's weed spot to get them something to smoke. "I need something to ease my nerves a lil bit." Lil Kilo said as they was getting into his car. By the time the two were pulling up to Big Ed's spot they had a plan formulated. "You right I don't think he'll show his face at school any time soon. We'll have a better chance catchin' him on the block like you said." Lil Fresh was saying as Lil Kilo was putting his car in park. "But like I said tho fool I know where his baby momma stay. I been over there before. A *few* times matta fact." Lil Fresh said. "I thought you said you know where his momma stay. You didn't say nothin' about his baby momma." Lil Kilo said. "Nawl fool I said I know where his baby momma stay at. But then again as mad as I was I probably did say his momma. Shid that bitch can get it too!" Lil Fresh said meaning every word. "Let's go grab this sack right quick. We'll finished talkin' bout this once we get back in the car." After serving them some weed Big Ed didn't waste any time asking them about earlier. "What's up with Lil Slim, he aite?" The question kind of caught them off guard. "Huh…?" Lil Kilo said giving Big Ed one of those 'What you talking about looks.' But the way Big Ed looked back at Lil Kilo let Lil Kilo know that he knew what was going on. "You heard bout what happened?" Lil Kilo asked. "Who haven't heard about what happened? This the hood. Shit spread like wildfire around here. Especially if it got something to do with somebody getting shot or the police taking somebody to jail." Big Ed said. "Yeah he aite. But the nigga who did it ain't gone be." Lil Kilo said thinking about how life would be if Lil Slim didn't make it. Big Ed then told Lil Kilo and Lil Fresh not to be running around talking about what they going to do to people. "It's best to keep it to yourself and just do it. Because the more people that know the greater the chance that somebody will tell. Real niggas don't talk about what they gone do anyway." Big Ed told them before asking them if they had any artillery. "I hope ya'll lil niggas strapped up because that lil nigga ya'll dealing with gotta fuckin' arsenal of guns. I know because I sold them to him over the years." Big Ed said trying to advise Lil Kilo and Lil Fresh not to go at Rachean playing because he was ready for war. Neither of them owned a gun. Better yet neither one of them have never even shot a gun so hearing Big Ed speak about it brought them to their senses. "Shit I ain't never held a gun." Both Lil Fresh and Lil Kilo was thinking at the same time. "You said you sold him his straps right?" Lil Kilo asked Big Ed. Big Ed nodded his head. "You got some mo' for sell?" Lil Fresh asked taking the words right out of Lil Kilo mouth. "I got all shapes and sizes for whatever type of damage ya'll trying to do. But they not here. Ya'll will have to follow me to my other spot." Big Ed said. "I can't risk the F.E.D's catching me with them. Shid they'll build a cell inside of a cell for my black ass if they caught me with the type of shit I got." Big Ed said. "Let me grab my keys and we can swing by there right quick if ya'll want to." Following Big Ed way across town to an apartment complex Lil Kilo pulled into the parking space next to Big Ed. "Believe it or not this the same apartment yo momma and daddy use to live in." Big Ed told Lil Kilo as he was unlocking the apartment door. Inside the apartment nothing gave the indication that guns were being stored there. Observing the apartment one would think that the apartment belong to a middle class single white woman from all the colorful decorations and the cleanness of the apartment. "Does anyone live here?" Lil Fresh wanted to know. "Nawl. I just make it look as if someone do so when the inspection people come in they want expect nothing to be in here that ain't supposed to be." Big Ed said leading them into the kitchen where he scooted the refrigerator away from the wall and unplugged it. "One of ya'll grab the backside of the frig and the other feel at the bottom for a lack and unlatch it." Lil Fresh grabbed the backside while Lil Kilo reached under the refrigerator feeling for the latch Big Ed was talking about. Lil Kilo found it and unlatched it then stood back up and dusted his shirt off. "Now do the same thing on this side Lil Kilo." Big Ed said. Lil Kilo unlatched the other side and the refrigerator made a *click* sound. "Stand back a lil bit Lil Kilo. Aite now, Lil Fresh wiggle yo side slowly like this until the back comes off." Big Ed said wiggling his side of the refrigerator showing Lil Fresh until the back came completely off. "Lean it against the wall Lil Fresh." Without the back part of the refrigerator on the refrigerator looked like a small closet with nothing but guns in it. "Man how you come up with this idea?" Lil Kilo asked looking at all the guns that fit perfectly in the back of the refrigerator. "It pays to know a few white boys that know a lil something. Now take your pick. I got everything from a .22 to a baby M-16 back here." Big Ed said. Lil Kilo settled for two .45 automatics with the lemon squeeze triggers, a .40 glock and a Mac-11. While Lil Fresh choose a P-89 Ruger with a 32 round clip, a glock .40 and the baby M-16 Big Ed had on display. "What's the ticket on these straps Ol' Man Ed?" Lil Kilo asked wanting to know how much Big Ed was charging them for the guns. Big Ed told them that the only thing he wanted from them was for them to stay alive. "I'm not charging ya'll nothing for the guns. They on me. All I want is for ya'll to stay alive. Now help me put this back on." Big Ed said grabbing the back side to the refrigerator. After putting the refrigerator back together Lil Kilo asked Big Ed did he mind if they smoke a blunt inside the apartment. "As long as I can hit that muthafucka I don't." Big Ed told Lil Kilo and Lil Fresh all type of stories about what type of niggas their daddies were while they was smoking. The story they wanted to hear twice about their daddy was the one he told them about how he was the one that fronted them their first pound of weed back in the day when they first started hustling. "It seem like just last year but that was damn near twenty years ago when they first came to me asking me to front them some weed. The next thing I know them boys blew up! I mean everything that moved thru the city was theirs." Big Ed said grabbing the blunt from Lil Fresh. "And they made sure everybody ate." Lil Kilo loved to hear stories about his daddy. "I done heard a lot of stories about our daddy and how big they were but what I don't understand is how don't nobody know who killed them." Lil Kilo said hoping Big Ed knew more than what he was telling them. "It's hard to say who killed them because everybody loved them. All we know is four dead bodies was found shot to death in a hotel room." Big Ed said passing the blunt to Lil Kilo. "Four dead bodies? Who was the fourth?" Lil Kilo asked dumping the ashes off the blunt. "There was ya'll daddy, Lil Slim daddy and they had another partna they use to run wit named Quick. I don't think Quick left any kids behind so when people speak about them to ya'll they probably just let ya'll know about ya'll daddy and forget to say something about Quick. But Quick was one of them." Big Ed said thinking about the movement their daddies had. "How come don't nobody know who killed them tho? That don't make sense. I mean somebody gotta know something." Lil Fresh said. "I think it's kinda crazy that don't nobody know anything about that myself." Big Ed said. "Me personally I believe they was plugged into some type of Mob or Cartel or something. Because to be able to keep a constant supply of dope at the price they had a real connect was needed. That's just common sense. But the reason they were killed or who was behind it is like trying to figure out if there's life on Jupiter nobody knows." After smoking and talking to Big Ed about their daddies a little while longer Lil Kilo and Lil Fresh headed out. "Good lookin' on these straps Ol' Man." Lil Kilo told Big Ed sticking the Mac-11 down the front of his pants. "No problem! Handle ya'll bizniz." Big Ed said as they were leaving out the apartment. "And remember the price." Lil Kilo dropped Lil Fresh off at home then pulled up to his house and noticed that his mother wasn't there. *I wonder if she's still at the hospital with Lil Slim's momma.* Lil Kilo thought pulling out his cell phone to call his mother but kept getting the voicemail on the first ring. Scrolling down his contact list to call his mother's other number Lil Kilo seen Ms. Brown name under his mother's name. Looking at the time on his phone Lil Kilo seen that it was fifteen minutes after one and debated on if he should call Ms. Brown or not. After his mother didn't answer her other phone Lil Kilo figured that she was still at the hospital with Lil Slim's mother. Getting out of his car walking in the house Lil Kilo called Ms. Brown just to see if she would answer. "She's probably sleep." Lil Kilo said to himself after Ms. Brown didn't answer the phone. Pulling the Mac-11 from out the front of his pants Lil Kilo walked up the stairs to his room. "Fuck that! If she is sleep she gone have to wake her ass up. I need somebody to talk to." Lil Kilo said out loud then called Ms. Brown again. Lifting his mattress up holding the phone with the side of his head and his shoulder Lil Kilo sat the Mac-11 and the two .45's down and layed the mattress back down just as Ms. Brown answered the phone. "Hello..!" Lil Kilo heard Ms. Brown say from the other end of the phone sounding like she was wide awake. "Hellooo…" Ms. Brown repeated after Lil Kilo hesitated to say something. "Uh… what's up Ms. Brown? This Keon. Was you sleep?" Lil Kilo said saying the first thing that came to his mind not thinking that Ms. Brown was going to pick up the phone. "Oh…hey Keon. Actually I just got in bed. What are you doing up this late? You trying to find you a booty call?" Ms. Brown asked kind of surprised that Lil Kilo was on the other end of her phone this late. "Nawl I ain't lookin' for a booty call. I need somebody to talk to. I been goin' thru it today." Lil Kilo said sitting down on the edge of his bed. "What's wrong Keon? Is everything okay?" Ms. Brown asked now sitting up in her bed with her covers wrapped around her. Lil Kilo told Ms. Brown that he didn't feel comfortable talking about it over the phone. "Would you like to come over and talk about whatever's bothering you Keon?" Ms. Brown asked in a voice that had worried all in it. Lil Kilo thought about it for a second. "I mean if its okay with you and as long I don't have to worry about yo ol' man beatin' on the door tryin' to get in as soon as I get over there." Lil Kilo said. "Yes it's okay with me Keon. And for the first and last time I don't have a man." Ms. Brown told Lil Kilo then gave him her address and hung up the phone. *'I need to take another shower now.'* Ms. Brown thought getting out the bed. Lil Kilo hung up the phone with Ms. Brown and grabbed him a change of clothes. "I hope she don't mind me takin' a shower over there." Lil Kilo said walking down the steps with a brand new pair of Balmain jeans, a brand new white t-shirt and a new pair of socks and boxers in his hands. After leaving his mother a voicemail saying that he was staying over Lil Fresh house Lil Kilo left out the house locking the door behind him. Before getting into his car Lil Kilo seen that he had two bullet holes at the bottom of his car door. "FUCK!" Lil Kilo said out loud rubbing the bullet holes. Throwing his change of clothes in the passenger seat Lil Kilo grab the .40 glock he got from Big Ed from under his seat and cocked it back. "He'll never catch me slippin'." Lil Kilo said looking around tucking his gun on his waistline. Halfway to Ms. Brown's house Lil Kilo's mother called him back after checking her voicemail. "Hey baby, I got your voicemail." "Hey ma. I was just letting you know that I was going to stay over Lil Fresh house tonight." Lil Kilo said switching lanes so that he could get ready to get off the interstate. "Is that where you're at now?" Lil Kilo's mother asked standing outside the hospital door so she could get some service. "Not yet. I just left the house. But what's up with Lil Slim momma, is he aite?" Lil Kilo asked. Lil Kilo's mother paused for a second before telling him the bad news. "Well Keon…" Lil Kilo's mother said then paused again. "The doctors just informed us that Issac's condition isn't getting any better and that his breathing has become very faint. I think he's slipped into a coma. Ivonne isn't taking this to well so I'm going to stay with her until the morning." Lil Kilo's mother told him. "So if you need me for anything this is where I'll be." After talking to his mother and hearing about Lil Slim and his condition worsening Lil Kilo smashed over to Ms. Brown's house with murder on his mind. "Ima make sure that nigga momma cry!" Lil Kilo thought thinking about Rachean. Lil Kilo pulled up to Ms. Brown's house twenty minutes after leaving his house and was knocking on her door holding his clothes in one hand and his cell phone in the other about to call Lil Fresh to let him know about Lil Slim when Ms. Brown opened the door wearing some blue sweat shorts and a tank top. Seeing Lil Kilo at her doorsteps and not in front of her desk felt kind of odd to Ms. Brown at first. Looking down seeing that Lil Kilo brought a change of clothes with him Ms. Brown used that to break the moment of silence between them. "I said that you could come over so we could talk, not that you could move in." Ms. Brown chuckled. Knowing that Ms. Brown was talking about the clothes he had in his hand Lil Kilo felt a tad bit embarrassed standing there with a hand full of clothes. *Something told me to leave this shit in the car.'* Lil Kilo thought then told Ms. Brown that he wasn't trying to move in. "That was a good one tho." Lil Kilo laughed to play it off. "I was just hoping that you didn't mind me takin' a shower over here that's all." Lil Kilo said walking into Ms. Brown's house. Ms. Brown lead Lil Kilo into her living room then told him to make his self at home. "You have to excuse my house Keon I haven't had the chance to clean up today." Ms. Brown said standing behind the leather sectional couch she had. "Would you like anything to drink?" Ms. Brown asked walking into the kitchen. "Nawl I'm cool. I 'preciate it tho. You don't mind if I make a call do you?" Lil Kilo asked looking back over the couch at Ms. Brown's ass as she walked into the kitchen. "Goodness!" Lil Kilo said under his breath. "No, go right ahead Keon. Just make sure it isn't one of your little girlfriends you're calling."

Ms. Brown said from the kitchen. "Why would I call you and I'm with you? That don't make any sense." Lil Kilo said back calling Lil Fresh. Ms. Brown was coming out the kitchen saying that she's to grown to be somebody's girlfriend but stopped talking when she heard Lil Kilo on the phone saying that Lil Slim had slipped into a coma. "My momma called and told me not to long ago. She said something about his breathing to…Yeah I know…Ima go back up there to see him tomorrow if he's allowed visitors…Yeah…Ima holla at you tomorrow about that…Aite bet." Lil Kilo hung up his cell phone and layed it on the table. "Ms. Brown!" Lil Kilo yelled not knowing that she was standing right behind him listening to his conversation the whole time. Lil Kilo kicked off his Timberland boots and pulled his hoodie over his head and felt the sack of weed he had bought from Big Ed earlier. "I hope she don't mind me smokin' in here either." Lil Kilo thought. "You need something?" Ms. Brown asked walking into the living room with a glass of tea. "I was just lookin' around at how neat you got things in here and you talkin' bout you haven't cleaned up today. It looks clean in here to me." Lil Kilo said looking up at Ms. Brown wondering how one person could possess so much beauty. "You fine as wine Ms. Brown." Lil Kilo said smiling not knowing what in the hell made him just say that. Ms. Brown couldn't do nothing but laugh. "Fine as wine? What T.V show you hear that on?" Ms. Brown asked still laughing. "But I see that you've gotten comfortable. And we're not in the classroom either Keon so you don't have to keep calling me Ms. Brown. That makes me feel like an old lady." Ms. Brown said sitting down on the couch beside Lil Kilo. "Well what you want me to call you then Ms. Brown?" Lil Kilo said then grinned. Ms. Brown punched Lil Kilo in the arm. "My name is Za'Mya or Mya. I prefer Mya unless we're in the classroom then it's Ms. Brown." Ms. Brown said. "Well since we're going on first name and nickname basis my name is Lil Kilo not Keon. And that's even when we're in class." Lil Kilo said back. Ms. Brown smiled. "I see that you are even more humorous in person than you are in the classroom Keon. Now tell me what's going on with Issac." "How you figure something is wrong with him?" Lil Kilo asked Ms. Brown caught off guard by the question once again. "I heard you telling somebody on the phone which I'm assuming was Marshawn that Lil Slim's conditions are getting worst. It doesn't take a rocket scientist to figure it out." Ms. Brown said pulling her legs up to sit Indian style on the couch. Lil Kilo thought about telling Ms. Brown a bunch of bullshit about what happened to Lil Slim but didn't, he told her the whole truth. Even the reason they were out there on the block in the first place. Ms. Brown remembered Maria saying something about one of the High School students getting shot and as Lil Kilo was talking she knew that it was Lil Slim that Maria was talking about when they were in the bathroom at the bar. "You know my friend was telling me something about one of the students getting shot and I'm sure he's exactly who she was talking about." Ms. Brown said taking a sip of her tea. "How many times did Issac get shot for him to be in the condition he's in?" Ms. Brown asked Lil Kilo who looked so hurt and full of pain. "He got hit four times in the chest, once in the leg, his shoulder and in the back. He lost a lot of blood and now that I think about it I know it's blood all over my back seat." Lil Kilo said as the scene from earlier played out in his head. "God please allow my nigga to pull through." Lil Kilo said silently. "That blood is going to be hard to get out once it stains you know that right?" Ms. Brown said. Just looking at Lil Kilo Ms. Brown could tell that the thoughts that were going through Lil Kilo's mind weren't pure. "Dear Heavenly Farther please be with Keon and his family and friends. God please. Amen." Ms. Brown prayed silently and fast after really just paying attention to Lil Kilo's facial expressions. "Yeah I know. I'm goin' to take it to the dealership tomorrow and switch it out for something else." Lil Kilo said knowing the dealership wouldn't have a problem switching out his car for him simply because he owned the rights to the dealership after his daddy was killed. Ms. Brown and Lil Kilo sat on the couch talking about a little bit of everything not worried about the time until Ms. Brown let out an unintended yawn. "Excuse me, I don't know where that came from." Ms. Brown said covering her mouth with her hand. Lil Kilo glanced at his watch and seen that it was a little after 3 in the morning. "I don't know if that was your cue to let me know you're tired of me or what but it's 3 o'clock in the morning. I hope you not thinkin' bout putting me out." Lil Kilo said. "You told me to make myself at home so I'm about to take me a shower then climb in yo bed and catch me some Z'zzz." Lil Kilo added matter of factly. Ms. Brown liked the boldness and confidence Lil Kilo had. It turned her on tremendously but she kept that to herself. "Let's back up a bit now big fella. I don't mind you staying over taking you a shower and catching you some Z'zzz but catching them in my bed?" Ms. Brown paused and pointed to herself with a look on her face that said 'You gotta be kidding me.' "I thinks not!" Ms. Brown chuckled. "There's some extra blankets in the hall closet and this couch is big enough and comfy enough I'm sure." Ms. Brown said getting up off the couch. "See you in the morning." Ms. Brown said then winked at Lil Kilo. Lil Kilo watched as Ms. Brown made her way to her bedroom staring at her ass once again. "Ms. Brown trippin' if she think I ain't funa lay next to that tonight." Lil Kilo thought to himself before getting up to go take a shower. After lathering up and rising his body four or five times Lil Kilo closed his eyes and stood under the shower head letting the water bounce off his chest and thought about everything that happened in less than 24 hours. Getting out the shower drying off with one of the towels from out the bathroom closet Lil Kilo slid on his boxers then lotioned his body with some of the cocoa butter Ms. Brown had sitting on the sink with the rest of her cosmetics. "I hope she don't think I'm sleeping on that couch for real." Lil Kilo said to himself leaving out the bathroom. Walking down the hall in his boxes to where Ms. Brown's room was Lil Kilo opened Ms. Brown's door expecting to see her sitting up in bed watching T.V or something but to his surprise the T.V was off and Ms. Brown was tucked under her covers snoring lightly. Lil Kilo pulled the door up behind him quietly and without thinking twice about it climbed in bed with Ms. Brown and pulled the silk satin sheets over his body and was out for the count before he knew it.

Chapter 5

The next day Ms. Brown woke up with Lil Kilo's arm wrapped around her waist and was glad she fell straight to sleep last night too tired to pull her clothes off and sleep naked like she normally do. *'I bet he would've loved that.'* Ms. Brown thought about to get out of bed but decided to move her backside against Lil Kilo to see if he had an early morning erection. Trying not to wake Lil Kilo Ms. Brown lifted her hip lightly off the bed and moved back slowly until she felt something poke her booty cheek. "I know that's not what I think it is?" Ms. Brown flinched which caused Lil Kilo to stir in his sleep and pull her closer to him. Ms. Brown's backside was now all on Lil Kilo and she felt exactly what she was intending to feel. Ms. Brown became wet between the legs feeling Lil Kilo's manhood poking her between her booty cheeks and the longer she layed there the wetter she became. Ms. Brown thought about turning Lil Kilo over on his back and climbing on top of him and giving him the ride of his life but didn't want Lil Kilo to get the wrong impression of her so she slid out of bed and into the shower where she played with herself pretending that it was Lil Kilo's hands that was all over her body instead of her own. Lil Kilo got up not to long after Ms. Brown got in the shower stretching, yawning and hungry as ever. "I wonder what she got to eat in there." Lil Kilo said then climbed out the bed and walked out the room in his boxers and up the hall into the living room where he slid on his Balmain jeans be brought over and his Timberland boots. Checking his cell phone Lil Kilo seen that he had four missed calls three of which was from Neka and the other one was a number he didn't recognize. *I'll call her later.* Lil Kilo thought putting his phone back on the table and walked into Ms. Brown's kitchen shirtless. Lil Kilo had Ms. Brown's freezer and refrigerator door wide open looking for something to eat. "I'm acting like I know how to cook. Let me quit playin'." Lil Kilo told his self and grabbed a box of cereal from off the top of the refrigerator and found the biggest bowel he could find and settled for a big bowl of Frosted Flakes. Standing in the kitchen going to work on the bowl of Frosted Flakes Lil Kilo didn't hear Ms. Brown walk in. Ms. Brown stood there for a second watching Lil Kilo eat that bowl of cereal like he haven't ate in days. "Slow down Keon. That cereal isn't going nowhere anytime soon and if it do you can always make you another bowl." Ms. Brown said laughing walking into the kitchen opening the refrigerator. "All this food in here and you fix a bowl of cereal? You must not know how to cook." Ms. Brown said looking back at Lil Kilo while taking out some eggs and turkey bacon out the refrigerator setting it on the counter. "Nope! Showl can't and you bet not laugh." Lil Kilo said turning the bowl up so he could drink the milk. "And where's the 'Good morning' at?" "Good morning to you sir…" Ms. Brown said noticing the portrait Lil Kilo had tatted on his side of his daddy's face with the words 'R.I.P Gone But Not Forgotten' around it and some other words that she couldn't make out. Ms. Brown told Lil Kilo that next time he better not come climbing in her bed while she's sleep unless she gives him permission to do so. "You lucky I didn't wake you up and do the things I wanted to do to ya. If yo bed wasn't so comfortable I probably would've but it seem like as soon as I layed down I was sleep." Lil Kilo said sitting the bowl in the sink about to head to the bathroom to wash his face and brush his teeth. "But there's a next time huh?" Lil Kilo said. Ms. Brown gave Lil Kilo her 'You got to be kidding me look' again but was saying 'There's a anytime for you' in her mind. "That came out wrong. What I was trying to say was…" "Yeah yeah yeah. You said it like you meant it so don't try to switch it up now. But I'm funa swing by the dealership to switch whips. We still goin' out tonight?" Lil Kilo asked now standing beside Ms. Brown as she was cracking the eggs open pouring the yoke into a bowl. Ms. Brown smiled but was shocked to hear Lil Kilo say something about them going out because she figured that Lil Kilo had forgot all about their date after everything that's been going on. "If you're not too busy we can. I know you'll be at the hospital with Issac and taking care of your business so we can go some other time if you want to." Ms. Brown said scrambling the eggs in the bowl. Lil Kilo told Ms. Brown that he shouldn't be at the hospital all day and that he would make time for her. "So don't go makin' no plans because I'll be back to get you." Lil Kilo said walking out the kitchen to the bathroom so he could wash his face and brush his teeth before he left. Ms. Brown thought that Lil Kilo's maturity level was beyond his age and that was nothing but another plus in her eyes. *'He acts twice his age.'* Ms. Brown thought to herself about to call Lil Kilo's name to tell him to be careful out there but he was calling her name. "Ms. Brown!" Ms. Brown heard Lil Kilo yell from the living room. "What did I tell you my name was?" Ms. Brown yelled back into the living. "My bad Za'Mya." Lil Kilo said walking back into the kitchen pulling his t-shirt over his head. "I guess you gone be calling me by my full name instead of Mya huh?" Ms. Brown said. "Yep! I can't be callin' you what everybody else be callin' you." Ms. Brown smirked. "What do you want boy?" "Boy?" Lil Kilo gave Ms. Brown a look that let her know that he didn't play about that word. *'Ohh... Keon don't like it when I call him boy I see.'* Ms. Brown thought to herself and became wet all over again. "I was bout to tell you that I was on my way out so you could come lock the door behind me but seein' you lookin' so good right here I now want a hug and a kiss before I leave." Lil Kilo said stretching his arms out. Ms. Brown gave Lil Kilo a hug and the way he held her made her feel protected so without evening realizing that she was going for his lips Ms. Brown kissed Lil Kilo's lips lightly then walked him to the door telling herself that it was something about Lil Kilo that she loved. "I don't know what it is just yet but I'm going to find out. He's just so young though." Ms. Brown thought. Before Lil Kilo pulled off from Ms. Brown's house he sat in his car rolling him a blunt and called Lil Fresh to see where he was at but Lil Fresh wasn't picking up his phone. After his blunt was rolled Lil Kilo fired it up and pulled off headed towards the dealership to get him another car. Getting on the freeway headed back across town Lil Kilo picked up his phone and called Neka on speaker phone then dropped his phone in his lap so he could drive, talk on the phone and smoke his blunt all at the same time. "What's up boo?" Lil Kilo said after Neka picked up. "Heeyy baby!" Neka said sounding happy and worried at the same time. "I heard about what happened to Lil Slim yesterday and tried to call you last night and this morning to make sure he was okay but you didn't answer." Neka said. "Is he okay?" Lil Kilo let Neka know what was going on with Lil Slim and Neka couldn't believe it. "Don't go tellin' everybody what I just told you either. Matta fact don't tell NOBODY that he's in the hospital. Keep that to yourself." Lil Kilo said seriously. Neka could tell by the tone of Lil Kilo's voice that he didn't want anybody knowing what was going on with Lil Slim so Neka promised him that she wouldn't say anything to anyone. "I won't tell nobody baby I promise." Neka said. "Will I be able to see you today Keon? I didn't get to see or talk to you at all yesterday. I miss you." Neka said sounding as if she were whining. "Ion know about today boo I have a few things I gotta take care of." Lil Kilo said then thought about it. "Where you at now boo?" Lil Kilo asked thinking that he could swing by and see her for a little while after he changed cars. "I'm at home. Can you come and see me before you start handling your business? Please..! I just want to hug you. I cried all night long when you didn't answer your phone." Neka said all in one breath sounding like she was ready to start crying again. "What I tell you about all that cryin', cry baby? You gotta be strong boo. Where yo muscles at?" Lil Kilo said making fun of Neka. "I'm not no crybaby and I am strong. I'm just weak for you and your well being." Neka said back. "As long as I know you're okay then I'm okay." Lil Kilo knew that Neka's love for him was true which made it easier for him to return that same love. "I just be messin' with you boo but give me a hour or so and I'll be over there, aite?" Lil Kilo said before he hung up and got off the freeway. Lil Kilo pulled into the dealership and parked his car in front of the building where it said Reserved then hopped out and went inside to holler at Cheese the cat his daddy had running the shop before he was killed. Cheese was sitting behind the counter talking on the phone when Lil Kilo came in so he walked over to the vending machine and got him a candy bar and a cold drink while he waited on Cheese to get off the phone. "What's up nephew? I haven't seen your face in a sec. What's good?" Cheese said as soon as he hung up the phone and seen Lil Kilo. Cheese made his way around the counter to give Lil Kilo some dap. "I need a new whip. My shit got bullet holes in it." Lil Kilo said giving Cheese some dap back. "Bullet holes? What you doing with bullet holes in yo whip nephew?" Cheese wanted to know sounding a little worried. "You not beefing with nobody is ya?" Lil Kilo sat his drink down on the counter. "It's a long story. I'm straight tho." Lil Kilo said opening the Snickers he just got out the vending machine and taking a bite. "I just can't be ridin' 'round with bullet holes in my shit. I need to switch whips. You got something for me?" Lil Kilo asked. Cheese told Lil Kilo that he could pull off the lot in which ever car he wanted to pull off in then asked him what he wanted to do with his car. "You want me to have it repaired and sprayed another color or what? I mean that is that Panamera." Cheese asked. "Yeah do what you do to it then spray it white. I was bout tired of that black color anyway." Lil Kilo said looking around the lot to see which whip he wanted to pull off in. Lil Kilo wanted something that wasn't to noticeable so he could blend in with majority of the traffic but looking around Lil Kilo noticed that everything on the lot would have him sticking out in traffic still. "I see that you don't have nothin' a nigga can just duck off in huh? Everything out there is a Benz or better." Lil Kilo said. "We have another car lot right around the corner with everything else on it." Cheese told Lil Kilo. "What you tryna duck off in?" Lil Kilo thought about it for a second. "Ion know. A new Camaro or something." "What color you want? I'm funa have my partna drop it off." Cheese said grabbing the phone off the counter. "See if he got a burnt orange one over there with some tints on it." Lil Kilo said eyeing one of those new Lexus coupes Cheese had sitting on the lot. Cheese made the call and told Lil Kilo that they didn't have a burnt orange one but he had a brand new maroon one with tinted windows that ain't never been drove. "Aite that's cool. Tell 'em bring it." Lil Kilo said then walked outside to his car to get his .40 glock from under the seat and his half of blunt out the ashtray. Ten minutes after Cheese hung up the phone his partner was pulling up. "A Unk hold that white Lex coupe for me. I'll be back to get it in a few weeks." Lil Kilo said getting into the Camaro. "Who is that lil nigga?" Cheese partner asked watching Lil Kilo back out the parking lot. "That's Kilo's son. You can't tell? That lil nigga look just like his daddy." Cheese said wondering why Lil Kilo was pulling back into the dealership. Lil Kilo hopped out walked over to his car and grabbed his cds. "I can't ride without that Gates in the deck. That satellite radio ain't gone get it." Lil Kilo said then hopped back in the Camaro and smashed off. Lil Kilo called Neka and told her that he was on his way then hopped on the interstate and opened the Camaro's engine all the up going as fast as the traffic would allow him to go. Lil Kilo pulled up to Neka's house in no time. Pulling out his phone to call Neka to tell her to come outside Lil Kilo seen that he had a missed call from Lil Fresh so he called him back and Lil Fresh picked up on the first ring. "What's up Lil Kilo? Where you at fool?" Lil Fresh asked. "I just pulled up over Neka's house." Lil Kilo said getting out his car walking up to knock on Neka's door. "Ima swing thru there once I leave from over here. You at home ain't cha?" Lil Kilo asked Lil Fresh knocking on Neka's door. "Yeah I'm at the house. You goin' to see Lil Slim today?" Lil Fresh asked. "Yeah. Soon as I leave from over here Ima come get you and we'll swing up there." Lil Kilo said hearing Neka unlocking the door. "Aite bet fool." Lil Fresh said then hung up. Neka opened the door smiling from ear to ear and gave Lil Kilo the biggest hug and kiss ever. "You huggin' me like you miss me. What's up sexy?" Lil Kilo said after Neka let him go and pulled him into the house. "I more than miss you baby! I've been worried sick thinking about you. I'm so glad that you are okay. My momma told me to tell you that she's sorry to hear about your friend. She caught me crying last night and asked me what was wrong." Neka said hugging Lil Kilo again. "All okay cool. Where my baby at anyway? I ain't seen her in a week or two." Lil Kilo said grabbing Neka's ass. "My momma is not your baby! I'm your baby! And I don't know where she's at. She said she was going to the store but that was an hour ago." Neka said happy that Lil Kilo was over there with her. "So what do you have planned for the day?" Neka asked because normally on Saturdays her and Lil Kilo spent time together. "I got some lil bizniz to take care of then me and Lil Fresh gone go up to the hospital to visit Lil Slim." Lil Kilo said then reached out and grabbed Neka's ass cheek again and told her that he wouldn't mind doing her today. "I wouldn't mind either but I'm not sure where my mother is and I don't want to get caught in the act or even worst I don't want to start something we can't finish." Neka said pressing her body against Lil Kilo's sliding her hand down his pants. "You better quit then because if he get hard you gone have to get him back soft." Lil Kilo said feeling his third leg rise. "Oh yeah..?" Neka said leading Lil Kilo into her room then layed him on her bed and pulled her pants off then pulled his pants and boxers down. Neka then sat on Lil Kilo's chest backwards and grabbed his dick and licked around the head of it with her tongue while pushing her pussy towards his face so they could please each other orally in the 69 position. Lil Kilo had to use his hands to hold Neka's ass cheeks and thighs open while he lick and sucked on all over her clit. After a few minutes of moaning and slurping all over Lil Kilo's dick and feeling Lil Kilo's tongue all on her clit Neka couldn't hold back anymore and exploded her juices all over Lil Kilo's face. "Ummm…" Neka moaned feeling Lil Kilo's legs stiffen which let her know that he was on the verge of exploding his self. Neka opened her mouth a little wider and sucked her jaws in then started deep throating Lil Kilo using her hand slightly until he came all in her mouth. Neka sucked and swallowed everything Lil Kilo shot out then got up and got a soapy rag and wiped Lil Kilo off. "I love you Keon." Neka said as Lil Kilo was fixing his clothes getting ready to head out the door. "I love you too boo." Lil Kilo told Neka looking her in the eyes. After leaving from Neka's house Lil Kilo swung by Lil Fresh house so they could go see Lil Slim. "Is this what money do? You just switch whips whenever you get ready to?" Lil Fresh said hopping in the Camaro with Lil Kilo. "You can do whateva you wanna do when you got money. You can drive a different whip every day of the week if you wanted to." Lil Kilo said. "One thing I've learned about money is it don't make you happy. It only make your life better. Remember that." Lil Kilo told Lil Fresh as he was pulling off. "But I switched whips because I had some bullet holes in my shit. Now that bitch ass nigga is clueless to what kind of car we'll be in." "That nigga probably out on the block like everything cool too." Lil Fresh said adjusting his seat so he could lean back a little bit more. "I swung thru there before I picked you up and he wasn't out there. You said you know where his baby momma stay at didn't ya?" Lil Kilo asked. "Yeah I know where her cum catchin' ass stay at if she haven't moved." Lil Fresh told Lil Kilo. "You strapped ain't cha?" Lil Kilo asked Lil Fresh. "Yeah fa show. Is you?" Lil Kilo pulled his gun from off his hip and put it on his lap. I'm keepin' mine on me from here on out. Ain't no tellin' where it might go down at." Lil Kilo said. "I feel ya. I ain't leavin' home without mine either. But have you heard anything else about Lil Slim?" Lil Fresh wanted to know. "Nawl but my momma stayed at the hospital with his momma last night. I'm funa call her and see what's goin' on." Lil Kilo said then called his mother to see if Lil Slim was doing any better only to find out that he wasn't. Lil Kilo's mother told him that Lil Slim was in the same condition and still wasn't allowed any visitors. After hanging up the phone with his mother Lil Kilo told Lil Fresh what his mother said then said a silent prayer for Lil Slim again then looked over at Lil Fresh and seen him wipe a tear from under his eye. "Ride thru the hood one more time to see if Rachean is standin' out." Lil Fresh told Lil Kilo. "That fool bet not be standin' out there. That's his ass if he is." Lil Kilo said making his way towards the hood. "He don't have enuff money to hide forever. He gone have to come out of hidin' one day." Lil Fresh said. Riding through the hood ducked off behind the dark tinted windows on the Camaro they couldn't find Rachean for nothing in the world. "Ride thru the block again and ask Percy have he seen him." Lil Fresh suggested. Lil Kilo rode back through the block and pulled up beside Percy and let his window down. "Let me holla at you for a second P." Lil Kilo said. Percy was leaning against the back of his car when a maroon Camaro pulled up beside him. Seeing the window drop Percy thought it was about to go down and started moving his hand towards his waistline until he seen Lil Kilo lean up and ask to holler at him for a second. "Man I thought ya'll was them jack boys from the other side of town." Percy said. "Yo that's fucked up what happened to Lil Slim too, he aite ain't he?" Percy asked walking towards the car. "Yeah he good. I'm lookin' for that nigga Rachean tho, you know where that nigga been hangin' at?" Lil Kilo asked Percy looking him in his eyes. "I ain't seen that nigga face since that shit happened but between me and you the word is he be out here late night hustlin' when everybody gone." Percy said looking Kilo right back in the eyes. "Is that right?" "That's what they sayin'. Ion know because Ion be out here late night no more. But what's up on the work, ya'll niggas still straight?" Percy asked trying to buy some more dope from Lil Kilo. Lil Kilo had completely forgot about selling drugs after Lil Slim got shot and hearing Percy ask to buy some more reminded him that the dope was still stashed at his house. "Yeah we straight. How much you tryna get?" Lil Kilo asked Percy. "I need like five or six of them thangs if they still twelve fifty." Percy said. "Yeah the prices are still the same. It's gone take me like 30 minutes to get it to you tho, I gotta go pick it up." Lil Kilo told Percy. "Bring me six of them then." "Aite bet. Give me like 30 minutes." Lil Kilo said letting his window back up then let it back down and told Percy not to tell anybody what kind of car he was in. After serving Percy the six ounces of crack and giving him a number to reach them at whenever he needed some more Lil Kilo and Lil Fresh continued to ride around looking for Rachean. They even parked a few houses down from where Rachean baby momma lived to see if he would come out of there but he never did. "Man we done searched high and low for this nigga. I'm bout ready to kick her door in to find out if he's in there or not." Lil Fresh said watching Rachean's baby momma house like a hawk. "I'm tired of sittin' out here watchin' and waitin'. Shid I'm starting to get hungry." "I am too. Let's swing by the Chicken Shack right quick." Lil Kilo said pulling off. Turning off Rachean's baby momma street Lil Kilo told Lil Fresh to call her and see if she would let him come over. "If she let you come then chances are that nigga not in there but if she act like she don't want you over there then we know that's where he been hidin' at." Lil Kilo said. "Nigga we should have done this a hour ago." Lil Fresh said pulling out his cell phone scrolling down his contact list and stopped on the name Kesha. "I can't remember if I saved her under

Kesha1 or Kesha2." Lil Fresh said calling Kesha2. Lil Kilo listened in on the conversation Lil Fresh was having and could tell that it was Rachean's baby momma on the other end of the phone. Lil Fresh carried on the conversation with Rachean's baby momma all the way to the Chicken Shack. "She said she wasn't home right now but would call me when she got there." Lil Fresh said after he hung up. "Did it sound like she was lyin' or what?" Lil Kilo asked pulling around to the drive thru. "It didn't sound like it but you know how that go. She could've been sittin' right there beside the nigga tryna bait me in." Lil Fresh said. After ordering their food Lil Kilo backed into a parking space in front of the Chicken Shack where the two sat and ate their food trying to figure out how they could catch up with Rachean. Leaving the Chicken Shack Lil Kilo remembered that he was supposed to be taking Ms. Brown out today. "Let me call Ms. Brown to see if she still want to go out before I forget." Lil Kilo said out loud grabbing his cell phone. "Man Ms. Brown ain't fuckin' with you fool." Lil Fresh said laughing picking the half of blunt Lil Kilo had in the ashtray up. "You wastin' yo time my nigga. You ain't smooth enuff like me to fuck with Ms. Brown." Lil Fresh said then fired the half of blunt up Lil Kilo had sitting in the ashtray. "Shid you must not know where I stayed at last night fool." Lil Kilo said then called Ms. Brown on speaker phone to make sure they were still going out. After confirming that they still had a date Lil Kilo swung by his house to change clothes. Grab my phone right there and see who callin'." Lil Kilo told Lil Fresh sliding on his red Gucci Supreme kicks. "It's Percy." Lil Fresh said tossing the phone on the bed beside Lil Kilo. "You gone have to get you a whip real soon so we can be in two places at once." Lil Kilo said after he got off the phone. Leaving out to go serve Percy another three ounces Lil Kilo told Lil Fresh that he would call his people tomorrow and see if they could put him in a whip. After serving Percy Lil Kilo dropped Lil Fresh off over the girl house from school then jumped back on the freeway and headed across town to Ms. Brown's house.

Chapter 6

"He think he slick." Rachean told his baby momma after she hung up the phone with Lil Fresh. "He think he gone catch me slippin' over here but just don't know what he walkin' into." Rachean said grabbing the AK-47 he bought from Big Ed that was stashed under the couch and checked the clip. "What do you want me to tell him if he calls back?" Rachean's baby momma asked holding their seven month old daughter in her hands. "Tell him that it's okay for him to bring his ass on over so I can teach him a lesson. But before he gets here I want you and Kerri to go over to your sister's house and ya'll stay there until I call and let you know what's up." Rachean told his baby momma then leaned over and kissed his baby girl on the cheek. "How about me and the baby go ahead and go over there now and I'll just call and let you know when he's on his way." Rachean's baby momma said not wanting to take a chance of Lil Fresh just popping up without calling her first. "Aite but I'ma drop ya'll off just in case I need to make a run." Rachean been staying over his baby momma house every since he shot Lil Slim because he knew that Lil Kilo and Lil Fresh would be looking for him.

Feeling like neither one of them would go to the police and tell because of the code of the streets they lived by Rachean was just waiting to catch them slipping. Before leaving out the house to drop his baby momma and daughter off Rachean grabbed his glock nine from off the table that he also bought from Big Ed and put it on his waist line then popped one of the x-pills that he had sitting on the table as well. On his way back from dropping his baby momma and daughter off Rachean stopped at the liquor store and bought him a bottle of Amsterdam and a pack of cigarettes. *'I need me some weed for the night now.'* Rachean thought walking out the liquor store getting back into his baby momma's gold four door Camry with tinted windows that he had darkened the tints on yesterday. Rachean called and got him a half ounce of weed from somebody he knew in the hood then pulled back up over his baby momma's house and went inside and sat his bottle of liquor on the table then sat down and rolled him a blunt. "I can't believe this bitch ass nigga called my baby momma tryna set me up?" Rachean said to himself filling the cigar up with weed. Feeling the effects from the x-pill he popped start to kick in Rachean cut the radio on and rapped every Boosie song that came on. Halfway through his blunt and five shots of Amsterdam later Rachean was thinking about calling his baby momma to get Lil Fresh number to see if him and Lil Kilo wanted to meet up and shoot it out but decided that wasn't a good idea. *'I would be askin' for it if I did that.'* Rachean thought waiting on nightfall so he could hit the block and hustle.

Lil Kilo took Ms. Brown to a Five Star restaurant he remembered eating at all the time when he was younger which impressed Ms. Brown because she was expecting Lil Kilo to take her somewhere a little less expensive. "I've never ate here before." Ms. Brown said when they pulled up to the restaurant. "I didn't even know this place exist." Ms. Brown wondered how Lil Kilo knew about such a nice restaurant that she never even heard of before. "My daddy opened this before he got killed. He use to bring me and my momma here to eat every Saturday. I haven't ate here in a while tho." Lil Kilo said. "I almost forgot about this place." Lil Kilo said and noticed that the restaurant was a little crowed and that the paint on the building was a different color. "So what made you remember it?" Ms. Brown asked looking at Lil Kilo being able tell that he missed his daddy beginning around from how much he talked about him. "I was thinkin' of somewhere special to take you. I didn't want it to be a place that you were use to and this place was the first place that came to mind." Lil Kilo said. Ms. Brown leaned over and kissed Lil Kilo on the cheek. "What was that for?" Lil Kilo asked parking the car. "That's for thinking of somewhere special to take me instead of taking me somewhere predictable." Getting out the car walking into the restaurant Lil Kilo seen that there was seven other people waiting to be seated. "This line is to long to be waitin' in." Lil Kilo said under his breath looking around trying to find somebody that worked there. A waiter walked up to show the next couple in line their table and Lil Kilo stopped her. "Excuse me Ms. Is the owner or manager in?" Lil Kilo asked the waiter figuring that she was new because he didn't remember seeing her face the last time he ate there. "Yes sir he is. Do you need help with something?" The waiter asked politely. "Could you tell him that Mr. Campbell is out here please?" Lil Kilo said. The waiter escorted the couple to their table then went and told her boss that there was a Mr. Campbell standing in line that wanted to speak with him. It surprised the waiter to see her boss that never moved from behind his desk get up when she said something about a Mr. Campbell. *'Mr. Campbell must be somebody important for him to be getting his lazy tail up.'* The waiter thought leaving out the office behind her boss. The waiter watched Mr. Campbell and her boss from a distance and could tell that Mr. Campbell was a *somebody* other than the 19 year old boy that he looked like. "Little Kilo! What's going on nephew? I haven't seen or heard from you in a while. How have your mother been?" The waiter's boss said to Lil Kilo hugging him by the shoulders. Lil Kilo told the manager that was actually his uncle that his mother was cool and that he wasn't trying to stand in that long line to get a table. "Is the family section still open Unk? I gotta very special lady with me that I'm tryin' to sit with and get to know a lil better while we fill our stomachs with some of the finest food in town." Lil Kilo said then introduced Ms. Brown to his uncle. "Yeah it's still open nephew follow me." Lil Kilo's uncle said then led Lil Kilo and Ms. Brown towards the back of the restaurant. Lil Kilo grabbed Ms. Brown's hand and followed behind his uncle feeling the eyes of almost everybody in the restaurant on them as they walked by their table. "This is very nice of you Keon." Ms. Brown said once they were seated in a secluded part of the restaurant that was much plusher than the rest of the restaurant. "I'm just trying to be a gentleman to

my woman." Lil Kilo said easing the my woman part in there.
"So now I'm your lady huh?" Ms. Brown asked figuring that
Lil Kilo figured that she wouldn't catch on to what he said.
"Yep!" Lil Kilo said nodding his head. "Just because you spent
the night over my house and snuck into my bed while I was
sleep doesn't mean we're together Keon." Ms. Brown joked.
"Besides it's going to take more than you being a gentleman
to win me over." Ms. Brown flirted. Lil Kilo grinned. "What
if I told you I was a light sleeper?" Lil Kilo said checking out
the menu that seem to have changed a little since the last
time he ate there. "What does being a light sleeper have to
do with anything?" Ms. Brown asked with a confused look
on her face. "You said it's gone take me being more than a
gentleman to win you over right?" Lil Kilo asked. "And…
your point is?" Ms. Brown asked with the same look on her
face. "My point is I wasn't fully sleep when you were tryin' to
be slick and see what I was workin' with this morning. I felt
you easing back." Ms. Brown was speechless. Lil Kilo felt her
moving back against him this morning and instead of lying
about it Ms. Brown just changed the subject. "Boy you crazy."
Ms. Brown said smiling. "What's the best cooked dish on this
menu Keon?" After ordering and eating their food Lil Kilo
ordered a bottle of Dom Perignon and they sat sipping the
wine making small talk for another hour or so.

"I know he should be done eating by now. He been gone
almost four hours." Lil Fresh said logging off Facebook.
Lil Fresh been waiting on Lil Kilo to come pick him every
since Lil Kilo dropped him off. "Let me call this nigga right
quick." Lil Fresh said pulling out his phone. Lil Kilo and Ms.

Brown was leaving out the restaurant getting back into Lil Kilo's car when Lil Fresh called. Lil Kilo told Lil Fresh that he would be to get him as soon as he dropped Ms. Brown off. On the way home Ms. Brown wanted to ask Lil Kilo was he going to stay the night at her house tonight or was he going home but she didn't want Lil Kilo thinking that she was trying to pressure him into staying with her. *'He'll ask if he want to stay over again.'* Ms. Brown thought as they was pulling up to her house. "I'll be home a lil later tonight so don't go to sleep on me." Lil Kilo said looking over at Ms. Brown. "Excuse me?" Ms. Brown said as if she didn't understand what Lil Kilo was saying. "I said I'm coming home tonight so don't go to sleep on me." Lil Kilo repeated. "Shouldn't you be telling your mother that?" Ms. Brown said. "Nawl I'm telling you that. Now like I said don't go to sleep on me." Lil Kilo said before Ms. Brown got out the car. Lil Kilo stopped and picked Lil Fresh up after leaving Ms. Brown house then stopped by his house to pick up some more dope for Percy and got a phone call from his mother as he was walking through the door. "What's up ma?" Lil Kilo answered pointing back at the door telling Lil Fresh to lock it behind him. Lil Kilo was hoping that his mother was calling to tell him that Lil Slim was doing better but could tell that wasn't the case from the sound of her voice. "Baby...." Lil Kilo mother said sounding doleful. "Mam..." Lil Kilo said walking up the steps to his rooms. "The police is down here trying to question Issac but he's still in a coma so they want to question you and Marshawn about the shooting to find out who shot him." Lil Kilo wasn't trying to talk to the police about what happened to Lil Slim because he didn't want them involved in what was going on so he told his mother to tell the police that they didn't know who shot Lil Slim or why. "That was my momma she said the police wanted to question us about Lil Slim's shooting." Lil Kilo told Lil Fresh after he hung up the phone with his mother. "I ain't got nothing to say to those folks. Shid they better off asking Stevie Wonder what he seen because I haven't seen nothing or heard nothing." Lil Fresh said sitting down on Lil Kilo's bed. "I told her to tell them we don't know who did it then I heard the police officer say "Well here's my card mam, call me if you hear anything or if Issac gets any better so we can question him." Lil Kilo said digging in the back of his closet for the dope they had stashed there. "It's a black kid that was shot so they ain't gone do too much investigating. They want easy answers." Lil Fresh said. After serving Percy Lil Kilo and Lil Fresh rode around trying to come up with a different plan to catch Rachean slipping after Lil Fresh said he didn't really trust Rachean's baby momma. "I know she knows what's going on, I mean who don't? We would be some fools to follow through with those plans." Lil Fresh said trying to think of another way to catch Rachean. "We could ride down on him tonight and do him in cause he don't know this car or we could park on the next street and come from behind one of those houses and light his ass up!" Lil Fresh suggested as Lil Kilo thought about what Lil Fresh was saying. "If we come from behind the house on that fool you gone have to have that M-16 you bought and I'm gone need my Mac-11 cause ain't no telling what that nigga gone have out there with him. So we gone have to come wit it when we come." Lil Kilo told Lil Fresh. By the time night fell Rachean was on two x-pills working on his fifth blunt and his second bottle of liquor feeling his self. "I'm takin' you with me tonight." Rachean said talking to his AK-47 he had sitting on the couch beside him. Before leaving his baby momma house Rachean changed into an all black Dickie outfit he put on every night to hustle in and grabbed his pistol and his AK-47. Thirty minutes later Rachean was laying his AK-47 in the grass on the side of the abandon house he be hustling in front of just as Lil Kilo and Lil Fresh was riding up the street. "Did you see him fool?" Lil Kilo asked Lil Fresh as they was turning off the street. "Man I didn't see nobody but a couple of junkies walking towards that abandon house Percy be standing in front of." Lil Fresh said. "They was probably on their way to where ever the dope at which is where Rachean at." Lil Kilo said. "Bust a block and ride back thru then. They gotta still be out there." Lil Fresh said cocking his gun back. "What's up Ray Ray you workin'?" One of the crackheads asked Rachean who was still standing on side of the house. "We got thirty bones." The crackhead said grabbing the money from the other crackhead. "Can you hook us up?" "Yea come around back. I don't trust that car that just rode up the street." While Rachean was around the back of the house Lil Kilo and Lil Fresh was creeping back up the street looking for the crackheads Lil Fresh saw. "They done disappeared." Lil Fresh said. "They can't be gone too far. Their either in one of these houses or behind one of them tryin' to get high." Lil Kilo said looking on the side of each house as they passed by. "Slow down a lil bit this the house I seen the crackheads standin' in front of." Lil Fresh said pointing at a abandoned house. Lil Kilo slowed the car down so that he could look in the direction Lil Fresh was pointing. "I don't see nobody on the side of the house maybe they're around back somewhere." Lil Kilo said. Rachean was watching the maroon Camaro with dark tinted windows slowly creep up the street and slow down. "Do ya'll know who's drivin' that maroon car that keep ridin' up and down the street?" Rachean asked the crackheads who could care less about who was driving the car now that they got some dope. "It might be Percy. You know he be out here ridin' around sometimes." One of the crackheads said. "Nawl that ain't Percy." Rachean said then told the crackheads not to walk back around front. "Go thru the back yard and down the alley. I think that car parked a few houses up." Lil Kilo parked to see if the crackheads would pop out from behind one of the houses so that he could stop and ask them who got some dope but the crackheads didn't come out so Lil Kilo pulled off. "I don't think that nigga out here. What time is it?" Lil Kilo asked Lil Fresh. "It's 10:55 almost eleven. I don't think that nigga out here either. The block dry. It ain't a soul out here." Lil Fresh said. "I don't see how he's hustlin' late night and ain't no money to be made." Lil Kilo said turning off the block. Lil Kilo told Lil Fresh they would look for Rachean tomorrow and asked him where he was staying at tonight so that he could drop him off. "Shid I'm staying over yo crib tonight." Lil Fresh said. Lil Kilo told Lil Fresh that he wasn't going home. "Where you goin' then nigga?" Lil Fresh asked. "I'm staying over Ms. Brown's house again. Shit I might just move in." Lil Kilo said chuckling. "Nigga she ain't funa let you move in with her you trippin'. But take me home I don't feel like being bothered with no hoes right now." Lil Kilo dropped Lil Fresh off and told him that he would come get him in the morning to take him to get a whip. After dropping Lil Fresh off Lil Kilo called Ms. Brown and told her that he was on his way then called his mother and told her that he was staying over Lil Fresh house again.

Chapter 7

The next day Lil Kilo took Lil Fresh to holler at Cheese to get him a car and was tempted to pull off the lot in the white Lexus coupe he seen the last time he was there. "I gotta have that Lex Coup Cheese don't get rid of it. I'll be back in a couple mo' weeks to get it." Lil Kilo told Cheese while they was waiting on Cheese partner to being Lil Fresh his car. Lil Fresh wanted a Camaro like the one Lil Kilo had but the car lot Cheese partner worked at didn't have any more in stock and had to order some which would take two to three weeks and Lil Fresh didn't want to wait that long so he settled or a black Dodge Challenger with black tints. "Whenever you ready for it come get it. Them bullet holes that was in your car door been fixed to. All I gotta do is have the car sprayed now." Cheese said watching his partner pull into the dealership in the Dodge Challenger Lil Fresh ordered. Leaving the car lot Lil Kilo followed Lil Fresh to the DMV so that Lil Fresh could get his drivers licenses then the two made their way up to the hospital to see Lil Slim. Parking in the hospital garage in the section where the visitors parked Lil Kilo and Lil Fresh got out and walked across the street into the hospital through the sliding doors. "May I help you?" A heavy set nurse sitting behind the counter ask them. "We're here to see Issac Cook Jr." Lil Kilo said walking up to the counter. The heavy set lady typed Lil Slim's real name into the computer to find out his room number and was red flagged. "I'm sorry but the person you're trying to see isn't allowed any visitors at this moment. He has a red flag by his name which means he's either undergoing surgery or something like that. Do you know what he's been admitted into the hospital for?" The heavy set nursed asked. "He got shot a few days ago." Lil Kilo told the heavy set nurse. "That may be the reason he has a red flag by his name sweetie." "So what we got to do to see him?" Lil Fresh asked. The nurse told them that she wouldn't be able to let them back to see Lil Slim because of the red flag by his name. "I'll give you four hundred dollars to give us his room number." Lil Kilo said sliding four one hundred dollar bills across the counter. The nurse looked around the room to make sure nobody was watching then grabbed the money off the counter and stuffed it in her bra. "Room 180." The nurse said then turned in her chair pretending to be checking some files. Lil Kilo and Lil Fresh slipped into room 180 and stood in the doorway for what seemed like forever watching Lil Slim lay lifelessly breathing though the respirator that he was hooked up to. Walking over to stand next to Lil Slim's bed Lil Kilo felt his heart sink seeing his nigga plugged up to a machine that was the only thing keeping him alive. Lil Fresh walked over and stood beside Lil Kilo. "This shit don't seem real man. Everything was all good just a week ago." Lil Kilo said. Lil Fresh looked at Lil Kilo and said in a hushed tone. "I know man. But don't worry bout Lil Slim he a soulja. He gone make it. Ain't that right Lil Slim?" Lil Fresh said to Lil Slim like he was going to talk back. "I know he gone pull through. I just never thought I'll see him like this. My nigga got tubes and I.V patches everywhere. And he's losing weight." Lil Kilo said wondering how the doctors fed patients that was in these conditions. Lil Kilo and Lil Fresh talked to Lil Slim and was praying for him when a nurse came in to do her check up and put them out. "You're not supposed to be in here. How did…" The nurse started saying until she noticed that they was praying. "We're so sorry mam but we had to see best friend so we snuck up here. We don't mean any harm and will be leaving now." Lil Kilo said with tears in his eyes looking down at Lil Slim one last time before leaving the hospital room. Out in the parking garage Lil Kilo and Lil Fresh sat talking about Lil Slim and his condition for a little while then hopped in their cars and went their separate ways with plans to meet up later on. Lil Kilo found his self talking to God again before he pulled out the garage. "God please allow Lil Slim to pull though, God Please." He repeated over and over again. Cutting his cell phone back on Lil Kilo plugged it into the car charger and seen that his mother had left him a voicemail which made him wonder about Lil Slim's mother and how she felt about her son being shot with the chances of not making it. Riding through the hood about to go holler at Big Ed Lil Kilo was juggling the thought of calling Lil Slim's mother to apologize but wasn't sure if Ivonne wanted to talk to him so he decided not to call. After hollering at Big Ed getting him something to smoke Lil Kilo pulled up at the corner store to get him something to drink and some cigars and was sitting in front of the store rolling a blunt when his phone rung. Looking at the caller ID on his phone he seen that it was Neka calling. "She probably mad that I haven't called her in a couple days." Lil Kilo said to his self before answering the phone. "What's up boo?" And just like he expected she wanted to know why he haven't called her. "I haven't heard from you in two days. Are you okay Keon?" Neka asked. "Yeah boo I'm good. Just been going thru a lot lately. What's up with you tho, you aite?" Lil Kilo asked licking the end of his blunt shut. *I'm glad Ol' Man got that Kush back in.'* Lil Kilo thought sitting his blunt in the ashtray. "Yeah, I'm aite." Neka said giggling trying to sound hood like Lil Kilo. "I've just been worried about you like always." Neka wasn't from the hood so she didn't understand what living or being from the hood was like. The only time she's ever in the hood is when she was with Lil Kilo. Other than that she was where the rich people lived and would've been going to school where the rich kids went but unfortunately there wasn't a high school for the rich kids in Youngtown. "What I tell you about worryin' and what it does to you?" Lil Kilo said. "I wouldn't worry so much if you picked up the phone and called me sometimes. And you don't have to worry about me worrying my hair out because I was thinking about getting it cut like Halle Berry got her hair." Neka said knowing that Lil Kilo didn't like short hairstyles. "Nawl don't do that boo. You know I don't like that look. Only Halle can get away with that. Besides when you get it cut short like that you have to keep it done or it don't look right. But when you got that long natural hair like yours you can always pull it back in a ponytail and still be fye!" Lil Kilo said looking for his lighter. "I can always grow it back." Neka said. "Yeah but that will take too long. Where you at anyway?" Lil Kilo asked Neka. "I'm at home. Why, are you coming over?" Neka asked. "I'm bout to come pick you up so put some clothes on." Lil Kilo said then hung up. "Where the fuck is my lighter at?" Lil Kilo said out loud lifting up to make sure he wasn't sitting on it. *'Lil Fresh dooty ass probably cuffed it.'* Lil Kilo thought getting out the car to run back in the store to buy another lighter. Pulling up at Neka's house Lil Kilo called and told her that he was outside then grabbed his blunt out the ashtray and fired it up. By the time Neka came out the house dressed in a red and white Dolce and Gabbana shirt and some white Dolce and Gabbana pants that hugged her cheerleading figure perfectly Lil Kilo was sitting in a cloud of weed smoke that smacked Neka dead in the face as soon as she opened the car door but Neka didn't care. She was so happy to see Lil Kilo that she hopped straight in and grabbed his blunt and put it out and was all over him. "What's wrong baby?" Neka asked sensing that something was on Lil Kilo's mind. "Ain't nothin'… I'm cool. What's up you hungry?" Lil Kilo said pulling off. "No not really but I'll sit down with you if you want." Neka said wondering what was on Lil Kilo's mind. "Is everything okay Keon?" Neka asked him after riding in complete silence for a few minutes. Lil Kilo told Neka that he just seen Lil Slim layed up in the hospital and how he was starting to feel like he was all his fault. "I've been thinkin' bout callin' his momma to apologize for what happened but I don't think she wanna talk to me right now." Lil Kilo said. "I think you should call her and apologize. She might need to hear that from you Keon." Neka told Lil Kilo hoping that he picked his phone up and called Lil Slim's mother to apologize. "I'll call if you get behind the wheel and drive while I finish smokin' my blunt." Lil Kilo said pulling over. Neka and Lil Kilo switched seats and Neka drove straight to the hood. "You like it in the hood don't you boo?" Lil Kilo asked as they were getting off the interstate. "Yep! These my people. Now sit up in that seat and call yo home boy momma and apologize fool." Neka said in her best hood rat voice. Lil Kilo shook his head and chuckled. "Don't be makin' fun of my peoples punk just cause you ain't from the hood." Lil Kilo said knowing that Neka was only playing because of her deep concern she had for the people that wasn't as fortunate as her. "Just because I'm not from the hood doesn't mean that I don't care about what goes on there." Neka said. "If I ruled the world there wouldn't be no hoods, poverty would just be a word and you and I would spend each day of our life together." Neka said then pulled into the Chicken Shack so Lil Kilo could get him something to eat. "Your down to earthiness if that's a word is what I love most about you boo. Most people that's lucky enough to be in your shoes turn their nose up at the ones below them. And that's something I've never once seen or heard you do." Lil Kilo said falling in love with Neka all over again thinking about her attitude and outlook on life. "Are you sure it's not my looks and the way I put it on you in the bed that you love most about me baby?" Neka asked pulling behind a car that was in the drive thru. "Nawl that ain't the reason. Just part of it." Lil Kilo said then told Neka to order him a number three when they got to the window. After Lil Kilo got his food him and Neka rode around the hood until Lil Kilo told her to stop over his house so he could pick something up. "You still haven't called Lil Slim's mother yet."

Neka said as they was getting out the car walking inside Lil Kilo's house. "I'm gone call as soon as we get inside." Lil Kilo said opening the front door to his house. "Momma!" Lil Kilo yelled standing in the living room of their house. "I know she hear me." Lil Kilo said then yelled momma again. "What is you doing all this yelling for boy? I'm on the phone." Kenya said walking into the living room with the phone to her ear. "Oh, hey Neka. I haven't seen you in a while. How have you been?" Lil Kilo mother asked Neka. "I've been doing okay Ms. Kenya and Keon is the one to blame for us not seeing each other. He act like he's been too busy to bring me by to see you." Neka said. "Don't blame it on me because I'm not the cause. Tell her the real reason why you haven't been by." Lil Kilo said walking up the stairs to his room because he already knew that Neka and his mother was about to start yapping. "Aw boy hush! You is the reason I haven't been seeing my daughter in-law." Lil Kilo's mother said to Lil Kilo as he made his way up the stairs. Lil Kilo pulled his bedroom door up behind him and sat his pistol on his bed then dug out the dope they had left and the money they made so far and sat it all on his bed then sat down and started counting the money. *'It's bout time to holla at Cutt again. We need some more dope.'* Lil Kilo thought after counting the money and seeing that they only had six ounces left. Lil Kilo called Cutt and told him that he needed another one and Cutt told him to come on. Just as Lil Kilo was putting the dope and money up Neka walked into his room and seen him in the closet and asked what he was doing. "Just puttin' something up. You bout ready to go? I gotta make a run right quick." Lil Kilo told her then grabbed his gun from off the bed and stuff the four ounces of dope the dude that be with Percy wanted in his boxers. Neka seen Lil Kilo's gun and knew why he had one so she didn't even ask about it. All she said was "Baby please be careful." After serving the dude that be with Percy the dope Lil Kilo dropped Neka off so that he could meet up with Lil Fresh so they could go holler at Cutt to reeup. Before Neka got out the car she made Lil Kilo call Lil Slim's mother to apologize. "You wasn't going to forget about that was you?" Lil Kilo said pulling out his cell phone. "Nope!" Neka said watching Lil Kilo dial some numbers on his cell phone then listened in on his conversation with Lil Slim's mother. It took a lot off Lil Kilo's chest after talking to Lil Slim's mother. Hearing her tell him that everything was going to be okay ment a lot to him and it showed on his face once he hung the phone up. Leaving Neka's house Lil Kilo met up with Lil Fresh and got in the car with him so they could meet Cutt at the Pizza Hut downtown. "I see you didn't waste no time changin' the scent in here." Lil Kilo said once he got in the car with Lil Fresh and smelled the strong weed odor that was in the air. "I smoked a blunt bout a hour ago. The smell should be gone by now." Lil Fresh said pulling off. "Where we 'pose to be meeting Cutt at?" Lil Fresh asked. Lil Kilo told Lil Fresh where they was meeting Cutt at then told him about the conversation he had with Lil Slim's mother. "I thought she was gone have a attitude or something but she didn't. She takin' it better than I thought she would be." Lil Kilo said. "It's good that she's in good spirits. I was thinkin' bout calling her myself. I might just swing by to see her tho." Lil Fresh said. After they met Cutt at the Pizza Hut Lil Fresh dropped Lil Kilo off at his car then followed him back to his house. "I don't know where we gone cook this dope at my momma still here." Lil Kilo said to Lil Fresh as they got out their cars. "Where ya'll cook it at last time?" Lil Fresh asked wondering if his momma was home. "Cutt let us use his spot. But that's way back across town and I ain't tryna risk ridin' dirty like that." Lil Kilo said. "I gotta lil freak that got a project on the Southside. I know she'll let us cook up over there." Lil Fresh said. "Who you talkin' bout Eva?" Lil Kilo asked hitting the name on the nose. "Yeah how you know?" "I guessed but call and ask her if we can use her kitchen for a couple hours. Tell her we'll give her a hunnit." Lil Fresh called and was denied until he said something about the hundred dollars Lil Kilo offered her. "She said it's all good but to make sure we got everything we need." Lil Fresh said after hanging up his phone. "Shid we don't need nothin' but a coffee pot, some baking soda, scales and a knife. Follow me to the store before we go over there." Lil Kilo said hopping back in his car. After getting everything they needed from the store Lil Kilo and Lil Fresh pulled up in the projects and parked in front of Eva's building. "Call and tell her to open the door." Lil Kilo told Lil Fresh as they was walking up the stairs to Eva's project. Eva opened the door with her hand out. "Ya'll ain't cumin' in til I get my money. Ya'll ain't funa trick me." Eva said standing in her door sounding real ghettoish. "I'ma give you two hunnit just let us in and get settled." Lil Kilo said moving Eva's hand that was blocking the door and walked into her house. "Don't cum bargin' in my house like you runnin' something Lil Kilo. You ain't runnin' nothin'." Eva said eyeing Lil Kilo's bankroll. Lil Kilo peeled off two one hundred dollar bills and handed them to Eva. "I see you haven't changed a bit with yo ghetto ass. But 'preciate you lettin' us use your spot." Lil Kilo said. "As long as ya'll paying ya'll can use my kitchen any time ya'll get ready." Eva said putting the money in her back pocket. Eva was one of them project chicks that thought she was better than everybody else but wasn't no different than the rest of them. Loud, ghetto and thick to death. "Where yo pots and shit at?" Lil Kilo asked walking into Eva's kitchen that was somewhat clean. "Look unda tha sink duh!" Eva said walking into the kitchen to be nosey more than anything. "Let me use yo bathroom right quick. I gotta piss." Lil Fresh said walking out the kitchen. "You know where it's at. Don't act like you forgot." Eva said bending over in front of Lil Kilo to get him a pot. "When you gone let me suck the cum outta that dick again Lil Kilo?" Eva asked Lil Kilo handing him a pot then reached for his dick with her free hand but Lil Kilo. Eva went to the same school Lil Kilo and Lil Fresh went to but dropped out after she got pregnant the second time. "You know you fuck with my nigga now and I don't get down like that." Lil Kilo said knocking Eva's hand down. Eva was one of those females that could trick a nigga that didn't know her because she wasn't ugly at all and on top of that she got a body like a model and a ass like Kim K. "I don't fuck with Lil Fresh like that. We just cool. Don't act like you don't miss skippin' class to get this head Lil Kilo." Eva said leaving out the kitchen as Lil Fresh was walking back in. Lil Kilo showed Lil Fresh how to cut the dope with the baking soda then cook it and bring back more. Lil Fresh caught on to how to cook the dope and the two was bringing back an extra two ounces of crack off every 4 ½ ounces of cocaine they cooked. After the whole brick was cooked they had a total of 44 ounces of crack instead of the 36 ounces of cocaine they started with. "I'm gone take 22 zips and give you 22 of them. That way you can do yo thing while I'm doin' mine." Lil Kilo told Lil Fresh leaving the mess they made behind for Eva to clean up. "Man I see how these niggas get rich off this shit! It's simple. Buy it low, cut it, stretch it, cook it and sell it high." Lil Fresh said. "It's more to the game than that. You gotta watch out for the police, the haters and the snakes." Lil Kilo said pointing to the living room where Eva was when he said the last part. Lil Kilo knew how his nigga was when it came to girls and planned on having a talk with him once they left Eva's house. "Let's get out of here." Lil Kilo said walking out the kitchen. Outside in the parking lot Lil Kilo and Lil Fresh ran into a couple niggas they went to school with that be doing a little hustling on the low and asked them how much was they paying for the work. After finding out they was getting taxed for it Lil Kilo gave them his cell phone number and told them that him and Lil Fresh would sell it to them cheaper then what they was getting it for. "Drop that work off then meet me at the Chicken Shack. I need to holla at you." Lil Kilo said as he was getting into his car. "Aite give me bout 20 minutes and I'll be there."

Chapter 8

After stashing the 22 zips in the back of his closet Lil Kilo sat on the edge of his bed and thought about his boy. "Man this shit fucked up." Lil Kilo said to himself after about 10 minutes of day dreaming. Getting up to go down stairs to get something to drink Lil Kilo passed his mother's room and heard her talking on the phone. "Yeah girl I know… I can only imagine your pain… Don't you say that… Issac will be just fine. He will be home to you sooner than you think." Lil Kilo heard his mother saying. Knowing that his mother was on the phone with Lil Slim's mother Lil Kilo could tell from what his mother was saying that Lil Slim's mother was having doubts on Lil Slim pulling through. *'Things must be getting worse for Lil Slim.'* Lil Kilo thought walking off from his mother's door. Just as Lil Kilo was about to open the refrigerator he felt his phone vibrating then heard it ding singling that he had a text message. Pulling his phone out his pocket to see who texted him Lil Kilo smile when he seen that it was Ms. Brown sending him a text telling him thanks again. "No thank you." Lil Kilo replied. Then got a bottled water out the refrigerator and before he could shut the door back he felt his phone go off again. "For?" Ms. Brown asked. "For listening to me get things off my chest the other night." Lil Kilo hit send then sent Ms. Brown the heart emoji. After going back and forth with Ms. Brown Lil Kilo called Lil Fresh to see where he was at. "I'm about to leave my house in bout 5 minutes." Lil Fresh told Lil Kilo. "Bet." Lil Kilo said then hollered up the stairs and told his momma that he'll be right back. "Hold on before you leave out the house." Lil Kilo mother said walking out her room. "I want to talk to you." Lil Kilo mother said coming down the stairs. Lil Kilo could tell from the sound of his mother voice that something wasn't right. Reaching the bottom of the stairs Lil Kilo's mother broke down crying. "Don't cry momma it's gone be okay." Lil Kilo said hugging his mother. "Don't cry." "Keon... I... sniff sniff... I want you to know that I love you." Lil Kilo mother's said squeezing him tightly. "I love you too momma." Lil Kilo said back hugging his mother. "I just got off the phone with Ivonne... and... and... she's still at the hospital..." Lil Kilo's mother was saying. "Momma please tell me that Lil Slim is aite." Lil Kilo said feeling tears start to roll down his face. Lil Kilo's mother just held him still crying. "Ivonne said that she don't think Issac is gone make it baby." Lil Kilo's body stiffened and everything around him seemed as if it had stopped. Not wanting to believe what his mother was saying Lil kilo wiped his tears. "Stop crying momma Lil Slim gone be okay. God got 'em." Lil Kilo said then kissed his mother and told her that he'll be back. "I need some fresh air." Hopping in his whip Lil Kilo grabbed his gun from under the seat and put it on his lap. "Bitch ass nigga made my momma cry. I'ma make sure his momma cry." Lil Kilo though while pulling out his phone to call Lil Fresh. Sitting in the back of the Chicken Shack picking with his food Lil Kilo just stared out the window. "You aite?" Lil Fresh asked sensing that something was bothering his nigga. "Nawl man I ain't." Lil Kilo said then let out a deep breathe. "My momma said Lil Slim momma said that he might not make it." What?" Lil Fresh said not believing his ears. "They said he might not make it fool." Lil Kilo said fighting back tears. Lil Kilo, Lil Fresh and Lil Slim been around each other since birth so they were like brothers. Anytime you seen one you seen the others. "I can't believe this shit." Lil Fresh said pushing his food in front of him. "Me either." Lil Kilo added. "Life wouldn't be the same without Lil Slim." Lil Kilo said. Lil Fresh and Lil Kilo sat there in silence both lost in their own thoughts after Lil Kilo said that life wouldn't be the same without Lil Slim. "Sorry to hear about your friend." Hearing this broke both of them out of their train of thoughts. Looking up seeing a beautiful short Puerto Rican girl that looked like she was mixed with black and her friend standing there they both just stared. "We didn't mean to interrupt you or wasn't trying to be rude. We just wanted to say sorry." They Puerto Rican girl said before her and her friend walked off. Lil Kilo and Lil Fresh both followed the two girls with their eyes and watched as they walked out of the Chicken Shack and got into a white C380 Benz coupe. "You know them?" Lil Kilo asked Lil Fresh. "That's umm…umm… damn! What's her name? She use to go to middle school with us." Lil Fresh said trying to put a name with a face. "Middle school? Nigga the only person I remember from middle school is Neka." Lil Kilo said. "I forgot you wasn't getting no play back then and Neka was the only girl that wanted you." Lil Fresh told Lil Kilo still trying to figure out what the Puerto Rican girl name was. "Nigga I could have had any bitch I wanted in middle school but none of them was as cute as Neka." Lil Kilo said then took sip of the Ice Tea he was drinking. "I can't remember her name but she was in one of my classes." Lil Fresh said trying his best to remember the Puerto Rican girl's name. "It'll come to me. But why did you want to meet me here? To tell me about Lil Slim?" Lil Fresh questioned. "Nawl. I wanted to talk to you about the game." Lil Kilo said remembering the real reason he told Lil Fresh to meet him at the Chicken Shack. "The game? What about the game fool?" Lil Fresh asked. "This is a whole different ball game we dealin' wit. This shit is serious. It's more than just money that comes with it." Lil Kilo was telling Lil Fresh looking him square in the eyes to make sure he was understanding what he was saying and what he was about to say. "I know its serious fool. You don't think I know that?" Lil Fresh said feeling a little offended. "I'm just making sure you do. The game we playin' if we're not smart about our every move could leave us dead or in jail." Lil Kilo was saying then paused. "I mean look at Lil Slim. He's layed up in the hospital with seven bullet holes in him from us not being smart. That situation could have been handled differently and none of that would've happened." Lil Fresh nodded his head which let Lil Kilo know that he understood what he was saying. Lil Kilo then asked Lil Fresh if he knew the only reason they were selling dope to begin with. "Yeah, me and Lil Slim talked about it." Lil Fresh said thinking about what Lil Slim told him. "It's just me and you out here now tho so I'ma need you to stay focused." Lil Kilo told Lil

Fresh. "And leave these bitches alone." Lil Kilo added knowing how his nigga was with females. "I got you." Lil Fresh said reaching across the table to give his nigga some dap. "You think Lil Slim gone make it tho?" Lil Fresh asked Lil Kilo with concern all in his voice. Lil Kilo looked up at Lil Fresh and said with more hope than anything "Yeah... I think he gone make it. God got em." After leaving the Chicken Shack with Lil Fresh Lil Kilo thought about calling Neka to see what she was doing but called Ms. Brown instead only to get her voicemail. "She must be busy." Lil Kilo said to himself then sent her a text message and said 'Call me when you get a chance.' Riding through the city unintentionally looking for Rachean Lil Kilo found himself busting blocks through the hood in complete silence thinking about Lil Slim. *Let me call Big Ed and get me a sack. I need to clear my mind.'* Lil Kilo thought. Pulling out his cell phone to call Big Ed Lil Kilo seen that he had a missed FaceTime call from Neka. "I'll call her back in a sec." Lil Kilo said then called Big Ed. "What's up Ol' Man you got some of that shit the rappers smoke?" Lil Kilo asked after Big Ed picked the phone up. "It just depends on which rapper you talkin' bout. Not all rappers smoke strong. A lot of them just rap about it." Big Ed said joking around with Lil Kilo. "I need some of that shit Snoop Dogg, Lil Wayne and Wiz Kahlifa be smokin'." Lil Kilo said. "You know where I'm at." Big Ed said then hung up. Not even fifteen minutes later Lil Kilo was sitting on Big Ed's couch passing a blunt back and forth. Big Ed told Lil Kilo that the word on the street was him and his niggas were the ones to see if you were looking for some work. "They say ya'll keep that white girl and got the cheapest price going." Big Ed told

Lil Kilo dumping the ashes off the blunt. Lil Kilo never really had a real conversation with Big Ed other than the ones they had about his daddy or the amount of weed he was buying to smoke. But for some real reason Lil Kilo felt that he could talk to Big Ed so he did. Lil Kilo told Big Ed everything and Big Ed listened and understood why Lil Kilo and his niggas started selling dope now. "When I first heard that ya'll niggas was selling dope it confused me." Big Ed said. "I was thinking that ya'll niggas were playing follow the leader or some shit." "Follow the leader?" Lil Kilo said then laughed. "I mean I know that neither one of ya'll lil niggas gotta be out there so I figured ya'll were influenced by other niggas." Big Ed said passing Lil Kilo the blunt. "Nawl we weren't influenced. There's a purpose behind us being out there." Lil Kilo said then took a hit from the blunt. Out of nowhere Big Ed felt like this was Déjà vu. "You remember when I told you I was the nigga that fronted yo daddy his first pound of weed?" Big Ed asked Lil Kilo. "Yeah I remember." Lil Kilo said wondering where Big Ed was going with this. "Well I'm going to tell you the exact something I told him." Big Ed said then thought back to the conversation he had with Lil Kilo's daddy. "Once ya'll decided to join the streets ya'll put ya'll self in men shoes, so that's how ya'll will be treated. That age shit means nothing. You hear me Lil Kilo?" Big Ed questioned. "Yeah I hear you." Lil Kilo said back passing the blunt thinking about what Big Ed said then thought about Lil Slim. "Ain't no love in these streets. NONE! It's nothing but hate, jealousy, snakes and rats. You have to be on point at all times. You never know who's out to get you." Big Ed said then took a short pull from the blunt. "You ever seen that movie Paid in Full?" Big Ed asked Lil Kilo. "That's a classic. You can't be from the hood and haven't seen that." Lil Kilo replied. "Why you ask me that?" "To remind you that there are Rico's everywhere you go. So don't go making new friends. Keep yo circle tight." Big Ed told Lil Kilo. Lil Kilo listened to everything Big Ed was telling him and grew a liking to him even more after Big Ed gave him a real life lesson before he left. "And one other thing before you leave." Big Ed told Lil Kilo as he was putting his jacket on. "What's up Ol' Man?" Lil Kilo said. "Stay in school. I'm gone tell you something real valuable that the rich parents teach their kids that the poor parents don't." Big Ed said dropping the blunt roach in the ashtray. "You know what the rich people teach their kids?" Big Ed asked Lil Kilo looking him square in the eyes. Lil Kilo thought about it for a second. "Nawl I don't." Lil Kilo said really wanting to know what Big Ed was about to say because he knew that his mother wasn't rich or poor and conversations like these were never talked about at home. "Check this out. The rich people tell their kids to go to school get a good education to CREATE their own job. While the poor parents teach their kids to go to school to get a good education so that they can find a good job." Big Ed said then paused for a second to see if what he said registered to Lil Kilo. And it did. "I see what you saying. That's deep." Lil Kilo said giving Big Ed some dap. "Create your own job like your daddy did baby boy because I'm telling you right now that these streets are washed up. Ain't no future in them." After leaving Big Ed's spot Lil Kilo thought about everything he was saying. Checking the clock on the dash seeing that it was 6:38 Lil Kilo tried to Facetime Neka back but she didn't answer. Feeling like he needed someone to talk to Lil Kilo decided to go back up to the hospital to see if he could sneak back into Lil Slim's room to talk to him. *'I hope Big Momma working today.'* Lil Kilo thought thinking about the heavy set nurse that gave him and Lil Fresh Lil Slim's room number the last time. Parking his car in the garage Lil Kilo walked across the street towards the hospital and noticed that it was packed on the inside. "Damn it's a lot of people in here tonight." Lil Kilo said under his breath walking through the front door of the ER room. Looking towards the front desk seeing four people waiting in line Lil Kilo looked over their shoulder to see if Big Momma was there. *'Damn she not working at the front desk.'* Lil Kilo thought seeing an elderly white lady sitting behind the desk. "I know she ain't goin'." Lil Kilo said talking to his self but figured it was worth a try. Standing in line waiting to try to run game on the old white lady sitting behind the desk Lil Kilo scanned the waiting room with his eyes. *'Man these people look crazy as hell in here.'* Lil Kilo thought. *'Why in the hell is she wearing that mask, why is both his legs and arms in a cast, what the hell could possibly be wrong with this winning as baby, why haven't the doctors took granny to the back yet, and why in the hell is this old white man staring at me.'* Lil Kilo chuckled. "Yes, how may I help you sir?" The old white lady sitting behind the desk asked talking to Lil Kilo. "Oh... Umm... Hi... I'm here to see Issac Cook Jr." Lil Kilo said than smiled. "Okay, I'll just need to see a photo I.D." The old white lady said then hit a few keys on the keyboard. *'Shit, I might not have to run game to see my nigga after all.'* Lil Kilo thought pulling his driver licenses out. Just as Lil Kilo was about to hand her his driver licenses the old white lady looked up and said "I'm sorry young man but Issac has a red flag by his name and isn't allowed any visitors." "Damn!" Lil Kilo let the words slip out his mouth. "Excuse my language mam. I'm just a little frustrated. I really need to see my brother." Lil Kilo said thinking about bribing the old white lady until she said something about the hospital policy and her losing her job. "I understand. Thanks anyway." Lil Kilo said then tucked his licenses back in his wallet and headed towards the doors. Exiting the hospitals doors Lil Kilo was about to cross the street until he heard someone say "Hey." Lil Kilo looked back and seen the heavy set nurse that gave him and Lil Fresh Lil Slim's room number sitting in the smoking area smoking a cigarette. "You must be here trying to see your friend again?" The heavy set nurse asked Lil Kilo. "Yeah but the white lady at the front desk following all the rules." Lil Kilo said walking over to where the heavy set nurse was sitting. "That's Ms. Nancy. She's been here almost 25 years. She follows the policy very precisely. But what happened to your friend anyway?" The nurse wanted to know. Not really wanting to tell the nurse to much "He got shot" was all Lil Kilo said. "Can you help me get to his room again?" Lil Kilo asked. "You got four hundred dollars again?" The nurse asked then thumped the ashes off her cigarette. Not wanting to pay the heavy set nurse $400 dollars again but wanting to see his nigga Lil Kilo handed it to her. "You showl don't mind charging a nigga lights out do ya?" Lil Kilo said watching the nurse fold the money up and stick it in her bra. "Not when I can lose my job doing this. Now look, take my I.D. badge go down those steps right there and you'll be on the first floor." Ms. Heavy Set said pointing to a set of steps behind them. "Once you get to the door put my badge up to the lock pad and the door will open. Leave the door cracked with a rock or something so I can get in." The nurse told Lil Kilo. "And then just leave my badge under the sink in his room and I'll get it." Lil Kilo laughed. "You giving instructions like you've done this before. Umm…what's your name?" Lil Kilo asked never getting the name of the heavy set nurse. "I'm giving instructions like I don't want to get caught and lose my job." The nurse said with a slight attitude. "And my name is Candy." "My bad Ms. Candy I was only jokin'." Lil Kilo said walking towards the steps. '*Why all big girls name gotta have something to do with food?*' Lil Kilo thought walking down the steps. Inside Lil Slim's room Lil Kilo stood by the door for a brief second watching Lil Slim lay spiritlessly in the dimly lit room. Walking over to stand next to Lil Slim Lil Kilo bowed his head and said a quick prayer. "Dear God, please watch over my friend, please God. He don't deserve this. He's only 16 and his mother needs him God. God I call upon you asking you to allow Lil Slim to be okay. In God's name I pray amen." Lil Kilo prayed then wiped the tears from his eyes. Standing there looking at all the tubes and I.V. patches that was connected to Lil Slim's body Lil Kilo began to wonder how things would be without his nigga again but just as quick as the thought ran across his head it was gone and Lil Kilo caught himself reaching down to grab Lil Slim's hand. "Let me wash my hands." Lil Kilo thought needing to relieve his bladder as well. Lil Kilo pulled the bathroom door open and was shutting it behind him when he heard the door to Lil Slim's room open. "Room 180. Issac Cook Jr." Lil Kilo heard a female voice say then heard the door shut. "Shit!" Lil Kilo said under his breath not really knowing what to do because of there being nowhere to hide in the small ass bathroom he was in. "Do you mind changing the I.V. bag while I check Mr. Cook's heartbeat?" Lil Kilo heard the same female voice ask whoever was in the room with her. "I don't mind." The other voice said which was another female voice that didn't sound like Candy the heavy set nurse who's been helping Lil Kilo. *'I mightis well leave her ID under the sink before I forget.'* Lil Kilo thought to himself trying to make the least noise as possible. "Do you think that this little boy will make it out of this coma?" Lil Kilo heard the second female voice ask. "His mother asked me this question yesterday. I told her all we can do is pray. Because with his condition he doesn't seem to be getting any better. Without this ventilator that he's hooked up to he'll surely die." The first voice said writing something on the clipboard she was holding. "There is power in prayer. Hold on little man God is with you." The second voice said rubbing Lil Slim's forehead." "All done in here. Three more rooms and I'm off." The first voice said. After hearing the voices leave the room Lil Kilo took a piss washed his hands and was standing right back next to Lil Slim praying again this time holding Lil Slim's hand. "Dear God, it's me again Lil Kilo. I mean Keon. I know I just prayed maybe 10 minutes ago but I want to pray one more time to ask you to please watch over Lil Slim… I mean Issac, please… Thank you God… Amen." Lil Kilo prayed then noticed that he was squeezing Lil Slim hand kind of tight. Not wanting to let go of Lil Slim's hand Lil Kilo told Lil Slim to squeeze his hand back if he could understand what he was saying. Hoping that Lil Slim would respond with the slightest squeeze Lil Kilo closed his eyes and concentrated on any type of movement. After about five minutes of pure concentrating Lil Kilo opened his eyes and looked at Lil Slim. "What's up Lil Slim? You been in here to long nigga. You gettin' comfortable or something fool?" Lil Kilo told Lil Slim wanting to have a conversation with him so bad that he just started talking to him like wasn't nothing wrong with him. "Don't let me find out ain't shit really wrong with you and you layed back here on PC (protective custody)." Lil Kilo found his self joking and laughing with Lil Slim. "I got yo back fool. You ain't gotta be scared." After about two minutes of joking around with Lil Slim Lil Kilo stopped after seeing that his nigga wasn't joking back. "Lil Slim I don't think I've ever told you this but I love you fool. And I mean that from the bottom of my heart. I love you like a brother that I've never had and losing you is something I'm just not ready to deal with." Lil Kilo was so engulfed in his conversation with Lil Slim that he never heard the door open and someone walked in and close it behind him. "I really hate seeing you layed up like this man. We need you to get well." Lil Kilo said letting his tears flow freely down his cheeks dropping on Lil Slim's bed. Lil Kilo grabbed Lil Slim's hand again then leaned over his bed and kissed Lil Slim on the forehead. "I love you." Lil Kilo said then whispered in Lil Slim's ear. "We can't found out who killed our daddy until you come home." As Lil Kilo was raising back up he thought that he felt Lil Slim gently squeeze his hand but brushed it off thinking that his movements may have made it feel that way. "I love you Lil Slim." Lil Kilo said once more turning to walk out not knowing that someone was watching him from the door until the person broke down crying. Lil Kilo stood still.

"Ms. Ivonne?" Lil Kilo said trying to make out the silhouette that was standing next to the door. "Is that you Ms. Ivonne?" Lil Kilo asked walking towards the door. "Yes, this is me Keon." Ivonne said walking out so that Lil Kilo could see her. Ivonne grabbed Lil Kilo and hugged him tightly. "Keon, I don't want you walking around here feeling like this is all your fault because it's not. God has a reason for it all." Ivonne said wiping her tears looking over at her baby. Lil Kilo told Ivonne that he was sorry for everything still and that everything was going to be okay. "How long have you been in here?" Lil Kilo wanted to know. "I left to go get me a bite to eat and came back and seen you praying it looked like so I didn't interrupt." Ivonne told Lil Kilo then walked to stand next to her baby. Lil Kilo looked on and began to wonder just how much pain Ivonne was in seeing her son layed up in the hospital fighting for his life knowing that Lil Slim was all she had.. "I can only imagine how you feel right now Ms. Ivonne." Lil Kilo said walking over to stand next to Lil Slim's mother. "I love you Ms. Ivonne." Lil Kilo told Lil Slim's mother. "I love you too." Ivonne told Lil Kilo before he left.

Chapter 9

"I'm telling you it'll work. Trust me." Rachean was telling his homeboy named Fat Chubb. "Ain't nobody gone be there. I've been putting this together for a few days now. I done scoped the scene and everything." Rachean said passing Fat Chubb a blunt. Fat Chubb was one of those roguish fat black ugly ass niggas that didn't have a lick of hustle so he robbed. Taking the blunt from Rachean Fat Chubb took a hit then blew the smoke in the air. Rachean and Fat Chubb was sitting in Rachean baby momma's living room smoking and drinking talking about how they needed to make some extra money. "I'm not saying it won't work. All I'm saying is you tryna kick a nigga door in broad day light?" Fat Chubb said hitting the blunt again. Fat Chubb kind of put you in mind of a younger Beanie Sigel with his facial hair and hair on his head that look as if the last time it was touched was when his mother brushed it when he was a baby. "This shit is sweet." Rachean said getting excited knowing how easy his plan was. Rachean got tired of hustling at night because he wasn't making the kind of money he made during the day so he linked up with Fat Chubb and started robbing niggas around the way.

And now he wanted to kick Lil Kilo's mother door down and rob Lil Kilo because of the word on the street that Lil Kilo got it. "How you even know that he got somethin' in there?" Fat Chubb asked Rachean passing him the blunt back. "Everybody know Lil Kilo and 'em keep some work. I asked around to see if they had a spot and everybody I asked said 'Not that they know of.' Rachean said then hit the blunt. "And if a nigga don't have a spot and still stay at home with his momma where else the work gone be?" Rachean asked the question then dumped the ashes from the blunt inside a cup that they were using as an ashtray. "You right. But shid he might got it over one of his lil hoes house." Fat Chubb said pouring him a shot of Hennessy. "This lil nigga 16-17 he ain't thinkin' like that. I guarantee you everything is over his momma house in his room somewhere." Rachean said wondering where Lil Kilo was stashing his dope. "Aite look we can kick the door but if ain't nothin' in there I'm takin' everything of value. I know his momma got all type of ice layin' around wit her fine ass." Fat Chubb said throwing the shot of Hennessy back. "Aite let's do it Friday morning. Today is Tuesday. He'll be at school and his momma will be at work." Rachean said passing the blunt back then poured him a shot of Hennessy. "Why wait til Friday? Let's do it tomorrow." Fat Chubb said ready to hit another lick. "I want to peep the scene a little bit longer to see what time his momma leave the house and stuff." Rachean said. Rachean and Fat Chubb sat and talked about robbing Lil Kilo and some other niggas from the hood that was supposed to be getting money.

"RingRingRing…RingRingRing…RingRing…" Lil Kilo hung up the phone just as soon as the answering machine was about to pick up. "Why the fuck this nigga ain't picking up the phone?" Lil Kilo said out loud. "Who are you calling?" Neka asked from the passenger side of Lil Kilo's whip. "Lil Fresh. I need to talk to him about something." Lil Kilo said sending Lil Fresh a text message. "Maybe he's busy. He'll call you back. How is Lil Slim doing?" Neka asked wondering who Lil Kilo was texting. "He good. I went to see him yesterday." Lil Kilo said then asked Neka if she was hungry. "Umm… No not really I'm just ready to see Kevin Hart's new movie." Lil Kilo and Neka was on their way to the movies something Neka wanted to do to take Lil Kilo's mind off everything he's been going through for a while and to be up under him at the same time. "Cool. We'll just snack on some popcorn when we get there." Just as they were pulling up to the movie theater Lil Kilo's text message went off. Thinking that it was Lil Fresh Lil Kilo pulled out his phone and seen that it was Ms. Brown and slide his phone back in his pocket. "Who was that Keon?" Neka wanted to know because normally he responded to almost everybody that texted him. "Nobody." Lil Kilo said getting out the car. Not really wanting to start nothing but wanting to know who texted Lil Kilo Neka asked "Would you disrespect me and text another female in front of me Keon?" Lil Kilo kind of figured that Neka thought that he was texting another female when he texted Lil Fresh so he told her no he'll never disrespect her in that manner then pulled out his phone and showed her where he texted Lil Fresh. Neka wanted to ask Lil Kilo so bad who just texted him but left it alone. After the movie Lil Kilo dropped Neka off at home and tried to call Lil Fresh again and the phone just rung. '*What in the hell do this nigga got goin' on?*' Lil Kilo thought then decided to drive over to Lil Fresh house to see if he was there. Not seeing Lil Fresh car in the drive way but seeing his mother's car there Lil Kilo knocked on the door. . "Hey Ms. Mikayla, how you doing? Is Lil Fresh home?" Lil Kilo asked knowing the answer to his question. "I haven't seen him since earlier. He came in and left right back out." Lil Fresh mother said then added "He said he lost his phone and gave me a new number. Do you have his new number?" Lil Fresh mother asked Lil Kilo. "No Ion have it. I didn't know he lost his phone. What's his new number?" Lil Kilo asked pulling out his phone. "I'll have to get it out my phone. Come in for a sec." Lil Fresh mother said then opened the door for Lil Kilo. After getting the number Lil Kilo pulled off and called Lil Fresh new number and Lil Fresh picked up the phone on the second ring. "Hello." "What up fool? What you got goin' on?" Lil Kilo said turning off Lil Fresh street headed home. "Not shit fool. I lost my phone earlier and didn't know your number by heart. What up tho?" Lil Fresh said jumping back in his car leaving the corner store getting him some cigars. "I've been tryin' to hit you up all day to see if you needed some more work." Lil Kilo said pulling up at the corner store to get him some cigars to roll him a blunt. "I got like 10 of them thangs left. So I should be cool for a few days but I got something I need to tell you about ol' boy." Lil Fresh said pulling off. "Aite bet. I'll see you at school tomorrow and we'll chop it up then." Lil Kilo said then hung up and called Ms. Brown back to see what she was doing but didn't get an answer so Lil Kilo walked in the gas station and got him something to drink and some cigarillos. Sitting in his car rolling him a blunt Lil Kilo contemplated on pulling over to Ms. Brown's house but thought against it. *I'm funa take my ass in the house I got school in the a.m.* Lil Kilo thought then fired his blunt up and hit the interstate. The next day at school Lil Kilo and Lil Fresh was sitting in the cafeteria kicking the shit tripping off one of the funniest niggas in the school named Thump. Thump was a light skinned slim nigga that had the funniest jokes ever. This nigga will literally fry anybody and today he chose to fry the school security guard and had the whole cafeteria in tears talking about the security guard's work boots. "So what up Lil Fresh? What did you have to tell me?" Lil Kilo asked Lil Fresh after the lunch bell rung signaling that lunch was over. "Aw yeah. You know freaky ass LaLa that stay on the block? I think she's a senior or somethin'." Lil Fresh asked Lil Kilo as they were leaving the cafeteria. "You talking about thick ass LaLa that wear glasses? That stay in the brown house?" Lil Kilo said trying to think of who Lil Fresh was talking about. "Yeah her. You know I be knockin' her off from time to time and I was over there last night and she was tellin' me that Rachean done started hangin' with her baby daddy robbin' niggas." Lil Fresh said waving at a mixed chick named Samone that walked by. "For real... who is her baby daddy?" Lil Kilo asked. "Some nigga named Fat Chubb. She said he be on the Northside." Lil Fresh said stopping to hug some other girl named Ashley that seemed like she was gone have a heart attack if Lil Fresh didn't stop. "So this nigga robbin' now huh?" Lil Kilo said. "His pockets must be hurtin'." "Yeah they gotta be. She said that he don't be on the block nomo every since he hooked up with Fat Chubb. That's probably why we haven't seen him out there." Lil Fresh said giving Lil Kilo some dap so that he could head to his next class. "That nigga can't hide forever but meet me over my house after school so we can count up." Lil Kilo said then headed up the stairs to Ms. Browns class. The bell rung again signaling that all students should be in class as Lil Kilo walked in the door. "Just in time Mr. Campbell." Ms. Brown said to Lil Kilo as he was making his way to his desk. "Today were going to have a small pop quiz on things we should already know being that this will be your last year as High School English Students." Ms. Brown said after Lil Kilo sat down and she had everyone's attention. "I'm going to ask a question and randomly pick people to answer them. If you don't get it right you'll have to write me an essay on whatever it is I asked. Now is everybody ready?" Ms. Brown asked looking at Lil Kilo. Lil Kilo winked knowing that Ms. Brown wasn't going to call his name while everyone else in class said "Yes Mam." Ms. Brown asked about eight questions and everyone answered them correctly. *So he really gone pull out his cell phone when I texted him last night and he didn't text or call me back until two hours later.* Ms. Brown thought thinking of something to ask Lil Kilo. "Okay let's go back to the basics." Ms. Brown said. "What is a conjunction?" Scanning the room with her eyes like she didn't know who name she was about to call Ms. Brown said "Keon Campbell. What's a conjunction?" Hearing his name being called Lil Kilo slide his phone back in his pocket and looked up at Ms. Brown with a 'You kidding me right' face. *Don't look like that your ass should have texted me back.'* Ms. Brown thought but said "Mr. Campbell if you don't mind will you stand up and remind the class just what a conjunction is." All eyes were on Lil Kilo now being that he was the most popular kid in the school and this being the first time his name was ever called to participate. Still sitting down Lil Kilo pointed to his chest as if he was asking 'You talkin' to me?' "Yes, Mr. Campbell. Now please rise and inform the class on conjunctions." Ms. Brown said now wondering if Lil Kilo knew the answer to the question she asked. Lil Kilo slide out of his seat and stood on side his desk and could feel every set of eyes staring at him. "What's is a conjunction?" Lil Kilo repeated the question. "Ms. Brown you know English is my favorite subject right?" Lil Kilo asked then fixed his collar on his Polo shirt that didn't need to be fixed. "No I didn't know that Mr. Campbell." Ms. Brown said feeling herself getting wet between the legs looking at Lil Kilo and all the confidence he gave off. "Yes. I love English and was hoping you didn't call me for such an easy question. But since you did ummm… let's see… conjunctions are the words used to connect clauses or sentences or to coordinate words in the same clause. Words like and if and *but* are considered conjunctions." Lil Kilo said putting emphasis on the word but then winked at Ms. Brown before he sat down. "Good job. Okay now class I've wrote your class work on the board and I'll pass around worksheets that'll also be due by the end of class." Ms. Brown said needing to go to the bathroom to wipe the wetness from between her legs. *'Handsome, hood and educated. I'm going to fuck his lights out as soon as I get the chance to.'* Ms. Brown thought thinking about Lil Kilo watching him complete his work from her desk. After school that day Lil Kilo and Lil Fresh sat in Lil Kilo's room counting the money they both had made off the 44 zips they had split. "I got 19 thou right here." Lil Fresh said. "And still got 10 zips at the house." "I counted eighteen-five on my end." Lil Kilo said. "I think I got eight or nine zips left myself. Let me check." Lil Kilo checked the back of his closet and counted out 8 zips. "Yeah I got 8 left." "A fool, I got a question." Lil Fresh said wondering where in the hell Lil Kilo got all this money from but knowing that it had to come from his daddy. "Where in the hell is you gettin' all this money from?" Lil Fresh asked. "How did I know you was about to ask that fool?" Lil Kilo said then told Lil Fresh that his daddy left him a half a million in cash in the trunk of the Porsche Panamera he gave him. "My momma said that it had to be something special about that car because in the will he left in bold letters that nobody was to touch that car but me once I got my licenses." Lil Kilo said remembering the day he first popped the trunk on the Porsche and seen two large briefcases sitting there with a note on top that said "If you're reading this my time has expired son. I love you…Be great." Then at the very bottom of the note were some Spanish words that Lil Kilo paid no mind to at the time. "Shit 500 thou. Pops blessed you. My daddy left me a quarter million and a few bizniz's but I can't get it until I'm 18. That's a year and a half from now." Lil Fresh said. "Yeah I remember you tellin' me that. Lil Slim daddy left him a whole lot of shit behind too that he can't touch until he's 18. But I'm about to call Cutt so we can ree-up." Lil Kilo said pulling his cell phone from his pocket. "We need to find out a way to cut Cutt out and get to the source. He probably

makin' something off us every time we call." Lil Kilo said
then called Cutt and told him to call his people and see if
they was good. "Aite. Ima call you right back." Cutt said then
hung up. "Yeah he gotta be making something. This nigga
get excited every time I talk to 'em." Lil Kilo told Lil Fresh
who was rubber banding up the money. "Shid you really
can't blame 'em. He gotta eat to." Lil Fresh said. "You right
but I'm funa find out who he's gettin' it from to cut all the
extra stuff out." Lil Kilo said waiting on Cutt to call back.
"What we gone do bout Rachean tho? This nigga probably
think this shit over with." Lil Fresh said. "His day comin'
and real soon. I promise." Lil Kilo told Lil Fresh. Lil Fresh
told Lil Kilo that Fat Chubb baby momma might set Rachean
up for them and Lil Kilo told Lil Fresh that he didn't want
everybody in their business. "We'll catch and do his ass in.
The nigga gone slip up and when he do that's his ass." Sitting
around waiting on Cutt to call Lil Kilo and Lil Fresh started
playing a game of 2K. Half way through the game Cutt
called Lil Kilo and told him that his people said that they
should be back on deck tomorrow. "Cutt said that his people
talkin' bout tomorrow. We should be cool until then tho."
Lil Kilo said pausing the game so he could stash the money
him and Lil Fresh counted out back in the closet. "We need
a real plug." Lil Kilo said unpausing the game. Lil Fresh
asked Lil Kilo how long did he plan on selling drugs and Lil
Kilo told him that he really haven't thought about it. "But
you know the only reason we sellin' dope is to find out who
killed our daddies anyway so probably once we find out.
Why you ask that?" Lil Kilo said. "I was just wondering
because I ain't gone lie I done made a whole lot of fuckin'

money off this shit." Lil Fresh said then told Lil Kilo that he appreciate him putting him in the position to make his own money. Lil Kilo never thought about it like that because he was doing it so that they could find out who was behind their daddies murder. But now that Lil Fresh mentioned it, it made him think. "You good fool. You my nigga. And when I eat we all eat." Lil Kilo said giving Lil Fresh some dap. After beating Lil Kilo in the game Lil Fresh told Lil Kilo that he was about to go pick his girlfriend up and grab a bite to eat. "I'm bout to starve fool. You hungry? Call Neka up and let's double date." Lil Fresh said standing up so he could stretch. "Nawl I'm good I ain't really hungry. I might call Ms. Brown and see what she doin'." Lil Kilo said then asked Lil Fresh if he had his strap on him. "Ion leave home without it." Lil Fresh told Lil Kilo then lifted his shirt showing it. After Lil Fresh left Lil Kilo went downstairs to get him something to drink and looked at the time on the stove and seen that it was almost six o'clock. *Where the hell is my momma at?'* Lil Kilo thought pulling out his phone to call her and she picked up on the first ring. "Hey baby." Lil Kilo's mother said. "What's up momma? Where you at?" Lil Kilo asked but figured that she was either at the nail or beauty salon after hearing the women talking in the background. "I'm over here at Keisha's getting my hair done." Lil Kilo mother said and started to give Lil Kilo the worried mother questions until he cut her off. "What's wrong? Are you okay? Are you hungry? It's some..." "Momma... Momma... Momma... everything is fine. I'm not hungry. I was just callin' to see where you was at because you weren't here." Lil Kilo said walking into the living room to check on his money that he had stashed. "Well okay momma I love you and tell Keisha I said I'm still waiting on my date." Lil Kilo said laughing. "Boy hush! Keisha not worried about you." Lil Kilo's mother said before she hung up. Lil Kilo scooted the all-white leather sectional off the white and black Persian rug that was in the center of the floor. *'Who in the hell puts a silk Persian rug in the middle of the floor?'* Lil Kilo thought remembering asking his mother that same question. "I do! And I bet not catch you standing on it with your shoes on or your dirty socks. Yo daddy spent more money on that darn rug than he did on this sectional." Was her response. Moving the rug out the way Lil Kilo examined the hardwood flood carefully looking for a design in the hardwood that resembled an eye. Finding it Lil Kilo pressed down on it three times and a square of the hardwood popped up. Then he press down on the square next to it twice and it popped up as well. "This is one cold ass hiding spot Pops." Lil Kilo said out loud. Lil Kilo remembered seeing his daddy get into the hiding spot a few times and finally found it one day after two hours of crawling on the floor a few years back and found close to four hundred thousand in it. Seeing that his money was just the way he left it Lil Kilo pushed down on the hardwood closing it back then straightened everything back to the way his mother had it. "400 thou wrapped in saran wrap, I'll send a hit and get you touched I'm the man now..." Lil Kilo rapped making up his own lyrics to his own song while pulling out his phone to call Ms. Brown and seen that he had a text message from his momma. "Ivonne told me to tell you thank you again for going up there to check on Issac. Love you. Be home soon." "Tell her I said no problem. I love you too." Lil Kilo texted back then called Ms. Brown. "Well if it isn't Mr. You Know English My Favorite Subject." Ms. Brown answered the phone excited to hear Lil Kilo's voice. Lil Kilo laughed. "You crazy. I hope you didn't think I was gone get that answer wrong, did ya?" Lil Kilo asked sitting on one of the stools his mother had in the living room. "I was hoping you didn't because I would've hate giving you that essay." Ms. Brown said. "You really think I would've done that darn essay?" Lil Kilo asked. "I know why you called on my name anyway." Lil Kilo said. "And why is that Mr. Campbell?" "Because you probably thought I was textin' a female or somethin' because I had my phone out." Lil Kilo said hitting it right on the money. "You damn right." Ms. Brown said laughing. "You not gone be texting your lil girlfriends in my class." Lil Kilo chuckled. "What you doing tho gorgeous? It sound like you in the car." Lil Kilo said hearing music in Ms. Brown's background. "My friend Maria called and asked if I could pick her daughter up from school because she was running behind. Why? What you doing?" Ms. Brown asked Lil Kilo. "I'm at the house bored. I was about to come over your house but you not there." Lil Kilo said. "Aw so you call me when you bored huh?" Ms. Brown questioned. "Nawl I call when I'm thinkin' bout you." Lil Kilo said then told Ms. Brown to call him when she got home. *'I mightis well chill and wait on tomorrow to ree-up.'* Lil Kilo thought grabbing him a bottled water out the refrigerator then headed upstairs but didn't make it to his room before his phone rung. "What's up fool?" Lil Kilo answered. It was Lil Fresh calling telling him that he needed to holler at him again. "In person tho fool." Lil Fresh said. "Aite where you at?" Lil Kilo asked hearing the urgency in Lil Fresh voice. "I'm at the new Chicken Shack they just built on the West Side." Lil Fresh said. "Give me 20 minutes and I'll be there." Lil Kilo said then hung up. Lil Kilo grabbed one of his .45's from under his mattress and tucked it on his hip and was out the door and was pulling up to the Chicken Shack 15 later banging Yo Gotti's CM9 cd. "Damn ain't no parking spots." Lil Kilo said backing into a handicap parking spot by the door. Looking inside the restaurant Lil Kilo seen Lil Fresh getting up from the table telling him to hold on with his finger. "I be right back boo. I gotta holla at my nigga real fast." Lil Fresh told the light skinned girl he was with then walked out to Lil Kilo's car. "I swear you got mo hoes then you do clothes. Who is that you got in there?" Lil Kilo asked after Lil Fresh got in the car. "All that's B lil sister." Lil Fresh said giving his nigga some dap. "B? Who the fuck is B nigga?" Lil Kilo questioned looking back at the girl Lil Fresh was with to see if she looked like anybody he knew. "Beyoncé nigga! Look at her, you can't tell?" Lil Fresh said bragging. "Nigga get the fuck outta here with that bullshit!" Lil Kilo laughed. "She cute but probably slower than a turtle crossin' the street." Lil Kilo joked. Lil Fresh laughed. "Nawl she gotta head on her shoulders. She graduate from Liberty High this year and gotta full scholarship to Youngstown State. She might be who I end up with." Lil Fresh said. "You endn' up in a committed relationship?" Lil Kilo laughed again. "Nigga yeah right. That'll be the day hell freeze over. Fuck all that tho. I didn't come here to talk about you and that bobble head. What's good?" Lil Kilo asked Lil Fresh grabbing the half of blunt that he always seemed to have in the ashtray. "Aite so me and

Ol' Gal was sitting at the table waitin' on our food and this fine ass waitress comes out and ask me could she talk to me in private. So I give her that 'You gotta be kidding me look' and she apologize to Ol' Gal tellin' her that she wasn't tryin' to be rude or wasn't on nothing slick." Lil Fresh was saying. Lil Kilo just looked and listened wondering what in the hell was so important. "Then she said it's about Issac." Lil Fresh said and got Lil Kilo's full attention. "What she say about Lil Slim fool?" Lil Kilo asked reaching in his pocket for his lighter. "After I heard Lil Slim's name I patted my hip to make sure my banga was there then asked her what about him. Long story short I rapped with her and she was sayin' that her mother use to work for our daddy and she could get to Rachean quicker than we could and all type of shit." Lil Fresh said. Lil Kilo fired the blunt up letting everything Lil Fresh was telling him sink in. "And she told you all of this because of what? That bitch might be tryin' to set us up." Lil Kilo said wondering who this fine ass waitress was Lil Fresh was talking about. "Ion think she tryin' to set us up fool. I didn't get that type of vibe from her. But then again I was tryna figure out how she knew about Rachean." Lil Fresh said then grabbed the blunt from Lil Kilo. "She left me her number and everything. She said her momma want to talk to us." Lil Fresh added before he hit the blunt. "What she say her name was?" Lil Kilo wanted to know. "I never got her name but her name tag had Zelle on it. Let me see what she wrote on the paper she handed me with her number on it." Lil Fresh said pulling out a brown napkin from out his pocket. "It have the same name on here. Zelle." Lil Fresh said handing the napkin to Lil Kilo. Lil Kilo stared at the number thinking about the worst case scenario if he called and met up with her. "Aite, we'll call and see what they talkin' bout after school tomorrow. If they want to meet up we'll tell them to meet us right back here." Lil Kilo said then folded the napkin and put it in his cup holder. "Aite bet. We still reeing up tomorrow ain't we? Because I'm down to six zips. Percy called right before I picked her up and wanted four more." Lil Fresh said. "Yeah, hopefully that nigga people ready for us. But I hope you handled your bizniz first then picked shorty up fool." Lil Kilo said hoping Lil Fresh wasn't letting his hoes know what he was doing. "Come on now Lil Kilo. You know I wouldn't dare let a bitch know what I got goin' on." Lil Fresh said. Lil Kilo told Lil Fresh that he would get with him tomorrow so they could handle their business. "Looks like Ol' Gal startin' to get a lil impatient in there anyway." Lil Kilo said pointing at Lil Fresh friend who was sitting at the table on her phone. "She'll be aite." Lil Fresh said then hopped out and went back into the Chicken Shack. "My bad boo I didn't mean to keep you waitin'." Lil Fresh said sitting back down at the table. "Ummhmm… it must have been important." The next day at school Lil Kilo couldn't stop wondering who this waitress and her momma was. Meeting up with Lil Fresh by the gym after fourth period Lil Kilo asked Lil Fresh "Did the waitress gal from yesterday say what kind of work her momma did for our daddy?" Lil Fresh thought about it for a second. "Nawl she just said that her momma worked for them." Lil Fresh said pulling out the new Iphone and sent a text message. "She probably was the driver or some shit. Or they probably used her spot to cook at." Lil Kilo said then noticed Lil Fresh had a new phone. "So you went and upgraded on me and didn't tell me so I could upgrade with cha?" Lil Kilo said pulling out his Iphone and texted Cutt to let him know that they would be ready soon as school let out. "You know I gotta keep the latest." Lil Fresh said waving his phone around so that Lil Kilo could see it. "If it ain't the newest Lil Fresh just can't do it." Lil Fresh said. Lil Kilo laughed. "Nigga you always makin' yo words rhyme like you a pimp or some shit." Lil Kilo said. "I am a pimp fool. Quit actin' like you don't know bout me." Lil Fresh said as the bell rung. "Meet me over my house after school so we can take care of this bizniz." Lil Kilo told Lil Fresh before heading to his next class. After school let out Lil Kilo and Lil Fresh was upstairs in Lil Kilo's room stuffing the $32,000 dollars for the brick in a duffle bag so that they could go meet up with Cutt. Pulling up at the Pizza Hut on the other side of town Lil Kilo spotted Cutt's Infiniti truck and pulled in beside him. "I'm funa see if I can get his plug while we right here too." Lil Kilo said then grabbed the duffle bag off the backseat and hopped out and jumped in the passenger seat of Cutt's whip. "What up Big Dawg?" Lil Kilo said giving Cutt some dap after he shut the door. "What's good fool?" Cut said back dapping Lil Kilo. "Same shit ain't much changed. You think yo people got another one of these for me tho?" Lil Kilo asked Cutt grabbing the sack that Cutt had sitting on the middle console with the brick of dope in it. "I can call him and see. You just let me know when you ready." Cutt said wondering where Lil Kilo was getting this type of money from. "I'm ready now. All I gotta do is swing by my lil spot and grab the bread." Lil Kilo said throwing my lil spot in there to throw

Cutt off. "Aite bet go grab the bread and I'm gone holla at my people while I'm droppin' they money off." Cutt said grabbing the duffle bag Lil Kilo was handing him. "Cool. But tell yo people that I said I want a sit down with them. I like to know who I'm doin' bizniz wit." Lil Kilo said. "If they don't wanna sit down Ion wanna do bizniz with them nomo." Lil Kilo said then hopped out of Cutt's whip and jumped back in his car and pulled off. "What he talkin' bout?" Lil Fresh said sliding the bag Lil Kilo gave him under the seat. "I told him to tell his people we want to sit down and if they don't want to sit down than we don't want to continue to do bizniz with them." Lil Kilo said jumping on the interstate. "You think that's gone work?" Lil Fresh asked. "Yeah it should. Even if it don't shid we ain't losin' nothin'. They need our money more than we need their dope. So we good either way it go." Lil Kilo said switching lanes. After about 15 minutes of bobbing and weaving in and out of traffic Lil Kilo pulled up to his house and seen that his mother was there. "Ion know who black truck this is parked behind my momma. Bet not be a nigga tho." Lil Kilo said pulling beside his mother's all white Bentley coupe that was one of Lil Kilo's daddy's favorite cars before he was killed. "I think that's Lil Slim's momma truck fool." Lil Fresh said grabbing the sack from under the seat and sticking it down the front of his pants. "It showl is." Lil Kilo said then chuckled. "I'm trippin'." Walking inside the house Lil Kilo and Lil Fresh went straight upstairs to Lil Kilo's room after speaking to Lil Slim's mother. "When the last time you seen Lil Slim?" Lil Fresh asked Lil Kilo pulling out the sack from in front of his pants. "I went up there a week ago and caught hell tryin' to get to his room." Lil Kilo said then told Lil Fresh the story on how the fat nurse named Candy got him out of another four hundred dollars. "Next time we go up there I'ma try to take her fat ass out to eat so she want charge us nomo." Lil Fresh said causing both of them to crack up laughing. "You might have to put that meat in her fool." Lil Kilo said laughing even harder. "Nawl she can't get the wennie fool. I might tease her wit it tho." Lil Fresh said causing Lil Kilo to fall over on the bed holding his stomach laughing. "Boy you a fool." Lil Kilo said sitting up on the bed wiping tears out his eyes. "For real fool. She too big for me. You might be able to do something with her tho. You know you ain't fuckin'." Lil Fresh said. "Nawl I can't do nothin' with all that. That's too much ass for me." Lil Kilo said then told Lil Fresh to call the waiter to see what she was talking about. "I gave you the number yesterday fool." Lil Fresh said sitting down at Lil Kilo's computer logging on Instagram. "Damn. It's still in the car sitting in the cup holder. I'm funa go grab it." Lil Kilo said opening the door to his room. Walking down the steps Lil Kilo heard his mother and Lil Slim's momma talking about Lil Slim. "I told you not to talk like that. God has his hands wrapped all around Issac. Now wipe those tears away and smile girl." Lil Kilo heard his mother say. "I know Kenya it's just that...that...the doctors are saying that he's not getting any better." Lil Kilo heard Lil Slim's momma say then heard her burst into tears. "He's been sniff... sniff... in a coma for over two weeks now. God please don't take my baby away from me God please...I lost my baby girl to a bullet and their father to a bullet already God. I don't think I can take anymore." Lil Kilo heard Lil Slim's mother saying then said another quick prayer and eased out the door to his car. Looking across the street Lil Kilo seen a gold car with some tinted windows that looked out of place. "I ain't never seen that car parked over there." Lil Kilo said to himself and noticed he didn't have his gun on him. Easing back in the house and up the stairs Lil Kilo looked out his window to see if the car was still there. "Who you lookin' fo' fool, the mail man?" Lil Fresh joked. "Nawl it was a gold car with some tinted windows sitting across the street when I went to get the number out the car." Lil Kilo said shutting his blinds. "Is it still there?" Lil Fresh asked getting up to look out the window. "Nawl it's gone now." Lil Kilo said handing Lil Fresh the napkin with the number on it. "Ain't no tellin' who that was fool. Probably was one of big dude that live there hoes bringing him something to eat." Lil Fresh said sitting back at the computer dialing the number that was on the napkin. "I ain't never seen that car over there tho." Lil Kilo said then took and slide the dope they just bought under his bed. "Yeah this me." Lil Kilo heard Lil Fresh say then mouthed the words "Put her on speakerphone." Lil Fresh put his phone on speaker then asked "How you know this was me?" "Because this is a unsaved number calling and I don't give my number out. That's how." "All okay…" Was all Lil Fresh got out before Lil Kilo grabbed the phone. "Where yo momma at?" Lil Kilo said trying to sound like Lil Fresh. The phone got silent for a second. "This must be Kilo Jr." Lil Kilo looked at Lil Fresh stunned. "Hello…" The voice on the other end of the phone said. "Yeah this me… where yo momma at?" Lil Kilo said trying to figure out how in the hell she knew his voice. "I noticed the voice change and figured it was you. She's right here." The waiter said then paused. "She said that the two of you can come over here so we can talk because she's sure that your mother is home so we can't come there." Lil Kilo paused again. "Nawl we don't want to meet over there. We don't know ya'll like that." Lil Kilo said. The phone got silent again. "My mother said that she would rather not meet in public if that's where you were trying to meet up at. Hold on she wants to talk to you." Lil Kilo heard the phone being passed then heard a voice say "Hey you are very safe with me. I use to work for your daddy. If you don't feel safe you can bring your gun, how about that?" The lady on the other end of the phone said. "How I know me and my nigga ain't walkin' into a trap?" Lil Kilo questioned. "You don't but you haven't done nothing to me to trap you. I'm here to help you. But if you tell me that your mother Kenya isn't home I'll come to 809 Montgomery Dr. That is your address right?" "How in the fuck do you know where I stay?" Is what Lil Kilo wanted to say then thought about how secretive his momma was about everything that goes on in her life and figured that whoever was on the phone had to know his daddy personally. "Aite look what's yo address? Me and my nigga bout to roll thru but if we sense any bullshit we gone chop that shit up over there." Lil Kilo said. After getting the address Lil Kilo hung up and made sure Lil Fresh had his strap on him. "You ain't even gotta ask that fool. I told you I keep mine." Lil Fresh said. Lil Kilo stood up and lifted his mattress. "Grab that Mac-11 for me." Lil Kilo said then layed the mattress back down. "I'm ridin' with this Mac today. If you see anything that look funny shoot that shit up." Lil Kilo told Lil Fresh before they left out. "Let's hop in yo whip. Yo tints a lil darker than mine fool." Lil Kilo said walking towards Lil Fresh car. "And a lil faster since I put that Hemi under the hood." Lil Fresh said hitting the automatic starter starting his car from the outside. "I'ma teach 'em how to stunt." Lil Fresh said getting inside his car. Lil Kilo typed the address into the google maps on his phone then said "They 17 minutes away. Jump on the interstate like you going to Southern Park Mall it's back that way." Fifteen minutes later they were turning on the street. "What's the address?" Lil Fresh asked looking out his window. "1718. There it go right there on yo side. Go down there and turn around." Lil Kilo said pointing to the end of the street. Pulling up to the address Lil Kilo called and told them they were outside. "Okay pull up to the garage I'm about to open it." Lil Kilo hung up and pulled his Mac-11 from under the seat. "I'm shootin' clean thru the wind shield. They bet not try nothin'!" Lil Kilo said cocking his Mac-11 back. Inside the garage Lil Fresh parked next to an all-white Audi A7 that had light tints on it. "I think this is the car she pulled off in that day." Lil Fresh said as the garage door slide down behind them. Lil Fresh cocked the hammer on his P-89 ruger back just as the door to the house opened. "Is that her?" Lil Kilo asked gripping the Mac-11 with both hands ready to shoot. "Yeah that's her." Lil Fresh said. Lil Kilo and Lil Fresh just sat there. "Is ya'll gone just sit there looking stupid or is ya'll gone get out?" The waiter said standing in the door with a blank look on her face. "We had to make sure wasn't nobody gone jump out from the other side of this car." Lil Kilo said after he got out and shut the door. "We know everything about the two of you. Why would we give our address to do something when we have yours?" Lil Kilo thought about that and felt a little better. "And please put that Mac-11 and P-89 ruger up." The waitress told them. "How you know what kind of gun I got?" Lil Fresh wanted to know. Lil Kilo looked down and grinned because he was still holding his Mac-11 with two hands. "I love guns." The waitress said moving back so that Lil Fresh and Lil Kilo could get in. Standing in the kitchen Lil Kilo scanned the entire house. "Damn ya'll shit layed up in here." Lil Fresh said looking around. "It's a mess in here. Follow me." The waitress said then started walking out of the kitchen. "What's yo name if you don't mind me askin'?" Lil Kilo said still looking around at all the expensive paintings and furniture that was on the walls and in the house. "Ja'Zelle. It's pronounced Ja'Zale but spelled J-a Z-e-l-l-e. You can call me Zelle." The waiter said sounding so sweet and innocent. Lil Kilo looked the waiter in the face for the first time paying attention to her looks and seen that Zelle was pretty but gave off a I ain't to be fucked with vibe. "Momma…!" Zelle yelled up the stairs not knowing that her mother was in the living room. "I'm in the living room chile stop yelling like you crazy." Ja'Zelle's mother yelled back. Walking into the living room the first thing Lil Fresh and Lil Kilo noticed was the huge elephant head chandelier that was hanging from the high ceiling. After about 30 seconds of standing around looking amazed at how top of the line everything looked Lil Fresh blurted out "This shit tight! Looks like some shit from the movie Belly when they was in DMX crib fool." "Yeah it is layed in here." Lil Kilo said looking at the lady that was sitting across the room in a recliner reading a book. "Would

ya'll like something to drink?" Zelle said. "Nawl I'm cool."
Lil Kilo said. "Bring me a soda or something." Lil Fresh said
looking back at Zelle admiring her beauty as well. *'Damn you
fye gurl and thick as shit just like I like 'em.'* Lil Fresh thought
watching Ja'Zelle walk off. Ja'Zelle stood about 5'7 and
weighted close to 160 pounds, had light brown eyes and
almond brown skin and kind of looked like Taraji P. Henson.
"Would ya'll like to sit or is ya'll gone stand the entire time
and look around like ya'll haven't seen a nice house before."
Ja'Zelle's mother said then sat her book on the table next to
her and told Ja'Zelle to bring her a bottle of wine and her
wine glass. Walking around the dark brown love seat to get
fully into the living room Lil Kilo glanced at the pictures
that were sitting on a mantle and seen a picture of his daddy
then stopped and walked over to the mantle and picked it
up. "What kind of bizniz did you do for my daddy?" Lil Kilo
asked turning to face Ja'Zelle's mother who looked like she
couldn't have been no older than 35. "I was the clean up
lady." "The clean up lady?" Lil Fresh said louder than he
intended like he couldn't believe what he just heard. "So you
tellin' me that you use to work for our daddy and all you did
was clean up?" Lil Kilo asked the question as if his time has
been wasted. "Let me guess you cleaned up the trap spots
twice a week?" Lil Fresh said. Ja'Zelle's mother laughed.
"Have a seat and I'ma tell you what kind of cleaning I did."
Ja'Zelle mother said grabbing the wine bottle and glass from
her daughter. "Don't let this pretty face fool you. My aim
good. I can knock the wing off an eagle. I was the one your
daddy called when it was time for someone to meet their
maker." Ja'Zelle's mother said. Lil Kilo's eye brows went up

when he heard that. Lil Fresh popped open the Coca-Cola Ja'Zelle brought him and took a sip then sat back. "So you tellin' me when my daddy wanted somebody killed he called you?" Lil Kilo questioned. "Every time." Ja'Zelle mother said then poured herself a glass of wine. "And you know why?" She asked then took a sip of the wine and looked both Lil Kilo and Lil Fresh in the eyes. "Because I got the job done." Ja'Zelle mother said never batting an eye. Lil Kilo could tell that whoever this lady was sitting in front of him was serious. "She mean bizniz fool." Lil Fresh said sensing the same thing Lil Kilo sensed. "Yeah I know." Lil Kilo said to himself then asked "So why are you telling us all of this? Ummm…what's yo name?" Lil Kilo asked. Ja'Zelle's mother then broke down to Lil Kilo and Lil Fresh everything she knew about their daddies from the time she first met them at the Chicken Shack up until they got killed. "We grew a bond. It was love between us. I could count on them just like they could count on me. I tried like hell to find out who was behind their hit and even to this day no one knows." Ja'Zelle's mother said sipping her wine. "Do you think the police had something to do with it?" Lil Kilo asked then seen a silver weed bong sitting next to the table where Ja'Zelle mother was sitting. '*I wonder who smoke?*' Lil Kilo thought as Lil Fresh asked the question. "Like I said nobody knows." Ja'Zelle's mother said then told them about the police officer that their daddies had working for them that disappeared after their daddies was killed. "But did you ask me who bong this is Lil Fresh?" "Ummm…yeah or is that decoration?" Lil Fresh said. "Decoration my ass. You want to hit it?" Ja'Zelle mother asked then told them they looked exactly like their daddies.

"I bet ya'll got their ways to." Lil Kilo watched as Lil Fresh grab the bong from Ja'Zelle's mother thinking about everything he just heard. "So…you never said what the reason behind this meeting was." Lil Kilo said looking back over at Ja'Zelle's mother. "I loved ya'll daddies like brothers. I was their protector and I feel it's only right for me to watch over their sons who from what I've seen and heard are filling their daddy's shoes." Lil Fresh and Lil Kilo listened. Lil Kilo heard the name Quick and asked what all she knew about him. Ja'Zelle's mother told them the same thing Big Ed told them about Quick. "If I'm not mistaken Quick had a daughter, I believe. I'm not sure who it was by. But you can ask anybody about Quick and I guarantee you they'll say 'You talkin' bout Kilo, Quick, Slim and Fresh?'" Ja'Zelle momma said. "You gone fire that bong up fool or what fool?" Lil Kilo asked Lil Fresh watching him just hold it. "Shit I'm tryin' to figure out what she got stuffed inside this bitch. I think I'm high off the aroma." Lil Fresh said reaching in his pocket for a lighter then fired the bong up and coughed immediately. "So let me make sure I got this right." Lil Kilo said. "You sayin' you gone be our clean up lady now?" Lil Kilo asked Ja'Zelle's mother who chuckled. "No not me… her." Ja'Zelle mother said then pointed behind Lil Kilo and Lil Fresh. They both looked back at the same time and seen Ja'Zelle standing there. "Her?" Lil Kilo said. "Look we understand that she's yo daughter and that she may have some of you in her but…" Lil Fresh said until Ja'Zelle's mother held up her hand silencing him. "Trust me she's everything like me and exactly what you need on your team." Ja'Zelle's mother said then told Lil Kilo and Lil Fresh how

Ja'Zelle killed her own daddy after he came home drunk one night and tried to put his hands on her. "Hold up." Lil Fresh said. "I know I ain't that high. Did she just say you killed your daddy?" Lil Fresh asked Ja'Zelle who was not sitting on the couch across from them. "Yep… sure did. He should have never put his hands on my momma." Ja'Zelle said sounding innocent again. *'Damn she heartless.'* Lil Kilo thought. After passing the bong around a few times skipping Ja'Zelle because she didn't smoke and making mostly small talk about their daddy Lil Kilo's phone rung. "That's Percy callin'. He probably tryna get straight." Lil Kilo said to no one in particular. "Percy is a okay dude. It's the Busta dude that I don't trust." Ja'Zelle's mother said picking up her wine glass and book off the table like she was getting ready to leave the room. "This is a good ass book your daddy wrote too." Ja'Zelle mother told Lil Kilo. "Yeah I know I read it two or three times." Lil Kilo said. "Yo daddy wrote a book fool?" Lil Fresh asked sounding surprised. "Yeah, I told you that a long time ago." Lil Kilo told Lil Fresh. "Ion remember. What's the name of it?" Lil Fresh asked. "The Longest Drought Ever." Lil Kilo said then told Ja'Zelle's mother to show Lil Fresh the cover. "I almost forgot to ask about Lil Slim. How's he doing?" Is he still in a coma?" Ja'Zelle's mother asked. Lil Kilo told Ja'Zelle's mother that Lil Slim was doing better and would be home soon not knowing that she knew more about Lil Slim's condition than he did. "Okay well I'm about to take me a shower and relax. I'll let the three of you discuss business on Rachean." Ja'Zelle's mother said watching Lil Fresh watch her thighs as she walked in the workout shorts she had on. "Just like your daddy I see."

Ja'Zelle's momma told Lil Fresh then laughed. Before
Ja'Zelle's momma could get all the way out the living room
Lil Kilo turned and couldn't help but to notice how fat her
ass was in those shorts. "You never told me your name Ms."
Lil Kilo said. "Jaz." Was all Ja'Zelle's mother said before she
disappeared up the steps. Lil Kilo turned around and said
"Yo momma don't be bullshittin' do she?" "Hell nawl she
ain't bullshittin'." Lil Fresh added thinking with his lil head
while Lil Kilo was talking about her killer instincts. After
talking with Zelle for another 30 minutes about taking hits
for them starting with Rachean Lil Kilo told her to lock his
number in her phone and call him Saturday so they could
meet up and finish talking business.

Chapter 10

Friday morning Lil Kilo was up a little earlier than he normally be after waking up out of a nightmare. "Damn." Lil Kilo said sitting up in bed. Looking at his phone to see what time it was Lil Kilo pulled his wife beater over his head and wiped the sweat from his back, chest, arms and legs then laid back down staring straight up at the ceiling. *'I gotta tell Lil Fresh about this.'* Lil Kilo thought then closed his eyes and tried to go back to sleep but couldn't. Lil Kilo tossed and turned until he heard his mother bang on his door. "Keon..! Wake…" "I'm up momma." Lil Kilo said cutting his mother off. "I'm just laying here." "Are you okay?" Lil Kilo's mother asked sensing that something wasn't right with her baby. "Yeah I'm cool. I just couldn't sleep. You headed to work?" Lil Kilo asked throwing the covers off him. "Yes, I get off at 3 then I'm going to the hospital to sit with Ivonne for a little while. If you need me just call me. If I don't answer leave me a voicemail or send me a text message." Lil Kilo mother said checking herself in the mirror that was hung in the hallway. "Okay momma." Lil Kilo said smiling knowing how over protective and worried his mother be. "Okay I love you. I didn't get to fix breakfast

this morning. If you hungry eat some saug…" Lil Kilo mother
was saying before Lil Kilo cut her off again. "Momma! Go to
work lady. I love you and will see you later." After finding him
something to wear Lil Kilo jumped in the shower and got out
to his phone ringing. *Who in the hell is this callin' this early.*
Lil Kilo thought walking out the bathroom into his room.
After seeing that it was Lil Fresh calling Lil Kilo called him
back then put him on speaker phone and continued to dry
off. "What up fool?" Lil Kilo said once Lil Fresh picked up
the phone. "Nigga that's not how you answer the phone at 7
something in the morning. Where's the good mornin' at?" Lil
Fresh said putting his dreads up in a ponytail. *It's bout time
to get my shit twisted again.* Lil Fresh thought looking in his
full length mirror that hung on his door. "Nigga you ain't my
bitch. I ain't tellin' you good mornin'." Lil Kilo said sliding
on a fresh pair of Rock Revival jeans and grabbed the jacket
that matched it. Lil Fresh laughed. "Nigga you got some
smoke? I ran out last night and you know I gotta get my mind
right before I get my day started." Lil Fresh said. "I got a lil
bit. Pull up and we'll both just hop in my whip." Lil Kilo said
before he hung up and grabbed his .45 and tucked it. 20
minutes later Lil Fresh called Lil Kilo letting him know that
he was outside. Sitting in Lil Kilo's driveway rolling a blunt
Lil Kilo asked Lil Fresh what he thought about Ja'Zelle. Lil
Fresh told Lil Kilo that Ja'Zelle seemed cool or whatever but
a girl doing their dirty work just didn't sit right with him.
"But if our daddy had her momma takin' hits for them then
she might be able to get the job done. Shit she did her own
daddy in so she gotta have a icebox where her heart use to be."
Lil Fresh said trying to sing Omarion's song messing it up

completely. "I think she's a natural born killa. Look at her momma." Lil Kilo said firing up the blunt he just rolled then backed out the driveway. Turning off his street Lil Kilo seen the same gold car that was sitting across the street from his house a few days ago turn on his street. "There go his bitch ass right there headed to school." Rachean told Fat Chubb watching Lil Kilo slow down. "It look like they slowin' down." Fat Chubb said looking out the back window of Rachean's baby momma gold Camry. "I see him hittin' the brake lights." Rachean said looking out the rearview mirror. "He kept going tho." Rachean said then pulled to the end of the street and turned around and pulled into Lil Kilo's driveway next to Lil Fresh Challenger. "I think that's Lil Fresh car right there." Rachean told Fat Chubb then pulled his hood over his head. "You ready fool?" Rachean asked Fat Chubb who was looking out the window checking the surroundings. "Fa sho…" Was all Fat Chubb said before opening his door and got out and walked to the front door of Lil Kilo's house dressed in all black. "Step back." Fat Chubb told Rachean then took two huge steps and on the third step kicked the door with his right foot as hard as he could. "BOOM…" Fat Chubb kicked it again and the front door flew straight in. "Let's ram shack this bitch. I know he got somethin' in here." Rachean said handing Fat Chubb a garbage bag running up the stairs. Rachean opened the first door he seen which was the bathroom then moved to the next room which was Lil Kilo's mother's room. "Check that room." Rachean said then rushed down the hall to the next room. "Holla if you find somethin'." Fat Chubb yelled going straight for the closet. Rachean busted in Lil Kilo's room and the first place he checked was under the bed.

Scooting all of Lil Kilo's shoes from under the bed Rachean seen a Nike shoe box and slide it from under the bed. *'Gotta be money.'* Rachean thought opening the shoe box only to find out that it was full of old basketball, football and baseball cards that Lil Kilo use to collect when he was in middle school. *'The fuck this bitch as nigga doin' collecting cards?'* Rachean thought wanting to fling the box of cards across the room. Meanwhile Fat Chubb was moving like the Tasmanian Devil in Lil Kilo's momma room tearing shit up looking for anything of value stuffing every piece of jewelry she had in his pockets. By the time Fat Chubb was coming down the hall Rachean was in Lil Kilo's closet. "Jackpot!" Rachean yelled eyes big as hell looking at all the dope and stacks of money Lil Kilo had barricaded in the back of his closet. Hearing Fat Chubb yelling Rachean grabbed a stack of the money and stuffed it in the front of his boxer briefs then yelled "I found the stash fool it's in here!" Rachean was stuffing his garbage bag when Fat Chubb walked in with an empty garbage bag. "That bitch didn't have shit in there." Fat Chubb said pulling out all of Lil Kilo's drawers throwing everything on the floor finding more jewelry. "This lil nigga got some hella ice tho." Fat Chubb said holding one of Lil Kilo's chains in the air. "Throw it in the bag. I got everything outta here. Let's go!" Rachean told Fat Chubb pushing off the side of the wall in the closet to stand up then heard something click. *'What the hell was that?'* Rachean thought looking back into the closet seeing that the wall had a crack going down the middle of it. "Chubb…check this shit out fool." Rachean told Fat Chubb who was now trying to flip Lil Kilo's mattress. "Grab that end. This shit heavy." Fat Chubb said holding the top end of the mattress up. Rachean grabbed the bottom end and they flipped the mattress. "Bingo!" Fat Chubb said grabbing Lil Kilos Mac-11 and .45 off the box spring. "He want be needin' these." Fat Chubb said then tucked the guns. "Fuck them guns! I think I've found the real stash spot!" Rachean said then showed Fat Chubb how the wall had cracked opened after he pushed on it trying to stand up and get out of the closet. "It's kinda dark in here. Where yo phone?" Fat Chubb asked wondering what was behind the wall. "I left my phone in the car. Just try to slide the wall apart and see what happens." Rachean said kneeling down so that he could see into the closet more. Fat Chubb took and slide the hands between the crack of the wall and pulled the wall apart. "Oh shit!" Fat Chubb said seeing the stacks of money stacked neatly up the wall. "Grab anotha bag fool to put this money in." Fat Chubb said then thought about shooting Rachean in the back of the head and running off with all the money but didn't. After cleaning out Lil Kilo's closet Fat Chubb pulled the closet walls back together and just like that they were gone. Sitting in Ms. Brown's English class Lil Kilo wasn't paying attention to nothing she was saying. All he was thinking about was that gold car with tinted windows that he seen again this morning turning on his street. "Ion know what it is about that car that's fuckin' with my intuition but something ain't right about it." Lil Kilo told Lil Fresh four or five times on their way to school that morning. The bell rung signaling that class was over and Ms. Brown asked Lil Kilo to stay after. "What's up Za'Mya?" Lil Kilo asked then smiled remembering Ms. Brown telling him that she liked the way he pronounced her real name. Ms. Brown smiled. "I noticed that you were looking a little spaced out today. Is everything okay?" Ms. Brown questioned being able to tell by just looking at Lil Kilo that something has been bothering him. "I'm good boo. Just got a lot on my mind that's all." Lil Kilo said looking back at Ms. Brown then smiled for the second time that day. "What you smiling about Keon...I mean... Lil Kilo." Ms. Brown said then smiled again herself. "Ion know. Just lookin' at your beautiful face made me smile." Lil Kilo said starring Ms. Brown in the eyes. "Boy please. I was rushing this morning. I didn't even get a chance to do my hair." Ms. Brown said thinking about how she just pulled her hair into a ponytail this morning and kept it pushing. *I need to schedule me an appointment with Keisha.* Ms. Brown thought. "That's when you're the prettiest I hope that you don't take it wrong like Drake said." Lil Kilo told Ms. Brown then asked her what she had planned for the weekend. "Nothing serious." Ms. Brown told Lil Kilo who then made plans to hook up Saturday before he headed to his next class. After school Lil Kilo and Lil Fresh was walking out the building headed to Lil Kilo's car tripping off Lil Fresh talking about he was going to fuck the principles daughter if the principle kept messing with him. "Keon..." Lil Kilo heard his name being called and knew from the voice who it was. Lil Kilo turned around "What's up baby girl?" Lil Kilo asked. "Can you take me home today? We don't have practice today and my mother is still at work and I don't want to ride the bus." It was Neka walking towards him looking like one of those models straight out of a Vogue magazine. Lil Kilo repeated everything Neka said picking with her. "Leave me alone." Neka said punching Lil Kilo playfully in the arm. "Hey, Lil Fresh." Neka spoke.

"What up Nek Nek?" Lil Fresh spoke back. "Yeah I'll take you home under one condition." Lil Kilo said then hugged Neka. "What's the condition? Let me guess… I drive while you and Lil Fresh smoke?" Neka said already knowing what Lil Kilo was about to say. "Damn you smart." Lil Kilo said then laughed. "I just know you better than you know you that's all." Neka said. Pulling out of the school parking lot Neka drove straight to the hood before dropping herself off. "You know I had to swing thru and see my people first." Neka joked putting the car in park. "I should've known…" Lil Kilo laughed then got out to give Neka a hug. "Ima buy you a car boo. That way you ain't gotta wait on yo momma or ride the bus." Lil Kilo told Neka then kissed her on the forehead and hopped back in the driver seat of his car. Back at Rachean's baby momma house Rachean and Fat Chubb had split everything up except for the money Rachean had stashed in his boxers and the jewelry Fat Chubb had stuffed in his pocket. "I told you that stupid ass nigga didn't have a stash house. This nigga had 250 g's hidden in his wall. Not to mention the extra 40 g's and the 36 ounces of dope sittin' in the back of his closet." Rachean said to Fat Chubb thinking about the other 10 thousand he had cuffed and didn't tell Fat Chubb about. *I got a hunnit and fifty five thou and a half of brick. I'm the man now.* Rachean thought rolling another blunt of loud out the pound they just bought from Big Ed. "That shit was easy. Like takin' candy from a baby. I wonder what Lil Fresh bitch ass got in his house." Fat Chubb said thinking about the $155,000, the half a brick of dope and all of Lil Kilo's mommas jewel he got in his pocket that he didn't tell Rachean about. "That nigga probably ain't got much in

there but shid we can kick his door in too if you want to."
Rachean said then thought about the guns they found under
Lil Kilo's mattress and told Fat Chubb that he could keep the
Mac-11 since he got a AK-47 already. "Just give me the hand
gun." Rachean said. "Girl it's Friday and you telling me you
staying in the house? Girl be ready by eight. I'm coming to
get you. I need me a drink." Maria was telling Ms. Brown
standing in her closet trying to find her something to wear.
"I have some studying to do. Girl this veterinarian work ain't
no joke." Ms. Brown said sitting in the middle of her bed
taking notes from a textbook that was as thick as a phonebook.
"Girl I told you to study law and I'll get you in there." Maria
said picking up a brown and gold Coach dress putting it up
to her body. "I know you've told me that and if you say it one
more time I might just take you up on your offer." Ms. Brown
said closing her book flopping back on the bed. Ms. Brown
and Maria talked for another 15 minutes with Maria trying
to convince Ms. Brown to go have a drink with her but Ms.
Brown just wasn't feeling it. "How about you come over
Sunday and we have some girl time." Ms. Brown said but
Maria just wasn't having that. "Okay how about I just stop
by the liquor store and get us some wine and come by your
house and we have a drink there?" Maria suggested. "Girl you
must really need a drink huh?" Ms. Brown said laughing at
Maria. "It's not funny Za'Mya." Maria said in Spanish like
Ms. Brown didn't understand what she said. All the years
from being around Maria Ms. Brown began to pick up on a
little Spanish. "Girl bring yo ass on sounding like a baby that
can't have her way." Ms. Brown said. "But please don't bring
that same wine you brought last time. That crap had my

stomach doing flips the next morning." After school let out that day Ms. Brown came straight home to study for her veterinarians test Monday but her friend Maria called interrupting her. *'It's not even five o'clock and Maria trying to have a drink something must be wrong.'* Ms. Brown thought climbing out of her bed to slide on some tights before Maria got there. Pulling up at Lil Kilo's house after leaving Big Ed's spot getting them something else to smoke Lil Kilo was telling Lil Fresh to call Eva to see if they could use her kitchen again to cook the brick they bought from Cutt the other day. "Speaking of Cutt that nigga still haven't called me back yet about the meetin' with his people." Lil Kilo said parking next to Lil Fresh car. Getting out the car Lil Fresh popped his trunk to throw his backpack in there and noticed that his back tire was flat. "What the fuck!" Lil Fresh said slamming his trunk. "What's wrong fool?" Lil Kilo asked following Lil Fresh eyes to the flat tire. "My mufucken tire flat. It look like somebody sliced it." Lil Fresh said bending down to look at it. "Yeah that mufucker been sliced. Which one of yo hoes you done made mad." Lil Kilo joked then realized that Lil Fresh car been parked at his house the entire time they were in school and don't neither one of Lil Fresh hoes know where he live at. "Let's go check the camera right quick fool to see who the fuck been in my driveway." Lil Kilo said now looking up and down the street to see if anybody was outside. Walking to the door Lil Kilo stopped mid step and pulled his gun out. "Somebody been in here." Lil Kilo whispered looking back at Lil Fresh pointing to the door that was cracked. Lil Fresh pulled his gun out and whispered back "I hope they ass still in there." Creeping up to the door Lil Kilo noticed two foot prints near the lock then pushed the door open slowly with the tip of his gun. Entering the house with both their guns pointed Lil Kilo checked the kitchen and living room with Lil Fresh right behind him. Seeing that everything was still in place Lil Kilo pointed to the stairs with his gun then took a few steps towards them then stopped to see if he could hear anything. Creeping up the stairs with their guns still pointed Lil Kilo made his way pass the bathroom then looked inside his mother's room and felt a sense of rage inside of him seeing his mother's room tore to pieces. "Somebody gone die tonight!" Lil Kilo said looking Lil Fresh in the eyes. "Who in the fuck would…" Lil Fresh was about to say but Lil Kilo cut him off. "I don't give a fuck who it is. They gone die!" Leaving out his mother's room headed to his room to see if they found his stash Lil Kilo already knew what it was once he seen his mattress flipped over and his closet door open. "Shit! Them bitches found our stash. They got everything fool." Lil Kilo said moving everything around in his closet. "Who you think did this shit? You think somebody been watchin' you?" Lil Fresh asked walking over to the window looking out of it. Lil Kilo stood up and seeing Lil Fresh look out the window made him think about that gold car. "Ion know who did this shit but I'm about to find out. Help me slide this mattress back on the bed. Them bitches took my Mac-11 and my other .45." Lil Kilo said sliding the mattress on his bed then noticed that all of if his drawers was pulled out on his dresser and ran to it hoping they didn't find his necklace that belonged to his daddy before he was killed. Seeing that the necklace was gone too angered Lil Kilo even more. Walking over to the computer stand Lil Kilo cut it on then clicked a few buttons and the camera screen popped up. "I hope these niggas don't think they got away." Lil Kilo said rewinding the footage until he seen him and Lil Fresh pulling out his driveway this morning headed to school. "I didn't even know you had cameras on the house. I need to get me some." Lil Fresh said standing beside Lil Kilo watching the computer screen. "Lil Slim gave me the idea back when we first started hustlin'. Good thing I listened." Lil Kilo said eyes glued to the computer. "Ding." Lil Kilo's text message went off. Looking back on the floor by the closet Lil Kilo seen his phone and was about to ignore it until another text message came through. "Tell me if you see anything." Lil Kilo said walking to grab his phone off the floor to see who was texting him. "Damn. I forgot that I gotta tell my momma bout this." Lil Kilo said reading her messages letting him know that she'll be home a little later. "I forgot all about lettin' moms know too. Shit what you think she gone say?" Lil Fresh asked watching the gold car that Lil Kilo was talking about ride pass the house. "Oh shit. Look fool there go that gold car from earlier." Lil Kilo rushed back to the computer screen thinking of something that he could tell his mother. "I don't know what she gone say or how she gone take it but I have to tell her." Lil Kilo said watching the screen seeing the gold car creep back up slowly then turn into his drive way. "I fuckin' knew something wasn't right with that fuckin' car when I first seen it." Lil Kilo said loudly poking the computer screen hard enough to crack it. Lil Fresh told Lil Kilo to calm down and stay cool and that whoever it is that hop out the car was a dead man walking. It took whoever it was in the car a few minutes to get out and when they did Lil Kilo snapped. "Rachean! Fat Chubb! How the fuck they know where I live at?" Lil Kilo said looking up at Lil Fresh. "Ion know how they know fool." Lil Fresh said. Lil Kilo's phone rung and thinking that it was his mother calling Lil Kilo was prepared to tell her the truth. "It's Zelle callin'." Lil Kilo said then hit ignore. "You should've answered it. She might know somethin'." Lil Fresh said still watching the computer screen. "I'll call her back in a minute. I need to call my momma to let her know what's goin' on." Lil Kilo said dialing his mother's number nervously and got the voicemail then sent text her a message telling her to call him ASAP it's important. "I forgot she told me that she was goin' to the hospital to sit with Lil Slim's momma when she got off work." Lil Kilo said then call Ja'Zelle back. "What's good Zelle?" Lil Kilo said into the phone. "Meet me at the Chicken Shack in 20 minutes. It's business." Ja'Zelle said and was about to hang up but Lil Kilo stopped her. "Now is not a good time. Gimme bout a hour or so and I'll call you back and let you know where to meet me at." Lil Kilo told Ja'Zelle. "I know exactly what's going on. I'll be there at the Chicken Shack in less than 15 minutes." Ja'Zelle said then hung up the phone. Lil Kilo looked at the phone for a split second then slide it in his pocket. "What she say?" Lil Fresh asked watching Rachean and Fat Chubb run out the house and jump back into the gold car with tinted windows. "You see them fools run out the house?" Lil Fresh said wondering what was in the big bag Fat Chubb was toting. "Check this out fool. This nigga gettin' back out the car." Lil Fresh said watching Rachean hop out the car with a knife in his hand and walk to his back tire and slice it. "I can't believe this bitch ass nigga sliced my tire. What type of shit is that?" Lil Fresh said shaking his head.

Lil Kilo told Lil Fresh what Ja'Zelle said about knowing exactly what was going on. "She tryna meet up at the Chicken Shack." Lil Kilo told Lil Fresh. "Shit, she don't know nothin' we don't know. What we need to meet her fo'?" Lil Fresh said then told Lil Kilo that them niggas was probably over Rachean's baby momma's house chilling like everything was cool. "I know that's where they bitch ass at. We should swing by there and wet both they ass up!" Lil Fresh added. Lil Kilo was ready to do exactly what Lil Fresh said but used his better judgement and told Lil Fresh that they were gone meet up with Ja'Zelle to see what she was talking about. Before leaving to go meet up with Ja'Zelle Lil Kilo straightened his mother's room a little after putting everything in his room back the way he had it. Pulling up at the Chicken Shack Lil Kilo seen that Ja'Zelle was already there backed into a parking spot by the door waiting on them. Lil Kilo backed in beside Ja'Zelle's Audi and she hopped out and climbed in the back of Lil Kilo's Camaro. "The sooner we get to him the better the chance of ya'll getting most of ya'll stuff back." Ja'Zelle said getting straight to business. Lil Kilo looked back at Ja'Zelle. "How you know what's goin' on and this just happened?" Lil Kilo questioned. "How I know is not what's important. Now all I need is the word and I'll have everything taken care of by the morning." Ja'Zelle said sounding like she had everything mapped out already. Lil Kilo wanted to continue with the questions but could tell that Ja'Zelle wasn't going to tell him anything so instead he told her to handle her business. "Do me one favor tho." Lil Kilo said then got quiet. "Call me before you kill him. I want to be there." Stepping out of the hospital to check her phone Kenya got Lil Kilo's text message and called him back immediately. "Hey baby is everything okay? I just got your message." Kenya said after Lil Kilo picked up the phone. Lil Kilo paused then stuttered. "Umm… ummm…no it's not momma. Some…body…umm…broke into our house." Kenya panicked. "Oh my God! Keon are you okay? Was you in the house when they broke in?" Lil Kilo's mother asked sounding as if she was about to have a panic attack. "I think it happened while I was in school. I came home and seen it. But I'm okay. Me and Lil Fresh headed back over there now." Lil Kilo told his mother. "Oh my lord. Call the police. I'm on my way." Lil Kilo's mother said then hung up before Lil Kilo could tell her not to call the police. 'Shit!" Lil Kilo said then smashed the gas pedal trying to beat his mother home. "What?" Lil Fresh asked ready to put his seat belt on. "My momma tryna call the police and I'm not tryin' to get them involved." Lil Kilo said doing 90 in a 55. "Slow down fool!" Lil Fresh told Lil Kilo. "I'm tryna beat her to the house so I can convince her not to call the police." Seven minutes later Lil Kilo was pulling in his driveway and not even two minutes after that his mother was pulling up. "Keon…!" Kenya yelled looking around downstairs. *What did they take?*' Kenya thought seeing that nothing was out of place in the living room. "KEON…!!!" "Mam…!" Lil Kilo yelled down the stairs hearing his mother rushing up the steps. "Are you okay? What did they take?" Lil Kilo's mother asked the questions back to back. "I'm not sure what they took outta your room. But they took…" Lil Kilo was saying. "Oh lord please don't tell me they took my jewelry that your daddy left me." Lil Kilo's mother said then rushed into her room and broke down crying as soon as she saw that her stuff was all over the place. Walking over to her jewelry box seeing that it was empty caused even more tears to flow down Kenya's cheeks. "They did...they got all that I had left of him." Lil Kilo's mother cried. "Don't cry momma. Ima get it back." Lil Kilo said ready to kill Rachean for making his mother cry. Kenya looked at Lil Kilo with tears falling nonstop and asked him how. "How Keon...how are you going to get my jewelry back? Do you know who done this? Have you done something to somebody?" Lil Kilo's mother asked holding her jewelry box. "No momma." Lil Kilo said. "Is somebody looking for you? Do this have anything to do with Issac?" Lil Kilo just stood there. "Answer me!" Lil Kilo's mother snapped. "I'm goin' to get all of our stuff back, I promise. I just don't want you to call the police." Lil Kilo's momma looked him dead in the eyes and said "Please don't tell me you are in the streets. Please! I lost your daddy to the streets and will be damned if I lose you the same way." Not really wanting to lie to his mother Lil Kilo said "You want lose me to the streets momma." Which made Kenya think. "Is that why you changed cars? Is that why you had all that money in your closet?" Kenya asked sternly. "Keon don't you fucking lie to me! If you want to live a street life like your daddy you will not... and I repeat... You will *NOT* do it here." Lil Kilo's mother said and broke down crying again. Hearing his mother curse for the first time in a long time Lil Kilo just stood there then walked over to where his mother was and hugged her knowing that she was hurt. "Momma..." Lil Kilo said not really knowing what to say next but knowing that he did not want to hide anything from his mother so he told her the truth about everything that been going on. "It's too late momma. It's too late for me to change anything." Lil Kilo told his mother who couldn't believe what her son just told her. "Son you will not be able to find out who killed your daddy. The police have been trying to figure this out for over 10 years now and they still don't have a clue. So what makes you think that you'll be able to?" Lil Kilo told his mother that the police probably stopped looking after the first week. "It's probably marked as an unsolved murder in their books. Another unsolved black murder." Lil Kilo said then told his mother not to worry about him. "I can hold my own momma I promise." For some reason Lil Kilo's mother felt that no matter what she did or said that her son had his mind made up on what he wanted to do and just like his daddy once their mind was made up there was nothing no one could do to change that. Not even God. Lil Kilo's mother wiped her eyes and told Lil Kilo that she loved him but he was just like his daddy so she wasn't going to try to stop him. "All I ask is that you finish school son. Please don't drop out. I've worked my tail off to raise you right and keep you away from that mess but I see that it found you still. I'll always be here son." Lil Kilo's mother said then told him that she will be moving within a few days because she no longer felt safe where she lived at now. Lil Kilo told her that he understood then left the room and come back with a hand full of money. "Here's $100,000 dollars towards the house." Lil Kilo said then sat the money on the bed. "It's some of the money daddy left me." Lil Kilo sat and talked with his mother trying to convince her that everything was going to be okay with him until she asked him where he was going to be staying at. Lil Kilo hadn't thought about where he would be staying and all type of thoughts jumped through his head. "Maybe I can stay with Lil Fresh." But as soon as that thought came it left. *'Nawl cause then Ms. MiKayla would want to know what's going on.'* Lil Kilo thought then thought about Neka but didn't want her mother all in his business because he knew that where ever he went all his dope, money and guns was coming with him. "I'm going to stay with my teacher." Lil Kilo said not knowing what made him think of Ms. Brown. Kenya looked at Lil Kilo like he was crazy. "Your teacher?" This made Kenya crack a smile for the first time that day. "How old is your teacher Keon?" Lil Kilo looked in the air like he had to think about it. "Ummm…" Lil Kilo said not really knowing how old Ms. Brown was. "I think she 25." Kenya laughed this time. "So you really think your teacher is going to let you come live with her?" Lil Kilo's mother asked. "I don't plan on movin' with her forever. Just for a few days until I can find my own." Lil Kilo said then thought about the houses his daddy left his momma. "Unless you let me get one of those houses daddy left?" Lil Kilo said. Kenya told Lil Kilo that the houses his daddy left are being rented out but one of them would be available in the next month or so. "Mr. Ridley and his wife are moving out of town soon but if I did let you move in don't think that you'll be living rent free. Your ass will be paying $1,600 a month just like them." Lil Kilo's mother said. "Come on ma, I know you wouldn't charge your baby boy." Kenya gave Lil Kilo a look that said 'Try me.' Sitting on the edge of his bed feeling a little better after talking to his mother Lil Kilo couldn't decide if he should text or call Ms. brown. "Fuck it. I'ma call her." Lil Kilo said looking out the window watching Lil Fresh and the tow man change his tire. "Hello…" Ms. Brown answered. "What's up Za'Mya?" Lil Kilo said then wasted no time telling Ms. Brown what was going on. "Ooo… Kay…?" Ms. Brown said sounding confused. "I was wonderin' would you mind if I came and stayed with you for a few days until I found my own place?" Lil Kilo said still looking out the window. Ms. Brown thought that Lil Kilo was joking and told him that if he wanted to spend the night with her all he had to do was ask. Lil Kilo then let Ms. Brown know that he was serious and she agreed. "I'm about to run to the grocery store. I should be back by the time you get here." Ms. Brown said then hung up. After throwing a couple of outfits in his LouieV suitcase Lil Kilo walked back to his mother's room and seen her holding a picture frame of his daddy and a bible praying. Not really being able to make out what she was saying but figured she was asking God and his daddy to watch over him Lil Kilo just watched. Lil Kilo walked in once she was done. "You okay momma?" Lil Kilo asked. "Yes, I'm fine baby…" Kenya said then told Lil Kilo that she was moving into the mini mansion tomorrow his daddy use for his man cave since it was already fully furnished. Lil Kilo told his momma that his teacher said that he could come stay with her for a few days. "I want to meet this teacher of yours." Lil Kilo's mother said hugging Lil Kilo telling him to protect his self. Kenya kind of felt bad for not being able to do more for her baby but knew that no matter what she did that her son had his daddy ways and all she could do was pray that God and his daddy watched over him.

Chapter 11

Sitting on the front porch of Rachean's baby momma's house Rachean and Fat Chubb passed a blunt back and forth talking about how easy it was robbing Lil Kilo. "Nigga I ain't never had this much money." Rachean said feeling like he was on top of the world. "Shit me either fool. I robbed a nigga for 10 stacks bout two months ago." Fat Chubb said reaching in his fifth pocket pulling out a folded $20 dollar bill. "What's that some molly fool?" Rachean asked Fat Chubb who now had his I.D out scraping the dollar. "Nawl this that straight pure Colombian. This that shit that numbed Scarface." Fat Chubb said chopping the powdery substance then snorting some. "Coke?" Rachean asked. "At its finest…Sniff… Sniff… you wanna hit it fool?" Fat Chubb said trying to pass the twenty dollar bill and his I.D to Rachean. "Nawl Ion fuck with that shit. I thought it was some molly." Rachean said pulling out his phone to call him up some molly. "Damn fool look at Lil Momma walkin' up the street." Fat Chubb said. "You know her?" Rachean looked up to see who Fat Chubb was talking about then squinted his eyes like he needed some glasses or something. "Hell nawl Ion know her but I'm about to get to.

Watch this." Rachean said feeling his swag a little more knowing that he was fresh to death and had a pocket full of Lil Kilo's money. "What's up wit it baby girl?" Rachean said once the girl got a little closer. Rachean and Fat Chubb both gazed at the girl's body. "Damn she thick…Damn she fye… I'll fuck the shit outta her." Were both of their thoughts as the girl stopped looked and smiled then pointed to herself as if saying "Who me?" "Yeah you. What's up? What's yo name baby girl?" Rachean said listening to Fat Chubb tell him to tell her to come here. "Jewel." The girl said then acted as she was about to walk off. "Get her fool. Tell her come here." Fat Chubb was saying lightly so only Rachean could hear him. Rachean wanted to turn around and tell Fat Chubb to shut his fat ass up but asked Jewel where she was headed instead. "Down here to my suga daddy house. He funa give me some money." "She sellin' pussy fool. Tell her we got some money fo' her." Fat Chubb was whispering again. Fat Chubb was one of those fat freaky ass niggas that never seemed to get any pussy unless he paid for it. "How bout you come chill with me and my nigga and let us be yo suga daddy." Rachean said looking at his watch to see what time it was. '*We got bout two hours before my baby momma get off.*' Rachean thought. "I don't know about that. Ya'll might not treat me like he treat me. He's a real suga daddy." The girl said licking her lips that had just enough lip gloss on them to make them shine. "You tell us what you want then." Rachean said pulling out a bankroll of money. "$500 dollars apiece if that's not out of ya'll range. This ass right here ain't cheap." Jewel said turning sideways so Fat Chubb and Rachean could see how fat her ass was in the stretch pants she had on. "I got $500." Fat Chubb blurted out letting it be known that he was going to give her five hundred dollars to fuck. Jewel walked in the yard making her ass bounce with each step then asked them was they ready once she got up on them. "Damn right we ready!" Fat Chubb said standing up forgetting that his powder was sitting in his lap and spilled it all on the porch. "Shit!" Fat Chubb said picking up his I.D and the twenty dollar bill putting them both in his pocket. "Don't worry baby I got some more of that." Jewel said then pulled out a white plastic bag from her bra. Inside Rachean's baby momma house Rachean was trying to run a train on Jewel, pay her her money and put her ass out before his baby momma came home but Jewel wasn't going for that. "It's gone cost $500 more dollars apiece for both of ya'll to fuck me at one time." Jewel said. "Or me and Big Daddy can go in the bathroom so I can rock his world first…" Fat Chubb knew that he had a little dick and didn't want Jewel to say it in front of Rachean so he acted like he wasn't going to pay a thousand dollars for some pussy. "I got $500. Ion got a thousand. Let's gone to the bathroom." Fat Chubb said ready to fuck the shit out of Jewel. Inside the bathroom Jewel unzipped her jacket and placed it on the towel rack then pulled her shirt over her head and undid her bra. "You so got damn fye! I'll suck the shit outta that pussy and eat that ass." Fat Chubb said feeling his self get aroused. Jewel grabbed Fat Chubb's hand and massaged her titties with it then moaned. "Ummm…" Then slide his other hand down between her legs allowing him to feel her wetness. "You like that Big Daddy?" Jewel said pulling his hand from between her legs so he could taste his fingers. "I want to feel daddy's dick." Jewel said rubbing Fat Chubb's dick through his pants. "But I want Big

Daddy's dick to stay hard for me." Jewel said grabbing the plastic bag from out her jacket then opened it. Fat Chubb was so horny listening to Jewel talk nasty to him that he could've exploded just thinking about how good her pussy was. "I want you to snort some of this off my titties while I tease the head of that dick daddy." Jewel said pouring way too much powder on her chest than Fat Chubb could sniff. But Fat Chubb tried it anyway and stuck his face right between Jewel titties and sniffed his life away. Then done it again. "Ohh, yes daddy." Jewel moaned a little louder hoping that Rachean heard her. Seeing Fat Chubb eyes roll in the back of his head Jewel covered his mouth and nose with her hand stopping his breathing completely. "Umm… yes daddy give me that dick… UhhhUhhUhh… You gone make me cum daddy… yes fuck me!" Jewel moaned laying Fat Chubb lifeless body down on the bathroom floor then patted him down and found a rusty .38 revolver. "Thanks lil dick." Jewel said then moaned again. Rachean could hear Jewel moaning from the living room and thought *Fat Chubb must be in there punishin' her big booty ass.* Hearing the bathroom door open then the water in the sink start to run Rachean kicked his Jordan's off that he bought earlier that evening with Lil Kilo's money. "I hope you ready in there." Rachean heard Jewel say walking up the hall. "I been ready!" Rachean said leaning over to put Lil Kilo's .45 on the table then pulled his pants off and grabbed his dick through his boxers. "I hope so." Jewel said back. "This is easier than I thought it would be." Jewel said to herself hearing Rachean kick his leg up on the couch. "Stay yo bitch ass just like that." Jewel said stepping in the living room fully dressed pointing Fat Chubb's rusty .38 at Rachean.

"Any sudden movements and you'll feel how hot these bullets get." Rachean looked up stunned. "Bitch do you know..." "Shut the fuck up... I know exactly who I'm fucking with." Jewel said then stepped over to the table and grabbed Rachean's gun and felt Rachean was about to try something. And he did. Rachean tried to dive over and grab his gun. "BOOM!" "I told you to stay yo bitch ass just like you were." Jewel said shooting Rachean in the thigh. "Aww...Fuck..!" Rachean said grabbing his leg falling back on the couch. "The next one want be a leg shot." Jewel said then told Rachean to shut the fuck up while she make a call. Lil Kilo and Lil Fresh was on their way to see Lil Slim when Ja'Zelle called. "I can finish the job if you want me to." Ja'Zelle told Lil Kilo still pointing the gun at Rachean hoping he did something foolish so she could shoot him again. "This personal. Keep him alive." Lil Kilo said. Ja'Zelle told Lil Kilo where she was and ten minutes later Lil Kilo and Lil Fresh was standing in front of Rachean. "So the day has finally come huh? I knew I'll see you again." Lil Kilo told Rachean then cracked him clean across the head with the same .45 he stole from him. Rachean hollered in pain. "You ain't soundin' so tuff now. Talk that gangsta shit you was talkin' when you shot my nigga seven times." Lil Kilo said raising back to smack Rachean with the butt of his gun again. Rachean flinched. "Where the fuck my shit at nigga?" Lil Kilo said cocking his gun back sticking it in Rachean's face. "Talk nigga! You took 50 g's and a brick and I want all my shit back." Lil Kilo said watching Ja'Zelle walk off and come back in the living room with some salt. "Ion know what you..." Rachean was about to say. "Bitch..!" Lil Kilo said then smacked Rachean in the mouth with the barrel of the gun causing blood to fly out and get all over the couch. "I ain't gone ask you again." Lil Kilo said. "Uggh..." Rachean groaned. "This may burn a little." Ja'Zelle said then walked over and poured some salt all over Rachean's gunshot womb. "AAUGH...FUUCCK!" Rachean screamed feeling like the salt made his entire leg catch on fire. "Now tell me where my shit at and I'll let you live." Lil Kilo said watching Rachean wobble back and forth on the couch holding his leg. Knowing that Lil Kilo wasn't going to let him live Rachean filled his mouth with blood and spat "Suck my dick nigga!" Then tried to spit at Lil Kilo but the force from one of the .45 bullets hitting him in the neck stopped him. "BOOM..." "Watch yo mouth nigga." Lil Kilo said. "BOOM...BOOM...BOOM... BOOM...BOOM..." Lil Kilo killed Rachean then looked at Lil Fresh and told him to search the house. After about three minutes of searching Lil Fresh found exactly what he was looking for. "Lil Kilo!" Lil Fresh yelled from the back. "Grab a trash bag. I found it plus some!" Lil Fresh said looking at all the money not knowing that it came from out Lil Kilo's closet. Stuffing everything inside the trash bag Lil Kilo and Lil Fresh made their way back towards the front where Ja'Zelle was emptying Rachean's pockets. "Check Fat Chubb's pockets. He's in the bathroom stretched out. I'm sure he got some money on him to." Ja'Zelle said handing the wad of money to Lil Kilo that she got out Rachean's pockets. Lil Fresh rushed back to the back and found Fat Chubb layed out on the bathroom floor with white shit all over his face. "BOOM..." Lil Fresh planted a bullet in the center of Fat Chubb's forehead after taking everything out of his pockets including Lil Kilo's mother jewelry. "Lil Fresh!" Lil Kilo yelled making sure Lil Fresh was straight. "I'm good. I was just makin' sure fat boy wasn't." Lil Fresh said walking back in the living room. After setting Rachean's baby momma's house on fire the three jumped in Lil Kilo's car and speed off. Pulling up at Ja'Zelle's house Lil Kilo counted out twenty thousand dollars and handed it to Ja'Zelle. "That's 20k right there." Lil Kilo said after Ja'Zelle grabbed the money. "Is that cool?" Lil Kilo asked. Ja'Zelle told Lil Kilo that she would have took this hit for free just because that one was personal for her as well. Lil Fresh looked back at Ja'Zelle. "I use to like Lil Slim." Ja'Zelle said then grinned a grin that was more of a blush. "But to bad I don't mix business with pleasure." Before Ja'Zelle got out the car her and Lil Kilo talked and agreed that 20 thousand a kill was a reasonable price and just like that Ja'Zelle aka Jewel was a part of the team. After pulling off from Ja'Zelle's house Lil Kilo told Lil Fresh that they was going to get up with Cutt tomorrow so they could ree-up. "I ment to ask you about that situation with you and moms yesterday. You good on that end fool?" Lil Fresh asked Lil Kilo who looked like he had a lot on his mind. "Yeah everything straight. She moved into my daddy old mansion." Lil Kilo said feeling like he needed a blunt right then and there. "Word. So where you stayin' then fool? You know my house is yo house." Lil Fresh told Lil Kilo. "Preciate that love fool but you know I can't be cooped up in the room with yo ass." Lil Kilo said then laughed. "Nawl but I stay with Ms. Brown now." Lil Kilo added slick bragging. "Get the fuck outta here with that bullshit nigga." Lil Fresh said not believing Lil Kilo. "I ain't bullshittin' fool. Watch this." Lil Kilo said then pulled out his cell phone and called Ms. Brown on speaker phone. Ms. Brown picked up on the third ring. "Hey Keon, what's up?" "Is that how we doin' it Za'Mya?" Lil Kilo asked. Ms. Brown busted out laughing. "I mean Little Kilo." Ms. Brown said. "I see somebody got jokes. Where you at tho sexy?" Lil Kilo questioned looking over at Lil Fresh nodding his head. Lil Fresh hit Lil Kilo with a stale face. "I had to run down to the bank before they close. Why, you ready to come *home*?" Ms. Brown said putting emphasis on the word home. "I was gone head that way in less than a hour but if you not gone be there I'll wait." Lil Kilo told Ms. Brown then looked at Lil Fresh again and smirked. "Give me a minute. I'm going to stop at the hardware store and get you a key made so we want have this problem again." Ms. Brown told Lil Kilo then asked "Have you ate? I was thinking about making my famous tuna casserole. But I wasn't sure if you eat fish or not." Ms. Brown slide the last part in the air to see if Lil Kilo would catch it. And he did. "You damn right I eat fish. Just not errbody's because errbody fish ain't good for you." Lil Kilo said then told Ms. Brown to call him once she was headed home and hung up. "Don't ever doubt my mackin' fool." Lil Kilo said then asked Lil Fresh if he had something to smoke on as he pulled up behind his car. Lil Fresh ran in the house and came back out with a fat blunt of Purp. "Just what I needed." Lil Kilo said. Half way through the blunt jumping from conversation to conversation mainly talking about the murders they just committed Lil Fresh paused. "Do you think Lil Slim gone make it tho Lil Kilo?" Lil Fresh asked Lil Kilo. Lil Kilo could hear the doubt in Lil Fresh's voice and knew that he missed Lil Slim just as much as he did. "To be honest I know my dawg gone be aite. That's just how much faith I got even tho it ain't looking too good for him right now." Lil Kilo said then grabbed the blunt from Lil Fresh. "Lil Slim a soulja." Lil Kilo said. Before Lil Kilo pulled off he took and split the money they got out of Rachean's baby momma house and told Lil Fresh that after school let out Monday that they were going to change cars again. "Ain't no tellin' who seen what earlier." Lil Kilo said. Later on that night Lil Fresh tossed and turned all night thinking about Lil Slim and the next morning as soon as he got up and got dressed Lil Fresh drove straight to the hospital to see his nigga. Pulling up at the hospital Lil Fresh was about to call Lil Kilo but seen that is wasn't even 7:00 am yet so he decided against it. *That nigga probably still sleep or knee deep in Ms. Brown.*' Lil Fresh thought parking his car in the handicap spot so that he could be right by the door. Trying to remember the fat nurse lady name Lil Kilo said the day he was telling him the story about the last time he was up there Lil Fresh hit the handicap button by the door so that the doors would open automatically. Walking in Lil Fresh noticed that there were only two people waiting in the lobby. *Damn it's dry in here this mornin'.*' Lil Fresh thought. "It usually look like the Happy Hour up in here." "Hello, how may I help you?" The lady sitting behind the desk said. Leaning down on the counter Lil Fresh told the lady sitting behind the desk that he was there to see his friend then gave the lady Lil Slim's real name. "Umm…Issac Cook Jr…let me see." The lady said then told Lil Fresh "I'm sorry sir but I'm afraid that I'm not going to be able to let you back to see Issac. It look like he's being or has been delivered to another room. Sorry." The lady said giving Lil Fresh a "Sorry sir there's nothing I can do" face. "What is they movin' him for? Is he aite?" Lil Fresh asked starting to panic a little. "I'm sorry but that's confidential." The lady said then got up and walked through the set of double doors that was behind her. Lil Fresh looked around the waiting room trying to find the fat nurse that helped him and Lil Kilo the last time they was there but didn't see her. *'Confidential my ass.'* Lil Fresh thought then snuck through the other set of double doors and down the hall to room 180. Halfway to Lil Slim's room Lil Fresh heart dropped and everything around him seemed as if it had slowed down after he seen two doctors pushing a hospital bed with a sheet covering the body pass Lil Slim's room. "Nooooo…!" Lil Fresh yelled then took off running towards the doctors pushing the hospital bed but was scooped clean off his feet by the two security guards that was working that floor. Lil Fresh flipped out and started kicking and wiggling his body trying to get free. "Put me down! That's my brother they pushin'." Lil Fresh said now in tears. "Please put me down sir! Please!" Lil Fresh begged. "I just wanna see my brother one last time…please put me down." Lil Fresh pleaded still kicking and wiggling. Lil Fresh's pleads was the only noise being made on that floor and every nurse that was working that shift looked on heartbroken seeing Lil Fresh begging to see his brother one last time. "I'm sorry young man but I don't have that type of authority." One of the security guards told Lil Fresh. "I'm also sorry for your lost but I'm afraid that we're going to have to put you in back of one of our cop cars if you don't calm down." The security guard said easing Lil Fresh to his feet. Lil Fresh had a face full of tears. "Fuck you! You racist ass pig! You probably don't care because he's black!" Lil Fresh spat jerking away from the security guard who was about to jack Lil Fresh back up until the other security guard stopped him. "He's grieving. Leave him alone." Sitting in his car Lil Fresh cried his heart out thinking about the times him and Lil Slim shared. Lil Fresh called Lil Kilo's phone over twenty times leaving a voicemail accidentally each time Lil Kilo didn't answer. Hearing his phone go off the last two times Lil Kilo wondered who was calling his phone so early and why. Looking at his phone seeing that he had twenty two missed calls from Lil Fresh Lil Kilo jumped up and walked in the living room to call Lil Fresh back. All Lil Kilo could hear when Lil Fresh picked up the phone was crying. "A…yo…Lil Fresh…what's wrong fool?" Lil Kilo asked trying to keep his voice down so that he wouldn't wake Ms. Brown. "HE'S GONE! Lil Slim is gone fool!" Lil Fresh said unable to hold back his tears. "I'm up here now. I seen…sniff sniff… them push him out on the hospital bed…sniff sniff… and every…" Lil Fresh just broke down crying again and couldn't even finish his sentence. "Hold up. Slow down because you cryin' and talkin' at the same time and I can't understand you." Lil Kilo said understanding everything Lil Fresh was saying but wanted him to repeat it because he didn't want to believe him. Lil Fresh wiped his face with the bottom of his shirt then opened his door so he could spit. "He's gone man. Lil Slim is gone." Lil Fresh said then told Lil Kilo everything that happened even the part where the security guards jerked him up. Lil Kilo felt tears well up in his eyes then fell to his knees and let his tears fall freely. "Tell me you playin'." Lil Kilo said feeling as if his whole world just came crashing down. "Let me call my momma real fast to see what happened." Lil Kilo said then hung up and tried to call his mother but couldn't control his tears. "Why God?" Lil Kilo repeated over and over. After about 20 minutes of nonstop crying Lil Kilo gathered up enough strength to dial his mother's number without crying. The phone rung twice and went to voicemail. And not even a full minute later Lil Kilo got a text from his mother. "Hey baby?" "What's going on with Lil Slim momma?" Lil Kilo replied. 30 seconds later Lil Kilo got another text from his mother. "I know baby. Ivonne called me this morning and told me. I cried then had to get myself together because I'm at work. TTY on my lunch. Love you." Lil Kilo read his mother's text message and squeezed his phone so tight that he almost cracked it. "Is everything okay Keon?" Ms. Brown asked standing behind Lil Kilo in her night grown. Lil Kilo just sat there crying. He didn't turn around and acknowledge Ms. Brown or nothing. "Keon…" Ms. Brown said softly walking into the living room to face Lil Kilo. Dropping down to her knees Ms. Brown grabbed Lil Kilo and held him to her chest. "It's okay to cry baby. He's in a better place now." Ms. Brown said. "I heard you talking to Lil Fresh about Issac. It's going to be okay." Ms. Brown told Lil Kilo rocking him back and forth as tears continued to flow down his face. Ms. Brown knew what it was like to lose someone close after losing her father to a heart disease last year. "I know how you feel Keon. But you have to stay strong." Ms. Brown said feeling her eyes tear up holding Lil Kilo. Lil Kilo wiped his face and called Lil Fresh back and still haven't said a word to Ms. Brown. Lil Fresh picked up on the first ring and told Lil Kilo that he was about to go holler at Big Ed to get him something to smoke. "Pull up over here when you're done hollerin' at Big Ed." Lil Kilo told Lil Fresh then gave him the address and jumped in the shower and cried his heart out some more. "God why did you have to take Lil Slim? He didn't deserve to die God." Lil Kilo cried. Ms. Brown stood in the doorway listening to Lil Kilo cry and found herself undressing to get in the shower with him. "Lord knows that it's too early for him to be seeing me naked but…" Ms. Brown tried to rationalize with herself knowing that she was ready for Lil Kilo to not only see but have her body as well just under better circumstances. "Can I get in with you?" Ms. Brown asked Lil Kilo watching the steam from the hot water rise above the shower curtain. Lil Kilo said nothing even after Ms. Brown asked him again. "Can I?" Ms. Brown asked again halfway in the shower now. Still Lil Kilo said nothing. Once she was completely in the shower Ms. Brown took the rag Lil Kilo was holding and lathered it with the Dove body wash that was sitting on side of the tub and started to wash Lil Kilo's back and worked her way around his neck and chest. Ms. Brown could feel Lil Kilo's body start to relax a little so she turned him around to face her and said "I'm here for you Keon" then continued to wash down his chest pass his stomach with the rag. Not wanting to be sexual but wanting to clean Lil Kilo's manhood Ms. Brown took the rag across his pubic hairs then started to bring it back up until Lil Kilo pushed her hand back down. Grabbing Lil Kilo's dick with her free hand Ms. Brown then lifted it up so she could wash his balls and felt herself getting wet. "This is not the time for that little lady." Ms. Brown said talking to her pussy who didn't seem to listen. "Umm…" Ms. Brown heard Lil Kilo moan lightly then realized that she was slowly stroking the shaft of Lil Kilo's dick with a tight grip. "Umm…" Ms.

Brown moaned back lightly feeling Lil Kilo grab and caress her left nipple. Ms. Brown then took her thumb and rubbed it across the tip of Lil Kilo's dick and felt it twitch. Wrapping her hand around Lil Kilo's hand Ms. Brown moved his hand down between her legs. "Ohhh…" Ms. Brown moaned then leaned in and tongue kissed Lil Kilo still holding his dick in her hand thinking about dropping down to her knees sticking it all in her mouth. "You have a nice…" Ms. Brown was about to tell Lil Kilo how big his dick was until they heard somebody banging on the door. "Doom Doom Doom Doom Doom!" *'Damn!'* Lil Kilo thought. "Shit!" Ms. Brown said to herself ready to bend over and tell Lil Kilo to just stick it in but knew that Lil Kilo wasn't going to leave Lil Fresh at the door knocking. "That gotta be Lil Fresh." Lil Kilo said ready to tell Ms. Brown to bend over so he could stick it in real fast but wasn't gone leave his nigga outside for a piece of pussy. "I guess we have some unfinished business to take care of later on." Ms. Brown told Lil Kilo as he was getting out the shower then told him to shut the door behind him so she could finish washing up. "I'm comin' fool." Lil Kilo yelled speed walking to the door with nothing but a towel wrapped around his body. "Doom Doom Doom!" Lil Kilo yanked the door open. "My bad fool. I was in the shower." Lil Kilo looked at Lil Fresh and could tell from the puffiness and redness of his eyes that Lil Fresh had been crying nonstop. "You aite man?" Lil Kilo asked knowing the answer to his question. Lil Fresh shook his head no. "It hurts Lil Kilo. My fuckin' heart hurts man. I've never felt this much pain before." Lil Fresh said with tears welling up in his eyes again. "Let me put some clothes on. Hold on right quick." Lil Kilo said as Lil Fresh walked into the house. Not even five minutes later Lil Kilo was walking back into the living wearing some Jewel House sweat pants and some Nike flip flops and sat down beside Lil Fresh and hugged him and told him that he loved him. "I love you too fool but this shit is fucked up. I can't stop crying. Just imagine how his momma feel fool." Lil Fresh said looking at Lil Kilo who was trying to hold back his tears. "She done lost her baby girl, her baby boy and her man." Lil Fresh said shaking his head. "All to a bullet." Lil Kilo just sat there lost in his thoughts thinking about the pain that Lil Slim's mother must be in right now. Hearing his phone vibrate on the table brought Lil Kilo out of his trance. "Grab that for me fool." Lil Kilo told Lil Fresh who was sitting directly in front of his phone. Grabbing his phone from Lil Fresh Lil Kilo seen that it was his mother calling him back. "Hello…"

Chapter 12

"Loreli…!" Maria yelled down the hall to where her daughter's room was. "LO-RE-LI!" Maria pronounced each syllable to her daughter name louder after she didn't respond. "I'm coming mami." Maria heard her daughter say. "You said that 15 minutes ago. Girl bring yo butt on." Maria said back adjusting her Michael Kors watch. Walking out of her room dressed in a grey and pink Pink sweat suit and some pink and white Jordan's Loreli asked her mother could they go to the mall after seeing her daddy. "It took you seventeen hours to put on a jumpsuit Loreli?" Maria said shaking her head. Loreli laughed because she knew that she could take forever getting dressed. "I had to do my lashes, fix my hair and find something to put on. If you would've took me with you when you went and got your hair and lashes done I would've been ready you know, MA-RI-A!" Loreli said knowing that her mother hated it when she called her by her name. Maria looked back at Loreli with a "Don't play with me" look on her face. "Well, if someone wasn't out eating with their friend then somebody would've had their hair and lashes done." Maria said grabbing her jacket out the hallway closet. "Momma me and Mia ran around the corner to the Chicken Shack then I dropped her off and came home and you were gone." Maria laughed. "That's not funny momma!" Loreli said in Spanish. Loreli looked just like her mother but you could tell that she was mixed with something while Maria looked pure Puerto Rican. "I don't know why you just don't book your own appointments Loreli shoot." Maria said. "You are grown right?" Loreli told her mother that she liked going together so they could have their girl time together like they use to do all the time when she was a child. "But I will start booking my own if you want me to momma." Loreli said trying to sound sad walking out the door behind her mother. Hearing that Maria told Loreli that she was sorry for leaving her and that from here on out they would get their hair, lashes and nails done together again. Pulling up to visit her daddy and pulling off was never the same for Loreli. "Can I ask you a question mom?" Loreli asked her mother who couldn't help but stare out the window every ride back from seeing Loreli's dad. "Yes baby you may." Loreli's mother said. "Do you ever miss daddy being home?" Silence fell in the car. Maria started to think about the very first day she met Loreli's dad. Sitting across from her brother in the visitation room Maria could feel the eyes staring at her from across the room. "You know those guys sitting over there?" Maria asked her brother who was doing a life sentence for a King Pin charge. Maria's brother followed her eyes to the table where two dudes was sitting with a cat named Kilo that he knew from the unit. "No. Not the guys sitting at the table." Maria's brother said in a voice that let Maria know that he was still over protective. "Why?" Maria's brother asked still looking at the two dudes as if they may have said or done something to his sister. Maria laughed which caused her brother to look back at her. "Why you laugh?" Maria's brother asked in a deep low-toned Spanish voice. Maria told her brother that she could see the lion come out of him when she asked him did he know them. "I see somebody is still very overly protective of their little sister." Maria said then cut her eyes back at the table where the two guys was sitting only to catch eyes with the same dude again. "Yes I am. This place doesn't stop nothing. I still do everything I want to do!" Maria's brother said putting emphasis on his last sentence. Maria knew from experience that her brother would do whatever to whoever to keep her happy. Even if that meant killing. "You see that Spanish chick sitting three tables over?" The dude that's been catching eyes with Maria asked his homeboy who was locked up for a year for a gun charge. "Yeah I seen her up here a few times visiting José. I think that's his sister or something because I never seen them kiss or hold hands." "Who is he?" The other nigga asked who was sitting at the table. "A Drug Lord. He got a King Pin charge. I think he got two life sentences. Word been said that he got the guards on his payroll and he's plannin' an escape." "Momma…Momma…MA-RI-A!" Loreli said trying to get her mother's attention. "Huh…what…oh shoot…Girl I was in a whole nother world. What did you say?" Maria asked Loreli now thinking about the times when Loreli's daddy was home. "I forgot now." Loreli said not really forgetting but wanting to change the subject because she knew how her mother got once she started thinking about her daddy. "Can we go get something to eat then go to the salon?" Loreli asked knowing that she usually got what she wanted after visiting her daddy.

"Hello…" Lil Kilo repeated after his mother didn't say nothing and was just holding the phone crying. "Momma… stop cryin' momma." Lil Kilo said feeling tears well up in his eyes again and fall down his cheek listening to his mother cry. "I can't help it…sniff…Keon. Issac is in a better place now." Hearing his mother say that caused Lil Kilo to drop his phone and cry tears of pure pain. "Keon…Keon!" Lil Kilo heard his mother yell his name through the phone. "Mam…" Lil Kilo said after he picked his phone back up. Tears running down his face and his heart feeling like it's been ripped out of his chest Lil Kilo blanked out for a split second until he felt Lil Fresh shake him. "He is allowed visitors for the next hour." Was all Lil Kilo heard his mother say before getting off the phone with her. Lil Kilo told Lil Fresh what his mother said about Lil Slim being able to have visitors for the next hour then got up. "I'm bout to take a quick shower to try to pull myself together a lil bit." Lil Kilo said walking to the back into Ms. Brown's room where she was layed across the bed in some purple boy shorts and his wife beater. Knowing that Ms. Brown just heard him pouring his heart out again Lil Kilo told her that he was about to go visit Lil Slim's body at the hospital. "I'll be back a lil later." Lil Kilo said walking towards the closet. "I don't know how much time I got left with my nigga. Ion got time to take another shower." Lil Kilo thought sliding off his Nike slippers stepping into a pair of all white Air Force 1's. Lil Kilo grabbed his Jewel House shirt tucked his strap kissed Ms. Brown on the cheek then was standing in the living room telling Lil Fresh to "Come on". Not really wanting to drive Lil Kilo hopped in the car with Lil Fresh. The entire ride to the hospital neither Lil Fresh nor Lil Kilo said a word. Lil Kilo stared out the window the entire ride feeling like all of this was his fault while Lil Fresh sat still trying to figure out how Lil Slim's mother felt losing her son. "God please give Ms. Ivonne the strength she needs to carry on." Lil Fresh prayed. Lil Fresh was about to ask Lil Kilo how he think Lil Slim's mother felt losing him, his sister and his daddy to a bullet but didn't after seeing Lil Kilo staring out the window with tears still falling from his eyes. "This don't seem real fool." Lil Kilo said through his tears. "Life seems fake. It's not real. Tell me this shit not real Lil Fresh." Lil Kilo said tears falling even harder. Lil Fresh really didn't know what to say because he was feeling the complete opposite about life right now. "I wish I could tell you that Lil Kilo but this shit real fool. Everything gone be okay tho. We still gotta a mission to set out on. It's what Lil Slim would want." Lil Fresh said trying his best to console Lil Kilo with his words. Hearing how strong Lil Fresh seemed to be made Lil Kilo realize how weak he was but at the very moment he really didn't care. Fifteen minutes later they were pulling up at the hospital. "I haven't felt this much pain since my daddy died fool. I forgot this type of pain even existed." Lil Kilo said stepping out the car to get his self together a little before they walked in the hospital. Before walking in to see Lil Slim one last time Lil Fresh and Lil Kilo made a vow that no matter the situation or the circumstance that they would always be there for each other no matter what. "I love you fool." Lil Kilo told Lil Fresh after embracing him with a tight hug. "I love you too." Lil Fresh said looking Lil Kilo in the eyes. Walking to the entrance of the hospital Lil Kilo texted his mother to find out Lil Slim's room number. "Room 180." Lil Kilo's mother texted back. *'I wonder what made them put him back in the same room?'* Lil Kilo thought crossing the street watching a man carry a car seat into the hospital then wondered if it was true that every time a person die a baby is born. "What room he in?" Lil Fresh asked. "180." Lil Kilo said. Entering the hospital Lil Kilo and Lil Fresh both stopped about a foot away from the front desk and scanned the waiting room with their eyes. "Damn it's packed in here." Lil Fresh said. "I was thinkin' the same thing." Lil Kilo said trying to find a nurse. "Excuse me Ms…" Lil Kilo said to a nurse that was walking by pushing an elder white lady in a wheelchair. "Yes, how may I help you?" The nurse asked stopping. "Umm…we're here to see our friend. He's in room 180." Lil Kilo told the nurse then looked down at the lady in the wheelchair and noticed that she had a very faint smile on her face. Lil Kilo smiled back. "What's your friend's name?" The nurse asked unclipping her walkie talkie from her waist. "Issac Cook." Lil Kilo and Lil Fresh both said. The nurse said a few words over the walkie talkie and a few seconds later told Lil Kilo that someone would be at the front desk in just a minute to help them. Not really having too much to say they both just stood there. After what seemed like forever a chubby red haired white nurse who seemed like she had an attitude emerged from behind the doubled doors. "Can I help you?" "Yes bitch you can!" Lil Kilo wanted to say but held his tongue. "Yes mam, we're here to see Issac Cook. I believe he's in room 180." Lil Kilo said instead. "I'll need to see both your ID's and the both of you will need to sign in on that clipboard sitting in front of you." The red haired nurse said pointing at the clipboard as if Lil Kilo and Lil Fresh was blind. "You want to be smart. I can be smart too." Lil Kilo said to himself then signed his name across three lines then handed the clipboard to Lil Fresh who grinned once he seen Lil Kilo's name then signed his name the same way. The red haired nurse handed them their ID's back then pointed to the same double doors Lil Fresh snuck in earlier and said "That way!" Walking through the doubled doors then down the hall to Lil Slim's room Lil Fresh seen the same security guards that escorted him out and to his surprise they waved. Not really feeling the security guards from his last visit Lil Fresh threw his head up at them. "That's the same two monkey ass guards that put me out." Lil Fresh told Lil Kilo who was struggling to hold back his tears. "Everything gone be aite Lil Kilo. You still got me. Lil Slim will be with us forever." Lil Fresh said after seeing nothing but sadness all over his homie face. Lil Kilo said nothing as they walked pass room 174.

After eating Pappadeaux Maria was sitting inside Keisha's Hair Salon getting Loreli's nails, feet and hair done listening to Keisha and another girl that worked at the shop named Ronda go back and forth about everything under the sun. Everything that didn't have nothing to do with either one of them. "I know you heard about what's been going on with Money Man Zed and Nivia?" Ronda said braiding her client hair down. Ronda was one of those chicks that knew about *EVERBODY'S* business before they even knew about their own business. It seemed like she knew about stuff before it even happened. "UnUn girl what happened?" Keisha asked not really caring about what happened but knew Ronda was gone tell her anyway. "Whaaat...gurl you haven't heard?"

Ronda said like this was something that made the news. "Girl you know Money Man supposedly been fucking one of Nivia's friends and got her pregnant." Ronda said then immediately changed the subject and started talking about some chick name Donna that *supposedly* got put out of her house. *'And this is exactly how rumors spread.'* Maria thought. "People telling other people what *supposedly* happened to the next person." After sitting in the salon for a little over two hours Maria was ready to go home take her a long hot bubble bath, sip her some wine and climb in bed but not before Loreli begged her to take her shopping. "Look chile, you not about to work my nerves today. Today is my off day." Maria told Loreli. "But this could be a early birthday present momma. Please!" Loreli begged and wined at the same time because she knew her mother usually gave in when she did. "Don't try that on me Ms. It's not going to work this time." Maria said trying not to look at Loreli because she knew for sure that her daughter would have her sad puppy dog face on. "Okay momma we don't have to. I understand that you are tired. Thank you for getting my hair, nails and feet done." Loreli said. Maria looked over at Loreli and thought *'Lord if this child don't get her persuasiveness from me.'* "Okay Loreli, its 3:34. I want to be sitting in my tub by 6." Maria said which caused Loreli to smile. "That's two hours and twenty six minutes. Plenty of time to shop." Loreli said then leaned over and kissed her mother on the cheek. "And get her quick adding and subtracting from her daddy."

Standing in front of room 180 for what seemed like eternity Lil Kilo took a deep breath then tried to push the door open.

"It's locked." Lil Kilo told Lil Fresh who tried to push the door open but the door didn't budge. Checking the door number to make sure they were at the right room Lil Kilo started to knock but hesitated. "What if I'm not ready to see Lil Slim for the last time?" Lil Kilo questioned himself. Then a million other what if's ran through his head. "You have to push on the latch to open the door." A nurse whispered to Lil Kilo and Lil Fresh as she walked by. "Oh…thanks." Lil Kilo said after seeing the latch the nurse was talking about. Taking another deep breath and exhaling slowly Lil Kilo pushed the door open slowly and noticed his hands start to sweat a little. *'I'm not sure if I'm nervous or scared.'* Lil Kilo thought feeling his chest fall to his stomach as the door opened wide enough for him to walk in. Lil Kilo took a step into the room then paused after seeing another nurse standing beside Lil Slim's hospital bed checking something on a clipboard. Lil Fresh stood behind Lil Kilo trying to look over his shoulder wondering why he stopped. "Go fool." Lil Fresh whispered nudging Lil Kilo in the back. "It's a nurse in here fool." Lil Kilo turned and whispered back taking another step into Lil Slim's room so that Lil Fresh wouldn't be on his back. Hearing some commotion towards the door the nurse looked up and smiled then waved Lil Kilo and Lil Fresh over. "You aite fool?" Lil Fresh asked Lil Kilo who was just standing there still. "My shoes feel like they got concrete in them. Ion think I wanna see my nigga like this." Lil Kilo told Lil Fresh looking him in the eyes. Lil Fresh seen that Lil Kilo was on the verge of tears again. "Don't cry fool. Lil Slim was called home for a reason. He our angel now." Lil Fresh said now holding back his own tears that seemed to have formed out of nowhere. "Are you here to see Issac?" They both heard the nurse ask. "Um…yes mam. We can still see him right?" Lil Fresh asked stepping around Lil Kilo and on into the room. "Yes you may." The nurse said sticking her hand out to shake Lil Fresh and Lil Kilo's hand. "I'm Laura." The nurse said introducing herself. "I just got done checking all his vital signs and he's doing very well." The nurse said. The only thing Lil Kilo heard was "Yes" while Lil Fresh listened and heard every word clearly. "Wait a minute…did you say that he's doin' well?" Lil Fresh asked the nurse to make sure he heard her correctly. "Yes he is!" The nurse said then smiled again. Lil Kilo looked at the nurse like she was crazy. '*We must be in the wrong room.*' Lil Fresh thought then said "We're here to see Issac Cook Jr." The nurse told Lil Fresh that she knew exactly who they were there to see. "A.k.a Lil Slim." The nurse said trying to joke a little to lighten the mood in the room. Looking pass the nurse Lil Kilo tried to make out Lil Slim's face but couldn't because the bed was to far away. '*Why am I scared to see my nigga and I was just up here seeing him the other day?*' Lil Kilo thought still haven't heard nothing the nurse and Lil Fresh was talking about as he made his way further into the room and over to Lil Slim's bed. "Well I'll let the two of you spend some time alone with Lil Slim." The nurse said before leaving out the room. "How in the hell do she know Lil Slim's nickname?" Lil Fresh wondered walking over to Lil Slim's bed to where Lil Kilo was. "I told you God got him fool! I told you!" Lil Fresh said excitedly now standing right beside Lil Kilo. "Man nigga you don't know how I'm feelin' right now!" Lil Kilo said after he fully realized that Lil Slim was still alive. Lil Kilo grabbed Lil Slim's hand then closed his eyes and said a quick prayer thanking God. Just as Lil Kilo was about to let Lil Slim's hand go he felt Lil Slim squeeze his hand back gently. "I love you." Lil Kilo whispered looking down at Lil Slim. "He can hear us talkin' to him fool. I just felt him squeeze my hand." Lil Kilo told Lil Fresh laying Lil Slim's hand back down. Seeing Lil Slim alive and not dead was like a breath of fresh air to Lil Kilo. "I already knew my nigga was gone shake back because my nigga a straight soldier! Ain't that right fool?" Lil Fresh said looking down talking to Lil Slim. Lil Slim's leg flinched. "You see that?" Lil Fresh asked Lil Kilo. "I told you my dawg a soldier." Lil Fresh said smiling from ear to ear. They both got quiet for a second staring down at Lil Slim thinking the same thing 'This nigga blessed and strong as hell to survive the shots he took.' "Ima have my nigga a smoke fest once they let my nigga up outta this bitch. We gone have weed, bitches and bottles." Lil Fresh said as the door opened behind them. Looking up to see his mother and Lil Slim's mother coming through the door Lil Kilo and Lil Fresh both took a step back so that Lil Slim's mother could see her son but Lil Slim's mother told them that they didn't have to move. "Me and Kenya been here since he woke up. The two of you go ahead. I'm sure Issac is tired of hearing my voice anyway." Lil Slim's mother told Lil Fresh and Lil Kilo causing both of them to snicker a little. Lil Kilo looked Lil Slim's mother in the eyes and told her that he was sorry that she had to go through this. "We all go through certain things in life Keon and we all have our struggles. It mainly depends on the person and how they deal with situations which determine if they'll be okay or not." Lil Slim's mother said. "And I'm ready for every single lemon life throws at me." Lil Slim's mother words alone let Lil Kilo and Lil Fresh know just how strong of a woman she was. Lil Kilo told Lil Slim's mother that he loved her and that he promise to never let nothing happen to her son again. "And I'm sure you haven't had a good night of sleep since he been here. So tonight I want you to go home and climb in your own bed and get you some rest." Lil Kilo said. "Me and Lil Fresh will stay the night with him tonight."

Chapter 13

Two months later

"Okay what about this?" The physician said then took the reflex hammer and hit Lil Slim's other knee with it. Lil Slim didn't flinch either time just kept staring out the window. "I'm assuming you didn't feel anything Mr. Cook?" The physician asked Lil Slim. It's been 60 days since Lil Slim was released from the hospital and after being told that he'll never walk again Lil Slim got his mother to hire him a personal therapist. "I'm not listenin' to those doctors momma. I know that I'll walk again one day." Lil Slim told his mother the first day he was home. Seeing the fight in her son eyes and knowing that he didn't want to have to depend on others to care for him Lil Slim's mother hired him the best physical therapist in the state. "Mr. Cook?" The therapist said snapping Lil Slim out of his train of thoughts. "Yes, I felt it." Lil Slim lied. "Which knee did you feel, the left or the right one?" Lil Slim's therapist asked. "I felt both of them." Lil Slim said knowing that if he said he didn't have any feeling in his legs then his therapist wouldn't even attempt to start the learning how to walk process. After an hour and forty five minutes of therapy and having to be helped with a bath Lil Slim sat on the couch talking to his mother about life. "Yes I believe in God baby." Lil Slim's mother said. "God pulled you through all of this." Lil Slim's mother told him rubbing his hand holding back tears. "God please be with my baby and give him the strength he needs to become mentally and physically strong again. God please." Lil Slim's mother prayed silently. Listening to her baby talk Lil Slim's mother knew that him being in a wheelchair and being told that he'll never walk again has taken a toll on him. "I know there's a God momma but..." Lil Slim was saying before he heard somebody knocking on the door. Lil Slim paused then looked at his mother. "I'll get it. It's probably Lil Kilo and Lil Fresh comin' to check on me. Lil Kilo texted me bout a hour ago and said he was comin' over." Lil Slim said then turned around in the wheelchair and rolled himself to the door. It took everything in Lil Slim's mother not to break down and cry knowing that it was only so much that she could do for her baby. "I can't let him see me crying." Lil Slim's mother told herself getting up headed upstairs so that Lil Slim could have some privacy with his friends. "Hey Ms. Ivonne." Lil Fresh and Lil Kilo said at almost the exact same time. "Hey boys." Lil Slim's mother said back then asked them where their mothers were. "Ion know where Kenya at. Probably at work." Lil Kilo joked calling his mother by her name. "Let me try to call her. I need to talk to her about something. I'll be upstairs if you need me Issac." Lil Slim's mother said halfway up the stairs. "What up fool, how you feelin'?" Lil Fresh said then tried to push Lil Slim back into the living room but Lil Slim didn't let him. "I got it fool." Lil Slim said then rolled his self back in front of the couch. "What ya'll niggas been up to?" Lil Slim asked grabbing the remote off the table. Lil Kilo could tell that being in a wheelchair was messing with Lil Slim's self-confidence and seemed to have him feeling a bit insecure so Lil Kilo started joking. "We ain't been doin' shit fool. Just been waitin' on you to quit actin' like you were in a coma when you know you were really scared the whole time." Lil Kilo chuckled which caused Lil Fresh to laugh and slide him a joke in there. "Yeah fool the big nurse named Candy told us how you use to open your eyes and move your hands and shit once your visitors left." Lil Slim laughed already knowing that his niggas loved to play around and crack jokes. "Ya'll niggas got me fucked up." Lil Slim said chuckling a little not even realizing that was his first time smiling since he been home. "I ain't neva scared." Lil Slim said then fell silent for a second. "But that bitch ass nigga that shot me…I wanna see the look in his eyes when I stand on top of him." Lil Slim said. Lil Fresh gave Lil Kilo a 'should we tell him' face and Lil Kilo shook his head no then pointed up the stairs with his eyes letting Lil Fresh know that Lil Slim's mother might be listening. "Don't worry bout that situation right now fool. You just worry about gettin' better and gettin' the hell up outta that wheelchair." Lil Fresh said. "Yeah that's all you need to worry bout right now fool." Lil Kilo added then told Lil Slim that him and Lil Fresh was coming back Friday to get him out the house. "Ion know about that fool. I got therapy everyday but Sunday." Lil Slim said not really wanting to leave the house until he was able to walk again. "I ain't tryna hear all that." Lil Kilo said. "Yo therapist ain't gone be here all day fool." Lil Kilo told Lil Slim. "So like I said, we'll be here Friday around fo'." Lil Kilo said. "Ya'll ain't gone let a nigga…" Lil Slim was about to say something but Lil Fresh cut him off. "Nawl we ain't gone let you sit around and be a house nigga. We comin' to get you Friday fool so be ready." Lil Fresh said. "Ya'll niggas just make sure ya'll got something to smoke then." After leaving Lil Slim's house Lil Fresh dropped Lil Kilo off at his whip and before Lil Kilo got out they sat there talking for a second. Mainly about Lil Slim. "Did you notice how Lil Slim wasn't makin' any real eye contact when he was talkin'?" Lil Kilo asked Lil Fresh. "Yeah I peeped that. It's like he embarrassed because he in a wheelchair or something." Lil Fresh said lifting up his arm rest grabbing the bag of weed that he got from Big Ed earlier. "Damn! Don't tell me I'm outta gars." Lil Fresh said then told Lil Kilo to check inside his glovebox and see if he had any cigarillos in there. "I should have some in my car." Lil Kilo said after seeing that there wasn't any inside the glovebox. Lil Kilo hopped out and searched his car and came back with one. "I had one left fool. Roll a fat one up. Shit Ion think I smoked nothin' all day." Lil Kilo said then heard his cell phone go off. Pulling out his phone Lil Kilo seen that it was Percy calling. "You got some work on you?" Lil Kilo asked Lil Fresh before he answered his phone. "Hello…what up fool…yeah how much…two of 'em?" Lil Kilo said looking at Lil Fresh to see if he had two ounces of crack on him. Lil Fresh lifted his arm rest again and checked his stash then held up one finger to let Lil Kilo know that he only had a zip on him. "I got this one on me right now." Lil Kilo said into the phone. "Shid it's gone take me bout a hour or so to get the other one…aite bet. Meet me at the Chicken Shack on the Northside." Lil Kilo said then hung up. "Percy tryna grab that one. He gone meet us at the Chicken Shack around the corner in 15 minutes." Lil Kilo told Lil Fresh who was stuffing the cigar with weed. Lil Fresh finished rolling the blunt then handed it to Lil Kilo and told him to fire it up while he hopped out and dusted his self off. "I'm bout outta work to fool. I think I got a fo' way left." Lil Fresh told Lil Kilo when he got back in the car. "I'm bout out my damn self. I'll call ol' boy back tomorrow so we can ree-up. He slick been bullshittin' lately." Lil Kilo said. After serving Percy Lil Fresh pulled back up to Lil Kilo's whip which was parked at Lil Kilo's old house and the two finished smoking the rest of the blunt watching a comedian name GoGo Ugly and another comedian name SlickShit on YouTube on the flat screen Lil Fresh had installed in his car. "What you bout to get into fool?" Lil Kilo asked Lil Fresh checking his watch seeing that it was a little after six. "Shit Ion know. I might hit the mall right quick. I told lil gal from school that I'll take her out tonight." Lil Fresh said pulling out his phone to send the girl from his school a text message to see if they were still going out. "Cool." Lil Kilo said reaching in his pocket pulling out a wad of money and counted out seventy five twenties and handed them to Lil Fresh. "Stop in Neiman Marcus and grab Lil Slim a pair of Bally's and a fit to put on Friday while you at the mall fool." Lil Kilo told Lil Fresh before he got out the car. Before pulling off from his old house Lil Kilo went inside to check on his money that was still in the floor. *I need to count this shit to see how much bread I got in all anyway.* Lil Kilo thought getting down on one knee getting ready to start counting. "This might take me a minute. I need to get comfortable." Lil Kilo said out loud as his text message went off. Pulling his money towards the couch Lil Kilo sat down then checked his text message. "How's your day going Mr. Campbell?" It was Ms. Brown. "Better now that I've heard from you." Lil Kilo texted back with the heart emoji at the end of his sentence. Before Ms. Brown could respond Lil Kilo sent another text. "Wyd? Wya? I need yo help." Ms. Brown responded immediately. "I'm at home. What's wrong? Is everything okay?" Lil Kilo read that and smiled then shook his head. *'How come every time you tell a female you need their help they automatically assume the worst?'* Lil Kilo thought then texted and told Ms. Brown that everything wasn't okay and that he'll be over in just a second to talk about it. "I'm funa make her ass help me count this shit." Lil Kilo said then ran upstairs to find something to put the money in. Looking around Lil Kilo noticed that his mother didn't take anything with her when she moved. *'She mightis well let me have this spot.'* Lil Kilo thought walking into his room grabbing a Supreme duffle bag he had in the closet while making a mental note to talk to his mother about letting him have the house. After stuffing the money he had sitting on the living room floor into the Supreme duffle bag he got out his closet Lil Kilo was headed out the door. Lil Kilo hopped in his whip and threw the duffle bag on the backseat and was about to pull off until he remembered that he needed some more cloths to change into while he was at Ms. Brown's house. Walking back into the house to grab him some more clothes Lil Kilo's phone rung. Seeing that it was his mother calling Lil Kilo answered. "Great minds think alike?" "What you talking

about boy?" Lil Kilo's mother said sitting inside the custom
built library Lil Kilo's daddy had built inside the mini mansion
before he was killed. "I was just about to call and check on
you. I haven't heard from you in a few days." Lil Kilo said
walking back out the house with another duffle bag filled
with clothes. "I was startin' to miss my favorite lady." "I'm
only your favorite lady when you want something." Lil Kilo's
mother said. "What you need now Keon?" Lil Kilo's mother
added jokingly. "How you know I need something? I could
be..." "Boy I've been knowing you almost 19 years. I know
when you want or need something. Now what is it Keon L.
Campbell?" Lil Kilo couldn't do nothing but laugh at the fact
that his mother always knew when he needed or wanted
something. "Well I was gone ask if I could have our old house
since ain't nobody staying there?" Lil Kilo asked smoothly.
"That house is sold already Keon." Lil Kilo's mother said.
"Hold up wait...don't tell me the school teacher done put you
out already?" Lil Kilo's mother asked in a joking way but was
serious at the same time. "No momma." Lil Kilo chuckled. "I
just want my own spot." "Oh, I was going to say, you know
momma will always have a bed for her baby." Lil Kilo's mother
said kind of missing her baby boy staying with her. "Well I
was just calling to check on you son and to tell you that I love
you. I didn't want much. Talk to you later." Lil Kilo's mother
said before she hung up and thirty five minutes later Lil Kilo
was pulling up to Ms. Brown's house after stopping by Big
Ed's to get him a smoke sack. "Well it's about time you got
here Keon." Ms. Brown said opening the door for Lil Kilo
before he could even knock. Lil Kilo could see the word worry
written all over Ms. Brown's face which caused him to crack

a smile because he forgot all about telling Ms. Brown that everything wasn't okay. "What you smiling for Keon?" Ms. Brown asked. "I'm just happy to see your face that's all." Lil Kilo said walking into the house. "Because I know you bout to make my life a whole lot easier." Ms. Brown was confused. "You mind letting me know what you're talking about?" Ms. Brown asked Lil Kilo following him down the hall to her room. "This is what I'm talkin' about. I had to do what I had to do for this money." Lil Kilo said trying to make it seem like he just robbed a bank or something as he unzipped the duffle bag with the money in it and dumped it all over Ms. Brown's bed. Ms. Brown stood still for a second then walked over to the bed. "Where did you get all this money Keon?" Ms. Brown asked looking Lil Kilo in his eyes. "And don't you lie to me either." Ms. Brown said thinking the worst. *I hope that he haven't done anything crazy or harmed anybody for this money.* Ms. Brown thought looking at all the money that was piled up on her bed. Lil Kilo could tell that Ms. Brown was worried about where the money came from so instead of continuing to play with her Lil Kilo told her the truth. Ms. Brown picked up a stack of one hundred dollar bills and threw them at Lil Kilo. "Keon! Don't play with me like that." Ms. Brown pouted. "You had me thinking something was really wrong." Lil Kilo laughed. "Something is wrong boo." Lil Kilo said looking at the stacks of money that was on the bed. Ms. Brown gave Lil Kilo a 'Stop playing with me' look. "I'm serious boo. I need yo help countin' this. Last time I counted it was $380,000 thou." Lil Kilo said grabbing a stack of fifty dollar bills that was stuck in the corner of the duffle bag. After explaining where the money came from for the fourth time Ms. Brown finally agreed to help Lil Kilo count his money. *'I can't believe he trust me enough to show me this much money.'* Ms. Brown thought looking at the stacks of twenty, fifty and one hundred dollar bills that had rubber bands wrapped neatly around them. "Keon..." Ms. Brown said taking a rubber band off the end of a stack of twenty dollar bills. Lil Kilo was thumbing through a stack of hundred dollar bills and didn't want to miss count so he kept counting until he was done. "What's up boo?" Lil Kilo said putting a rubber band back around the stack of hundred dollar bills he had in his hand. "Ummm..." Ms. Brown said forgetting what she was about to ask Lil Kilo. "You trust me enough to show me all this?" Ms. Brown asked remembering what she was going to ask holding up a stack of money. Lil Kilo sat the stack of one hundred dollar bills that he just counted behind his back picking up another stack while thinking about his answer before he said it. "Look Ms. Brown I'm gone be all the way real with you..." Lil Kilo said then explained to Ms. Brown why he didn't mind letting her help him count his money and Ms. Brown shook her head in understanding once Lil Kilo was done. "Like I said, I don't trust nobody when it comes to this shit tho boo." Lil Kilo said pointing at the stacks of money that was in front of them. "Money breeds jealously and hatred." Lil Kilo told Ms. Brown. "It'll turn people that you thought loved you cold hearted. Did you hear about the lady that just killed her husband for his life insurance policy in Tennessee?" Lil Kilo asked Ms. Brown who was listening to Lil Kilo but knew deep down that she'll never do nothing like that. "That type of stuff happens all the time." Lil Kilo said. Ms. Brown sat the stack of money she had in her hand down. "Well if you don't trust me why would you bring all of this over my house and ask me to help you count it?" Ms. Brown asked sounding a bit offended. "Because I'm comfortable with you." Lil Kilo said knowing that Ms. Brown was feeling some type of way when he told her that he didn't trust nobody. "Now come here and let me show you how to count money." Lil Kilo said then reached over and pulled Ms. Brown next to him and kissed her on the cheek. "I know how to count this bread foo." Ms. Brown said trying her best to sound hood as she grabbed a stack of fifty dollar bills and popped the rubber band the same way she seen Lil Kilo do it. Lil Kilo busted out laughing. "What's funny foo? Lemme show you how to count this bread. One two...1...one two...2...one two...3. That's $300 right there homie." Ms. Brown said laying the money she was counting out in front of her. Lil Kilo shook his head then chuckled. "You crazy boo. Let me find out you really from the hood." Lil Kilo said then grabbed another stack of hundred dollar bills and popped the rubber band off it. "Take notes." Lil Kilo said then counted out fifty one hundred dollar bills and asked Ms. Brown how much was it. "50 x 100 is 5,000." Ms. Brown said doing the math out loud. "So if I counted out 100 hundred dollar bills how much would that be?" Lil Kilo asked trying to sound like a college professor. "Ooooo...I get it." Ms. Brown said punching Lil Kilo in the arm playfully and not because she understood his method of counting money but because she got wet at the thought of Lil Kilo teaching her something. '*I think I've waited long enough to flex my skills.*' Ms. Brown thought thinking about what she was going to do to Lil Kilo just as soon as they were done counting the money. Three hours and forty five minutes later Lil Kilo was stuffing the last stack of twenty dollar bills back into the duffle bag. '*I think I'm gone buy me a money counter tomorrow. My hands done started crampin' after countin' out $380 thousand in cash.*' Lil Kilo thought standing up to stretch. Lil Kilo zipped the duffle bag up and slide it under Ms. Brown's bed. "I'll grab that in the mornin'." Lil Kilo said to himself then turned around and seen Ms. Brown standing there in her panties and bra. Ms. Brown walked over to Lil Kilo real slow and seductively then reached for his belt. Lil Kilo just stood there as Ms. Brown unbuckled his belt then whispered in his ear and told him to lay back on the bed. "You n…" Lil Kilo was about to say something but Ms. Brown placed her finger over his lips. "Shhhh…" Ms. Brown said softly then pushed Lil Kilo back onto the bed and started to undress him. "Don't say a word." Ms. Brown said then pulled Lil Kilo's shirt over his head and started to kiss down his neck and chest. Lil Kilo bit his bottom lip and let out a light moan looking Ms. Brown in her eyes as she kissed her way down towards his belly button. Feeling his manhood rise Lil Kilo started to say something but remembered Ms. Brown telling him not to say a word so instead he kicked his shoes off and got comfortable. Ms. Brown stripped Lil Kilo down to his boxers and could see the pre cum leaking through. Reaching her hand down Lil Kilo's boxers Ms. Brown started to rub the pre cum around Lil Kilo's dick making him moan. "Shit girl…" Lil Kilo said as Ms. Brown started to jack his dick slowly. Lil Kilo reached around and undid Ms. Brown's bra then pulled her down on top of him so that he could suck her titties. "You see how wet you got me..?" Ms. Brown moaned sliding Lil Kilo's hand down between her legs. "Ummm…" Ms. Brown moaned again feeling Lil Kilo rub his finger against her pussy lips. "You like that?" Ms. Brown asked spreading her legs wider. "Damn this pussy wet girl." Lil Kilo said sliding his middle finger inside Ms. Brown which caused her to moan a little louder. "Ouuu…Keon…" Ms. Brown moaned then slide down Lil Kilo's body stopping directly on top of his erection and opened her mouth biting softly on Lil Kilo's dick through his boxers. Ms. Brown then pulled Lil Kilo's boxers down around his ankles and grabbed his dick and started to rub his pre cum around the tip of his dick again causing more to flow out. "Ummm…" Ms. Brown moaned feeling Lil Kilo's dick twitch in her hands then slowly moved her head down so that she could stick the head of Lil Kilo's dick in her mouth slowly wrapping her tongue around it. "Mmmm…" Ms. Brown heard Lil Kilo moan which turned her on even more. "You like that Keon..?" Ms. Brown asked Lil Kilo with the tip of his dick still in her mouth. "MmmHmm…" Lil Kilo moaned feeling Ms. Brown slide her mouth all the way down on his dick then come back up slowly. "Suck that dick just like that girl." Lil Kilo moaned and Ms. Brown did just that. "Aaaah… shit girl …you gone make me…ummm…" Lil Kilo moaned louder as Ms. Brown sucked and slobber all over his dick. Ms. Brown felt Lil Kilo's leg stiffen and knew he was on the verge of exploding. "Ummhmm…ummm…" Ms. Brown moaned getting her mouth even wetter wrapping her hand around Lil Kilo's shaft now sucking it and jacking it off at the same time. "You gone make me cum…Ohh shit girl…Ms. Brown…yes..!" Lil Kilo moaned watching Ms. Brown's hand and mouth work magic. The more Lil Kilo moaned the more Ms. Brown was turned on which made her keeping sucking until Lil Kilo exploded all in her mouth. "Damn girl!" Lil Kilo said. "You tryna make a nigga fall in love ain't cha?" Ms. Brown stood up and smiled. "Follow me." Ms. Brown told Lil Kilo then lead him into the bathroom where she washed him up in her Jetted Whirlpool tub that had a built in Jacuzzi. After washing Lil Kilo's body Ms. Brown slide down on top on him and started grinning hard and slow until Lil Kilo's manhood stood back up and slipped inside of her.

Chapter 14

Two days later Lil Kilo, Lil Slim and Lil Fresh were all sitting in Ms. Brown's living room laughing and joking. "Stop lyin' nigga." Lil Slim was telling Lil Kilo. "I heard you standin' over me cryin' sounding like O-Dog in Menace 11 Society when Cain got shot." Lil Slim said laughing. "Talkin' bout don't die Slim…don't die…" Lil Kilo couldn't help but laugh knowing that Lil Slim was telling the truth. "Nigga I didn't say that bullshit." Lil Kilo said still laughing. Ms. Brown watched and listened to the three of them from the kitchen and could tell that they missed each other. "That nigga called me damn near every night cryin'." Lil Fresh said lying on Lil Kilo. "Maannn this nigga floggin'." Lil Kilo said. "Tell him about that time I pulled up on you in the hospital parking garage so we could go see him and you was bangin' yo head on the steerin' wheel like a white boy. Talkin' bout you can't take the pain anymore." Lil Kilo told Lil Fresh causing him and Lil Slim to bust out laughing. "Nigga stop stuntin'. I wasn't bangin' my head on the steerin' wheel." Lil Fresh said as Ms. Brown came into the living room with a tray full of hot wings, rotel and Doritos. "Will you move that remote and those cup holders Keon?" Ms. Brown asked Lil Kilo smiling knowing that he wanted to be called by his nickname. Lil Kilo looked at Ms. Brown sideways. "So we back on that Ms. Brown?" Lil Kilo said clearing the table so she could sit the food down. *'Shit, the way you had that dick in my guts I started to call you daddy.'* Ms. Brown thought then cracked a smile. "That slipped my bad Lil Kilo Campbell." Ms. Brown said messing with Lil Kilo. "Aite Za'Mya." Lil Kilo said back. Ms. Brown laughed. "Would ya'll like some juice, water or a cold drink Lil Fresh or Lil Slim?" Ms. Brown asked leaving Lil Kilo's name out. "I'll take a bottled water." Lil Fresh said. "Me too." Lil Slim said never looking up at Ms. Brown. Ms. Brown could tell that being in a wheelchair was messing with Lil Slim's pride so after she went and grabbed two water bottles and a glass of Apple juice for Lil Kilo Ms. Brown handed Lil Slim's his and told him how blessed he was to still be here. "So keep your faith in God and remember that you can do anything you want to do." Ms. Brown said patting Lil Slim's knee to let him know that she was referring to him walking again. "Thank you." Lil Slim told Ms. Brown as she was leaving out the living room. "Don't thank me thank God." Ms. Brown said winking her eye at Lil Slim then told Lil Kilo if he needed anything that she'll be in the back. "I bet you still ain't hit that." Lil Fresh said to Lil Kilo once Ms. Brown was out of sight. Lil Kilo laughed. "Nigga if I told you what happened two nights ago you gone tell me I'm lyin' so Ima keep it to myself." Lil Kilo said grabbing a hot wing. "Man fuck all that." Lil Slim said. "What's been goin' on in the streets?" That question caught Lil Fresh and Lil Kilo off guard. "Ya'll niggas still hustlin'?" Lil Slim wanted to know. Lil Kilo brought Lil Slim up to speed on what's been going on in the streets then told him about Rachean and how they met the person who use to take hits for their daddy. Lil Slim couldn't believe his ears. "So you tellin' me a bitch name Jaz use to take hits for Pops 'em and now her daughter takin' hits for us?" Lil Slim questioned rolling over to the table dipping a Dorito in the rotel. "Man I didn't believe the shit either until me and Lil Fresh went over there." Lil Kilo said then told Lil Slim about the visit him and Lil Fresh had with Jaz and her daughter. "So Rachean dead?" Lil Slim asked. "As a doe nob." Lil Fresh said grabbing a hot wing off the table. Lil Slim didn't know if he should be mad or glad that Rachean was dead because he wanted to be the one who stood over him. "You ain't got nothin' to worry bout fool." Lil Kilo said looking at Lil Slim. "That nigga gone." After eating damn near all the hot wings and most of all the rotel the three sat there talking about what their next moves should be. "We gotta get out here in there streets." Lil Slim said. "If we gone connect these dots properly and find out who killed our daddy we gone have to be on top of everything movin'." Lil Slim said as Lil Fresh and Lil Kilo listened. "We gotta lock our city down section by section." Lil Slim told Lil Kilo and Lil Fresh. Hearing Lil Slim talk let Lil Kilo and Lil Fresh know that he was still *wit it.* Lil Kilo told Lil Slim that him and Lil Fresh would hold shit down until he was able to walk again and Lil Slim snapped. "Fuck that! I don't give a fuck if I'm never able to walk again. Ima be right there with ya'll niggas." Lil Slim said noticing that he had balled his fist up out of anger because he knew that his feelings was causing him to contradict his actions. *'I'm tellin' them that I want to be right there with them but tellin' myself that I don't wanna be out until I'm walkin' again.'* Lil Slim thought. Lil Kilo told Lil Slim that he understood what he saying and how he was feeling. "Them bullet holes ain't stopped nothin' I see." Lil Fresh told Lil Slim. "Nawl that shit ain't stopped nothin'. I'm still that same ol' G. Now roll some weed up." Lil Slim said back laughing. In the middle of smoking a big fat ass blunt of purple dro that Lil Kilo had rolled and laughing and kicking the shit with each other they heard a knock on the door. "DOOMDOOMDOOOM…" "Who the fuck is that knockin' like they the police?" Lil Slim asked looking at Lil Kilo. "Ion know who that is. You got yo stick on you Lil Fresh?" Lil Kilo asked realizing that he left his gun in Ms. Brown's room. "You better know it." Lil Fresh said pulling his gun from his waist line. "I got it…!" They all heard Ms. Brown yell coming down the hall. "DOOMDOOMDOOM…" Whoever was at the door banged again. Lil Fresh slide his gun back on his waist line after hearing Ms. Brown say she got it. "It's my crazy ass Puerto Rican friend." Ms. Brown said walking towards the door unlocking it. "Girl why you banging on the door like you the PoPos or something?" Ms. Brown said opening the door. Ms. Brown's friend Maria walked straight in sounding real ghetto. "I smelled that smoke from the mailbox. Shit I was trying to get in rotation before it was gone. Now where it at?" Maria asked looking dead at Lil Fresh because he was the one holding the half of blunt they were smoking before she started banging on the door. *'Yo ass can get in rotation aite…'* Lil Fresh thought looking at how gorgeous Maria was standing there in a simple

Gucci dress and sandals with her hair pulled back tightly into a ponytail. "Must be ya'll last blunt or either ya'll thinking I'm a detective and don't want to pass the bud." Maria said causing Ms. Brown to laugh. "Girl you know you don't smoke quit playing… Heeyyy Loreli." Ms. Brown said excitedly seeing Maria's daughter come through the door holding Ms. Brown's mail. "Heeyy Ms. Za'Mya…" Maria's daughter said hugging Ms. Brown handing her her mail. "Here's your mail and that smell is strong. I didn't know you be getting your puff on." Maria's daughter said not noticing that Lil Kilo, Lil Fresh or Lil Slim was sitting in the living room. "My momma do to." "I done asked them to hit their lil weed but they being petty." Maria said looking over at Lil Kilo and them again. Maria's daughter Loreli followed her mother's eyes to the living room. "Girl I didn't know you smoked." Ms. Brown said locking the door then sat the mail down. "And you still don't." Maria said laughing. Lil Kilo, Lil Slim and Lil Fresh just watched. Maria looked and seen the way that her daughter was staring at somebody on the couch. "You know them?" Maria asked her daughter. "Umm…Oh I think we went to middle school together." Maria's daughter said breaking eye contact with Lil Slim. "Middle school is the only place you better have went with them little stingy heffers." Maria said. Lil Kilo couldn't help but laugh. "You showl is wearin' us out." Lil Kilo told Maria. "I sure am since ya'll being petty with ya'll lil weed." "Girl you really want to puff that weed with them don't you?" Ms. Brown said getting ready to walk out the living room. "Damn right I do. Do you smell how strong that shit is?" Maria said laughing. "We got plenty more if you want to roll one up."

Lil Fresh said blinking his eyes for the first time. "You must don't think I can roll a joint?" Maria told Lil Fresh then winked her eye at him walking into the living room sitting her Gucci clutch bag on the arm of the couch next to where Lil Kilo was sitting. "Where the papers at? And don't keep staring at my daughter... ummm...." Maria said asking Lil Kilo what his name was after she said ummm. "Yo daughter look familiar." Lil Kilo said trying to remember where he seen Loreli's face not to long ago. "She said you all went to Middle School together. So that's probably where you recognize her face from. Now where this lil weed at that ya'll been trying to save." Maria asked now looking at Lil Fresh catching him looking at her titties. 'It's not school tho.' Lil Kilo thought as Maria's daughter came into the living room and sat on the white leather love seat that sat across from them. Ms. Brown asked if anybody else wanted anything to drink while she was in the kitchen and Loreli asked if she had any tea. Lil Fresh looked up and across the table paying attention to Loreli for the first time then started patting his leg lightly. "That's Ol' Girl from umm... umm...damn!" Lil Fresh said unable to remember where he seen Maria's daughter at. "The Chicken Shack..." Loreli said telling Lil Kilo and Lil Fresh where they seen her at not to long ago. "Exactly!" Lil Kilo said remembering her walking up to the table while him and Lil Fresh was eating and asked them about Lil Slim. "I remember now. Ya'll pulled off in a Benz coupe didn't ya?" Lil Kilo said remembering the whip Loreli pulled off in. "You were looking pretty hard huh?" Maria asked Lil Kilo then asked Lil Fresh for a cigar to roll the weed up in. After grabbing the cigar from Lil Fresh Maria told him to break the weed down for her so she could roll up. "Girl I did not know you smoked for real." Ms. Brown said watching Maria lick the end of the cigar before filling it with weed. "Let me find out you being high at work is the only reason you take me out to lunch every day." Ms. Brown and Maria both laughed. "So this is Keon aka Lil Kilo, that's Marshawn aka Lil Dirty and that handsome young…" Maria was saying making sure she knew who Lil Slim, Lil Fresh and Lil Kilo was but Lil Fresh interrupted her after she called him Lil Dirty. "Get my name right wit yo sexy ass before I have you screaming my name." Is what Lil Fresh wanted to say to Maria. "I see somebody got jokes." Is what Lil Fresh said trying his best to come up with something slick to say to let Maria know he was feeling her but couldn't think of anything. "Sure do." Maria said then smiled. "Now like I was saying, that handsome young man that my daughter keeps staring at must be Issac aka Big Slim." Maria said walking around the front of the couch so that she was able to give Lil Slim a hug and tell him how strong of a person he was. Maria could tell that Lil Slim's self-esteem level was kind of low from the way he hugged her so she squeezed him a little tighter. Sitting down next to Lil Slim Maria handed Lil Fresh the blunt she rolled perfectly and told him to fire it up then looked Lil Slim in the eyes and told him how blessed he was to be alive. "You got shot nine times like Fifty and survived." Maria told Lil Slim which caused Lil Slim to smile because he kind of figured that's what she was trying to make him do with the 50 Cent joke because he was shot seven times. "God saved you for a reason." Maria told Lil Slim then told him that it was up to him to find out the reason. Lil Slim thought about what Maria said and nodded his head in agreement. "My nigga way passed blessed. My nigga a straight solider." Lil Fresh said handing Maria the blunt to see if she was gone hit it and to his surprise she did. Maria took two small puffs from the blunt then passed it to Lil Slim. "Damn that's strong." Maria said coughing just a little after blowing the smoke in Lil Fresh face. Ms. Brown laughed then asked Maria did she think that she'll be able to help her with all the paper work to open her own law firm while she was high. Maria looked at Ms. Brown and smiled. "Girl I only took two puffs." Maria said feeling a buzz from the weed already. "I'm not that damn high yet." Maria said standing up walking towards the kitchen. "Damn!" Maria heard Lil Fresh say then looked back just in time to catch him looking at her ass. "Damn my phone goin' dead." Lil Fresh said then winked his eye at Maria and grinned. '*Cute.*' Maria thought then asked Loreli if she wanted to come to the back with her while she helped Ms. Brown. "No, I'm fine mami. I'll be okay right here." Loreli told her mother then cut her eye at Lil Slim as he was pulling out his cell phone checking his text messages. '*I wonder who's texting him?*' Loreli thought. "I think my babi like Lil Slim." Maria told Ms. Brown leaving out the kitchen headed up the hall with a sprite and brownie in her hand. "And I think you got the munchies." Ms. Brown joked. "Damn yo momma fine! Give me 5 minutes maybe even 4." Lil Fresh told Loreli joking sounding like Chris Tucker on Friday as Lil Slim passed the blunt to Lil Kilo so that he could text his mother back. Loreli laughed. "You smoke?" Lil Kilo asked Loreli grabbing the blunt from Lil Slim. "Ion wanna be rude and not let you hit it." Lil Kilo said trying to

pass Loreli the blunt before he sat back down. "Oh…umm…
no I don't smoke but thanks." Loreli said hoping that Lil Kilo
didn't just catch her staring at Lil Slim. "What's yo name by
the way?" Lil Kilo asked Loreli. Loreli said her name and it
sounded as if she was speaking Puerto Rican. Lil Kilo tried
to pronounce it and had it all wrong. Loreli chuckled. "No
crazy it's Loreli, like low-rail-lee." Loreli said saying her name
slowly breaking down the syllables cutting her eyes at Lil
Slim to see if he was paying attention but seen that he wasn't.
'I wonder who he's texting?' Loreli thought trying to figure
out a way to get Lil Slim's attention. *'I know just the way.'*
Loreli thought then stood and acted as if she was setting her
tea down on the table. "Umm…your colostomy bag needs to
be changed Issac." Loreli said pointing to the bag that was
sitting beside Lil Slim in the wheel chair. *'What am I doing?'*
Loreli thought right before hearing Lil Fresh say "His what
need to be changed?" Lil Slim glanced down and seen that
his bag was halfway full. "Fuck!" Lil Slim mumbled. *'How
did I forget to change this stupid ass bag?'* Lil Slim thought.
"His colostomy bag or you may know it as a shit bag." Loreli
said still trying to figure out why she was so interested in Lil
Slim. "Help him change it." Lil Kilo said looking at Lil Slim
grinning knowing that if this nigga wasn't in that wheelchair
he would've been snatched Loreli up. "Nawl I'm good fool.
I got it." Lil Slim said getting ready to roll himself to the
bathroom but Loreli was right there whispering in his ear
before he could move. "Let me help you." While Loreli was
helping Lil Slim change his bag in the bathroom Lil Kilo told
Lil Fresh to roll another blunt. "You heard bout what
happened to Ol' Boy that be with Percy?" Lil Fresh asked Lil

Kilo. "Yeah Percy told me he got his shit pushed back a few days ago but didn't tell me why." Lil Kilo said wondering what Maria and Ms. Brown was back there doing. *'I hope Ms. Brown don't play with me bout my money.'* Lil Kilo thought making a mental note to put his money back up. "What?" Lil Fresh said like he couldn't believe that Lil Kilo haven't heard the news. "Listen to how crazy this shit is fool." Lil Fresh was saying as Loreli was pushing Lil Slim back into the living room. "The nigga baby momma set the nigga up to get robbed by her other baby daddy, the nigga wasn't goin' so the otha baby daddy popped 'em." Lil Fresh told Lil kilo as he was breaking down another blunt to roll up. "Who ya'll talkin' bout fool?" Lil Slim asked after thanking Loreli for helping him. *'I'm glad that all she had to do is unlatch the old bag throw it away and replace it.'* Lil Slim thought still feeling a bit embarrassed. "You remember that nigga name Byrd that use to run wit Percy fool?" Lil Fresh asked Lil Slim who noticed that Loreli sat down on the couch beside him instead of sitting back on the love seat. "Byrd… Byrd…" Lil Slim said trying to remember who Lil Fresh was talking about. "The brown skin tall nigga fool. The only nigga that's ever with Percy." Lil Kilo added. "Aww… yeah I know exactly who ya'll talkin' bout. Damn that nigga done got his shit pushed back?" Lil Slim asked looking at Lil Kilo shaking his head. "That shit crazy. How long ago was this?" "This shit happened like a week ago. The nigga got killed by his baby momma other baby daddy is the crazy part." Lil Kilo said then shook his head. "That's why Ion trust these hoes fool." Lil Fresh said licking the end of the blunt shut. "These hoes scandalous. I told ya'll that's why I fuck em, feed em and leave em." Lil Fresh said. Everybody in the living room laughed even Loreli. "Youa fool boy." Lil Slim told Lil Fresh as he fired the blunt up. Halfway through the bunt they were smoking Lil Kilo was about to ask Loreli was she feeling Lil Slim because every time Lil Slim asked them to get something for him she made it her business to do it for him. "Let me find out that you like my nigga." Lil Kilo told Loreli right before Ms. Brown and Maria walked back into the living room laughing off something Maria said. "What you over there smiling for Loreli?" Maria asked her daughter noticing that she was now sitting beside Lil Slim. "Estos Chicos estan loco." Loreli said in Spanish knowing that her mother and Ms. Brown were the only ones that would understand what she was saying. "Asi que necesitas alejar tu trasero de ellos, especial mente ese." Maria told Loreli pointing at Lil Fresh. Ms. Brown and Loreli busted out laughing. "Le gustas…" Ms. Brown added. "Creo que a ella le gusto!" Ms. Brown said pointing at Lil Slim. "I see." Maria said. "What in the hell are ya'll sayin' bout us?" Lil Kilo wanted to know blowing out a thick cloud of weed smoke. "Y el esta enamorado de ti." Maria added in Spanish causing Ms. Brown to chuckle a little thinking about how she put it on Lil Kilo the other night. After Maria and Loreli left Ms. Brown went back into her room to finish studying. "What else ya'll niggas been up to tho fool?" Lil Slim asked Lil Kilo and Lil Fresh. "I haven't heard not one phone go off about some money." Lil Slim said grabbing the blunt from Lil Kilo. "I ain't gone lie fool every since you got hit our mind haven't really been on it." Lil Kilo said. "We really been servin' the same mufuckers. Percy and a few other niggas from around the way." Lil Kilo said. Lil

Slim let Lil Kilo and Lil Fresh know that as soon as he was able to walk again that it was on. The next day while Lil Slim was in the living room with his therapist he heard somebody knocking on the door and figured that it was for his mother. "Okay good. Now tell me if you feel this…" Lil Slim's therapist said then hit Lil Slim in the left knee with the small hammer. Lil Slim had no feelings in his legs but would tell his therapist every time that he hit one of his knees that he could feel it. "Look Doc, I'ma keep it real with you…: Lil Slim said then told his therapist the truth about him not being able to feel anything when the hammer hit his knee. "I been lyin' this whole time Doc. I can't feel shit in my legs." Lil Slim said with tears in his eyes. "Don't cry Issac you have to fight. But I'm glad you finally told the truth." The therapist said rubbing Lil Sim's shoulders. "I knew you were lying my first visit here." The therapist added then told Lil Slim how he acted as if he hit his knee with the hammer but never did. "I asked you did you feel that and you said yes so I figured you were joking so I took another fake swing at the other knee and you told me you felt that too." The therapist said then asked Lil Slim did he feel anything either time he hit him. "No…" Lil Slim said in a voice that sounded like it had no life at all. The therapist then told Lil Slim that he had already informed his mother about the situation. "She said that it was up to you if he wanted to continue seeing a me or not?" The therapist told Lil Slim. Lil Slim sat silent for a second then looked at the therapist and told him that he appreciate everything that he have done. "But I don't want to be bothered right now." Lil Slim said sounding very depressed. "I have your number. I'll call you in a few weeks."

Lil Slim told the therapist who in return told Lil Slim that he understood but not to give up on life. "That shit easy to say when ain't shit goin' wrong in your life." Lil Slim said then rolled over to the 650 gallon fish tank his mother had custom built into the wall with all type of exotic fish floating around in it. Before leaving out the room Lil Slim therapist gave Lil Slim a life lesson in two sentences. "I'm gone tell you like this, just because a person isn't in the same condition as you doesn't mean their situation isn't worse. Not even six months ago I lost my wife, my son and my house to a house fire." Lil Slim's therapist said packing his stuff. "And you sitting right here acting like life is over for you just because there's a *possibility* that you won't walk again." Lil Slim's therapist said putting emphasis on possibility. Lil Slim stared at the fish tank thinking about what his therapist said and just as soon as he looked up to apologize he realized that the therapist was gone and somebody else was standing there which caused Lil Slim to become a little uneasy. "What you doin' here?" Lil Slim questioned trying to figure out what the hell was going on. "So you're a quitter? You just gone give up on life?" The person said still standing in the doorway to the living room. "Who let you in my house?" Lil Slim started to say but seen that his mother had walked up and was now standing behind the person. "What's this about momma, you know her?" Lil Slim asked now trying to play it cool. "I do now." Lil Slim's mother said. "Loreli seems like a nice girl. She even brought you a gift." Lil Slim's mother said then walked over to where Lil Slim was and gave him a kiss on the cheek. "I love how spacious and neat everything is in here Ms. Ivonne." Loreli said looking around while Lil Slim was trying to figure out how Loreli knew where he lived. *'Had to be either Lil Kilo or Lil Fresh that let her know.'* Lil Slim thought sliding out his phone sending both of them a text. "Thank you baby. I haven't had time to clean up much. I've been busy the last few weeks." Lil Slim's mother told Loreli then told her to make herself at home. And Loreli did just that.

Chapter 15

Over the next few weeks Loreli made it her business to see Lil Slim every single day. Monday through Sunday Loreli was over Lil Slim house. It got to the point where after school she wasn't even going home first anymore. She would drop her friend off at home and drive straight over to Lil Slim house. Lil Slim seen what was going on after Loreli's fourth visit and asked her what she was doing. "I mean you done came by every day this week." Lil Slim told Loreli. Loreli didn't know what it was that had her so attached to Lil Slim, the only thing she knew is she was. "Umm… I'm just coming to check on my friend. I mean you are my friend aren't you?" Loreli said looking Lil Slim in the eyes with a look of love. Lil Slim was confused about the whole situation and thought that Loreli had a motive behind coming to see him every day so one day Lil Sim asked his mother how she felt about Loreli. "Momma can I ask you something?" Lil Slim asked while they were both sitting at the kitchen table eating dinner one night. "Sure baby what's going on?" Lil Slim's mother said thinking that Lil Slim was about to ask her something about his daddy. "Uh… you know Loreli right?" Lil Slim said trying to figure out how to ask his mother how she felt about her. "Yes, I know Loreli." Lil Slim's mother said chuckling. "What's funny?" Lil Slim asked looking at his mother sideways. "I just knew you were about to ask me something about your daddy." Lil Slim's mother said. "Why say that?" Lil Slim asked. "Because every time you get quiet or when you're in deep thought you make the same facial expressions your daddy use to make." Lil Slim mother said then told Lil Slim how she felt about Loreli. Lil Slim looked at his mother like she was crazy. "I'm serious son I know. I'm a woman with an intuition out of this world." Lil Slim's mother said pushing her plate in front of her. "Especially when it comes to my baby." "So you think Loreli really like me?" Lil Slim asked then took a bit of the stuffed chicken breast his mother cooked. "Issac you're all I have in this world. I've lost both your daddy and your sister. I do not want to lose you. I wouldn't tell you nothing wrong. As a matter of fact I actually think Loreli have some type of love for you." Lil Slim just listened and thought about changing the subject until his text message went off and he seen that it was Loreli. "Hey, D'juan I'm sorry I couldn't make it by to see you today. I started working with my mami today and I don't know my schedule yet but hopefully I can make it tomorrow. I miss you. Well I'm going to bed ttyl. *P.S.* If I told you I love you would you believe me?" After reading Loreli's text message Lil Slim looked up at his mother. "I know you not playin' a trick on me is ya?" Lil Slim asked looking around to see if Loreli was somewhere hiding. Lil Slim's mother laughed. "That must be Loreli?" Lil Slim showed his mother the message and all she said was "I told you so." The next day Loreli was walking through Lil Slim's door dressed as a nurse in a white scrub outfit with a Michael Kors tote bag hanging from her arm. "You must be comin' to see me before you go to work?" Lil Slim said after opening the door letting Loreli in. Lil Slim caught his self smiling admiring Loreli's beauty even in a plain white scrub. *'I got me a Puerto Rican nurse.'* Lil Slim thought. "I skipped work today to nurse you back to health." Loreli said pushing Lil Slim into the living room. "Now come on Mr. Cook we have some work to do." Inside the living room Loreli pushed Lil Slim next to the couch then sat her bag down and unzipped it and pulled out the same exact reflex hammer that his therapist used and some type of oil it looked like. Loreli seen that Lil Slim still had a smile on his face and said. "You must have missed me." Lil Slim was caught off guard with that statement. "Huh… what you talkin' bout boo?" Lil Slim said then let out a light chuckle. "I seen the way you were just looking at me." Loreli said then put her hand on her hip and turned around in a small circle showing off her beauty and body in the scrub she had on. "It's okay because I missed you too big head." Loreli said giving Lil Slim a hug squeezing him tightly. When Loreli did her fashion show spin Lil Slim seen how fat her ass really was in those scrubs and was turned on even more than he already was from just seeing her beauty. "You crazy." Was all Lil Slim said. After taking a few more things out of her Michael Kors tote bag Loreli sat it on Lil Slim's mother white and black Connie sectional that costed somewhere around eleven thousand dollars. "Where's my bestie at by the way." Loreli questioned. Lil Slim knew Loreli was asking where his mother was but acted as if he didn't. "I'm not sure. You didn't drop her off after school?" Lil Slim said trying to keep a straight face. Loreli laughed then told Lil Slim to see if he still had jokes after she gave him his shots. Lil Slim grinned.

"Nawl tho she's still at work. She called right before you got here and said that she'll be a little late gettin' home today." Lil Slim said then asked Loreli what she planned on doing with all the doctor utensils she had. "I'm going to be your physical therapist from here on out." Loreli said holding up the reflex hammer. "Oh...umm...one second please." Lil Slim said then acted as if he was about to roll out of the living room and away from Loreli. Loreli laughed. "Get back in here Mr! I'm not going to hurt you." Loreli said wheeling Lil Slim back next to her bag. *'I wonder have he bathed yet?'* Loreli thought noticing that Lil Slim had on a pair of polo pajama pants and a white beater. *'I'm glad I washed my ass this morning.'* Lil Slim thought as Loreli walked around to the back of his wheelchair. "Today were going to do a feeling check." Loreli said placing the reflex hammer on the arm of the couch. "I'm going to touch you without letting you know I'm touching you and if you feel me touching you make a noise or something like that so I'll know you feel me touching you." Loreli said sounding just like a nurse. "Ahhh..." Lil Slim said soon as Loreli stopped talking. Loreli noticed that her hand was on Lil Slim's shoulder then pinched him. "I haven't started yet punk." Loreli said jokingly. "Okay, now do you feel this?" Loreli asked pretending to be touching Lil Slim. Lil Slim sat there for a sec not feeling anything. "Nope!" But I thought I was supposed to tell you when I felt you touching me lil booty." Lil Slim said looking back at Loreli. "Lil Booty? You must be running a fever?" Loreli said putting her hand over Lil Slim's forehead then walked around his wheelchair twisting making her ass bounce every time she stepped. "I'm Puerto Rican and black so you know my ass fat." Loreli said laughing. "That mufucker showl is fat…" Lil Slim mumbled. Standing back behind Lil Slim Loreli lightly rubbed her finger across Lil Slim's ear and Lil Slim wiggled his head." Okay Mr. Cook I'm assuming you felt that." Loreli said sounding just like a nurse again. Lil Slim remembered Loreli calling him by his middle name in her text message yesterday and asked her how did she know it. "I know a lot about you D'juan and as time go by I'll get to know everything." Loreli said calling Lil Slim by his middle name again. Lil Slim wanted to know how in the hell Loreli knew so much about him and they never talked before. "Is that right?" Lil Slim said. "Yep! And in case you're wondering what my whole name is its Loreli Marie Sanchez born September fifth nineteen ninety nine." Loreli said then rubbed her finger lightly across Lil Slim's neck. "I felt that Marie." Lil Slim said calling Loreli by her middle name. Loreli then told Lil Slim that she believed that the only place he didn't have feeling was his lower body then started to massage his shoulders. "Damn that feel good." Lil Slim said feeling the tension leave his body as Loreli's soft hands massaged his shoulders then made their way down to his chest. "You like that?" Loreli asked Lil Slim watching him lean his head back. "Ummhmm…" Lil Slim said closing his eyes as Loreli lean down a little closer and put her nose in the crease of Lil Slim's neck and inhaled slowly. "Don't worry baby I'm going to be here for you. I'll never leave your side." Loreli whispered in Lil Slim's ear. And for some reason Lil Slim believed every word Loreli said. "Okay now back to the therapy session." Loreli said after kissing Lil Slim's neck. "I know I didn't pee on myself." Loreli said to herself feeling her wetness soak through her panties. Grabbing her reflex hammer from off the couch Loreli walked around Lil Slim's wheelchair and was about to pop Lil Slim in the knee but noticed his pajama pants bulging in the front. "I see somebody got some feeling in this area right here." Loreli said pointing at Lil Slim's manhood with the reflex hammer giggling. Lil Slim looked down and shook his head. "Ion know how that happened." Lil Slim said then laughed to play it off. "I know how it happened." Loreli said then winked her eye at Lil Slim. *'Damn girl!'* Lil Slim thought thinking about how Loreli's mouth would feel wrapped around him right now. Holding the reflex hammer with her right hand Loreli ran her left hand up Lil Slim's thigh as if she was reaching for his dick then stopped. "Did you feel my hand rubbing up your thigh?" Loreli asked wondering if Lil Slim had feeling in his thighs. Lil Slim shook his head yes to let Loreli know that he felt her rubbing his thigh. "Well you sure didn't say nothing." Loreli said. Lil Slim laughed. "You had my mind somewhere else." Lil Slim said as Loreli tapped his knee with the reflex hammer kind of hard. Lil Slim looked at Loreli. "I guess you thought I was gone forget to say something that time too?" Lil Slim said rubbing his knee. Lil Slim then paused. "Wait." Lil Slim said then told Loreli to hit his knee again. Loreli hit Lil Slim's knee again but this time a little softer to see if he would still feel it and to her surprise he did. "I felt it again!" Lil Slim said excitedly not understanding why he didn't feel it when he had a therapist. Loreli tapped the other knee and smiled. "What you smiling fo' boo?" Lil Slim asked rubbing his other knee. "Because you haven't stopped smiling." Loreli said then tapped Lil Slim's knee again. "I can't do nothing but smile. The doctor told me that I'll never walk again. And feeling you hit my knee gave me hope." Lil Slim said pulling out his phone to call his mother to tell her the good news but she was coming through the door. "Issac!" That night Lil Slim sat talking with his mother trying to figure out what it was about Loreli that he was starting to like other than her somehow giving him feeling in his legs. "Listen son." Lil Slim's mother said looking him in the eyes. "God bring people into our lives for a reason. I don't believe that she have a motive as to why she's over here almost every day. I really think Loreli genuinely likes you for you." Lil Slim's mother told him. "I know momma… but it's like…" Lil Slim started to say but his mother cut him off. "But it's like nothing Issac. Don't let your emotions distract your heart. You must learn to balance out your mind and your heart son." Lil Slim's mother said. "Your daddy use to always tell me 'Ivonne, stop following your heart and follow your mind.' I never understood what he meant until he passed away." Lil Slim's mother said trying to hold back her tears but couldn't. Lil Slim hated to see his mother cry. "It's okay momma. You don't have to cry. Daddy still with us." Lil Slim said then reached out and grabbed his mother's hand. After wiping her tears Lil Slim's mother told Lil Slim what his daddy meant by following your mind and not your heart. "Sometimes son your heart needs more time to accept what your mind already knows. Listen to your mind and your heart shall follow son." The next day Lil Kilo was out handling business with Lil Fresh trying to find some more work. "Man this shit crazy." Lil Kilo said hanging his phone up. "What he talkin' bout fool?" Lil Fresh asked scrolling down his Instagram. "He said it ain't lookin' to good on his end and that it might be a few days before he can get his hands on something." Lil Kilo said scrolling down his contact list. "A few days? What type of shit is that?" Lil Fresh asked looking up from his phone. "Ion know but the way he was talkin' shid it might be longer than that. That nigga kept talkin' bout the drought." Lil Kilo said. "I'm bout to call Cutt to see if he know somebody else with some work tho." Lil Kilo said dialing some numbers on his phone. "His phone goin' straight to voicemail." Lil Kilo said then tried to call back and got the voicemail again. "Fuck!" Lil Kilo said getting frustrated. "Be cool fool we gone find some." Lil Fresh said then told Lil Kilo to swing by Big Ed's spot so they could get something to smoke and not even fifteen minutes later they were sitting on Big Ed's couch passing a blunt back and forth. "I see ya'll handled ya'll bizniz like gangstas." Big Ed said out the blue. Lil Kilo and Lil Fresh both gave Big Ed a 'What chu talkin' bout' look." "What you talkin' bout Ol' Man?" Lil Kilo asked grabbing the blunt from Lil Fresh. "The situation with ol' boy." Big Ed said pulling his finger back and forth like he was shooting a gun. Lil Kilo and Lil Fresh knew exactly which situation Big Ed was talking about seeing him move his finger. Lil Kilo hardly ever thought about Rachean although him and Lil Fresh killed him. "Shit I damn near forgot about that lil altercation with ol' boy to be honest." Lil Kilo said sitting back on the couch hitting the blunt. "Shit me too." Lil Fresh said. "That's that killer instinct that's been instilled in ya'll that ya'll daddy once had." Big Ed said then told them the story they daddy told him about a nigga in Detroit that tried to rob them. "So my daddy knew a bitch that had a cuzzin' that stayed in The D that supposedly had some work?" Lil Fresh said chuckling knowing that he got his ways from his daddy. "Yeah but the cold part is how they said they put Jaz, a bitch that use to take hits for them on him." Big Ed said grabbing the blunt from Lil Kilo. Hearing Big Ed say something about Jaz caused

Lil Kilo and Lil Fresh to look at each other and grin. "Since we on the subject bout our daddy and some work…" Lil Kilo said as Big Ed hit the blunt. "We havin' trouble gettin' our hands on some work as we speak. I know you know somebody that know somebody Ol' Man." Lil Kilo said hoping Big Ed knew somebody that had some dope. Big Ed paused for a second to think about his answer then dumped the ashes. "One of my partnas be doing his thang name Lil Jimmy." Big Ed said. "I can call him and see what he talking bout if you want me to." Big Ed said. "Yeah see what that nigga talkin' bout for me." Lil Kilo told Big Ed just as his phone rung. Pulling out his phone seeing that it was Neka calling Lil Kilo shot her a text and told her he'll call her back in a second. "I usually don't do this but I know ya'll solid." Big Ed said then grabbed his cell phone off the table and made the call. After what seemed like the forth ring to Lil Kilo Big Ed started talking. "What's good my brother…I been good man still hangin' slangin' and staying away from danger… fa show… fa show…" Big Ed said into the phone then paused for a minute while his partner Lil Jimmy was talking. Big Ed busted out laughing. "It's a cold world. You know you gotta wrap that thang up. But check this out…" Big Ed said then told Lil Jimmy about Lil Kilo and Lil Fresh. "Yeah…these lil niggas tryna go fishin'." Big Ed paused again then asked Lil Kilo how much dope he was trying to get. "Two bricks." Lil Kilo said in a straight whisper. Big Ed put the phone back to his ear and said "This lil nigga might know what he doing too. He told me he caught two 36 pound catfish the last time he went." Big Ed said talking in codes. "Okay cool just hit me when you touchdown tomorrow." Big Ed said then hung up. "He said that he out in Cali right now but he'll be back sometime tomorrow evening." "That's cool just hit my line whenever you hear somethin'." Lil Kilo said getting up to leave. "Sell me a quarter of some of that same shit we just smoked Ol' Man." Lil Fresh said reaching in his pocket. "Lemme get a quarter too. I damn near forgot about the weed after hearin' about the dope." Lil Kilo said. After leaving Big Ed's spot Lil Kilo and Lil Fresh popped up on Lil Slim to see what he had going on and just as they were pulling up they seen the same white C380 Benz coupe parking. "I know that ain't..." Lil Kilo said then stopped once he seen the driver door open. "This nigga think he slick." Lil Fresh said watching the female pop the trunk and grab his wheelchair then roll it around to the passenger side door. "Come on fool lets help him." Lil Kilo said cutting his car off and hopped out. "I'll help him into his wheelchair." Lil Kilo said walking up to the passenger side door. "Oh... hey Lil Kilo... I was wondering who ya'll was. I couldn't see through those dark tints." "What's up Loreli?" Lil Fresh said walking up. "Hey Lil Fresh." Loreli said back. "What ya'll fools doin' poppin' up on a nigga?" Lil Slim said jokingly. "Ya'll like to got dumped at." Lil Slim added laughing. "You ain't strapped nigga how you gone dump?" Lil Fresh joked helping Lil Kilo put him in his wheelchair. "Shid just cause I ain't strapped don't mean that pretty ass Puerto Rican ain't." Lil Slim said then pointed at Loreli who in return smiled an innocent smile. "Help her grab those bags off the back seat Lil Fresh. I had to go tear the mall down. I couldn't fit none of my clothes." Inside Lil Slim's house they all sat around in the living room talking shit and laughing. "A tho Lil Slim..." Lil Kilo said seriously. "What up fool?" Lil Slim said noticing the seriousness in Lil Kilo's voice. "You ain't switched up on us have you." Lil Fresh looked at Lil Kilo like where that come from. "Nigga I'll neva switch up." Lil Slim said feeling a little offended. "Them shots made me wiser fool." Lil Slim said wondering what made Lil Kilo ask him that. "I was just makin' sure." Lil Kilo said then told Lil Slim about the work they were picking up tomorrow. Finding out who killed his daddy never left Lil Slim's mind not even when he was layed up in the hospital bed fighting for his own life. "That's why you asked have I switched up huh?" Lil Slim said then told Lil Kilo that he was still just as serious as he was before he got shot about finding out who killed his daddy. "Let me get out this wheelchair onto crutched and I'll be ready." Lil Slim said seriously. "You ain't walkin' yet fool?" Lil Fresh joked. "Shid I'm damn near." Lil Slim said back. "I gotta professional personal therapist that put Roselyn Sanchez looks to sleep." Lil Slim said cutting his eye at Loreli to see if she caught that. Loreli blushed. "She gave me feelings in places where I couldn't feel shit." Lil Slim added. *I hope he's talking about in his heart.* Loreli thought cutting her eye back at Lil Slim. Lil Slim found his self taking a liking to Loreli after seeing that she would sometimes go out her way to see him. "I see you done switched tho fool." Lil Slim told Lil Kilo. "I had to. I was stickin' out like a sore thumb in that Panamera. I had to get something I could duck off in. Plus I had bullet holes and blood all on my back seat." Lil Kilo said. Hearing something about bullet holes and blood made Lil Slim think back to the day he got shot. "That nigga had some nuts." Lil Slim said thinking out loud then thought about how Rachean stood on top of him and emptied his clip. "I think that bitch ass nigga tried to kill me." Lil Slim said feeling his anger rise. "Ion think that nigga had no nuts. I think that nigga was just embarrassed.

You damn near stomped his brains out in front of everybody on the block and in order for him not to look like a bitch he had to do something. So he did what all cowards do, went and got a gun." Lil Kilo told Lil Slim. "Well that bitch ass coward want pull another gun." Lil Fresh said. "His gangsta got turnt all the way down." Hearing his niggas talk let Lil Slim know how much love they had for him and at that very moment Lil Slim grew a whole new wave of loyalty for them. "Ya'll niggas handled the bizniz and didn't think twice about it." Lil Slim said as Loreli got up to go in the kitchen. "You want anything D'juan?" Loreli asked. "Nawl I'm cool boo." Lil Slim told Loreli then looked at both Lil Kilo and Lil Fresh and told them "That shit there was way pass love. That shit is loyalty. There ain't a dollar amount big enough to repay ya'll niggas for what ya'll done for me." Lil Slim said then paused. "But shit even if it was I wouldn't repay ya'll niggas with it." Lil Slim said. "Shid why not fool." Lil Fresh said joking causing Lil Slim and Lil Kilo to laugh a little. "There's only one way to reward loyalty my nigga and that's with loyalty." After leaving Lil Slim's house Lil Kilo dropped Lil Fresh off at home and was on his way to Ms. Brown's house when Neka called. Not really feeling like being bothered Lil Kilo just let it ring. *I haven't talked to my lil baby in a few days let me call her back to see what she got goin' on.* Lil Kilo thought turning down his radio. Just as Lil Kilo was about to dial Neka's number she was calling him back. "Hello…" Lil Kilo answered. "I'm mad at you." Lil Kilo heard Neka say sounding sad. "What you mad at me fo' boo? I ain't done nothin'." Lil Kilo said already knowing why Neka was mad. "Don't play dumb Keon. You know why I'm mad at you." Neka said now sounding like she was getting mad. "Yeah I know why you mad boo… I apologize bae… where you at I'm funa pull up on you?" Lil Kilo said. "I'm not at home right now. I'm in Cincy with my friends." Neka told Lil Kilo. "What you doin' in Cincinnati?" Lil Kilo questioned passing the exit to Neka's house. "Tomorrow is my friend Kandise birthday. She's having her party here. But it's not like you care anyway, I haven't talked to you in two days Keon." Neka said feeling like the connection she once had with Lil Kilo wasn't there anymore. "Keon…" "What's up boo?" Lil Kilo said knowing that Neka was about to ask him something serious from the tone of her voice. "Do you still love me?" Neka asked Lil Kilo. "Of course I do." Lil Kilo replied. "Why you ask me that?" "Because I've been feeling like you don't. You don't call or text me like you use to. We use to go out at least once a week and now I barley even see you once a week." Neka said now sounding like she was about to cry. "If you don't want this anymore Keon just let me know instead of dragging me along." Lil Kilo could tell that Neka was feeling some type of way so instead of lying Lil Kilo kept it real with her. "I love you too much to see you hurtin' boo…" Lil Kilo said then told Neka everything he could over the phone then let her know that once he seen her he would tell her the rest. '*Should I tell her about Ms. Brown?*' Lil Kilo thought. "Oh my God! Somebody broke into your house Keon?" Neka said in disbelief. "Did they take anything or harm anybody? Was Ms. Kenya there?" Neka asked. "Everything's okay boo. Nobody was hurt." Lil Kilo said hearing the worry in Neka's voice. Lil Kilo was almost at Ms. Brown's house so he told Neka that he would talk to her a little later. "Keon…" Neka said before Lil Kilo hung up. "What up boo?" Lil Kilo said turning on Ms. Brown's street. "I love you baby. And please take care of yourself." Neka said. "I love you too and don't worry bout me baby. I promise to take care of myself. You just make sure you continue to take care of yourself hittin' that gym doin' those squats to keep that ass fat." Lil Kilo said back to lighten the mood before he hung up.

Chapter 16

"Where the fuck this nigga at?" Lil Kilo said out loud then hung up his phone and called again. "I told this nigga to be ready in the mornin' so we could go holler at Big Ed people." Lil Kilo said to his self getting Lil Fresh voicemail again. '*This nigga bet not be layed up with a bitch.*' Lil Kilo thought getting mad because Lil Fresh wasn't picking up his phone. "Guess I'll have to go holla at this nigga by myself." Lil Kilo said then pulled out his phone to call Big Ed to see where they was meeting at. Big Ed told Lil Kilo that he would call him right back to let him know. "Aite bet." Lil Kilo said then hung up and tried to call Lil Fresh again and still didn't get an answer. '*I hope my nigga aite. This ain't like him.*' Lil Kilo thought starting to worry a little because he knew that if Lil Fresh was with a bitch that he would at least text back and say that. Lil Kilo was just about to call Lil Slim and ask him have he heard from Lil Fresh but Big Ed was calling him back. "He said we can pull up to his house instead of meeting in public if that was cool with you?" Big Ed said into the phone. "At his house?" Lil Kilo said sounding a bit skeptical. "You sure this nigga straight?" Lil Kilo asked. "I'm positive." Big Ed said then told Lil Kilo that the only reason he told them to meet him at his house was because he felt comfortable with them. "He was good people with yo daddy." Big Ed said. "Me and my daddy are two different people but I'ma take yo word for it. Ima ride with you over there. Lemme slide my shoes on, grab the bread and I'll be there." Lil Kilo said then hung up and slide his phone in his pocket. After sliding his shoes on Lil Kilo walked to the back to grab his money. *'I'm glad she still gone.'* Lil Kilo thought opening Ms. Brown's closet door to get his money. "And I'm only takin' sixty. He either gone take it or leave it." Lil Kilo said then grabbed six stacks of twenty dollar bills. "I know he ain't funa turn down these 3,000 $20's." Lil Kilo said looking for something to put the money in and spotted Ms. Brown's small black Coach tote. After making sure he put everything back how it was Lil Kilo was headed out the door but not before grabbing his gun from under the couch. *'Can't trust nothin'.'* Lil Kilo thought headed out the door locking it behind him. On the way over to Big Ed's spot Lil Kilo tried calling Lil Fresh again and still didn't get an answer so he called Lil Slim. Lil Slim picked up on the second ring. "What up fool?" "Not shit bout to handle that lil bizniz I was tellin' you about yesterday. I been tryin' to call Lil Fresh all mornin', have you heard from 'em?" Lil Kilo asked Lil Slim who had just got done with his therapy session with Loreli. "Nawl I ain't heard from that nigga since ya'll left yesterday. What's goin' on?" Lil Slim asked pointing at the water bottle on the table asking Loreli to get it for him. "He was 'pose to ride with me to pick this work up but he ain't picking up the phone." Lil Kilo said jumping on the interstate. "I been callin' that nigga all mornin'." "I ain't heard from Lil

Fresh." Lil Slim said opening the bottled water Loreli handed him. "Try to call his momma and ask her if that nigga over there sleep. Knowin' him he was probably up late last night tryna freak." Lil Slim said. Lil Kilo laughed. "Ima try to call that nigga one more time after I get done handling this biz. If he don't pick up I'ma call his momma to see what's goin' on." Lil Kilo told Lil Slim then hung up and called Big Ed to tell him that he was about to pull up. "Is everything okay?" Loreli asked Lil Slim after he hung his phone up and sat it on the table. "Yeah. Lil Fresh not answerin' his phone. Lil Kilo said he been tryin' to call him all mornin'." Lil Slim said then turned the bottled water up. "Well it is still kind of early so he might still be sleep." Loreli said. "Shid its 10. That nigga usually up by 8." Lil Slim said as Loreli lifted his left leg into the air slowly then let it down and done the same thing to his right leg. Loreli was over Lil Slim's house every single day doing everything she could to help him walk again. Lil Slim was starting to feel so much feeling in his legs that one day he had his mother buy him some crutches to see if he could use them but his legs wasn't as strong as he thought they were after he fell taking the first step. "I'm starting to get hungry." Lil Slim said. "What do you have a taste for? I can make some breakfast or some lunch or we can go get something." Loreli told Lil Slim grabbing the empty water bottle out of Lil Slim's hand so she could throw it away. "You can make something boo we don't have to leave out." Lil Slim said then asked Loreli to see if they had everything they needed to make some of her famous chicken and cheese breakfast burritos. Meanwhile Lil Kilo and Big Ed were pulling up in a gated community on the lower eastside of town. "Let me call this

nigga to let him know we pullin' up." Big Ed said then dialed
some numbers on his phone. Lil Kilo sat on the passenger side
of Big Ed's Cadillac truck wondering who in the hell sold
dope out of a gated community then thought about how
smart that really was. "Can't have yo spot on the block where
it's hot at." Lil Kilo told his self. Driving around to the last
house on the street Big Ed pulled up and dropped his window
by the key pad then pressed the call button. "I see this nigga
done changed his gate again." Big Ed said noticing that the
once wooded fence was now a stainless steel and black color.
A few seconds later the gate opened and Big Ed pulled in and
up the drive way to where two all-black SUVs with dark
tinted windows and a Mercedes Benz truck was parked. "This
nigga move like the president don't he?" Lil Kilo said. "Those
are probably trap cars. I've never known Lil Jimmy to be
flashy." Big Ed said watching the front door open. "What you
mean his trap cars? What he do ride around sellin' dope out
of these cars?" Lil Kilo questioned watching a big black
muscular bald headed dude step onto the porch wearing a
black and white suit. "Something like that." Big Ed said
parking his truck behind the black SUVs. "I'll tell you bout
it once we leave." Hopping out the truck Big Ed and Lil Kilo
made their way towards the porch where the big black bald
head muscle dude was still standing waiting on them. Walking
pass the white Mercedes Benz truck Lil Kilo tried to peep
inside but couldn't see nothing but a reflection of his face.
'Damn those tints dark.' Lil Kilo thought. "Ima have to see if
Cheese know bout this Benz truck at the shop." Once Big Ed
and Lil Kilo made their way to the porch the big black muscle
headed dude opened the door and signaled for them to go in

without saying a word. Lil Kilo thought he was tripping once he got inside the house because standing in front of them was another big black muscle dude with suits on that looked exactly like the one that let them in the house. Without saying a word the muscle head that was in the house already walked up and searched Lil Kilo and Big Ed. The muscle head searched Lil Kilo and felt the gun on Lil Kilo's hip and removed it so fast popped the clip out cocked it back caught the bullet that jumped out the chamber then told Lil Kilo "Yu wan bee need diz…" In a thick Jamaican accent. Walking down the wide long hallway beside Big Ed Lil Kilo took in the entire scene. *'Damn this house big.'* Lil Kilo thought looking at all the stylish stuff that hung from the walls. Looking over his shoulder out of habit Lil Kilo seen one of the muscle heads standing at the end of the hall watching them. "Who are those big black strong bald headed ass dudes that let us in, his bodyguards or something?" Lil Kilo asked Big Ed. "Bodyguards, security guards and hit men. Shit them niggas will do anything Lil Jimmy tell them to do." Big Ed said as they got to the end of the hall. Looking down inside the den Big Ed seen that Lil Jimmy was at the bar making him a drink. "We just in time…" Big Ed said loud enough for Lil Jimmy to hear him and turn around. Lil Jimmy was damn near 50 but the only way you would be able to tell that is if he told you. "You damn right ya'll just in time." Lil Jimmy said. "What you drinking or should I ask what are ya'll drinkin'?" "You know I'm a Cognac man. What you got new over there?" Big Ed asked as him and Lil Kilo sat down. "You want a drink?" Big Ed asked Lil Kilo. "Nawl I'm good. Ion drink." Lil Kilo told Big Ed. *'This nigga must be a Saints fan.*' Lil Kilo thought noticing that everything in the den was black and gold and the chandelier that hung from the high ceiling was the same shape as the Saints symbol. "I got some Louis XIII I brought back from Cali. I got some Remy, Henn and D'usse. Shit I even got a bottle of Bourban over here." Lil Jimmy said holding up a big bottle of Jim Bean. "Lemme get some of that D'usse. I'm cool on that Bourban." Big Ed said chuckling a little. Lil Jimmy handed Big Ed his glass then sat the bottle of D'usse down on the table. "This must be Kilo Jr...they call me Lil Jimmy." Lil Jimmy said sticking his hand out to shake Lil Kilo's hand. Lil Kilo gripped Lil Jimmy's hand firmly and looked him in the eyes. "I'm Lil Kilo." Lil Kilo said letting Lil Jimmy's hand go. "Lil Kilo, Kilo Jr. Baby Kilo it don't matter what name you go by you the son of a legend. Muthafuckers should feel honored to meet you." Lil Jimmy said sitting back on the couch. Lil Kilo knew that his daddy was a big shot but thought that Lil Jimmy was talking to be talking when he said people should be honored to meet him. "Nawl I ain't nobody special." Lil Kilo said. "Stop!" Lil Jimmy said holding his hand out. "Did you hear what I just said about yo daddy? That nigga was a fuckin' great! Somebody that was well respected everywhere he went and he left his legacy to you. Ratha you know it or not yo name already hold weight in the streets." Lil Jimmy told Lil Kilo. Lil Kilo thought about what Lil Jimmy was saying and could see how his name could hold weight in the streets being that his daddy was the man. "Yeah but just because my daddy was well respected don't mean these niggas will have the same level of respect for me. I still have to let these niggas know." Lil Kilo told Lil Jimmy who in return understood what Lil Kilo was saying.

"You right." Lil Jimmy said. "Niggas ain't gone have that same level of respect but all you need in this game is a small amount of respect to gain respect." Lil Kilo was confused. "What you mean?" "What I mean is, with that small amount of respect you will definitely have somebody try to test yo gangsta and when they do..." Lil Jimmy paused then poured him a shot. "You make an example outta they ass. And watch a whole new level of respect be gained from the public." Lil Kilo understood what Lil Jimmy was saying now and for some reason wanted to know what kind of relationship he had with his daddy and how they met. "It's crazy how me and yo daddy met. I could sit here for days telling you stories." Lil Jimmy said then shoveled the big bowl of moon rocks and a cigar that was sitting on the table towards Big Ed and told him to twist one up. "Me and yo daddy was tight. Kilo was that nigga even as a lil nigga. Yo daddy had one of those names that everybody and I mean everybody knew but could never put a face with it." Lil Jimmy said. "That's how you know you doing something major in these streets when muthafuckers know yo name but don't have a clue as to what you look like." Lil Kilo just listened. "I was hearing this nigga name so much it made me want to meet him. This how crazy this nigga grind was tho..." Lil Jimmy said pouring another shot of D'usse. "Kilo use to get the work from me and my nigga Heavy then before we knew it we were getting work from him and his niggas." Lil Jimmy said. "That nigga went to jail came home and took shit over." Big Ed added firing up the blunt he just finish rolling. The room got silent for just a second. "Kilo, Slim, Fresh, and Quick..." Lil Jimmy said their names as if he were missing them. "Them was some good niggas.

Everybody and their momma loved them niggas. All the dope boys, all the kids, shit even the junkies loved them because they knew they could ask for something and get it from either one of them niggas." Big Ed said talking to Lil Jimmy passing him the blunt at the same time. "Them niggas had a heart of God's in their chest and they showed love and gave back to the hood more than the government." Lil Jimmy said as he grabbed the blunt from Big Ed. "But you know what I think got them niggas that big in the game?" Lil Jimmy asked Big Ed taking a pull from the blunt. "What's that?" Big Ed asked sitting back. Lil Kilo sat listening and observing paying close attention to everything Lil Jimmy was saying. "Loyalty. Them niggas stuck together like peanut butter and jelly. Not only was they loyal amongst each other but they had to have shown their plug how loyal they was to have them drop that bag off on them like that." Lil Jimmy said then looked Lil Kilo in the eyes and asked him was he sure he was ready for this cold game. And without batting an eye or thinking twice about it Lil Kilo's only words were "This shit personal." Lil Kilo then told Lil Jimmy the same thing he told Big Ed a while back. "I'm in it to find out who killed my daddy." Lil Jimmy could hear the coldness in Lil Kilo's voice and knew that if he was anything like his daddy then he wasn't going to stop going after whatever he's after until he got it. Lil Jimmy told Lil Kilo to let him know if there was anything he could do to help him find out. "Ion care what it is just let me know." Lil Jimmy said. Lil Kilo then told Lil Jimmy that he appreciate him wanting to help and if he needed him he would let him know. "But let's get to the real reason of why I'm here." Lil Kilo said just as somebody appeared in the doorway of the den. "Come on in nigga you just in time." Lil Jimmy told the person who was now walking into the den. "Heavy this is Lil Kilo Jr. Lil Kilo this my main man Heavy." Lil Jimmy said introducing Lil Kilo to his partner in crime. "Shid you didn't have to tell me who that lil nigga was. He look just like his daddy." Heavy said then gave Lil Kilo and Big Ed some dap. "Long time no see my nigga." Heavy told Big Ed. "You know it's hard for a small fry like me to keep up with the big wigs like you and Jimmy." Big Ed said messing with Heavy. Lil Kilo was peeping the way Lil Jimmy and Heavy dressed and really couldn't tell if they had money or not because they both were dressed in sweat pants and white tees. *It's their aura that speaks money.* Lil Kilo thought. "I'm not into the flashy, flamboyant lifestyle anymore. That shit draw to much attention." Lil Jimmy would later tell Lil Kilo in a conversation on down the line. "When you getting *REAL* money you don't wanna look like it." "So you coming to take the game over huh?" Heavy asked Lil Kilo. "Me and my niggas come to do what muthafuckers haven't done yet and it's been damn near 20 years." Lil Kilo said with just a pinch of anger in his voice. "And what's that?" Heavy asked thinking that Lil Kilo was about to say something about putting an end to the drought. "Find the muthafuckers that killed our daddy. Now let's talk bizniz." Lil Kilo said now looking back at Lil Jimmy pulling his money out Ms. Brown's black Coach Tote then sat it on the table. From the little time that Heavy been in Lil Kilo's presence he took a liking to him. "I like this lil nigga. He remind me of his daddy." Heavy said remembering how Kilo handled business when it was time to handle business. Heavy then told Lil Jimmy that they weren't going to make any money off Lil Kilo when he came to ree-up. "So we gone let 'em get 'em for what we get 'em for?" Lil Jimmy asked Heavy making sure he heard him correctly. "Yeah, this one fa Big Kilo." Heavy said. After leaving from hollering at Lil Jimmy and Heavy Big Ed and Lil Kilo headed back across town to Big Ed's spot. "Those niggas good people." Big Ed said pulling up to his spot. "You ain't got nothing to worry about fucking with them." Big Ed added then asked Lil Kilo if he wanted to smoke one before he left. "Not this time Ol' Man I gotta go drop this sack off and see what's going on with Lil Fresh. This nigga ain't picked up the phone all mornin'." Lil Kilo said then pulled out his money and peeled off a thousand dollars and handed it to Big Ed. "What's this for?" Big Ed asked. "For comin' thru on yo end the way you did." Lil Kilo said then told Big Ed he didn't have a choice but to take the money after he seen that Big Ed was about to decline his offer. "Shit I probably owe you that plus some anyway from all them free half a quarters you done gave me over the years." Lil Kilo said then chuckled and stuffed the money in Big Ed's hand. 'I wasn't looking for nothin' in return. I did that from the hea…" "And I'm doin' this from the heart." Lil Kilo said grabbing the dope he just bought from Lil Jimmy and Heavy off the backseat. "I'll swing back by a little later so we can blow one." Lil Kilo told Big Ed then got out and hopped in his car. Sitting the small Louis V Duffle that Lil Jimmy handed him with the two bricks in it on the passenger seat Lil Kilo took out his phone and tried to call Lil Fresh again but still didn't get an answer. Getting a little worried Lil Kilo pulled off and called Lil Slim. "Yo…" Lil Slim answered. "What up fool? You heard from Lil Fresh yet?" Lil Kilo asked Lil Slim blowing his horn at Big Ed letting him know that he was gone. "Nawl, I called a few times after I talked to you but he didn't pick up so I called his momma." Lil Slim said watching Loreli bend his knee back and forth. "What she say fool?" Lil Kilo asked sliding on his seat belt as the state trooper passed him. "She said that she was on her way to Mahoning to pick him up." Lil Slim said. "Mahoning? That's the juvenile place ain't it?" Lil Kilo asked confused. "Yeah. She said she don't know what's goin' on yet but she would have Lil Fresh to call me once…" "This Lil Fresh callin' on the other line now. Lemme see what he talkin' bout and I'll hit you right back." Lil Kilo told Lil Slim then clicked over. "Hello…" Lil Kilo answered. "Man you ain't gone believe what happen to me today fool." Lil Fresh said as him and his mother crossed the street to her car. "Meet me over Ms. Brown's house in 30 minutes." Lil Kilo said turning his blinker on so he could get on the interstate. "It might take me a little longer than 30. I gotta go get my car outta the pound." Lil Fresh told Lil Kilo then told him that he would call him as soon as he got his car out. Lil Kilo hung up from with Lil Fresh and called Lil Slim back to let him know what was going on and was pulling up at Ms. Browns house 20 minutes later. *I need to find me a spot to handle my bizniz at.* Lil Kilo thought as he got out the car. "Lemme call Big Ed and see if he know any realtors." Lil Kilo said out loud pulling his cell phone out. Walking up the two small steps to Ms. Brown's front door Lil Kilo dialed Big Ed's number before letting his self inside the house. "You done handled yo bizniz already lil nigga?" Big Ed said after he picked up the phone on the third ring. Lil Kilo chuckled. "Nawl not yet. I called to see if you knew any realtors. I need me a spot." Lil

Kilo said walking pass the kitchen where he seen Ms. Brown standing in the refrigerator with nothing but her bra and panties on. Taking a step back Lil Kilo blew her a kiss then headed back to her room to put the dope he just bought up. "What he need a spot for?" Ms. Brown wondered shutting the refrigerator trying to ease drop on Lil Kilo's conversation some more. "Yeah I got a few realtors." Big Ed said trying to remember all of the realtors he knew by heart. "I gotta chick name La'Tesha that can get you in something real slick or if you tryna buy something I gotta partna name O that be flipping houses." Big Ed told Lil Kilo who was sliding the Louis Vuitton duffle bag under Ms. Brown's bed. "See what yo Ol' Gal got for rent and let me know ASAP." Lil Kilo said figuring that he rather rent than buy in case he had to run the spot hot. "Okay I'm about to check now. I'll call and let you know something." Big Ed said then hung up. "Ms. Brown!" Lil Kilo yelled coming out the room not knowing that Ms. Brown was listening to his entire conversation from the door. "So you about to get your own place?" Ms. Brown asked coming straight out with it. "What you talkin' bout boo?" Lil Kilo smiled figuring that Ms. Brown may have heard him talking. "I heard you talking to somebody about a realtor." Ms. Brown said. Lil Kilo couldn't tell if Ms. Brown was pouting or if she was sad or angry from the sound of her voice. "Stop acting like that boo. I got too much goin' on to keep stuff in here." Lil Kilo said then told Ms. Brown that he wouldn't want to put her in anymore danger than she's already in. "Now come give me a hug with yo fine ass." Lil Kilo told Ms. Brown admiring her smooth long legs that looked as if they had just been shaved and rubbed down with some coconut oil. "Damn girl…" Lil Kilo mumbled. "You look like a whole snack in this burgundy laced thong set boo." Lil Kilo said rubbing Ms. Brown's ass as she came closer to hug him. "I'm a full course meal." Ms. Brown whispered in Lil Kilo's ear then moaned lightly feeling Lil Kilo finger rub against her clitoris. Ms. Brown started to open her legs a little wider until she heard Lil Kilo's phone ring. "Shit." Lil Kilo said pulling his cell phone out. Seeing that it was Lil Fresh calling Lil Kilo answered. "What up fool?" "I just got my car out the pound meet me somewhere so I can let you know what's goin' on." Lil Fresh said. Lil Kilo could hear the seriousness in Lil Fresh voice. "Meet me at the Starbucks downtown." Lil Kilo told Lil Fresh then hung up and told Ms. Brown that he'll be right back. "You need anything while I'm out?" Lil Kilo asked Ms. Brown knowing that she didn't. 15 Minutes later Lil Kilo was pulling up at the Starbucks looking for Lil Fresh car but didn't see it. "Where you at fool?" Lil Kilo asked backing into a parking spot with Lil Fresh on speakerphone. "I'm like four minutes away. I had to stop and get some gas and bumped into Shon Gotti selling his cd's. That nigga gotta hustle outta this world." Lil Fresh said pulling out of the gas station putting the cd he just bought into his cd player and started bobbing his head immediately. Pulling up at Starbucks Lil Fresh spotted Lil Kilo's car and backed in beside him then hopped out and got in the car with Lil Kilo. "What's good fool?" Lil Kilo said giving Lil Fresh some dap. "Man you ain't gone believe what the fuck happened to me earlier." Lil Fresh said then asked Lil Kilo if he had a cigar. Lil Kilo pointed down towards the cup holder. "It should be one left in that pack." Lil Kilo said. Lil Fresh grabbed the cigar pack to make sure there was a cigar in there. "Yeah it's one left but check this out fool. I was headed to the store this morning to grab Moms something for her headache and them blue lights got behind me." Lil Fresh said breaking down the cigarillo and stuffing it with weed. "Don't tell me you got caught with yo stick fool?" Lil Kilo said knowing that Lil Fresh couldn't have got caught with no work because he just ree'd up today. "Nawl it wasn't my strap. It was a lil half a blunt I had in the ashtray." Lil Fresh said pulling his lighter out his pocket. "What! A half a blunt?" Lil Kilo said. "Yeah a half a blunt." Lil Fresh said firing up the blunt he just rolled. "But that's not the killer part. Check this out..." Lil Fresh added then took a pull from the blunt. Lil Kilo listened. "The bitch walk up and ask for my licenses and insurance. I asked her why she pulled me over she said I was doin' 55 in a 35 which was a damn lie." Lil Fresh said then hit the blunt again and passed it to Lil Kilo. Lil Kilo grabbed the blunt dumped the ashes and continued to listen. "This the part that's gone fuck you up fool. The bitch hollered out she use to work for our daddy and if I come up with $10,000 dollars she won't take me in and she'll start workin' for us." Hearing this made Lil Kilo choke. "She said what?" Lil Kilo asked making sure he heard Lil Fresh correctly. Lil Fresh repeated his self then said "I told that bitch suck my dick I ain't payin' you shit! She got mad and told me she gone make my life a livin' hell then cuffed me and took me in." Lil Fresh said thinking about how rough the officer was trying to be with him. "You 'member her name fool?" Lil Kilo asked Lil Fresh about to try to find out who the police officer is Lil Fresh was talking about. "Umm..." Lil Fresh thought. "Ms. Coldwater... Ms. Coolwater or something like that." Lil Fresh said looking up into the air trying to remember the name that was on the officer's badge. Lil Kilo pulled out his cell phone. "I'm funa call Zelle's momma Jaz to see if she know anything about Ms. Coldwater." Lil Kilo said dialing some numbers on his phone passing Lil Fresh the blunt back. "What's good Sharp Shooter?" Lil Kilo said into the phone. "I'm good but… umm… is yo momma 'round right now… good I need you to ask her a question about a lady cop name Ms. Coldwater or something like that." Lil Kilo said watching as two tall blonde headed white girls came giggling out of Starbucks. *'I wonder what they laughing bout?'* Lil Kilo thought as Lil Fresh dropped his window and tried to get them to come here. "Ima get me a white girl watch." Lil Fresh said letting his window back up after the white girls ignored him. "She said what now?" Lil Kilo said into the phone. "Okay cool. Tell her I said good lookin' and I'll hit you later to let you know what's up." Lil Kilo said then hung up. "Pops 'em wasn't bullshittin' fool." Lil Kilo told Lil Fresh reaching for the blunt back. "Why you say that?" Lil Fresh asked taking another puff from the blunt before passing it to Lil Kilo. "Jaz said that Pops 'em had her on the payroll too but she was really good for nothin' and probably the reason our daddies got killed." Lil Kilo said grabbing the blunt hitting it. "So what you wanna do?" Lil Fresh asked then reminded Lil Kilo that she was talking about making his life a living hell. "Ion know. She might come in handy so I ain't gone kill her just yet. Zelle's momma getting' all her contact info for me as we speak. Ima pull down on her to see what she talkin' bout." Lil Kilo said then hit the bunt. "Her name is Ms. Coolwater too." Lil Kilo added as his phone rung and he thought that it was Ja'Zelle calling back but it wasn't it was Big Ed calling back about the spot. "Ol' Man…" Lil Kilo answered. "She said she got a four bedroom condo on the lower east side of town and a four bedroom townhouse on the opposite side of town of that." Big Ed told Lil Kilo. "If I was you I'll go with the condo. It's in a more secluded area." Big Ed said. "Aite cool. Ask her when I can get the keys. I'm ready whenever she ready." Lil Kilo said smiling. Big Ed told Lil Kilo to hold on while he called her on his other phone. "She told me to give you the address and she could meet you over there now if you want." Big Ed said with both his phones to his ears. "Yeah tell her I'll meet her now." Lil Kilo said passing Lil Fresh the blunt back. "Aite. She just texted me the address. I'm about to forward it to you." Big Ed told Lil Kilo then hung up. "I'm bout to get us a spot too fool. I'm tired of askin' mufuckers to use they stove." Lil Kilo said as his text message went off. "That's exactly what we need too." Lil Fresh said then told Lil Kilo that he wanted to ride with him to check the spot out. "Aite follow me over Ms. Brown house to park yo whip. I need to get some bread anyway." Lil Kilo told Lil Fresh. Pulling up and pulling off from Ms. Brown's house Lil Kilo and Lil Fresh jumped on the interstate still smoking the same blunt from Starbucks. "You ain't been on that new Lucci mixtape?" Lil Fresh asked Lil Kilo who pulled out a stack of one hundred dollar bills and handed them to Lil Fresh and told him to make sure it was 15k. "Nawl I been on that Gates tho. Dude one of the sickest in the game to me, him and Lito." Lil Kilo said looking at the GPS on his phone to make sure he was going the right way.

Chapter 17

Meanwhile, back at Lil Slim's house Lil Slim and Loreli were having their first altercation all because Loreli told Lil Slim that she felt that he was becoming addicted to the medication his doctor prescribed him. "I'm telling you the truth Issac. I'm not judging you." Loreli tried to explain to Lil Slim after he told her to get out. "That's the only reason I asked you were you still in pain last week because I seen you pop two of those Percocet pills in less than 30 minutes." Loreli said on the verge of tears because she's never seen Lil Slim this hostile before. "You know what… Fuck these pills!" Lil Slim said then knocked all three of his pill bottles clean across the room with the back of his hand. "I don't need them or you!" Lil Slim snapped. "Like I said… you can get the fuck out! I didn't ask you to be here!" Lil Slim yelled grabbing his crutches from off the couch beside him so that he could leave out the living room. Lil Slim was just now starting to gain enough strength to use his crutches but was trying to move faster than he normally moved on the crutches and fell. "Aggh… fuck!" Lil Slim moaned in pain now embarrassed. "Issac!" Loreli screamed rushing over to help him up. "Are you okay baby?

I'm so sorry." Loreli said grabbing Lil Slim's arm but Lil Slim jerked away from her. "Don't touch me." Lil Slim said. "Matta fact… get out! I'll help myself up and teach myself to walk again." Lil Slim said then sat up and scooted himself to the edge of the couch and pulled his self up. Loreli looked on in disbelief trying to figure out why Lil Slim was treating her this way. "I don't know what I done that was so wrong." Loreli said with tears in her eyes. Not wanting to cause any more damage that's already been caused Loreli grabbed her keys and walked out holding her face trying to stop her tears from falling while Lil Slim acted as if he didn't care. Outside in the driveway Loreli sat there crying for almost 20 minutes straight crying her heart out and didn't even notice Lil Slim's mother pull up beside her. "TapTapTap…" Loreli heard someone knocking on her window and looked up then tried to hide her face. "Open this door girl." Lil Slim's mother said. "Why are you sitting out here crying? Is everything okay?" Lil Slim's mother asked Loreli hoping that everything was okay with Lil Slim. Loreli sniffed then tried wiping her face but the tears wouldn't stop. "It's (sniff sniff) Issac" Loreli said sobbing then told Lil Slim's mother everything that took place not even thirty minutes ago. "I really think he's becoming addicted to those pills so I told him and he talked crazy to me." Loreli said still wiping her tears. Lil Slim's mother laughed a little. "What's funny Ms. Ivonne?" Loreli asked grinning just a little. "Nothing, I'm just replaying this over in my head. I can see him now trying to be smart and fall." Lil Slim's mother said laughing. "I should've kicked his crutches hmmm." Loreli said snickering and pouting at the same time. "I would've. Now fix your face and lets go back in here and show him who's the boss." Lil Slim's mother told Loreli helping her out the car.

"Yeah I'm feeling this right here." Lil Kilo said looking around the condo that was semi furnished with a black and grey leather Kiva sectional that wrapped around the living room that had a kitchen and bedroom set to match. Walking over to the big glass window that stretched from one side of the living room to the other Lil Kilo looked back at La'Tesha the girl who was renting the condo and asked "How much?" La'Tesha who was very business savvy but had a bit of hood in her as well walked from around the sectional stopping in the center of the living room then replied "Well since Mr. Sims told me that you were his nephew I can do $3,000 a month. Which I normally rent this modern three bedroom, two and a half bath with a walk in shower in the master bedroom and Jacuzzi tub as well, eat-in kitchen and…" La'Tesha was saying before Lil Kilo cut her off. "You ain't gotta say nomo. I like what I see." Lil Kilo said pulling out a stack of money. "You said 3k a month right?" Lil Kilo asked watching La'Tesha watch his money. La'Tesha shook her head. "Okay cool. I got 12 g's right here. Nine is for the first three months and the other three is for you as long as you don't make me sign no paperwork." La'Tesha thought about what Lil Kilo said and already knew what he planned on using the condo for. "Shid you can put this shit in my name for 3 thousand fool." Lil Fresh said seriously but playing at the same time causing both Lil Kilo and La'Tesha to laugh. "You have a deal Mr. and for being so generous I'm going to return the favor and hook you up with my uncle. He do fake ID's, Birth Certificates,

Pass Ports, Licenses, fix credit and everything. And he's legit."
La'Tesha told them while grabbing the money from Lil Kilo.
"How we 'pose know this nigga shit legit?" Lil Fresh said
then told Lil Kilo that the living room had enough space for
a full size pool and ping pong table. "Yeah how do we 'pose to
know that we ain't gone get jammed up using the fake licenses
and shit?" Lil Kilo asked knowing that him and his niggas
could use some fake identifications. "I'm gone show you how
I know he's legit and know what he's doing…" La'Tesha said
pulling out her ID from her purse showing Lil Kilo and Lil
Fresh. "Okay here's one reason I know he's legit…the name
here say La'Tesha Mooreland born 10/13/96 right?" La'Tesha
said sticking the ID out more for them to see. "Well my
birth name isn't La'Tesha Mooreland its Lorine Johnson."
La'Tesha said sticking her ID back inside her wallet. "Just
because that nigga made a fake ID don't make him official."
Lil Fresh said. La'Tesha chuckled. "Okay what if I told you it's
because of him I have this condo for rent and nine others?"
La'Tesha said seriously. Lil Kilo and Lil Fresh both looked
confused. "He even fixed La'Tesha Mooreland's credit to
where I was approved for a $750,000 thousand dollar business
loan and from there I took a little over $107,000 thousand
and built seven condos just like this one from the ground
up. I just spent another quarter million getting two more
put up." La'Tesha said. Lil Kilo could tell that La'Tesha was
being real with them and told her he would appreciate it if she
hooked them up with her uncle. "Hell yeah put us in touch
with yo people." Lil Kilo said. "You think that shit justifiable
Lil Kilo?" Lil Fresh asked. "I'm 21 I been doing this since I
was 17 and haven't had not one problem. I'm not pressuring

ya'll to mess with my uncle. I just know what kind of business ya'll conduct and was trying to help." La'Tesha told Lil Fresh looking at Lil Kilo while taking the condo key off her key ring. "Yeah I think everything straight." Lil Kilo said. After getting everything squared away with La'Tesha Lil Kilo and Lil Fresh sat in the condo talking about their next moves. "This shit bout to get serious fool I hope you know that." Lil Kilo told Lil Fresh getting up to check out the condo again. "I got two bricks stashed at Ms. Brown's house that I need to go grab so we can bring back here and bust down." Lil Kilo said ready to get to business. Lil Fresh next words let Lil Kilo know that he was as solid as they come. "Aye Lil Kilo..." Lil Fresh said. Lil Kilo looked up. "I want you to know that I'll neva bend, break or fold. We got our first piece of pussy together, sold our first piece of dope together and caught our first body together. You my muthafucken brother till this shit over with." Lil Fresh said meaning every word he said. Checking his watch seeing that it was only 4:37 Lil Kilo told Lil Fresh to run to Walmart and grab doubles of everything they needed to cook the dope up with while he shot across town to grab the dope from Ms. Brown's house. "Aite bet." Lil Fresh said. Leaving the condo locking it up behind him Lil Kilo hopped in his whip and called Lil Slim to let him know what was going on but didn't get an answer. So he called back.

"Your phone ringing." Loreli told Lil Slim who was standing on his crutches in the kitchen acting like he was trying to find something to eat but was really embarrassed that his mother and Loreli came back in the house together and his mother was taking up for Loreli and not him. "It's Lil Kilo calling."

Loreli said picking Lil Slim's phone up off the couch. Not wanting to hop all the way in the living room to get his phone Lil Slim told Loreli to bring it to him. "Bring it to me. I'm tryna find me something to eat." Lil Slim said opening the refrigerator door. Loreli walked into the kitchen grinning knowing that Lil Slim was feeling some type of way that his mother was taking up for her instead of him. "Here you go." Loreli said handing Lil Slim his phone just as it stopped ringing. "Let me know if you want me to fix you something." Loreli said picking with Lil Slim. "Nawl I'm cool." Lil Slim said grabbing his phone from Loreli trying not to make eye contact with her. '*That nigga probably getting a leg massage or somethin'.*' Lil Kilo thought hanging up his phone about to sit it in the cup holder until it starting ringing. "What up my nigga?" Lil Slim said trying to hide the aggravation in his voice. "I got all types of good news." Lil Kilo said jumping on the interstate headed to Ms. Brown house. "Is that right?" Lil Slim said a little louder so that his mother and Loreli could hear him. "Come pick me up and tell me bout it. I need to get out the house for a second anyway." Lil Slim said knowing that Loreli and his mother was listening to him. "You sure?" Lil Kilo asked jumping back off the interstate. "Yeah. I'm bout to slide some clothes on now." Lil Slim said then hung up and hopped pass the living room and told his mother and Loreli that he'll be back. "He's doing this on purpose. Don't pay him no mind girl. I know my son." Lil Slim's mother told Loreli and fifteen minutes later Lil Kilo was helping Lil Slim into the car. "I see you movin' up in the world." Lil Kilo told Lil Slim pulling off. Lil Slim already knew what Lil Kilo was talking about. "I'll be back on my own two before you know it. It's just a matter of time. But shid what's good, what's goin' on?" Lil Slim asked. Lil Kilo then filled Lil Slim in on everything that been going on with Lil Jimmy and Heavy, the spot he just bought and Lil Fresh situation with the police. "Hol up…" Lil Slim said thinking about what Lil Kilo just said about Lil Fresh and the police officer. "So Lil Fresh was pulled over and the officer tried to get him out of 10 after tellin' him that she use to work for our daddy?" Lil Slim said. Lil Kilo just nodded his head. "Sounds like she just tryin' to get some money because if she had any kind of love for Pops 'em she'll be tryin' to help us find out who did this." Lil Slim said. Lil Kilo then told Lil Slim that he was waiting on Ja'Zelle's mom to get back with him with the police officer contact information so he could pull up on her. "Whenever you do make sure I'm with you. I want to hear what she gotta say." Lil Slim said. Hearing that made Lil Kilo realize how much he missed Lil Slim being around and the conversations they us to have. "Don't worry bout that lil situation. Just worry bout gettin' back on yo feet. I'll take care of it." Lil Kilo said just to see what Lil Slim would say. *I wonder if my nigga still got that same drive he had before he got shot to find out who killed our daddy.*' Lil Kilo thought jumping back on the interstate. "I'm not worried bout gettin' back on my own two feet as much as I'm worried bout who killed our daddy fool." Lil Slim said in an unfriendly voice. Those words alone let Lil Kilo know that his nigga was still on go. Pulling up to Ms. Brown's house seventeen minutes after picking Lil Slim up Lil Kilo pulled in the driveway and told Lil Slim that he'll be right back. "Bring somethin' to smoke back out fool." Lil Slim told Lil Kilo before he got out. Lil Kilo was in and out of Ms.

Brown's house in less than five minutes with Ms. Brown right behind him. "I tried to tell her you ain't wanna be bothered fool but she wasn't tryin' to hear it." Lil Kilo told Lil Slim as Ms. Brown rushed to Lil Slim's side of the car and opened his door. "Issac!" Ms. Brown yelled sounding as happy as a person could be. "How are you doing? Look at you! You looking sooo…" Ms. Brown said excitedly. "Za'Mya…" Lil Kilo said Ms. Brown's name as if she was bugging. "What's up Ms. Brown?" Lil Slim said tripping off how excited Ms. Brown was to see him like she didn't just see him a few weeks ago. "You're not in that wheelchair anymore. I'm so happy for you. Can I have a hug please…?" Ms. Brown said reaching in hugging Lil Slim before he could say yes or no. It took Lil Kilo and Lil Slim another five minutes of listening to Ms. Brown telling Lil Slim how happy she was for him before they was able to pull off. "Damn she act like she ready to give you some pussy now that yo ass out that wheelchair." Lil Kilo joked backing up out of the driveway. Lil Slim laughed. "You grab something to smoke?" Lil Slim said then asked Lil Kilo what was inside the small Louis Vuitton duffle bag he threw on the back seat. Lil Kilo told Lil Slim what was in the duffle then reached in his pocket and pulled out a fat ass stack of loud. "Damn that shit funky." Lil Slim said grabbing the bag of weed from Lil Kilo. That's some of Big Ed's finest right there." Lil Kilo said then handed Lil Slim a cigarillo. "You still know how to get tight don't cha?" Lil Kilo asked just as his phone started ringing. "Here go Lil Fresh callin' now." Lil Kilo said then picked up and told Lil Fresh that he was 20 minutes away. By the time Lil Kilo and Lil Slim got back to Lil Kilo's condo Lil Fresh was already there waiting on them.

"Bout time fool." Lil Fresh said as Lil Kilo got out the car. "I should have known you were giving me nigga time when you said 20 minutes." Lil Fresh told Lil Kilo wondering who in the hell was about to get out the passenger seat of Lil Kilo whip as the door opened. "Come help a real nigga out." Lil Slim said grabbing his crutches from off the back seat. "I know that ain't my mufucken nigga." Lil Fresh said recognizing Lil Slim's voice. "Aw shit the world done fucked up! My nigga bouncin' 'round this bitch on crutches now." Lil Fresh said joking with Lil Slim. "I hope you didn't think I was gone be in that wheelchair forever fool." Lil Slim said grabbing the door panel lifting his self out the car as Lil Kilo and Lil Fresh helped him. "I'll be off these crutches soon." Lil Slim said adjusting the crutches under his arms. Upstairs in the condo the three sat around kicking the shit tripping off Lil Fresh and how he said the police officer tried to slam his foot in the door. "You musta pissed her off terribly." Lil Slim said still laughing. "I told that bitch to suck my dick I ain't payin' you shit!" Lil Fresh said. "I thought that bitch was fuckin' my daddy and knew of me or some shit and was tryna get me out some bread." Lil Fresh said as Lil Kilo got up off the couch and walked towards the kitchen. "What all you get from the store?" Lil Kilo asked Lil Fresh. "Shit I forgot the damn bags in the car. That shit slipped my mind once I seen Lil Slim was with you." Lil Fresh said then told Lil Kilo that he was about to go grab them. "This spot right here ducked off fool. How you run across this?" Lil Slim asked getting up off the couch with the crutches and hopped to the kitchen bar where he could see straight into the kitchen. "Some broad Big Ed knew." Lil Kilo said then asked Lil Slim if he needed some help after he heard him moan in pain. "Nawl I'm good fool." Lil Slim replied then asked Lil Kilo what all he planned on doing with the spot. Lil Kilo told Lil Slim that he was tired of asking people to cook up over their house and tired of paying muthafuckers. "Plus I don't like muthafuckers all in my business." Lil Kilo said unzipping the Louis Vuitton duffle bag and pulling the two bricks of cocaine out. "I really just plan on cooking and stashing shit here really." Lil Kilo said as Lil Fresh came back through the door. "Man I just seen a bitch that look just like Ciara walking this lil bitty ugly ass dog out there fool." Lil Fresh said. "For real?" Lil Kilo asked not really caring about the girl Lil Fresh was talking about. "Hell yeah she was hard fool." Lil Fresh said walking into the kitchen putting the bags on the grey and black Island top that matched the furniture in the living room. "I hope you got everything we need." Lil Kilo said pulling everything out the Walmart bags Lil Fresh brought in. "Yeah I got everything. I even grabbed a couple box cutters to bust them thangs open with and some scales." Lil Fresh said reaching in a bag for the box cutters. "Ya'll funa be a while whippin' all that shit. Give me another cigar and some mo' weed so I can twist another one up." Lil Slim said laying his cell phone on the bar after checking to see if he had any missed calls. "We ain't gone be that long fool. I might just whip a baby outta both of them to make sure everything A1." Lil Kilo told Lil Slim handing him the weed and a cigar then cut the stove on medium. "You still know how to cook?" Lil Fresh asked Lil Slim. "What kind of question is that? Nigga you still know how to fuck don't you?" Lil Slim said breaking the weed down. Lil Fresh and Lil Kilo laughed. "Damn right I do. Shid I fucked something last night matta fact. But the question is do you still know how to fuck nigga." Lil Fresh said jokingly causing Lil Slim to chuckle. "I ain't gone lie fool I feel like a virgin. I ain't fucked since I been home." Lil Slim said causing everybody to laugh including his self. "Ion know why you ain't tried to knock that lil Puerto Rican chick off. She fye." Lil Fresh said talking about Loreli. "Man fuck her." Lil Slim said. Lil Kilo chuckled. "Why you say that fool? What she done done?" Lil Kilo asked Lil Slim as he was running some cold water slowly into the large Pyrex jar twirling the jar with his wrist. "This shit lookin' like it's stretchin' like the Jordan symbol." Lil Kilo said grabbing the dope out the jar sitting it on a paper towel so it'll dry. "One big bolder just like I like it." Lil Kilo rapped. "Lemme tell you what Loreli gone fix her face to tell me fool." Lil Slim said to no one in particular. "What she say fool?" Lil Fresh asked pouring some baking soda on the scale. "This bitch gone tell me she think I'm addicted to the percs I be taking for pain." Lil Slim said. Lil Kilo and Lil Fresh both laughed. Lil Slim then told Lil Fresh and Lil Kilo how he shot off on Loreli and tried to put her out and how she came back in the house not even 20 minutes later with his momma. "And my momma gone have the nerve to take her side. I was in that bitch pissed off. I was happy as hell you called fool." Lil Slim told Lil Kilo. "I figured somethin' wasn't right." Lil Kilo said grabbing the chunk of dope off the paper towel to weight it. "The first thing you said was come get me." Lil Kilo said dropping the dope on the scale. "125 to 185 still wet a little." Lil Kilo said grinning. "What's that 2 over?" Lil Slim asked doing the math in his head. "That shit jumped out the gym didn't it?" Lil Fresh said mixing the 21 grams of baking soda with the 125 grams of cocaine he had in the Pyrex together. "It's just my whip game fool." Lil Kilo said grabbing the half of blunt Lil Slim was smoking and fired it up after he washed his hands. "That ain't shit nigga. I can whip a baby and bring a baby." Lil Fresh said sitting the Pyrex in the pot of boiling hot water. After another hour of cooking the dope Lil Kilo gave Lil Fresh nine zips of hard and nine zips of soft. "What you want me to do with this coke fool?" Lil Fresh asked. "Sell it. I know a couple niggas that like to buy it soft so they can cook it and bring back their own overs." Lil Kilo told Lil Fresh sticking the other brick and a half in the cabinet beside the refrigerator. "I got the perfect name for this spot. Right here." Lil Slim said causing both Lil Slim and Lil Kilo to look at him. "We gone call this spot The Chop House. This where everything get chopped up at right?" Lil Slim asked looking at Lil Kilo. "Yeah I like that name. The Chop House." Lil Kilo said repeating the name Lil Slim said. "This spot right here we gone keep confidential. Ion want nobody knowing bout this spot but us." Lil Kilo said looking at Lil Fresh. "That means none of yo lil hoes fool." Lil Kilo told Lil Fresh with a straight face. After putting everything up the three headed out. "I'ma stop by Ms. Brown house to grab me some clothes then I'ma drop you off fool." Lil Kilo told Lil Slim after they were in the car. "Bet." Lil Slim said reclining back his seat back a little. On the way over to Ms. Brown house Lil Slim was telling Lil Kilo how they had to go hard in the streets to let niggas know that they wasn't here to play then his phone rung. Seeing that it was Loreli calling Lil Slim declined the call. "I come to fuck these streets up!" Lil Kilo said. "We funa take this shit over!" Lil Kilo said then reached over and gave Lil Slim some dap. Less than 30 minutes after leaving The Chop House Lil Kilo was dropping Lil Slim off. "Damn she still here." Lil Slim said as they pulled up to his house. "She waitin' on Zaddy..." Lil Kilo joked helping Lil Slim out the car. "I got it from here fool." Lil Slim said standing up on his crutches. "What you funa get into?" Lil Slim asked giving Lil Kilo some more dap. "Shid I'm funa swing back by The Chop House and finish cookin'." Lil Kilo told Lil Slim then watched him as he made his way towards the house. That night Loreli stayed with Lil Slim and the two made love until the sun came up.

Chapter 18

The next morning Lil Slim woke up in pure pain. "Aggh…
Aggh…shit." Lil Slim winched in pain waking up reaching
for his legs. "Issac…lay back down baby. I'll rub them for
you. Where does it hurt?" Loreli asked nervously. "Fuck!" Lil
Slim said sitting up putting his back against his headboard.
"My shins hurting. It's a sharp pain runnin' through them
boo." Lil Slim said damn near on the verge of tears. "You
need your medication baby. When is the last time you took
it?" Loreli asked getting out the bed in one of Lil Slim's shirts
then noticed her panties on the floor and smiled. *I know why
them legs hurting*. Loreli thought thinking about how she put
it on Lil Slim last night. "I haven't took any since yesterday.
Aggh…" Lil Slim said moaning as the pain felt like it was
getting worse. "I told you I'm not taking that shit anymore."
Lil Slim said remembering how he knocked his pills off the
table then poured them down the sink after he put Loreli
out yesterday. "Okay hold on then Issac. I know what will
work." Loreli said sliding on Lil Slim's Nike sweat pants then
left out the room and came back in with two steaming hot
towels. "Okay now stretch both legs out." Loreli told Lil Slim

placing a towel on each leg applying a little pressure at the same time. "Let me know if I'm squeezing to hard." Loreli said. "Ummm…no boo that feel good. Squeeze just a lil bit harder." Lil Slim said leaning his head back. After massaging Lil Slim's leg with the hot towel Loreli then went and got four large zip lock bags full of ice and sat them on Lil Slim's legs. "Damn that's cold boo." Lil Slim said moving his legs a little. "I know baby but the coldness also relieves the pain and inflammation from injuries. You need this. It'll help trust me." Loreli said taking one ice pack off Lil Slim's leg and rubbed it softly then done the same thing to the other one. "How you know how to do all of this?" Lil Slim asked looking Loreli in the eyes as she continued to rub his leg. "Your legs must be feeling better sir?" Loreli asked Lil Slim who in return just smiled. "I'm Puerto Rican and Black. There's nothing I can't do." Loreli said seductively then rubbed her hand up Lil Slim's thigh slowly causing his manhood to rise. "See…" Loreli said licking her lips.

"Hello…" Lil Kilo answered his phone standing in The Chop House kitchen bagging up a couple of orders he had after making a few calls to let his people know that he was back on. "It's all good… I was just lettin' you know that everything is back how it 'pose to be…yeah they still $1,250…yeah I can get it to you soft, what you tryna do?" Lil Kilo said into his phone. "Aite give me bout a hour and I'll be there." Lil Kilo said then hung up. "Aite that's four zips for Percy, four zips for Zed, a zip and a half for Mark and a fo' way of soft for Lil Redd." Lil Kilo said out loud separating the orders on the Island in the middle of his kitchen. '*That nigga Lil Redd ain't bullshittin'. That lil nigga be gettin' off.* Lil Kilo thought putting the 14 zips of dope off inside the same small Louis V duffle he got from Lil Jimmy. Leaving out the house walking towards his car Lil Kilo seen the same Ciara look alike walking the same ugly ass dog Lil Fresh was talking about. "Damn you fine boo." Lil Kilo said to himself as the Ciara look alike waved at him like she heard his comment. "Hi you doin'." Lil Kilo spoke waving back. "I'm fine…" The Ciara look alike said back as Lil Kilo was getting into his car. "You showl is…" Lil Kilo said starting his car up and pulling off. After dropping Zed, Mark, and Percy's pack off Lil Kilo pulled up on Lil Redd who hustled way across town on the North Side. "What up Lil Kilo?" Lil Redd said getting in Lil Kilo's whip giving him some dap. "You know what's up with me nigga, I'm out here gettin' this paper. What's good with you." Lil Kilo said dapping Lil Redd back. "That makes two of us then." Lil Redd told Lil Kilo pulling out a wad of money. "You ain't the only one catchin' plays 'round here fool." Lil Redd said then counted out the money he owed Lil Kilo and put the rest back in his pocket. "I been peepin' you lil nigga. I know you bout yo cake." Lil Kilo told Lil Redd. "I'll fuck wit you if you want me to and throw you whatever you buy on consignment." Lil Kilo told Lil Redd grabbing the money from him counting it out. "So if I buy a split you gone front a split is what you're sayin'?" Lil Redd asked making sure he understood what Lil Kilo was saying. "Yeah that's what I'm sayin' but I'ma let you know now that this shit ain't just about the money with my team." Lil Kilo said looking Lil Redd in the eyes. "Shid what it's about then fool? Cause this shit all about money with me." Lil Redd told Lil Kilo grabbing the four and a half zips that

Lil Kilo was handing him. "This shit bout loyalty. Either you loyal completely or not at all. Ain't no in between." Lil Kilo said clearly. "But as long as you loyal we definitely gone get this money." Lil Kilo told Lil Redd then told him that the next time he called him to ree up that he would bring him his pack on consignment. After Lil Kilo and Lil Redd finished chopping it up Lil Kilo decided to give Neka a call to see if she was back in town yet. Leaving from the North Side calling Neka Lil Kilo got on the interstate headed in Big Ed's direction and Neka picked up on the third ring. "Hey baby!" Neka said with a little zing in her voice. "What's up boo? I haven't heard from you since the party, how was it?" Lil Kilo asked wondering why Neka haven't called him. "It was okay baby but you know I'm not really into all that partying but it was cool for the most part, I guess. The only thing that was on my mind was things that I could have been doing or working on other than being there." Neka said remembering how she felt like she was out of place at the party. "That's why I love you girl, you're always focused. But it's okay to enjoy yourself sometimes boo." Lil Kilo told Neka. "Put some clothes on so we can go grab a bite to eat. I got some stuff I need to talk to you about anyways." Lil Kilo said. "Okay baby, is everything okay?" Neka asked. Neka could always tell when Lil Kilo had something on his mind and she knew that he trusted telling her any and everything. Neka have always showed her loyalty and commitment to Lil Kilo so in return Lil Kilo done the same. "Everything's okay boo. I just miss that beautiful face and smile of yours. Besides, you know I can't go to long without seein' you." Lil Kilo told Neka hearing his other line click. "I be there in a minute boo. This Lil Slim let me see what this nigga talkin' bout." Lil Kilo said. "Okay baby. I'll be ready whenever you get here." Neka said hanging up the phone with the biggest smile on her face. "Yo..." Lil Kilo said answering his other line. "Nigga you ain't gone believe what just happened fool." Lil Slim said into the phone excitedly. Lil Kilo tried to figure out what could've just happened that was causing Lil Slim to be so happy. "What nigga you just got some pussy?" Lil Kilo said then laughed. "Nawl nigga I did punish her ass last night tho." Lil Slim said looking back over the couch to make sure Loreli didn't hear his last comment. "Well shid if it wasn't the pussy that got you happy like this it better be that you done started back walkin' again." Lil Kilo told Lil Slim while trying to decide if he wanted to pick Neka up first or go holler at Big Ed. *I'ma gone pick her up first. I know she waitin'.* Lil Kilo thought. "I haven't started back walkin' completely but I just took my first step by myself my nigga!" Lil Slim said with the same amount of enjoyment in his voice. "Gimme bout another month and I'll be back 'round this bitch skip-ta-my-lou-ing." Lil Slim said causing Lil Kilo to laugh and swerve a little. "I can only imagine that feeling. I know that shit feel good tho." Lil Kilo told Lil Slim who paused briefly before he spoke. "I ain't gone lie fool." Lil Slim said. "Hearing the doctors tell me that I'll never walk again kinda done something to a nigga spirit. I didn't wanna believe that shit tho so I didn't. I just *knew* I was gone walk again fool. That's just how much faith I have in "*myself.*" Lil Slim said putting emphasis on the words knew and myself then told Lil Kilo to imagine how much better the world would be if everybody believed in themselves like he did. "Just think of all the joy a person would have knowing that they

believed in their self enuff to turn their dreams to realities."
Lil Slim added. Lil Kilo listened to what Lil Slim was saying
and could tell that his nigga was truly happy that he was
learning to walk again. "A nigga gotta start being thankful
for the small shit that we pay no attention to fool." Lil Kilo
said almost to Neka's house. "Have you ever thought about
how much joy a blind person would have if they was able to
see the world for just a hour fool." Lil Slim asked Lil Kilo.
"Nawl I ain't never thought about that fool. But I know they
whole world would change after seeing how beautiful this
world is." Lil Kilo told Lil Slim. "That's how I feel being able
to walk again fool." Lil Slim told Lil Kilo twirling his ankle
around as Loreli came back into the living room with another
set of hot towels for Lil Slim's legs. After getting off the phone
with Lil Slim Lil Kilo tried to imagine life without one of his
senses and couldn't. "Thank you God for my health." Is all
Lil Kilo could say thinking about all the people that have
disabilities. Pulling up to Neka's house about seven minutes
after getting off the phone with Lil Slim Lil Kilo pulled up
and was about to blow the horn to let Neka know that he was
outside but remembered how she felt the last time he done
that so he called her instead. "I'm out here boo." Lil Kilo said
as if Neka wasn't in the window waiting already. "Okay here
I come." Neka said shutting the curtains back grabbing her
jacket and telling her brother that she'll be back in a few
minutes. Neka was halfway to Lil Kilo's car when he dropped
his window and signaled her to come here. "I'm coming
baby." Neka mouthed smiling. '*What he getting out the car
for*?' Neka thought until Lil Kilo started talking. "Come holla
at me for a second Rell." Hearing her brother's name being

called Neka looked back and seen her brother standing in the doorway. "I thought you were talking to me when you let your window down." Neka said as she got close enough to hug Lil Kilo. Lil Kilo squeezed Neka tight and told her to get in the car while he hollered at her brother. Neka jumped straight in the driver's seat. "I didn't know who you was pullin' up in front of my momma shit like that fam." Neka's brother said walking up on Lil Kilo giving him some dap. "I see you done switched whips." Rell said stepping back checking out Lil Kilo's car. "Yeah I had to get ducked off nah mean." Lil Kilo said looking back at his Camaro noticing that he needed a car wash. "You be fuckin' wit the work don't ya?" Lil Kilo asked Neka's brother. "Nigga I'm from Cleveland. What kind of question is that?" Rell asked Lil Kilo. "Shid you know I can get you them thangs fa like twelve hunnit a piece straight glass." Lil Kilo told Rell cutting him a deal because he was Neka's brother. "Twelve hunnit? Shit I'm payin' $1,375 back home and that shit comin' put together already. Niggas yellin' $1,450 if you want it soft." Neka's brother Rell said then wondered if Lil Kilo was telling the truth before he started getting his hopes up. "I got ten-five for a nine right now." Rell told Lil Kilo who did the math in his head. "You can give me $10,500 and owe me three." Lil Kilo said. "If you want it now I can have my partna drop it off to ya." Lil Kilo added then knocked on his window and told Neka to hand him his phone. "If it's all brick and no shake hell yeah I want it right now." Rell told Lil Kilo then told him that if everything was proper with the work then he would be right back to get some more. "Because my nigga be fuckin' wit it too. I know he gone want him a fo' way or a lil nine or somethin'." Rell said pulling out his phone sending his partner a text message to let him know that he found some work cheaper than what they been paying. "Aite well I'm funa have my nigga to swing by here and drop that off to you and if yo people want some just let me know and I'll get him tight too." Lil Kilo said calling Lil Fresh to let him know what's going on. "My nigga said he'll be here in less than fifteen." Lil Kilo told Rell before he hopped in the passenger side of his whip and Neka pulled off. "How did I know that you'll be in the driver side when I got in boo?" Lil Kilo asked Neka looking over admiring her beauty. "Because you think I'm your personal chauffeur that's how." Neka said turning on the blinker and then scooted her seat up. "No you think you my personal chauffeur." Lil Kilo laughed. "I told you to get in the car and you jumped straight in the driver seat. But I gotta ask you a question about your brother." Lil Kilo said getting serious then asked Neka if she thought her brother was solid. "Solid?" Neka said in a confused voice. "You mean like working out solid or is you talking about some street stuff?" Neka asked. As serious as Lil Kilo was trying to be he couldn't help but laugh after Neka said that. "What..." Neka asked shrugging her shoulders. "Nothin' baby." Lil Kilo said. "Don't worry bout it boo." Lil Kilo chuckled as Neka reached over and playfully pulled his hair. "That's why you need your hair done." Neka said knowing that Lil Kilo was laughing at her because she knew nothing about street terminology. "Don't worry bout it, I gotta appointment with The Loc King tomorrow. Thanks for remindin' me." Lil Kilo said almost forgetting about his hair appointment. "I wonder how I'll look with this shit chopped off?" Lil Kilo said out loud unintendedly. "I don't know your head is kind of big Keon." Neka said cracking up off her own joke. "It wasn't that funny." Lil Kilo said watching as Neka got on the interstate headed in the opposite direction from the hood. "You ain't goin' to check on yo people today? I can't believe that." Lil Kilo told Neka whose whole mood just changed. "You okay baby?" Lil Kilo asked Neka who seemed to be a little sad now for some reason. "No I'm not Keon. I'm not happy anymore and I think we need to talk about it." Neka said. Once Lil Kilo heard Neka say that she wasn't happy anymore he already knew that it was because of him. "Look boo, I already kn…" "Shhhh…" Neka cut Lil Kilo off then told him she wanted to talk with him while they sitting face to face. "I don't want you to lie to me Keon because you know that's something that we never have had to do with each other." Neka told Lil Kilo hoping that he remembered what he always told her. "I promise to keep it real with you boo." Lil Kilo told Neka then told her to swing by Big Ed's spot before they sat down to talk. Neka jumped off the interstate and was headed back across town and was at Big Ed's spot in no time. "Hold on right quick boo, I'm funa run in and run out." Lil Kilo told Neka getting out the car. After leaving Big Ed's spot Neka was trying to think of a good spot where they could sit and talk in peace and winded up at a park not to far from where Lil Kilo use to live. "We haven't been to this park in a while boo. What made you come here?" Lil Kilo asked thinking about all the memories him and Neka had at that park. "We use to meet here almost every day after school. This where you gave me my first kiss. You remember?" Lil Kilo asked Neka. "Of course I remember. How could I forget?" Neka said parking Lil Kilo's car then watched as he rolled his blunt. "You use to talk to me about everything." Neka said. "We use to sit on that bench right over there and talk for hours." Neka said pointing at a bench that sat off to the side by itself. "But now it's like you don't talk to me at all. You don't call or text me like you use to or nothing Keon. We use to go on a date at least once a week and now I'll feel lucky to even see your face once a week." Neka said sounding heartbroken. "Lil Kilo could tell by Neka's voice that she was hurt. "Damn boo, I'm sorry." Lil Kilo said thinking about how him and Neka have became a little distance after everything that's been going on in his life. "It's just that…" Lil Kilo was about to say but Neka cut him off again. "Don't it's just that me Keon. Tell me the truth. I want to know what's going on." Neka said turning her full attention to Lil Kilo. Lil Kilo fired his blunt up and knew that he couldn't tell Neka a lie after looking into her eyes and seeing her hurt. "Ummm…" Lil Kilo mumbled trying to think of the right words to say. "Look baby I know that things may seem to be a little off for us right now but I promise you that my love for you hasn't changed." Lil Kilo said hitting his blunt. "Just because your love haven't changed doesn't mean that your feelings haven't." Neka told Lil Kilo. "Everything changed after Issac got shot. I don't even get good night calls or text messages anymore. Do you know when the last time we had sex Keon?" Neka asked wondering if Lil Kilo was having sex with someone other than her. "Almost two weeks ago." Lil Kilo said remembering the last time him and Neka had sex but couldn't really remember when. "Two weeks ago? Wrong person Keon. It's been a month and nine days since the last time we did anything. And that was only oral sex."

Neka said then asked Lil Kilo if he was having sex with anybody else. "Now you know that I save my love makin' for you boo stop playing." Lil Kilo told Neka knowing that if he told Neka about Ms. Brown that her heart would break all over again right then and there. "Keon…" Neka said "What's up boo?" Lil Kilo said knowing that whatever Neka was about to say was about to be serious by the way she called his name. "Why are you always over Ms. Brown's house?" Neka asked Lil Kilo who was totally unprepared for the question. "Huh?" Lil Kilo answered subconsciously. "What you talkin' bout boo?" Was all Lil Kilo could say. Neka asked Lil Kilo the same question again. "Keon please don't lie to me. Why are you always over there?" Neka asked Lil Kilo again. Lil Kilo took a long pull from the blunt he was smoking then exhaled slowly before he replied. "You still seem to find out everything you want to know I see." Lil Kilo said trying to find the right words to say next. "You keep it real with me and tell me how in the hell you know I be over there and I'ma keep it real and tell you what's been goin' on." Lil Kilo said trying to figure out how Neka always seemed to find out about everything he did. Neka didn't really want to tell Lil Kilo how she found out but also didn't want to lie or keep secrets from Lil Kilo so she told him. "Okay… well… see ummm…this is what happened." Neka said then laughed a little before she told Lil Kilo how she used his phone locater to locate him one night after he didn't answer the phone for the entire day for her. "I just wanted to make sure you were okay." Neka said telling Lil Kilo how she figured out the address to where his phone was located at. "Then I caught the bus to the address and seen your car parked in the driveway. I figured that maybe that was one of your friends house so I waited for you to come out but you never did." Neka said on the verge of tears then told Lil Kilo how she was about to go knock on the door and ask for him until she seen a silver two door Altima pull in the driveway and Ms. Brown get out the car and check her mailbox then let herself into the house with a key. Lil Kilo didn't know if he should be mad or laugh once Neka told him how she found out he was staying with Ms. Brown. "You know what bae…" Lil Kilo said the question as a statement. "I can't even be mad at you because that right there just let me know how much you really love me." Lil Kilo said then told Neka the reason he was staying with Ms. Brown in the first place. "You could've told me that Keon." Neka said. "If you needed somewhere to stay you know you could've stayed over my house. My momma wouldn't have cared. She loves you." Neka said. "I know I could've but I have too much goin' on and I wouldn't bring my situation over yo momma's house like that." Lil Kilo said thinking about how it would've been staying with Neka and her mother. After another forty minutes of trying to explain to Neka what was going on without telling her to much Lil Kilo's phone rung.

Chapter 19

"He didn't pick up but he gone call me back and when he do I'll just hit yo line and let you know what he talkin' bout." Lil Fresh said talking to a nigga from his hood name Coco who be getting money. "Tell that lil nigga I need a whole one with tha stamp still in the middle." CoCo told Lil Fresh who was sending Lil Kilo a text message. "I got cha. Whenever he call me I'ma call you." Lil Fresh said then gave CoCo some dap and leaned back against his car waiting on his sale to pull up. "Where the fuck this nigga at?" Lil Fresh said out loud checking his watch to see what time it was. *It's been damn near 20 minutes and this nigga talkin' bout he 5 minutes away.* Lil Fresh thought walking around to the driver side of his car about to get in and pull off. "This better be him right here or I'm gone." Lil Fresh said as a black Silverado truck bent the corner and pulled up beside him then dropped the window. "My bad fool I had to stop and get some gas. Hop in." "Nawl pull over and hop out them people been rollin'." Lil Fresh said stepping back onto the sidewalk lying about the police rolling. Just as soon as Lil Fresh got done handling his business with his sell Lil Kilo was calling him back.

"Meet me at The Chop House. Its bizniz." Lil Fresh said into the phone then hung up. *'What kind of bizniz this nigga talkin'?'* Lil Kilo wondered pulling off from Neka's house pulling up at The Chop House twenty three minutes later and seen that Lil Fresh was pulling in right behind him. "What up Doug E Fresh?" Lil Kilo said hopping out the car peeping how fresh Lil Fresh was. "This dat Supreme shit right here fool." Lil Fresh said turning his shoe game sideways so that Lil Kilo could see the Gucci imprint on them. "I see ya. Keep playin' and you gone make me go fuck a bag up in Bloomingdales." Lil Kilo said trying to remember if he had some cigars in his car. "But what's good tho fool?" Lil Kilo asked Lil Fresh giving him some dap. "My people hit my line for a juice earlier so I met him in the hood and bumped into CoCo." Lil Fresh said. "He was tryin' to get his hands on some work. He said Percy told him we had it." Lil Fresh said pulling out his cell phone. "What he tryna do?" Lil Kilo asked as they were walking towards The Chop House door. "He said he want a whole one so I called to let you know but you didn't answer." Lil Fresh said as Lil Kilo opened the door and walked in. "Shit Ion think it's a whole one left. Call and tell him that we got a half hard and a half soft." Lil Kilo told Lil Fresh walking into the kitchen where the dope was and pulled it out the cabinet to see what was left. "I cooked damn near all the coke and didn't leave nothin' but a half for us to piece." Lil Kilo said as Lil Fresh called CoCo to let him know what was going on. "He said he need it all soft fool." Lil Fresh told Lil Kilo moving the phone from his face. "Tell 'em it'll be tomorrow." Lil Kilo said thinking about calling Lil Jimmy and Heavy back to order four more. "He said what you gone charge him for it half and half?" Lil Fresh asked Lil Kilo after telling CoCo what Lil Kilo said. "Tell 'em I'll do $1,075 all way out or if he want to wait I can get him one still in the wrapper for $41,000." Lil Kilo said then listened as Lil Fresh told CoCo that everything they sold was proper. "He said he'll take it half and half long as everything was proper." Lil Fresh said after he hung up with CoCo. "Bet." Lil Kilo said weighing up the work for CoCo. On the way out the door Lil Kilo called Lil Jimmy. "I need fo' extra large t-shirts." Lil Kilo said into the phone letting Lil Jimmy know that he wanted four more bricks. "Okay gimme a few minutes and I'll be there." Lil Kilo said then hung up and told Lil Fresh to ride with him. "I think that powder move faster than that hard move." Lil Kilo told Lil Fresh after they were in the car. "I was thinkin' the same thing after I dropped that sack off to Neka's brother earlier." Lil Fresh said then told Lil Kilo to remind him to grab the money out his console once they got back. "I think we should start sellin' all powder. That way we don't have to worry bout the cook up." Lil Kilo said as Lil Fresh phone rung. "Shid nigga Ion know bout you but I got a couple white boys payin' eighteen hunnit for them thangs already ready." Lil Fresh said. "So I'ma at least need a nine piece to feed them with." "That's cool we'll just whip half a chicken then. That should be enuff for yo people and Percy 'em." Lil Kilo said then told Lil Fresh to call CoCo and let him know they was about to pull up. "He said pull around back when we get there." Lil Fresh said as his phone rung again. "Man Ion know who this is calling but every time I pick up they don't say nothin'." Lil Fresh said then blocked the number. "Probably one of those lil dusty feets you be smashin' fool." Lil Kilo said then laughed. "Dusty feets? A bitch can't even get my attention if she ain't a dime." Lil Fresh told Lil Kilo dusting his shoulder off like it was some lent on it. "You still ain't hit Ms. Brown for real either nigga. Lil Slim told me you told him the truth." Lil Fresh said lying on Lil Slim. "Shid nigga Ms. Brown back been broke." Lil Kilo said then told Lil Fresh about the time he was about to break her back again but he came knocking on the door crying. Lil Fresh laughed. "Don't act like you don't remember fool." Lil Kilo said. "It was right around the time Lil Slim was in the hospital." Lil Fresh continued to act like he didn't know what Lil Kilo was talking about. "Ion know what you talkin' bout." Lil Fresh said. "Slow down before you miss the turn tho fool." "I ain't gone miss the turn." Lil Kilo said turning into CoCo's back yard. "Call and tell him we out here." Lil Kilo said grabbing the sack with the work in it off the back seat as CoCo was coming out the door. "There he go right there." Lil Fresh said sliding his phone back in his pocket watching CoCo as he walked towards the car. "What up Big Dawg?" Lil Kilo said dropping his window shaking hands with CoCo. "Shid you tha Big Dawg with these Big Dawg prices." CoCo told Lil Kilo shaking his hand back. "What up Fresh?" CoCo said sticking his arm in the window to shake Lil Fresh hand. "Let me see what its lookin' like." CoCo said now talking to Lil Kilo who took a zip of hard and a zip of soft out and handed it to CoCo. "Errthing A1 fam trust me." Lil Kilo told CoCo who was untying the sacks to check the dope out. "You said $1,050 all way out didn't ya?" CoCo said trying to run game as he pulled out an Apple Crown bag with the money in it. "Nawl them thangs $1,075.

I wish I could do ten-fifty on them thangs tho." Lil Kilo said peeping game. "Aite that's cool. I got $38,000 right here. Lemme give you the other $700 in bout a hr." CoCo said handing Lil Kilo the Apple Crown bag full of money. "I'll fuck wit cha and let you owe us $700 I ain't trippin'." Lil Kilo said grabbing the bag from CoCo. "It's all here ain't it or do I need to run thru it right quick?" Lil Kilo asked peeping inside the Apple Crown bag. "Playin' with another man's money is somethin' you ain't gotta never worry bout me doin' all because I ain't gone let another man play wit mine. It's all bout respect in this game." CoCo said as Lil kilo handed him the bag of dope. After serving CoCo Lil Kilo swung by Ms. Brown's house to grab the money for Lil Jimmy and Heavy and was glad that she wasn't there when he pulled up. "I'm funa go grab this bread. I be right back." Lil Kilo told Lil Fresh about to leave his car running until Lil Fresh told him to bring him something to drink back. "You mightis well come in right quick." Lil Kilo said cutting his car off. Inside Ms. Brown's room standing at the edge of her bed Lil Kilo grabbed eight stacks of twenty dollar bills. "This 80 plus the 38 CoCo just gave me is all I need." Lil Kilo said putting the rest of his money back up. Leaving Ms. Brown's house headed to meet Lil Jimmy and Heavy Lil Fresh told Lil Kilo that he was going to take the money they got from Rachean and Fat Chubb and put it with his the next time he ree'd up. "That way we'll have plenty and won't have to keep making all these trips." Lil Fresh told Lil Kilo thinking about the $100,000 Lil Kilo gave him after they killed Rachean and Fat Chubb that's just been sitting. "Aite I'ma let you know when I ree up again." Lil Kilo told Lil Fresh. "The way this

shit been sellin' we might be makin' another trip tomorrow."
Lil Kilo said playing but serious. "You know Bria we go to
school wit?" Lil Fresh asked Lil Kilo. "You talkin' bout big
booty Bria?" Lil Kilo said. "Yeah. You know I be breakin'
her back right? So I pulled up over there the other day and
her brotha was there." Lil Fresh said. "Don't tell me you done
let her brother jerk you." Lil Kilo said laughing. "Hell nawl
nigga. I would've fired his big ass up!" Lil Fresh said then
told Lil Kilo how Bria's brother faded him about some work.
"That nigga said what?" Lil Kilo asked like he didn't just
hear what Lil Fresh had said. "That he heard we had it and
he was tryna get down with the team." Lil Fresh repeated.
"What you tell 'em?" Lil Kilo asked Lil Fresh. "Shid I told
that nigga that Ion know what he talkin' bout." Lil Fresh
said. "Good." Lil Kilo said. "Them the type of niggas you
gotta watch out for. One nigga like that will take down a
whole operation. Think about it. He don't even know us. Shit
we could be the police and he talkin' bout he ready to get
down with the team." Lil Kilo said. "Shid that nigga might
be the police come to think about it." Lil Kilo added. "If we
don't know them we ain't servin' them." After Lil Kilo and
Lil Fresh left from hollering at Lil Jimmy and Heavy and
hearing them talk about their daddies for almost an hour
again Lil Kilo and Lil Fresh pulled back up at The Chop
House just as the sun was going down. "Grab that cheese out
yo car fool and let's go cook a few of these zips to make sure
this shit straight." Lil Kilo told Lil Fresh hopping out the car
grabbing another duffle off the backseat from Lil Jimmy
except this one was a Gucci duffle. Shutting his car door Lil
Kilo jumped a little. "Hey handsome." It was the Ciara look

alike standing in front of him. "What up sexy?" Lil Kilo said back hoping that he didn't look startled. "Oh, I was just about to jog a little and seen you again and figured that I should introduce myself properly." Ciara's look alike said sticking her hand out. "I'm Amora." "I'm Keon." Lil Kilo said reaching out to shake Ciara's look alike hand. *'Why the fuck did I just give her my real name?'* Lil Kilo thought. "Well nice meeting you Lil Kilo. I stay two condos down. Let me know if you need anything." Amora said getting ready to start jogging. "Hol up..." Lil Kilo said thinking that he was tripping. "What you just call me?" Lil Kilo asked looking confused. Amora giggled then pointed at Lil Fresh who threw his hands up in the air as if he were saying "What?" "So he..." Lil Kilo started to stay but looked up and Amora was gone. "What was she pointin' at me fo'?" Lil Fresh asked smiling. "Nigga you know why." Lil Kilo laughed. "I tried to get her but she wanted you. Shid what was I to do and I ain't seen you with nothin' bad like that but Neka." Lil Fresh joked. "You gotta be Ray Charles lil brother then. Nigga you better check my palm pilot. I'ma pimp. Better ask Snoop about me." Lil Kilo said unlocking the door to The Chop House. "Roll one up while I drop a onion in the pot just to see what it do." Lil Kilo said as he sat the Gucci duffle on the cabinet and unzipped it. "Shid we might need to cook a juice out of each one to make sure all of 'em straight." Lil Kilo told Lil Fresh who done kicked his shoes off and propped his feet up on the table. "Bust them bitches open then fool. I'm right here chillin'." Lil Fresh said breaking some weed down on a fifty dollar bill. It took Lil Kilo close to an hour in the kitchen making sure the dope was good. "I deserve a gold metal (Olympics) the way I do my thang in the kitchen." Lil Kilo came out the kitchen rapping Yo Gotti's song which let Lil Fresh know that everything was all good with the work. "Instead of waitin' until we ree-up again I'll just sell you two of these bricks in here for the same thing I got them fo' if you want me to." Lil Kilo said. "Aite bet. I'll swing the bread back by tomorrow or something tho because ain't no way in hell I'm funa drive out the boon-docks to the boon-docks then back to the boon-docks." Lil Fresh said firing the blunt up. "Have you heard from Lil Slim?" Lil Fresh asked blowing out a cloud of smoke. "Yeah that nigga hit me and told me he was takin' steps now without the crutches." Lil Kilo said grabbing the blunt from Lil Fresh. "I can't wait til my nigga get right." Lil Fresh said smiling. "We gone be back 'round this bitch like the Three Stooges and tha Three Musketeers." Lil Fresh said thinking about how close him and his niggas was. Over the next couple weeks Lil Kilo and Lil Fresh was selling more dope than they ever have it seemed like after Lil Kilo walked across the stage with his High School Diploma. "We made it baby! We made it!" Neka said jumping in Lil Kilo's arms with so much excitement in her voice and tears of joy in her eyes. "Yes we made it baby!" Lil Kilo said. "I have a surprise for you." Lil Kilo told Neka leading her outside to the parking lot to where a cream colored Porsche Panamera was that had a big red bow on it. "Congratulations baby!" Lil Kilo told Neka handing her the keys. Lil Kilo remembered the first time Neka seen his car and told him that was her dream car so he surprised her with his for graduating. Lil Kilo's mother was so happy that her son walked across the stage and got his diploma that she cried the entire graduation. "Thank you baby for sticking in there and making momma proud." Lil Kilo's mother told him after finding him and Neka standing in the parking lot kissing. After all the celebrating and partying for graduating Lil Kilo hit the streets running. It got to the point where Lil Kilo was running back and forth across town so much to put work up and get work that he bought a spot closer to town and turned The Chop House into his house. One day while sitting at the kitchen table in Lil Kilo's new spot bagging up Lil Fresh came up with a nick name for that spot. "I got the perfect name for this spot right here fool." Lil Fresh said. "We gone call this the White House because it ain't nothin' but white in this bitch." Lil Fresh said joking talking about all the cocaine him and Lil Kilo had sitting on the table in front of them. Lil Kilo and Lil Fresh was running through the dope so fast that Lil Jimmy and Heavy thought that they were giving it away until they came and told them that they needed ten bricks instead of the four they normally bought. "They gone take this shit over just like they daddy did. Mark my words." Lil Jimmy told Heavy that day after Lil Kilo and Lil Fresh left. And sure enough as the sky is blue did Lil Kilo and Lil Fresh start to take over Youngstown. They had the cheapest prices in town. Lil Jimmy and Heavy wasn't even selling their dope that cheap but did the math one day and found out that Lil Kilo and Lil Fresh was making close to eleven thousand dollars off each brick they sold. "Shit those lil niggas making ten six off a brick and we make twenty two three but if you think about it shid they making way more than us because they runnin' thru it faster than we are." Heavy told Lil Jimmy one day after Lil Kilo and Lil Fresh ree'd up. "We might need to up the price a little." Heavey said throwing a shot of Hennessy back. "Next time they come I'ma tell 'em that its drying up out here so the price changed." Lil Jimmy told Heavy. "Thirty three thousand?" Lil Kilo said in an unbelievable voice after Lil Jimmy told him that the price went up on the dope. "That's a extra 5 g's on each brick." Lil Kilo told Lil Jimmy then thought about what his daddy taught him. "A business man with integrity will always look you in the eyes when he speak son and will greet you with a hand shake before and after ya'll conduct business." Lil Kilo remembered his daddy telling him when he was younger. *'And this bitch ass nigga ain't done either one.'* Lil Kilo thought. "Its business nothin' personal I promise." Lil Jimmy told Lil Kilo. *'Yeah I bet it is.'* Lil Kilo thought. "Aite well we gone finish the rest of the lil work we got and just come back with some extra bread." Lil Kilo said then waited an extra second to see if either Lil Jimmy or Heavy was gone give him or Lil Fresh some dap and just as he expected they didn't. "We should've at least grabbed two of them thangs." Lil Fresh told Lil Kilo once they got back in the car. "I got some plays lined up." Lil Fresh said. "Them niggas tried to play us like some suckas." Lil Kilo told Lil Fresh. "My daddy always told me that a business man with integrity will always greet you with a hand shake before and after the deal. And will always look you in the eyes when talkin'." Lil Kilo said. "I kinda peeped that something wasn't right once he got to talkin' bout the prices myself fool." Lil Fresh told Lil Kilo. "So what you wanna do?" Lil Fresh asked. "We gone bake a cake for them for tryna stop us from eatin'." Lil Kilo said wickedly. Three days later Lil Kilo, Lil

Fresh and Lil Slim was all in Lil Slim's living room talking about how they was gone get Lil Jimmy and Heavy. The day after Lil Jimmy tried to play them Lil Kilo called and told Lil Slim about it and Lil Slim told him that he wanted in. "Nawl that ain't gone work." Lil Kilo said after Lil Fresh suggested that they just kick the door down and start shooting. "I know just the way to get in there." Lil Slim said lightly limping on one crutch now looking at his wheelchair that he didn't use anymore sitting beside the stairs. Two days later Lil Kilo was calling Lil Jimmy back. "Tell me something good." Lil Kilo said into the phone as him Lil Slim and Lil Fresh sat at the kitchen table in the White House with stacks of money in front of them. "Damn I was hoping to hear that the t-shirt machine was fixed and that the price was back right." Lil Kilo said then paused listening to what Lil Jimmy was saying. "Okay that's cool but Lil Slim back movin' around and want five t-shirts pressed up too." Lil Kilo said back into the phone then paused and listened again while Lil Fresh and Lil Slim were both trying to make out what Lil Jimmy was saying on the other end of the phone. "Aite I'll bring him with me so you can see 'em." Lil Kilo said then hung up. "That shit fell in place like a puzzle. He wanna meet you anyway Lil Slim." Lil Kilo said looking at Lil Slim. "Stuff that $255,000 thousand in that Gucci duffle Lil Fresh. I gotta piss before we leave." Lil Kilo said getting up from the table. "That's 'pose to be half a ticket ain't it if we gettin' 15 of them thangs?" Lil Slim asked. "They'll never know because it's comin' back with us anyway." Lil Kilo said. "Dead people can't count no money." After putting Lil Slim's old wheelchair and three glock .45's with sound suppressors in the trunk they all hopped in Lil Kilo's whip and was pulling up at Lil Jimmy's spot in nineteen minutes flat. Lil Kilo and Lil Fresh both hopped out the car and walked around to the trunk and pulled the wheelchair out. "Sat two of the straps in the bottom of the chair so Lil Slim can sit on them and put the other one behind his back for me to grab." Lil Kilo told Lil Fresh as the front door opened and one of the big black muscle headed security guards came out and asked them if they needed some help. "Nawl we got it. Preciate it tho. Lil Jimmy 'em in there?" Lil Kilo asked turning the wheelchair backwards so Muscle Head wouldn't see the guns sitting in the wheelchair. "Yeah him and Heevy down in thee deen drenking. I gotta mak run. Be back in hour." Muscle Head said in broken English leaving the front door cracked so they could get in. "Shit!" Lil Kilo said pushing the wheelchair to the passenger side of the car. "What fool?" Lil Fresh asked. "That big black ass nigga a witness. He gotta die too." Lil Kilo said opening the door for Lil Slim. "Sat on these two and keep this right here in the small of yo back so I can grab it." Lil Kilo told Lil Slim helping him out the car and into the wheelchair adjusting the sound suppressor so that it was pointed downwards. "Let's do this." Lil Kilo said then told Lil Fresh to grab the duffle bag off the backseat and sat it in Lil Slim's lap. Lil Kilo and Lil Fresh been to Lil Jimmy's and Heavy's spot so many times that the pat downs at the front door was just that, a pat down. "Hey there Mon." The Muscle Head twin said wondering if he should pat Lil Slim down after giving Lil Kilo and Lil Fresh a lazy pat down. "You want to pat him?" Lil Kilo asked pushing Lil Slim up a little. "Yeeha mon. Mee got ta do mee job." Muscle Head said walking around Lil Slim's wheelchair acting as if he was searching then squatted down in front of him acting as if he was patting Lil Slim's legs down. '*Perfect…*' Lil Kilo thought reaching down in the wheelchair pulling his gun out in a matter of seconds. "PewPewPew." Lil Kilo let off three quick rounds into Muscle Head's skull killing him instantly. "Shit." Lil Slim said watching Muscle Head fall backwards and blood start to ooze from out his skull. "Good thing I got on black pants. This nigga blood squirted all over me." Lil Slim said watching as Lil Kilo took out his phone and took a couple picture of Muscle Head. "What's that for?" Lil Fresh asked. "Ima send those to Ja'Zelle so she'll know what his twin look like, he gotta die too." Lil Kilo said sliding his phone back in his pocket. "Lil Slim give Lil Fresh one of those straps you sittin' on." Grabbing the gun from Lil Slim Lil Fresh cocked it back then tucked it on his waistline. "Let's go." Lil Kilo said pushing Lil Slim down the hall towards the den where Lil Jimmy and Heavy could be heard talking loud about the basketball game they were watching. "Ya'll niggas must got some money on this game." Lil Kilo said standing in the den ready to handle his business. "This crazy ass nigga betted a thou with Bron against the Durantula and Curry." Lil Jimmy said sitting his glass of liquor down. "So we finally get to meet Slim Jim huh?" Lil Jimmy said then looked over at Heavy who was throwing the rest of his drink back. "Aww Shiitt…" Heavy said sounding as if he had one to many shots of liquor already. "We got the whole crew in here. Let's toast to that!" Heavy said making his way over to the bar to get some more shot glasses. "I can't drink right now because of the meds they got me takin' but I appreciate the offer tho." Lil Slim said as Lil Kilo pushed him down into the den. "What up Lil Jimmy… Heavy?" Lil Fresh said looking around the room trying to figure out where they would have the dope stashed. "We ain't really got much time to sit around and kick the shit we got a few people waitin' on us and plus Lil Slim gotta therapist appointment in bout a hour." Lil Kilo said cutting all the small talk off. *'I wasn't tryna chit-chat with ya'll lil niggas that long anyway. I'm just tryna get them extra 75 g's we taxed ya'll for.'* Lil Jimmy thought then told Lil Kilo them that him and Heavy started drinking and forgot that they were coming which was a lie. "Go grab that bag for them Heavy ain't no sense in worrying bout this game we up by 12 with two minutes left. This shit over!" Lil Jimmy said pouring him another shot. "So what they sayin' about you walkin' again Slim Jim?" Lil Jimmy asked Lil Slim as Heavy walked out the den talking shit with his glass still in his hand. Lil Kilo tried to play it off and looked back to see which way Heavy was going but missed which way he turned. "Everything's looking good. I'm 'pose to get my crutches tonight." Lil Slim said right before Lil Kilo pulled out his gun. "Shut the fuck up nigga! We don't wanna hear nomo of your fake ass concerns." Lil Kilo said pointing his gun at Lil Jimmy who dropped his shot glass shattering it "What's tha…" was all Lil Jimmy got out. "Pew…" Lil Kilo heard a gun go off behind him and seen Lil Jimmy's head jerk back. Looking back Lil Kilo seen Lil Slim holding his gun with one hand rolling towards him with the other hand. "You and Lil Fresh follow Heavy. Wherever he's goin' is where everything's at. That one was personal that bitch kept callin' me Slim Jim." "PewPewPew…Pew." Lil Kilo and Lil Slim looked back at the same time and seen Heavy's body drop. "I had to. He was comin' in." Lil Fresh said then told Lil Kilo to follow him. "I seen which room he came out of." Lil Fresh said then trotted out the den with Lil Kilo pushing Lil Slim right behind him stopping to grab the duffle bag Heavy had beside him. "Right here." Lil Fresh said pointing to a room on the left side of the long hallway. Lil Kilo pushed Lil Slim inside the room then stopped and looked around. "Damn this room big." Lil Kilo said watching Lil Fresh tear the closet up. "That shit in here somewhere. Check under the bed." Lil Slim told Lil Kilo. "I be right back." Lil Slim said then rolled out the room then back into the room four minutes later holding a DVR hard drive. "What's that fool?" Lil Kilo asked starting to get frustrated because they still haven't found anything. "The footage from the cameras. Ya'll still haven't found the stash yet?" Lil Slim asked rolling to the center of the room. "Nothin'!" Lil Kilo said pulling the drawers out the dresser. "I found the money!" Lil Fresh yelled from the walk in closet. Rolling his self to the closet Lil Slim seen the glass Heavy was drinking out of sitting on the side of a big jacuzzi bath tub in the bathroom and rolled into the bathroom and looked around. *It look like he came in here and sat his drink down then…* Lil Slim thought looking around some more trying to figure out what Heavy's glass was doing in the bathroom. "Lil Slim!" Lil Kilo yelled. "Come on fool. I think them bricks was all the dope they had. We got the bread." Lil Kilo said as him and Lil Fresh made their way to the bathroom both holding the duffle bags. "Hold on. That nigga was doin' something in here or his glass wouldn't be sittin' right here." Lil Slim said. "He probably had to piss fool, come on." Lil Fresh said ready to go. "What's that thin thing sitting beside his glass?" Lil Slim asked then told Lil Kilo to hand it to him. "Looks like a remote for the TV. Come on fool let's get up outta here." Lil Kilo told Lil Slim. Lil Slim knew that it was something else in that house. He could feel it. "Look around fool. There ain't one TV in this room. This remote is for something else." Lil Slim said grabbing the buttonless remote from Lil Kilo. "This might just be a senor or something fool because it don't have no buttons on it." Lil Kilo told Lil Slim watching him look at the remote then start pointing it at stuff. "I'm tellin' you whatever this is it opens something." Lil Slim said then shook the buttonless remote with a little more force and the steps to the Jacuzzi made a click noise. "I told ya'll…" Lil Slim said watching the Jacuzzi tub split down the middle then separate. "Go grab anotha bag Lil Fresh." Lil Kilo said walking into the tub grabbing the neatly wrapped bricks placing them on side of the tub beside Heavy's glass that was still half full. "Jackpot!" Lil Slim said. "Is that everything?" Lil Slim asked Lil Kilo. "Yeah. That's 21 extra bricks. I counted them as I took them out." Lil Kilo told Lil Slim as Lil Fresh came back into the bathroom holding a trash bag. "I couldn't find nomo duffle bags so I grabbed a trash bag from out the kitchen." Lil Fresh said noticing the bricks Lil Kilo had stacked up on the jacuzzi. "Damn they had all them inside that tub?" Lil Fresh asked holding the bag open for Lil Kilo. "Key word is *had* now hold that bag open so we can get the fuck up outta here." Lil Kilo said placing the bricks in the trash bag. "I got this grab those duffle's fool." Lil Kilo told Lil Fresh placing the trash bag on Lil Slim's lap then pushed Lil Slim out the room. Just as they were coming up the hall headed towards the door they seen the door open and seen Muscle Head's twin walk in and was about to pull his gun out once he seen his brother layed out but was a little to slow. Lil Slim had a police aim on him and let off three quick rounds. "PewPewPew…" One hitting him in the neck crushing his esophagus while the other two pierced his chest barley missing his heart. "Pew…" Lil Slim let off a single round into Muscle Head's forehead as they left out the door.

Chapter 20

"It's $195,000." Lil Kilo said. "And 36 bricks." Lil Fresh added pulling the last two bricks of dope out the duffle bag and stacked them up on the floor in front of the couch with the rest of the bricks. After leaving Lil Jimmy and Heavy's house Lil Kilo shot straight to The Chop House so that him Lil Fresh and Lil Slim could get low. "That's 12 bricks and 65 thousand a piece. Drought Season Over!" Lil Slim said. "You got damn right. We bout to fuck these streets up!" Lil Kilo said counting out sixty-five thousand dollars sliding it across the table to Lil Slim then counted out another sixty-five thousand dollars and slid it to Lil Fresh. "Split them bricks up Lil Fresh while I call Ja'Zelle to have her go clean that place up." Lil Kilo said getting up to get his cell phone out the kitchen. "Roll one up Lil Slim." The next day Lil Slim and Lil Kilo was riding through the city talking about how they was going to get some more dope when it was time for them to ree up again since they would no longer be able to ree up with Lil Jimmy and Heavy. "We might have to hit the road. "Lil Kilo told Lil Slim. "Ion think nobody in the city gone be able to fill our order once this shit gone." Lil Kilo said. Lil Slim thought about their options. "I gotta auntie that stay in Cashville. We can take a trip down thru that way to see what's up wit them niggas if we need to." Lil Slim said trying to remember the last time he seen his auntie. "We might have to cause I know this shit funa fly." Lil Kilo told Lil Slim knowing that almost everybody that use to cop dope from Lil Jimmy and Heavy would be shopping with them now. "Yeah I know because we bout to take all ol boy 'em clientele." Lil Slim said taking Lil Kilo's thoughts right out his head. "That's what I was thinking. But what's up with Loreli cuzzin'? He still want them thangs or what?" Lil Kilo asked Lil Slim. "That nigga texted talkin' bout a family discount. Said he got seventy." Lil Slim said. "Tell that nigga take that seventy to Texas. Them thangs forty a piece in the O. Ain't no discount bih like Plies said." Lil Kilo and Lil Slim both laughed. "Shid them seventy sound good right now." Lil Slim said still laughing. "Showl do I ain't gone lie. Shid that's 70 g's we talkin' bout. But it ain't bout the money fool don't forget." Lil Kilo told Lil Slim. "You told me that." Hearing that Lil Slim looked over and gave Lil Kilo some dap. "I remember nigga." Lil Slim said then told Lil Kilo to swing by Big Ed's spot. "I'ma be walkin' without those crutches in bout another month to fool so Ima need me a whip." Lil Slim said sitting outside Big Ed's spot waiting on him to pull back up from the store. Lil Slim was on the phone with Loreli while Lil Kilo was scrolling down Instagram ear hustling. Listening to the conversation Lil Slim was handing with Loreli let Lil Kilo know that his nigga was catching feelings. "What I tell you bout that word?" Lil Kilo heard Lil Slim say before he hung up. "Let me find out you in love fool." Lil Kilo joked as

Big Ed pulled up and hopped out holding a brown paper bag. "Ion know bout all that in love shit. I ain't gone lie thou fool I fuck with her tough. Gal all way one hunnit. She haven't left my side yet." Lil Slim told Lil Kilo. Inside Big Ed's spot Lil Kilo could tell that Big Ed had something on his mind. "You aite Ol' Man?" Lil Kilo asked. Big Ed sat back on the couch and took a deep breath. "Somebody killed Heavy and Lil Jimmy." Big Ed said with hurt in his voice. "We were just over their house not to long ago." Big Ed said looking at Lil Kilo. Not knowing if he should keep his mouth closed or let Big Ed know what was going on Lil Kilo's only words were "Cold game." And those words alone let Big Ed know that Lil Kilo had something to do with Lil Jimmy's and Heavy's death. "Cold game." Big Ed repeated back feeling somewhat better for some reason. "You'll be back on yo feet soon want you Lil Slim?" Big Ed asked Lil Slim to change the subject. "My personal therapist tell me she gone have me walkin' in less than 30 days but you know how that go." Lil Slim said bending his leg back and forth showing Big Ed that his feeling was coming back. "I see ya." Big Ed said. "Shit I ain't never broke a bone or been shot so I can only imagine yo pain." Big Ed added then pulled a big bottle of Patron out the brown paper bag he carried into the house. "How old is you Ol' Man?" Lil Kilo asked. "You mean *are* you?" Big Ed said then chuckled opening the bottle of Patron. "Shid bout 75." Lil Slim joked causing Lil Kilo to laugh. "I pray my higher power allow me to see 75. I was born in '63 tho. I'ma real OG." Big Ed said taking a shot of the Patron straight out the bottle. "'63? Damn I was born in '99 that mean you 36 years older than me... 36 plus 17 is 53." Lil Slim said breaking down the math out loud to find out Big Ed's age. "Yeah youa real OG that got some of that real OG to smoke I hope." Lil Kilo said. "We smoking Granddaddy today." Big Ed told Lil Kilo then pulled out a big zip lock bag full of purple weed and smelled it. "You can smell this shit through the bag." Big Ed said. "I know. I started getting a whiff of it that's what made me say something about it." Lil Kilo said grabbing the sack Big Ed was handing him then stuck his nose in it and inhaled deeply. "This shit smell like heaven. I might need to grab a lil QP of this to keep at the spot." Lil Kilo said. After leaving Big Ed's spot Lil Kilo told Lil Slim to call Lil Fresh and see what he had going on. "I think I'm Big Meech...Larry Hoover..." Is how Lil Fresh answered the phone. "You feelin' good over there ain't ya?" Lil Slim said putting Lil Fresh on speaker phone. "Whippin' work... Hallelujah." Lil Fresh said then chuckled. "Nigga my phone been goin' dumb. I'm bout ready to cut this bitch off for a second." Lil Fresh said. "Nigga you done pieced out a zip in grams and swear you been gettin' off. Cut it out." Lil Kilo said laughing. "It wasn't even a whole zip." Lil Slim added. "That nigga still gotta eight ball left." Lil Fresh laughed. "Where ya'll fools at?" Lil Fresh asked. "Just left Big Ed spot bout to hit Ms. Cooks to grab a plate right quick. Where you at?" Lil Slim asked. "I'm feelin' like DMX in Belly right now. I'm bout to shoot out West and pick my juvenile up." Lil Fresh said smashing the gas pedal opening the engine up in his Challenger. "I'll hit ya'll niggas when I'm done." Lil Fresh said then hung up. "Lil Fresh a fool." Lil Slim said sliding his phone back in his pocket then told Lil Kilo to swing him back by the crib after they was done eating. "Loreli said she was comin' by early for therapy. I think she funa go outta town or something." Lil Slim told Lil Kilo. "Stop lyin' nigga. If you tryna get next to yo lil boo thang just sat that fool." Lil Kilo said messing with Lil Slim. "Nawl but on the real tho fool Loreli people probably got that dope, you know they Mexicans." Lil Kilo told Lil Slim. Pulling up at Lil Slim's house a short while later Lil Kilo pulled in the drive way behind a brand new red Range Rover. "Moms gotta new whip didn't she fool?" Lil Kilo asked. "Ion know who whip this is. That ain't moms tho. She still at work." Lil Slim said wondering who's Range Rover was parked in his drive way. "That might be Loreli." Lil Slim said pulling out his phone about to call her until he seen her pop out the door smiling. "I figured it was her." Lil Slim said then dropped the window and told Loreli that he would be in the house in a minute. "Who shit she drivin' fool?" Lil Kilo asked. "Gotta be her momma shit cause she don't have no brothers or sisters." Lil Slim said before he hopped out and went in the house. Nineteen minutes into his therapy session Lil Slim's mother came in from work and asked Lil Slim was that his truck sitting in the driveway. "I know one person that drive a red Range Rover and the only time she drive it is when we're going out." Lil Slim's mother said walking into the living room. "Oh, hey Loreli. I didn't know you were here. Where's your car?" Lil Slim's mother asked Loreli after giving her and Lil Slim a hug. "It's in the shop. Something is wrong with my water pump I think I heard the man at the shop tell my mother." Loreli said placing Lil Slim's right leg back on the couch. "So I'm assuming you're driving that truck out there?" Lil Slim's mother asked Loreli sitting her mail down on the table. "Umm… yes mam." Loreli said applying a little pressure to Lil Slim's calf muscle. "That's actually my mother's truck that she never drive so she let me drive it until my car is ready." Lil Slim's mother looked up from separating her mail. "What's your mother's name chile?" "Why momma dang you nosey?" Lil Slim chuckled. "You don't know this girl momma." "Boy hush!" Lil Slim's mother told Lil Slim then looked back at Loreli. "Maria…" Loreli said. "Maria…? Maria Sanchez?" Is she Puerto Rican?" Lil Slim's mother asked sounding a bit excited. Loreli stopped applying pressure to Lil Slim's calf muscle and looked up shocked. "You know my mom?" Loreli asked. "Do I? That's my girl and she's my boss! I work with her at the law firm." Lil Slim's mother said now digging in her purse looking for her phone. "Let me call Ms. Maria to see if she know what's going on." "I just dropped her off at the airport about an hour ago. So she might not have any service." Loreli said more shocked than surprised that Lil Slim's mother knew her mother. "She did tell me that she was going to Phoenix but I thought that was next week." Lil Slim's mother said. "Man that's crazy." Lil Slim said thinking about how small the world seemed to be but how big it actually was. "So you really know her momma, momma?" Lil Slim asked his mother. "Yes, as a matter of fact I think I still have pictures from the last time we went out." Lil Slim's mother said then flipped through her photos. "See…" Lil Slim's mother showed Loreli and Lil Slim her phone. "Is that your mother?" Lil Slim's mother asked Loreli after she seen the picture. "What a minute…" Loreli said looking at the picture a little closer. "I remember her putting this outfit on because I helped her pick it out. She told me she had a date though." Loreli said. "We had a date alright." Lil Slim's mother said. "Your mother is crazy. If you talk to her before I do tell her you know me and watch what she say." Lil Slim's mother said before she walked off to go soak in the tub. "Small city huh?" Lil Slim said after his mother left. "Very small." Loreli said then told Lil Slim to stand up and take as many steps as he could towards her. After the therapy session Loreli and Lil Slim sat and talked about a little bit of everything. Loreli was mainly talking about her feelings she had for him while Lil Slim tried to avoid that conversation and talk about meaningless stuff because the only thing he could really think about was getting back out there with his niggas. "So you just gone avoid my question Issac?" Loreli asked after Lil Slim didn't respond to the question she asked him. "My bad boo, what you say? My mind was somewhere else." Lil Slim said. "I asked you do you think that you and I would make a good couple?" Loreli said rubbing Lil Slim's legs. "I'ma be real with you Loreli..." Lil Slim said then told Loreli everything he had going on. "And finding out who killed our daddy is my main focus and if I'm fully focused on that I know I want be able to give you the time and attention you'll be lookin' for from me." Lil Slim said knowing that Loreli felt some kind of way about him. "Issac, I know what's going on. I listen to the conversations you have with your friends. I just want to be by your side." Loreli said then promised Lil Slim that she wouldn't beg for his time or attention. "I'll be your Bonnie and hold you down. I promise." Loreli added meaning every word she said. "I love you Issac." Lil Slim wanted to tell Loreli that he loved her to because he did but instead told her how serious it was in the streets. "I got hit just as many times as 50 got hit all because a nigga couldn't take a beatin' like a man. Ain't nothin' nice about these streets boo." Lil Slim said letting Loreli know how serious things could get in the streets. Loreli in return told Lil Slim that she knew exactly how serious things could be in the streets then told him something that she have never told anybody else. "My daddy was in the streets too." Loreli told Lil Slim looking him in the eyes. "He wasn't just in the streets, he ran the streets. My momma don't think I know but I do." Loreli told Lil Slim sounding a bit emotional. Lil Slim figured that her daddy was probably just another nigga that worked for his daddy but didn't want to brush the conversation off because he could tell that Loreli missed her daddy just as much as he missed his daddy although she never said anything about him. "What's his name boo?" Lil Slim asked pulling Loreli closer. Loreli knew how big her daddy was in the drug game and knew that there was a chance that there daddies knew each other so she really didn't want to say her daddy's name. *Why did I even tell him about my daddy? I've never mentioned my daddy to anyone. Me and my mother don't even talk about my daddy unless we going to visit him.* Loreli thought then told herself that she would always keep it real with Lil Slim because of the love she had for him. *I wanted him to know that I know what it's like to lose your daddy.* Loreli thought reminding herself why she even brought her daddy up in the first place. *Yeah her daddy probably ran packs or worked in one of my daddy spots.* Lil Slim thought after Loreli got quiet. "His name was Lorenzo…" Loreli said saying her daddy's name like she was telling a secret. Lil Slim didn't recognize the name so to comfort Loreli Lil Slim pulled her up to his chest and kissed her lips softly. "I love you too baby." The next morning while Lil Slim and Loreli were in Lil Slim's room eating the breakfast Loreli cooked Loreli's mother called to let her know that her plane will be arriving one day early. "Okay so I'll need to be at the airport Tuesday instead of Wednesday right?" Loreli said into the phone. "Yes, Tuesday baby. Your uncles and everybody asked about you too. Well I love you baby. See you soon." Loreli's mother said then was about to hang up but Loreli said something just in time. "Mami…" "Yes baby?" "I didn't know that you and Issac's mother knew each other." Loreli said. "You talking about your friend Issac?" Loreli's mother asked knowing exactly who her daughter was talking about. "Yes…" Loreli said then told her mother everything Lil Slim's mother said and how she noticed her truck. "You're talking about Ivonne that works with me at the firm. Yes I know her. That's my girl." Loreli's mother said. "I knew that she had a son name Issac but I didn't know that her son was your friend. Tell Ivonne I said call me." Loreli's mother said. "Okay I will. Love you. Talk to you later." Loreli said before she hung up. "I guess they do know each other." Loreli said to Lil Slim who was sprawled out in the middle of his king size therapeutic adjustable bed staring up at his 60' flat screen that was mounted on his wall. "I guess so." Lil Slim said back turning to ESPN to see if the Bengals won yesterday. "You're not paying me any attention." Loreli said then snatched the cover off Lil Slim and rolled up in them so he couldn't snatch them back. "Okay… Okay… Okay… boo." Lil Slim said after he couldn't get the covers back. "I was tryin' to check the score." "The score is two to nothing. My way." Loreli said. "Huh?" Lil Slim said confused. "You heard me. I'm up two to nothing." Loreli repeated then told Lil Slim that she was talking about in the bed because she made him tap out both times they had sex. "Two?" Lil Slim chuckled. "You mean one to nothing don't you? I'll give you yo props, you done yo thang last night." Lil Slim said then grabbed Loreli's ass through the cover. "Nope twice." Loreli said smiling. "The first time I took it light on you but last night I rocked your world!" Loreli told Lil Slim rubbing his manhood through his boxers making him rise. "Nawl the first time didn't count. I was just makin' sure my nigga still worked." Lil Slim said laughing as his phone rung. "See who that is boo." Lil Slim told Loreli watching her get up out the bed in her panties and bra. "Damn that ass fat lil booty." Lil Slim said watching Loreli's ass bounce every time she took a step. "Stop looking at what you can't handle." Loreli told Lil Slim then stop and made her ass wiggle just a little as she grabbed his phone off his dresser. "It's Lil Fresh." Loreli said. "Answer it." Loreli answered Lil Slim's phone then tossed it at him. "What up fool?" Lil Slim said into the phone. "She done put that Puerto Rican pussy on ya now she answering yo phone." Lil Fresh joked laughing. "Damn right!" Lil Slim said back then busted out laughing. "Yeah aite lemme find out." Lil Fresh said then told Lil Slim that him and Lil Kilo made a bet on what kind of car he would want. "Ya'll did what fool?" Lil Slim questioned. "Lil Kilo bout to get you a whip and we bet a stack on which whip you would want. He said you would want a Camaro like his and I said that you would want a Challenger like mine." Lil Fresh said following behind Lil Kilo headed to the car lot where they got their whips from. "And I guess you want me to get that Challenger so you can win the bet?" Lil Slim said chuckling. "But both ya'll niggas wrong. I want that new Tahoe. That bitch wet!"

Lil Slim told Lil Fresh then hung up and called Lil Kilo and acted like he didn't know what was going on until Lil Kilo said the same thing Lil Fresh just said and tried to get him to pick the Camaro instead of the Challenger. "What's funny?" Lil Kilo asked smashing the gas a little seeing if Lil Fresh was trying to race. "Ya'll niggas crazy." Lil Slim said. "Lil Fresh just called me and said the same thing." Lil Kilo laughed. "Damn he beat me to it. That's how you know we been around each other to long. I should have known that nigga was gone call once he said bet a stack." Lil Kilo said looking back at Lil Fresh through his rearview mirror smiling. "Yeah you should've known that nigga had a trick up his sleeve." Lil Slim said then told Lil Kilo that he didn't want neither one of those cars they picked. "I want that new Tahoe fool. That mufucker slick." Lil Slim said watching Loreli's booty. "I think I seen one of them too. Them bitches is slick." Lil Kilo said then asked "So is that what you want? I'm bout to have Cheese order you one if he don't have one on the lot." Lil Kilo told Lil Slim. "Yeah. Make sure it's black with them presidential thangs on it tho." Lil Slim said before they hung up. "Get yo sexy ass back in this bed and talk that gangsta shit you were talkin' before we was rudely interrupted." Lil Slim told Loreli. Two days later while Loreli was at the airport picking her mother up Lil Slim was riding with Lil Kilo dropping packs off and picking up money. "How many more bricks you got left fool?" Lil Slim asked Lil Kilo. "That shit gotta be bout gone the way yo phone ringin'." Lil Slim said. "I got like 6 or 7 left. Why? What up you need some?" Lil Kilo asked Lil Slim as his phone rung again. "Nawl I'm good. I still got almost 10 of them left. I got off 2 of them on her cuzzin'. He came with 78 so I fucked with 'em. Other than that I got a few niggas callin' for lil zips that I be havin' Loreli take me to catch." Lil Slim said then told Lil Kilo that he really haven't been trying to go to hard just yet. "You trust Loreli?" Lil Kilo asked as soon as Lil Slim got his last words out. Lil Slim let Lil Kilo know that he trusted Loreli then for some reason told him what she said about her daddy. "Anit no tellin' who her daddy was. What was that nigga, a Mexican too?" Lil Kilo asked Lil Slim. "Nawl nigga they not Mexican they Puerto Rican fool." Lil Slim said laughing. "I think her daddy was black tho or either mixed with black or something because Loreli said she was mixed with black when I asked her. So Ion know if her momma got black in her or her daddy." Lil Slim said. "It gotta be her daddy because you can tell her momma sexy ass pure Puerto Rican." Lil Kilo said picking up his phone that started ringing again and told whoever it was to give him an hour. "What she say her daddy name was tho fool? Ima ask Ja'Zelle momma about him." Lil Kilo said. Lil Slim looked at Lil Kilo and said "Lorenzo…"

Chapter 21

"Lorenzo...?" Lil Kilo repeated. "That nigga didn't have a nickname?" Lil Kilo asked. "Ion know fool." Lil Slim said laughing at the way Lil Kilo said Loreli's daddy name. "I didn't ask. Shit I figured that he was another one of daddy 'em flunkies." Lil Slim said. "His name sound familiar for some reason. Hold up." Lil Kilo said then pulled out his cell phone and called Ja'Zelle but her phone was going straight to voicemail. "It might of been Big Ed saying something about a Lorenzo." Lil Kilo said out loud trying to figure out where he heard the name Lorenzo from. Lil Kilo called Big Ed. "What up Ol' Man?" Lil Kilo said into the phone. "You know a nigga name Lorenzo that supposedly held a lil weight back in the day but got killed?" Lil Kilo asked Big Ed. "I know one Lorenzo that was getting money back in the day." Big Ed told Lil Kilo. "And that was Quick the other nigga that use to hang with ya'll daddy. Quick real name was Lorenzo Edwards. He the only Lorenzo I know that was getting some real money back then." Big Ed said then asked Lil Kilo why he asked him that. "I'm just tryna figure something out." Lil Kilo told Big Ed before he hung up. "You heard that didn't ya?" Lil Kilo asked Lil Slim. "He said the only Lorenzo he know is Quick. The nigga that use to run with our daddy." "Yeah I heard him." Lil Slim said wondering if the Lorenzo Big Ed was talking about was Loreli's daddy. "What if the Lorenzo Big Ed talkin' bout is Loreli daddy fool? That'll be crazy." Lil Slim said. "Shid it's only one way to find out." Lil Kilo said then told Lil Slim to call Loreli and ask her if her daddy had a nickname. Instead of calling Loreli Lil Slim shot her a text message asking her what she was doing then after she responded saying she just made it home from picking her mother up from the airport Lil Slim asked her did her daddy have another name he went by. Loreli was sitting in her room going through her clothes trying to find something to pack into her sleeping bag to take over to Lil Slim's house when Lil Slim texted her. *'Of course he did…'* Loreli thought walking over to her dresser where her daddy's obituary was and picked it up. *'Lorenzo "Quick" Edwards'* Loreli mouthed her daddy's name then texted Lil Slim back. "Yes, his nickname was Quick." Loreli texted staring at her daddy's picture on the obituary and broke down crying. After unpacking her bags Maria was coming down the hall to ask Loreli was she hungry but stopped in the doorway when she seen Loreli on her knees in the middle of her floor holding her daddy's obituary crying. Maria had tears in her eyes as she walked over to Loreli and fell to her knees beside her daughter. Holding Loreli close Maria's tears started to fall nonstop as she thought about the secrets she's been keeping from Loreli about her daddy. *'Maybe if I tell her the truth about what happened to her daddy then maybe my heart wouldn't feel so heavy anymore.'* Maria thought. *'But how do I tell my baby that it was her uncle that murdered her father?'* Maria thought then found it in herself at that very moment to tell Loreli the truth about her father. "I'm telling you now fool her momma know something. Trust me." Lil Kilo was telling Lil Slim after Lil Slim told Lil Kilo that Loreli told him that her daddy name was Quick. "Think about it fool…" Lil Kilo said. "It took for yo momma to see her truck over there to realize that she knew Loreli's momma but ain't no tellin' how long Loreli momma been knowin' all this and just ain't said nothin'. Her momma probably been knowin' who you is. Shid she probably know who I am too and Lil Fresh…" Lil Kilo was saying until Lil Slim cut him off. "Ion wanna jump to conclusions. I'ma get the truth out of Loreli when she come over tonight." Lil Slim said. "I can tell you how it happened fool…" Lil Kilo said coming up with his own theory. "Quick met Loreli momma then they got close. She seen that he was a street nigga so she turned him on to her daddy, they get plugged in with the Mexicans and daddy 'em started gettin' to big so the Mexicans killed them." Lil Kilo said believing every word he said as he was sounding real convincible. "They not Mexicans tho fool." Lil Slim told Lil Kilo grinning and at the same time kind of seeing that what Lil Kilo said to be true a little. "Mexicans, Puerto Ricans, Egyptians, whatever the fuck they are they from where the dope is plentiful." Lil Kilo said causing Lil Slim to bust out laughing. "Boy youa fool! I'ma see tonight tho." Lil Slim said ready to call Loreli right then and there and ask her a million questions but instead pulled out a bag weed and started breaking some down. *I'm definitely gone find out tonight.'* Lil Slim thought. Loreli couldn't believe her ears as her mother sat there explaining to her the truth behind her father's death.

Loreli wiped the last tear out of her eyes and found herself boiling with anger and hatred towards her mother. "How could you?" Loreli said in a voice that was pure evil. "You've watched me cry all these years and still continued to lie to me!" Loreli said yanking away from her mother. "Is this why you get me everything I want... Huh?" Loreli yelled looking at her mother with fire in her eyes. "You thought this would mend my wounds, cure my broken heart?" Loreli's temperature was rising from her mother's silence. But Maria just couldn't find the right words to say. I mean what could she say to calm Loreli down after telling her that it was her brother that killed her daddy. "ANSWER ME!" Loreli yelled in full rage pulling her TV off the wall breaking it then knocking her dresser over before running out the house crying again. Since her car was still in the shop Loreli jumped in her mother's Range Rover and drove straight to her daddy's grave site and sat there for hours crying her heart out apologizing like it was her fault that he was dead. *'Protect yourself. It's not your fault or your mother's fault. Daddy's okay. I'm here with you...'* Loreli smiled lightly hearing a voice whisper into her ear as she was getting up to leave but not before kissing the angel that sat above her daddy's name on his tombstone like she always did. Getting back into her mother's truck Loreli noticed that she needed some gas but left her wallet at home and didn't want to see her mother's face or hear her mother's voice at the moment so Loreli cut the radio on and 615 Exclusive *'Missing Me'* song was on so she cut it up and sung along with him. Looking at the clock on the dash board Loreli seen that it was a little after six and decided to go see Lil Slim. *'He's probably the only person on earth that can comfort me right now anyway.'* Loreli thought headed in the direction Lil Slim lived in and was pulling up at his house at a quarter til 7. Noticing that Lil Slim mother wasn't there Loreli sat in the truck trying to get herself together. "I look a mess…" Loreli said looking in the mirror. How was she supposed to tell Lil Slim that it was her uncle that killed his daddy was all Loreli was thinking. *What if he try to hurt me because of what my uncle did?* Loreli thought but then figured that Lil Slim wouldn't do that because her uncle killed her father as well. *Well what if he wants nothing else to do with me?* Loreli then thought as a million other what if's ran through her head. Knowing that Lil Slim wanted to know who killed his father just as bad as she did Loreli use that as her motivation to get out of the truck and go knock on the door. After about the thirteenth knock Lil Slim finally came to the door with some Nike gym shorts on and his towel draped around his head. "I just got out the shower boo my bad. I worked up a sweat on that darn Bowflex Machine that came in today." Lil Slim said taking the towel rubbing his head with it. "It's okay." Loreli said softly walking into the house. "I see somebody is moving around pretty good without those crutches." Loreli told Lil Slim watching him limp into the living room. Lil Slim removed the towel from his head then looked back at Loreli after hearing her voice sound broken and noticed that she's been crying. "You okay boo?" Lil Slim asked Loreli who just broke down crying again putting her face in the arm of the couch. "You don't have to cry Loreli. Tell me what's wrong." Lil Slim said sitting down on the couch beside Loreli so that he could hold her. "What's wrong boo?" Lil Slim asked Loreli again after she said nothing just kept crying. Finally after about 10 minutes of sniffing and crying Loreli got up to get her some tissue to blow her nose then sat back down beside Lil Slim with tears still in her eyes. Loreli looked Lil Slim in the face. "My momma told me the truth about what really happened to my daddy." Loreli said fighting back tears and trying to control the snot from falling out her nose at the same time. Loreli's words stunned Lil Slim because he knew that if Loreli knew who killed her daddy then that meant that she knew who killed his daddy as well but Lil Slim wasn't sure if Loreli was aware of that or not. Not really knowing what else to say Loreli promised Lil Slim that she didn't know anything about this until today then told him everything her mother told her. Lil Slim still said nothing but knew that everything Loreli was telling him was true because it all added up especially when she told him that her uncle was part of a Cartel. *'That's how Pop's 'em was able to flood the streets the way they did. They were plugged into the Cartel.'* Lil Slim thought. "Issac I promise I'm sorry baby. I promise I never would've kept anything like this from you. I promise." Loreli told Lil Slim on the verge of tears again. Lil Slim told Loreli that everything was going to be okay and not to worry then thanked her for letting him know the truth. Lil Slim knew from that moment on that Loreli's loyalty for him was unbreakable knowing that she could've easily kept her mouth closed about the situation and just left him alone. "I promise to always protect you boo." Lil Slim told Loreli as he wiped her tears then kissed her on the forehead. That night Lil Slim and Loreli made love for hours to each other and once they were done Loreli's only words to Lil Slim were "Promise me you'll never leave me Issac." "I promise..." Lil Slim said before they both passed out. The next morning Lil

Slim woke up to his text messages going off. Rolling over grabbing his phone off the night stand Lil Slim seen that it was Lil Kilo texting him at 8:09 in the morning. "Look outside fool." The text message said. *'Look outside for what?'* Lil Slim thought looking over at Loreli seeing that she was starting to stir in her sleep a little. Climbing out the bed Lil Slim stretched and yearned them limped towards the window. "Where you going baby?" Loreli asked Lil Slim rolling over on her back. "Nowhere. I'm just looking out the window boo." Lil Slim said opening the blinds letting the sun shine through. "Good mornin' by the way sexy." Lil Slim said looking back at Loreli before he looked out the window and seen a brand new black Tahoe truck with dark black tinted windows sitting in front of his house with a big red bow sitting on top of the hood. "Oh shit!" Lil Slim said smiling from ear to ear. "What is it?" Loreli asked getting out of bed walking to stand beside Lil Slim. "Ohh… that's nice Issac. That's just like the one you said you wanted too." Loreli said wrapping her arms around Lil Slim as the passenger side window let down and Lil Fresh head popped out. "I think he's telling you to come out baby." Loreli told Lil Slim watching Lil Fresh wave his arm signaling Lil Slim to come here. "I didn't even think nobody was in there til the window dropped." Lil Slim said limping back to his bed to call Lil Fresh and tell him that he was about to jump in the shower real fast then he'll be out. "You gettin' in the shower with me?" Lil Slim asked Loreli knowing she was. After showering and sliding on some clothes Loreli told Lil Slim that he could go kick it with his friends and to just call her when he was done. "I'm going to go talk with my mother and apologize for being such a brat yesterday." Loreli said then kissed Lil Slim on the lips as they headed down the steps where Lil Slim grabbed one of his crutches for a little support before they left out the house. Sitting in the passenger seat after Lil Fresh hopped out and got in the back Lil Slim couldn't stop smiling. "This mufucker fully loaded too." Lil Slim said checking out the leather seats and the display screen that was in the center of the dash. "Yeah this bitch loaded." Lil Kilo said then hit a button to let the sun roof back. "I'm thinkin' bout gettin' me one." Lil Kilo said giving Lil Slim some dap. "Shit, I slick want me a truck now too." Lil Fresh said from the backseat. "It's so much room back here that I can knock all my lil dusty feets off back here instead of getting a room." Lil Fresh added causing Lil Slim and Lil Kilo to laugh. "Nigga I thought you didn't have no dusty feets?" Lil Kilo said still laughing. "I just startin' to realize that all these lil hoes dusty feets. Especially the ones that think they bad but got more miles than the interstate." Lil Fresh said. "What ya'll niggas done ate? Let's swing by my Granny's spot and grab some breakfast. I'm bout to starve." Lil Slim said rubbing his stomach. "I got some shit to tell ya'll anyway." As Lil Kilo pulled off from in front of Lil Slim's house Lil Slim thought about how he was gone tell his niggas that he knew who killed their daddy and realized that it was only one way to tell them and that was to be straight up with them. "Cut the radio down right quick fool." Lil Slim told Lil Kilo who looked over at him then asked him was he alright. "Yeah I'm good… I found out who killed our daddy tho." Lil Slim said looking back over at Lil Kilo then back at Lil Fresh. "You did what fool?" Lil Kilo asked as if he didn't just hear every word Lil Slim just said. "I know the truth now fool. I know what really happened." Lil Slim said then told Lil Kilo and Lil Fresh every single thing Loreli told him last night. "So that Lorenzo was her daddy then huh?" Lil Kilo said. "Yeah that's him." Lil Slim said. "So Quick the other nigga that use to run with daddy 'em is Loreli's daddy?" Lil Fresh asked confused. "And her uncle 'em ran the Cartel and wacked daddy 'em after daddy 'em got tired of playin' the game and tried to pay their way out, is that what you sayin'?" Lil Fresh asked Lil Slim sticking his head around the seat so that he could see Lil Slim's face. Lil Slim told Lil Fresh that that was exactly what he was saying. "She even told me the name of the Cartel." Lil Slim said then asked Lil Kilo what was he thinking after he got quiet. "Shid I know what I'm thinkin' bout..." Lil Fresh said. "Murda! I say we kill they whole fuckin' family. Loreli ass too." Lil Fresh said angrily. "Blood is definitely about to spill but I just thought of a plan that'll bring our daddies killers to us instead of us going lookin' for them." Lil Kilo said then paused to make sure he had Lil Fresh and Lil Slim's full attention before he spoke again. "If the person who killed our daddy is Loreli's uncle that makes him Loreli's momma brother..." Lil Kilo said then paused again confusing the hell out of Lil Fresh while Lil Slim thought he knew what Lil Kilo was getting at. "Her brother ain't gone miss her funeral." Lil Kilo said coldly causing the car to become completely silent. Lil Slim had a lot of love for Loreli and promised her that he wouldn't let anything happen to her but now that they knew the true story behind their father's death Lil Slim knew his niggas was ready to kill whoever whenever. No matter how the job got done Lil Slim knew that it was only a matter of time before Lil Kilo would be ready to put a plan in motion. "I guarantee you he will be there." Lil Kilo said then thought about how hard it was going to be to get next to Loreli's uncle or even close enough to kill him. "What if he make the funeral private where nobody but family can attend?" Lil Fresh said in the backseat thinking about the what if's. "What you think?" Lil Kilo asked Lil Slim who's only concern at that moment was saving Loreli's life. "However ya'll wanna handle this we can do it. But I got one request..." Lil Slim said looking Lil Kilo in the eyes again. "And that is that Loreli live." Hearing that let Lil Kilo know that Lil Slim not only cared for Loreli but loved her as well. "Fuck that! That bitch gotta die too." Lil Fresh snapped from the back seat. "She gone know we did it if her momma come up dead." Lil Fresh said. "He gotta point." Lil Kilo told Lil Slim as he was pulling into Ms. Cook's. "To be honest I don't think she would tell." Lil Slim said. "I mean think about it... why would she even tell me all this knowing that she's putting her family in danger?" Lil Slim said then told Lil Kilo and Lil Fresh how hurt Loreli was after being lied to for so many years by the person she felt she could trust. "Her love and loyalty is with me right now. Not her momma." "I understand that Lil Slim but we still don't wanna take a chance on her even having the chance to tell we did it." Lil Kilo told Lil Slim after backing into a parking spot by the door. "Because she gone tell. Then what?" Lil Fresh said not understanding why Lil Slim was trying to save Loreli's life. "Then I'll take the rap." Lil Slim said. "I'll say that ya'll had nothin' to do with it and I'll go lay down." "Man you willing to chance doin' a life sentence behind some pus..." Lil Fresh was about to say but Lil Kilo cut him off. "Ima take your word on this one Lil Slim." Lil Kilo said. "Loreli lives. But her mother must go. That's the only way I see us gettin' her brother to come straight out." Lil Kilo said as another idea came to his mind. "And if we make it look like a accident he might come unprepared and we may be able to catch him off guard a little easier." Lil Kilo told Lil Fresh and Lil Slim as they got out the truck to go in and get them something to eat. Lil Slim was able to smile a little knowing that he was just able to save Loreli's life. After eating breakfast at Ms. Cook's and deciding to let Ja'Zelle take care of Loreli's mother the three hopped back in the truck ready to smoke something. "I need a big fat ass blunt right about now." Lil Fresh said after Lil Kilo asked him did he have some weed on him. "Stop at the store to get some cigars. I'm funa tryta stuff this whole half a quarter in one rillo." Lil Fresh said unzipping a zipper on his Robin Jeans pulling out some of the Granddaddy purp he got from Big Ed. "I think we all need a blunt right about now." Lil Kilo said pulling down the street to where the Shell's gas station was then hopped out and went in the store to get some cigars. As Lil Kilo was coming out the store he seen Lil Slim limping around to the driver side of the truck getting in. *'He must had to see what that thang drive like.'* Lil Kilo thought smiling. "I had to..." Lil Slim said as Lil Kilo was getting in the passenger seat. "Put yo seat belt on Lil Kilo, you know this nigga ain't got no toes." Lil Fresh joked causing Lil Slim and Lil Kilo to bust out laughing. "Fuck you nigga..." Lil Slim said still laughing. "Roll that blunt up that's what you do." Lil Slim pulled off from the gas station and busted a couple blocks through the hood while they smoked. Turning on the same street he got shot on Lil Slim's mind took him back to that day. "Ol shit! He gotta gun fool run!" Lil Slim heard Lil Kilo telling him right before Rachean shot him. "Bitch ass nigga." Lil Slim mumbled as he passed the house he was layed out in front of. Lil Kilo was the only one that heard Lil Slim mumble and already knew why he mumbled. "You ain't gotta worry bout him nomo." Lil Kilo told Lil Slim passing him the blunt. Lil Slim rode around for another 20 minutes then pulled back up at his house listening to Lil Kilo talk to Ja'Zelle about dealing with Maria. "We want this one to look like a accident." Lil Slim heard Lil Kilo say as he was parking. After he hung up with Ja'Zelle he told Lil Slim and Lil Fresh that Ja'Zelle said that she would have everything taken care of within 48 hours. "She told me to tell you to make sure Loreli stay with you for the next couple days." Lil Kilo told Lil Slim. "No Problem." Lil Slim said knowing that it wouldn't be hard at all getting Loreli to stay with him. That night while Lil Slim was making love to Loreli Ja'Zelle was sneaking out of Loreli's closet and down the hall to her mother's bed room. Standing in Loreli's mother doorway dressed in black from head to toe with black gloves on Ja'Zelle had a wicked grin on her face thinking about how she was about to take Loreli's mother soul out her body. Easing her way over to Maria's bed like a thief in the night Ja'Zelle bent down and felt under Maria's bed for the jar of scentless ammonia and nitric acid and the rag that she had placed under there just hours before Maria got home. Ja'Zelle sat patiently for hours inside Loreli's closet waiting on Maria to fall asleep. *'She should be sleep in just a minute now.'* Ja'Zelle thought after she heard Loreli's mother playing with herself. Standing over Maria with the rag drenched with the scentless ammonia and nitric acid Ja'Zelle struck swiftly and made her move covering Maria's nose and mouth with the rag. Feeling something touch her face Maria woke up and panicked inhaling the scentless ammonia and nitric acid that Ja'Zelle was covering her face with. "Be still." Ja'Zelle whispered tightening her grip squeezing the rag a little so that some of the liquid from the rag could drip into Maria's mouth and down her throat. Maria tried her best to squirm out of Ja'Zelle's grip as she felt her body becoming weak but she just wasn't a match for the nitric acid and ammonia and after another 30 seconds of inhaling and swallowing the chemicals Maria's body fell limp. "Good girl." Ja'Zelle whispered into Maria's ear as she layed her head back down on the pillow. Ja'Zelle then ran downstairs to get a knife and came back up the stairs and wrapped the knife in Maria's left hand and made her cut her right wrist vertically then horizontally so that her vein would split wide open and blood would leak. After making Maria cut her wrist wide open Ja'Zelle then took the knife and made Maria push the knife directly through the center of her neck which caused blood to squirt and gust out the sides of the knife. Ja'Zelle ginned that same wicked grin feeling the knife rip through Maria's flesh. 'Perfect.' Ja'Zelle thought taking a step back looking at Maria's hand still wrapped slightly around the knife that was pushed halfway through her neck. "One last thing." Ja'Zelle said out loud looking for Maria's cell phone and found it laying on the pillow next to her dead body. 'Good thing she don't have a password.' Ja'Zelle thought as she opened Maria's phone and seen that Maria was still logged into Pornhub. "Somebody must like girls." Ja'Zelle said looking at a Puerto Rican girl lick a black girl's clit on Maria's screen. Going through Maria's messages Ja'Zelle texted Loreli acting as if she was Maria. *'Loreli I want to apologize for not being the mother I should have. I love you but I know you no longer love me and the pain I've been keeping bottled up over the years I could no longer endure. I'm gone to be with your daddy again. I promise to watch over you from above. Until we meet again my arms will forever be around you. Love always, Mom. P.S. Keep Issac close to your heart my dear.'* "Send..." Ja'Zelle said and placed Maria's phone back on the pillow then cleaned up all evidence that she was there then made her way down the stairs and out the house unnoticed the same way she came in, through the back window. The next morning Loreli woke up and seen that her mother had texted her at 2:31 in the morning and figured that she was just apologizing again so Loreli sat her phone back down without opening the message then got up to go use the bathroom. Coming back into the room Loreli was about to wake Lil Slim up to see if he was hungry until she heard her text message go off again. *'Don't tell me she's texting again.'* Loreli thought picking her phone up seeing that it was only her notification reminder reminding her that she had a text. *'I guess it won't hurt to read another one of her lies.'* Loreli thought sitting on the edge of Lil Slim's bed. Loreli read the first line *'Loreli, I want to apologize for not being the mother I should have'* and closed the text message back then deleted every single text message that her mother ever sent her. "I don't even know why I bothered." Loreli said waking Lil Slim up out of his sleep. Meanwhile Lil Kilo and Lil Fresh was headed to meet Ja'Zelle and was pulled over in the process. "Shit!" Lil Fresh said waiting on the officer to get out the car.

"We cool fool. Ain't nothin' in here but these 30 g's we bout to drop off to Ja'Zelle. Unless you got something on you?" Lil Kilo said looking over at Lil Fresh. "Nawl Ion got nothin' but this lil smoke sack and some pocket change on me." Lil Fresh said stuffing the half a quarter of weed he had in his pocket under his nut sack. "What you call pocket change fool?" Lil Kilo asked Lil Fresh pointing to the knot that was bulging out of his pants. "What the fuck takin' them so long to get out the car?" Lil Fresh said looking in the rearview mirror as the police door opened. "Here they come now." Lil Kilo said looking in his side view mirror and seen that it was a female officer approaching his car. "Damn she thick!" Lil Kilo said subconsciously. Hearing that made Lil Fresh turn his head to see and remembered the police officers face. "That's her fool! That's her!" Lil Fresh said louder than he intended. "That's who?" Lil Kilo asked Lil Fresh as the police officer was walking pass the back end of his car coming towards his window. "That's the bitch that pulled me over." Lil Fresh said as the police officer tapped on Lil Kilo's window. "Good evening Mr. Campbell. Licenses and registration please." The officer said after Lil Kilo dropped his window. Knowing that the police officer knew who he was Lil Kilo acted as if he didn't. "How you know my name Ms… Coolwaters?" Lil Kilo asked reading the officer ID badge like he didn't know what her name was already. *'Oh I…umm ran your licenses plate and your name came up.'* Is what Ms. Coolwaters was about to say but instead told Lil Kilo everything that she told Lil Fresh. "I was waitin' on you to tell a lie." Lil Fresh said ducking his head down from the passenger seat so that Ms. Coolwaters could see his face. "Oh hey there Mr. Morgan." Ms. Coolwaters said then told Lil Fresh that she meant every word that she told him. "So let me guess, you pulled me over to try to swindle me outta $10,000 dollars to?" Lil Kilo said looking up at Ms. Coolwaters. "It's not swindling when I'll be giving you information in return that'll keep you alive and free." Ms. Coolwaters said watching Lil Kilo shake his head in agreement. "You right. And as long as the information you got is accurate then we could definitely use you." Lil Kilo said then asked Ms. Coolwaters how much was she gone charge them for her services. Hearing Lil Kilo say that they could definitely use her services Ms. Coolwaters used the situation she had with Lil Fresh to charge them five extra thousand. "I would've been fine with ten thousand a month but Mr. Smarty pants over there kind of got under my skin the last time we talked so now it's fifteen thousand a month." Ms. Coolwaters told Lil Kilo while looking at Lil Fresh. "Come on now sexy…" Lil Kilo said. "15 thou? How about we do the 10 you said at first and I go grab you 20 for the first two months." Lil Kilo said trying to make a deal with Ms. Coolwaters. Ms. Coolwaters heard that and immediately agreed after acting like she didn't really want to cut them a deal. "Aite cool. It's gone take me at least 30 minutes to go grab the bread for you." Lil Kilo told Ms. Coolwaters then got her number so that he could call her once he picked the money up. "Ms. Coolwaters…" Lil Fresh said after she gave Lil Kilo her number and was about to walk off. Ms. Coolwaters took a step back then bent down to look into Lil Kilo's car at Lil Fresh. "I'll give you that extra 5 thousand you wanted if you let me see how big that ass really is outside them uniform pants." Lil Fresh said seriously. Lil Kilo chuckled. "I see you just like your daddy." Ms. Coolwaters said grinning as she walked off telling herself that she would fuck the shit out of Lil Fresh young ass for them five thousand dollars. "Man you funa give that bitch 20 g's?" Lil Fresh asked Lil Kilo as they were pulling off. "Hell nawl. I said that just to get away from her for a second. She fucked up when she said that the information she got will keep us *alive* and free. Shid if that was the case Pops 'em would still be livin'." Lil Kilo said smashing the gas pedal pulling up over Ja'Zelle's house a short while later. "I'm outside." Lil Kilo texted Ja'Zelle and a few minutes later Ja'Zelle came walking out the house looking innocent as ever. "I gotta another job for you too." Lil Kilo told Ja'Zelle after paying her for killing Loreli's mother. Lil Kilo told Ja'Zelle about Ms. Coolwaters then asked her did she think she could handle the situation for them. "We bout to meet back up with her in just a minute. You think you can take care of her then?" Lil Kilo asked Ja'Zelle who in return asked where they was meeting her at. "Ion know. Probably somewhere in public tho?" Lil Kilo said. "Shoot!" Ja'Zelle said. "What you ain't gotta enough skill to kill in broad daylight?" Lil Fresh asked jokingly. Ja'Zelle grinned. "Funny. I'll just have to follow her to where ever she's going." Ja'Zelle said then told Lil Kilo to let her out she could go change her cloths and was following behind Ms. Coolwaters not even thirty minutes later.

Chapter 22

After getting confirmation from Ja'Zelle that Ms. Coolwaters was dead Lil Kilo and Lil Fresh met back up with her to pay her the rest of her money. "Keep that twenty you got off Ms. Coolwaters and here go another ten for coming thru the way you did. Good lookin'." Lil Kilo told Ja'Zelle before him and Lil Fresh pulled off. "Take me to my whip fool. I gotta couple plays to catch." Lil Fresh told Lil Kilo. Lil Kilo dropped Lil Fresh off then called Lil Slim to see what he had going on and to let him know about Ms. Coolwaters but Lil Slim didn't answer so he called Neka to see where she was but she didn't answer either. *'Ain't nobody fuckin' wit me right now huh?'* Lil Kilo thought putting his phone down as Lil Slim was calling him back. "What up fool?" Lil Slim said into the phone once Lil Kilo picked up. "You ain't gone believe what happened to me and Lil Fresh today fool." Lil Kilo said. "I'm bout to pull up and holler at you for a second. Where Loreli at?" Lil Kilo asked making a U-turn at the stop light. "She just left. I was walking her to her car that's how I missed your call. But come on I'll be right here." Lil Slim said then hung up and limped to the kitchen to get him something to drink and fifteen minutes later him and Lil Kilo were sitting on the couch talking. Lil Kilo had told Lil Slim about Ms. Coolwaters pulling him and Lil Fresh over and was now telling him about Maria. "So if Loreli headed home, I'm sure she gone call you cryin' once she get there and see her momma layed up dead." Lil Kilo said. "Yeah I know. I just hope she don't call and ask me to come over there with her. I ain't tryna see a dead body." Lil Slim said knowing that he was going to be the first person Loreli called once she seen that her mother was dead. "Ja'Zelle said that she made it look like a suicide so Loreli might feel like it's her fault that her momma killed herself." Lil Kilo said as Lil Slim's phone rung. "That might be her right there." Grabbing his phone off the table Lil Slim seen that it was his mother calling. "It's my momma." Lil Slim said then answered the phone. "Hello…" Pulling up at home Loreli seen that her mother's car was parked in the driveway which was a little unusual being that it was going on 1 o'clock in the afternoon. *'She must have took the day off or either forget something this morning and came back on her lunch break to get it.'* Loreli thought getting out of her mother's truck headed in the house. Letting herself in the house Loreli felt a wave of gloominess pass through her body as she stood in the living room. "Why is it so quiet in here?" Loreli wondered then yelled her mother's name but didn't get an answer. "MAMI!" Loreli yelled a little louder. *'Or maybe she got a tummy ache and is upstairs on the toilet.'* Loreli laughed hanging her jacket on the back of one of the kitchen chairs then crept up the stairs trying to sneak up on her mother. Tip Toeing up the stairs trying her best not to make a sound Loreli could hear her mother's cell phone ringing. Thinking that her mother was about to bust out of the bathroom Loreli stopped on the third step from the top until she heard the phone stop ringing. "Nawl she left not to long ago...okay I'll call an see." Lil Slim said into the phone talking to his mother about to hang up. "Okay momma I'm not gone forget, I'm doin' it now...I love you too." Lil Slim told his mother then hung up. "She tryna see if Loreli was still here. She said that Loreli's momma haven't showed up to work yet and everybody there is worried about her because she ain't picking up the phone." Lil Slim told Lil Kilo getting up off the couch to take some meat out the freezer for his mother. "She asked me to call Loreli to make sure everything was okay." Lil Slim said from the kitchen pulling a pack of smoked Salmon out the freezer. "You might wanna call her and let her know what moms said just to play it off anyway fool." Lil Kilo said looking back over the couch into the kitchen. "Yeah you right. Bring me my phone right quick." Lil Slim said running some warm water in the sink to sit the Salmon in. After hearing her mother's phone stop ringing Loreli stayed still for another second or so to see if her mother would make some noise but heard nothing and was about to take another step up the stairs until she heard her phone ringing down stairs in her jacket pocket. '*He picked the perfect time to call.*' Loreli smiled knowing exactly who was calling from the ring tone. Debating on if she should go back down stairs to answer her phone or keep sneaking up on her mother Loreli decided to keep sneaking up on her mother once her phone stopped ringing. "She didn't answer fool." Lil Slim told Lil Kilo who was sitting on the edge of the couch right beside Lil Slim so he could hear the sound of Loreli's voice when she answered the phone. "Call back." Lil Kilo said. Halfway down the hall to her mother's room Loreli felt that same gloomy feeling she felt standing in the living room again and started to wonder why until she heard her phone ringing again then a few seconds later heard her mother's phone ring. *"What in the world is up with these phones?"* Loreli thought. Standing in the middle of the hallway Loreli just knew for sure that her mother was about to walk out of her room and catch her. "Shoot!" Loreli mumbled smiling feeling tickled from the feeling of being caught trying to sneak up on her mother. But her mother never walked out of the room so Loreli started back sneaking. Creeping up on her mother's door Loreli seen that the door was cracked opened so she put her back up against the wall right beside it and listened. *'She must be sleep. It's to quiet in there.'* Loreli thought leaning off the wall slightly to peep through her mother's door. "She still not pickin' up fool." Lil Slim said hanging up the phone. "She probably got her phone on silent or something." "That or either she done seen the aftermath of Ja'Zelle's work." Lil Kilo said wondering how Ja'Zelle left Loreli's mother looking before she left. "Did Ja'Zelle say what she did to her?" Lil Slim asked trying to figure out how did Ja'Zelle kill Maria and make it look like a suicide. "Nawl she didn't say what she did. She just said that she made it look like a suicide. She probably made her hang or herself or some shit." Lil Kilo told Lil Slim pulling out his cell phone to see who was calling him. "Here go Lil Fresh." Lil Kilo said then answered the phone. "What up, where you at fool?" Lil Fresh asked Lil Kilo. "Over Lil Slim house, what up?" "Man I'm bout outta work fool. I'm down to four eggs outta that dozen we had."

Lil Fresh said. "Yeah I know. We all bout out. Lil Slim got some people down in Cashville so might be taking a trip soon to see what them niggas talkin' bout cause ain't nobody in the city gone be able to fill our order once we get ready to ree up." Lil Kilo told Lil Fresh then told him that they would sit down and talk about that later. "I think Buck from Cashville. If we bump into him when we down there he should be able to point us in the right direction. He a real street nigga." Lil Fresh said. "We tryna see how shit funa blow over with Loreli right now." Lil Kilo told Lil Fresh. "I'm tellin' you Lil Kilo, she should've been sent bout her way to fool. But keep me informed." Lil Fresh said then hung up. "What he talkin' bout fool?" Lil Slim asked as his phone started ringing again. Seeing that it was his mother calling him back Lil Slim answered and told his mother that Loreli didn't pick up the phone. "I hope everything's okay. Maria still isn't answering either." Lil Slim's mother said sounding worried. "Don't worry ma. I'm sure everything's okay. Get some work done and I'll see you when you get home." Lil Slim told his mother then hung up and told Lil Kilo that he was about to try to call Loreli back one more time. Standing in her mother's doorway traumatized Loreli's heart dropped seeing all the blood that was all over her mother's bed and floor. Loreli tried to turn and run but her feet felt like they were bolted down to the floor so Loreli stood there frightful staring at her mother holding a knife that was sticking out of her throat. "This don't seem real..." Loreli said to herself taking a step into her mother's room unconsciously. "If this was real, why aren't I crying?" Loreli said talking to herself steady walking towards her mother's bed. Now standing on the side of her mother's bed Loreli didn't feel anything as she stared down at her mother's lifeless body. Reaching down to close her mother's eyes that were wide open Loreli began to pray and apologize to her mother at the same time. Hearing her phone ring again after she was done praying brought Loreli out of the hypnotic like state of mind she was in. Now somewhat in her right state of mind Loreli was about to go get her phone but seen her mother's cell phone laying on the pillow next to her and picked it up to see who was calling back to back while she was trying to sneak up the stairs. Checking her mother's call log Loreli seen that she had over 50 missed calls, most of them from someone her mother saved in her phone as Ms. I. *'I wonder if that's Ms. Ivonne?'* Loreli thought checking her mother's text messages out of curiosity and seen that she was the last person her mother texted. "I'm so sorry mami…" Loreli whispered falling to her knees apologizing as she felt her heart break into a million pieces remembering that she erased all of her mother's text messages this morning without even reading her mother's last words to her. "Mami please forgive me." Loreli said closing her eyes as tears started to fall freely from her cheeks. It seemed like Loreli was more hurt from not reading and responding to her mother messages then anything and probably because she knew that her mother probably wouldn't have killed herself if she did. After a few minutes of crying Loreli opened her mother's phone back up and read the last message her mother sent her. The last part of the message shocked Loreli. *'P.S Keep Issac close to your heart my dear.'* Loreli read that part over and over trying to figure out exactly what her mother meant by keeping Issac close to her heart.

Loreli got up to go get her phone from downstairs to call the police and was telling herself that none of this was real. Pulling her phone out Loreli found herself calling Lil Slim back first instead of calling the police. "This her callin' back fool." Lil Slim told Lil Kilo grabbing his phone off the arm of the couch. "Put her on speakerphone." Lil Kilo told Lil Slim sitting up on the couch. "Hello…" Lil Slim said putting his phone on speaker. "Hello…" Lil Slim said again after Loreli didn't say anything. Lil Slim looked at Lil Kilo ready to hang up and call Loreli back because she was saying anything. Lil Kilo shrugged his shoulders then mouthed "Say it again." Lil Slim repeated his self. "Hellooo…Loreli?" Lil Slim said saying Loreli's name in a question. "My mother killed herself last night." Loreli said sounding numb about what she just said about her mother. "Oh…ummm…shit, you okay? I mean…umm…Ion know what to say boo. You need me to…" Lil Slim said trying to sound concerned like he didn't know that her mother was dead already. "Ja'Zelle musta made it look like a real suicide." Lil Kilo whispered to Lil Slim so that Loreli couldn't hear him. Lil Slim looked at Lil Kilo and shook his head. "I think she had a guilty conscience that's been eating her up on the inside because she tried to slit her wrist but I guess that wasn't working fast enough because she then took the knife and pushed it through her throat." Loreli said in that same numb voice. Lil Kilo and Lil Slim both squinted their faces up thinking about a knife being pushed through somebody's throat. "You don't seem to be too mournful and sad, you okay over there boo?" Lil Slim asked Loreli wondering why she was sounding like she haven't cried not one time. '*Why am I not crying like*

I just lost my mother?' Loreli thought. *'Did the love leave my heart for my mother after she told me about my daddy?'* Loreli questioned herself then told Lil Slim that she think apart of her love died for her mother after she told her that she knew about what happened to her daddy. Lil Slim nudged Lil Kilo in the side with his elbow and grinned. "I told you nigga." Lil Slim whispered listening to Loreli talk about her mother. "D'juan…" Loreli said calling Lil Slim by his middle name. Lil Slim paused. "What up boo?" "Promise me that you'll never forsake me and leave me lonely in this world. Because you're all I have now." Loreli said into the phone now sounding like she was about to cry. "I promise baby…" Lil Slim said without even having to think about it because he meant every word. After hanging up with Loreli Lil Slim sat back on the couch. "I told you I got her heart and her loyalty fool. Now yall niggas mightis well get ready because it's about to go down." Lil Slim told Lil Kilo who was thinking of a way to get their daddy's killer. "I know *exactly* how we can get next to her uncle bitch ass now." Lil Kilo said then told Lil Slim to make sure he found out when the funeral was. "After the funeral we gone follow him to the burial to see what kind of entourage he brought with him. Hopefully it's just him and a bodyguard. That way we can trail him from the burial and cut his ass off in traffic and do his ass in." Lil Kilo told Lil Slim who was listening intensively. "Ion wanna kill him in traffic. I wanna tie his ass up and get some answers. I wanna know the real story behind our daddy being killed." Lil Slim told Lil Kilo. "So Ima be the driver." Lil Slim added knowing that he wouldn't be able to move as fast as Lil Kilo and Lil Fresh would be able to. "Ima cut his ass off at a stop light and you and Lil Fresh hop out with them thangs out and pull the driver out the driver seat and put one in his dome then one of ya'll hop in the driver seat while the other hop in the back to make sure her uncle bitch ass don't try nothin'. And Ima follow ya'll." Lil Slim said visualizing everything that he was saying in his head. "What if he is the driver fool?" Lil Kilo asked Lil Slim. "What boss you know on that kinda level drive they self around fool?" Lil Slim said. "You right but we need to run this shit by Lil Fresh so he know what's goin' on." Lil Kilo said as his phone started ringing. Seeing that it was Neka calling him back Lil Kilo shot her a text message and told her that he would call her back in a minute. "Call that nigga back right quick to see where he at." Lil Slim told Lil Kilo getting up to go pee. After getting everything set up and running everything by Lil Fresh when he pulled up the three sat smoking a blunt tripping off the way they found their daddies killer. "Ima tell yall niggas what we need to do tho…" Lil Fresh said as Lil Kilo passed Lil Slim the blunt. "What's that?" Lil Slim asked just knowing that Lil Fresh was about to say something crazy. "We need to find out where his bitch ass keepin' them bricks at." Lil Fresh said. "We is talkin' bout tying up the head huncho of a Cartel ain't we?" "I didn't even think about that. And we been tryin' to figure out where we gone get our next order from. Drought Season bout to be over wit for real!" Lil Kilo said wondering how many kilos of cocaine Loreli's uncle had. "Shid me either. The only thing on my mind was findin' out the truth about our daddies and murder." Lil Slim said passing Lil Fresh the blunt. "Loreli said something about him staying in Texas if I'm not mistaken. I'll ask her again to make sure tho." That night Loreli layed under Lil Slim and cried her heart out trying to explain to him that she was now motherless and fatherless and really didn't know what to do. After expressing the love she had for him Loreli then told Lil Slim that her uncle the one that killed their fathers told her that she could come down there and stay with the rest of her family. "In Texas?" Lil Slim asked to make sure that's where Loreli said her uncle lived at. "Yes. I told him that I didn't want to move to Texas and he told me that we'll talk about it a little more after my mother's funeral." Loreli told Lil Slim then asked him would he miss her if she moved to Texas. Lil Slim thought about how it would be if Loreli just up and moved to Texas on him. "Hell yeah Ima miss you boo." Lil Slim said seriously then kissed Loreli on the forehead. "If you leave me I might forget how to walk again." Lil Slim joked trying to make Loreli smile. "I don't know what I'll do without my *personal* therapist here with me. Without you here all the feeling in my legs might go back out." Lil Slim said. "Don't leave me! Please don't leave me…" Lil Slim said sounding like a kid that was begging his mother not to leave him at daycare on the first day. Lil Slim was dead serious about him not wanting Loreli to leave him even though he was making a joke out of it and Loreli knew it and couldn't help but smile. "I'm not going to leave you baby." Loreli told Lil Slim. Lil Slim layed his head on Loreli's stomach then looked her in the eyes and told her that he loved her. "Issac, can I asked you something?" Loreli said after telling Lil Slim that she loved him more. Lil Slim looked back up and raised his eye brows. "Before I walked in you and your friends were sitting in the living room talking and ummm…" Loreli said trying to figure out how to word what she was trying to say. "Were you all talking about doing something to my uncle when he come up here?" That question caught Lil Slim completely off guard and Loreli could tell by the facial expression that Lil Slim was making that he didn't even know he was making. "Huh?" Was all Lil Slim said. Loreli sat Lil Slim up so that they were looking each other in the face. "Issac listen to me, I know that you and your friends are seeking revenge on my uncle for what he has done but he is a very powerful and dangerous man. You all have to be careful if this is what you're planning to do." Loreli said then asked Lil Slim if they were planning on doing something could he not to do it at her mother's funeral. "Please Issac, if not for me do it out of respect for her." Then the room got quiet. Lil Slim was trying to figure out how in the hell did Loreli know what they were talking about before she walked in the house while Loreli was trying to figure out why she wasn't feeling any type of remorse for her family when she knew for a fact that Lil Slim and his friends was about to try to kill her uncle. Lil Slim remembered telling Loreli the reason him and his niggas was in the streets and figured that she just put two and two together. *'I hate that it had to come to this boo.'* Lil Slim thought thinking about how they had to kill Loreli's mother to get to their daddies killer. *'But it did.'* Loreli was starting to figure out why she was feeling so cold on the inside towards her family. *'My uncle killed my daddy, my mother knew about it the whole time but looked me in the eyes and lied to me every time I asked her about it.'* Loreli thought. *'How could I have any sympathy for my family when it seems like nobody had enough sympathy for me to tell me the truth about what happened to my daddy?'* Lil Slim wrapped his arms around Loreli then whispered in her ear and told her that he was truly sorry to hear about her mother and that he never wanted her to leave his side. Loreli leaned forward and kissed Lil Slim softly on the lips. "Be careful Issac..." Loreli said to Lil Slim in almost a whisper.

Chapter 23

Two days before the funeral

"Let me call this nigga to see if he still tryna hit the mall." Lil Fresh said to his self after dropping one of his girlfriends back off at home. Pulling though the Chicken Shack drive-thru Lil Fresh called Lil Kilo to see where he was at. "What up foolie?" Lil Kilo answered. "Not shit, funa grab a bite to eat right quick. You still tryna hit the mall?" Lil Fresh asked Lil Kilo then dropped his window and ordered a 3-piece wing combo. "Nawl go head. I'm just now makin' it over here to the shop. I'm hollerin' at Cheese now about gettin' us another truck so we don't have to use Lil Slim's then Ima swing by and holla at Ol' Man and grab a couple more of them heavy duty sticks he got." Lil Kilo told Lil Fresh. "Aite bet. Just hit me when you done then. And make sure whatever's hangin' out the bottom of them bitches curl and not curve." Lil Fresh said then hung up just as one of those new black Chevy Tahoe trucks pulled up beside him. Thinking that it was Lil Slim pulling up beside him Lil Fresh dropped his window and the driver door and the door behind the driver on the Tahoe

306

swung open and two masked gunmen hopped out holding assault rifles. "Oh shit!" Was all Lil Fresh was able to say before the gunmen pulled him out of his car and threw him in the back of the Tahoe and tied his hands together and blind folded his eyes. "Aite that's cool. Good lookin' too Cheese. I knew you was gone come thru fa me." Lil Kilo told Cheese after Cheese told him that the truck would be ready to be picked up tomorrow morning. "No prob nephew. The only reason you gotta get it in the morning is because of the extra bullet proof stuff you wanted on there. But my manz said no later than 12 it'll be here." Cheese told Lil Kilo then told him to be careful with whatever he was about to get into. Pulling off from the car lot Lil Kilo headed in Big Ed's direction to pick up two AK-47's and a AR-15 that Lil Slim wanted specifically. After meeting up with Big Ed Lil Kilo dropped the guns off at The Chop House and ran into Ciara's look alike on his way back out the house. *Man I think this bitch stalkin' me.* Lil Kilo thought as he was walking towards his car and she was walking pass. "Hey Lil Keon." Amora joked remembering the time she asked Lil Kilo for his name and he told her Keon but Lil Fresh had already told her his nickname. Lil Kilo chuckled. "I see somebody gotta lil sense of humor *and* a lil tooty booty." Lil Kilo joked back looking at Amora's ass from the front of her body. "Brains beat beauty any day. But you must wear glasses if you calling this a tooty." Amora told Lil Kilo then turned to the side so that he could see how round it was in the stretch pants she had on as if Lil Kilo haven't peeped it already. *I should grab that big mufucker.* Lil Kilo thought then laughed and asked Amora for her number so that he could call her. "I gotta make a run but if you want to we can get up a lil later." Lil Kilo said pulling out his cell phone. "You ever swam in the ocean?" Amora asked Lil Kilo after giving him her number. "I ain't never swan in the ocean but I swam like a whale tho." Lil Kilo told Amora letting her know that he could handle that ocean she was talking about before she jogged off. Pulling off from The Chop House making his way towards the interstate Lil Kilo was about to call Neka to see if she was hungry until he heard some police sirens and seen some blue lights in his rearview mirror. "Fuckin' unmarks!" Lil Kilo said out loud noticing that it wasn't regular police cars pulling him over. *I'm glad I got to put those guns up before these racists muthafuckers decided to fuck with me.'* Lil Kilo thought as the driver door opened on the unmarked police car and a Mexican looking police officer got out. "This nigga don't even look like he speak English." Lil Kilo said to himself watching through his rearview mirror as the passenger door opened on the unmarked police car and another Mexican looking police officer got out and approached his car from the opposite side. "Look at her lil short thick ass with her hand on her gun ready to shoot." Lil Kilo said now watching both of the police officers as they seemed to start taking their time. Still looking out his rearview mirror Lil Kilo wondered why was the officer that got out the driver side of the unmarked police car looking like he was calling for back up when it was two of them already. Cutting his eye from the rearview mirror Lil Kilo looked up just in time to see a black SUV with dark tinted windows pull up beside him and two masked gunmen jump out holding assault rifles. After leaving from Loreli's house helping her sort through some of her mother's belongings Lil Slim felt like going to pay his daddy a visit. *'I ain't been out there to see you in a second Pops. I got some things I need to holler at you about.'* Lil Slim said to himself wishing that he had a blunt rolled up already. Halfway to his daddy's grave site Lil Slim tried to call Lil Kilo to make sure that everything was set to go with the truck but Lil Kilo didn't answer. *'That nigga should be done by now.'* Lil Slim thought then tried to call back but got the voicemail again. "Let me call Lil Fresh right quick, I know he probably done talked to Lil Kilo." Lil Slim said then tried to call Lil Fresh but Lil Fresh didn't answer either so Lil Slim called Big Ed to get him a smoke sack since he was right around the corner from him. "Lil Kilo came by about a hour or so ago to buy some straps. Ion know what ya'll got going on but like I told him, staying alive is the goal." Big Ed told Lil Slim before he left. Leaving Big Ed's spot Lil Slim pulled up at the corner store to get him some cigars and something to drink and was sitting at the pump rolling him a blunt when he noticed two black SUV's with dark tinted windows pull in behind him. *'Something ain't right about them bad boys right there.'* Lil Slim thought starting his truck up looking in his rearview mirror trying to see into the truck behind him but couldn't because of the tint that was on the window. "That's either the jump out boys or them jack boys and I ain't tryna see either one." Lil Slim said catching a funny vibe from the trucks behind him so he pulled off. Looking in his passenger side mirror while pulling off Lil Slim seen that the second truck that pulled in was pulling around the first truck and tried to cut him off but was a few seconds to late. Lil Slim had already smashed the gas pedal screeching off. "I knew it!" Lil Slim said looking back seeing that the driver of the first truck was out of his truck kneeling down pointing a gun towards his truck. '*Who tha fuck is these people?*' Lil Slim thought trying to swerve a little to cause the other truck to run off the road and dodge a bullet at the same time. "BOOM!" Lil Slim heard the gun go off then felt his truck swerve. "FUCK!" Lil Slim yelled trying to gain control over his truck knowing that his tire was flat. "BOOM!" Lil Slim heard the gun go off again and felt his other tire pop which caused his truck to do a complete 360. "Shit!" Lil Slim said trying to figure out who the fuck was after him and how in the hell did they know what kind of car he was in. By the time Lil Slim's truck stopped spinning both of the trucks that pulled in behind him at the gas station was now blocking him off and four masked gunmen hopped out walking towards his truck all holding assault rifles. Feeling as if they've been tied up for hours Lil Kilo, Lil Fresh and Lil Slim all sat next to each other trying to figure out what was going on. No one being able to talk or see because of the thick cloth that covered their mouth and eyes they all just sat there not even knowing that they were beside each other. Hearing the door shut to whatever room they were in Lil Kilo counted the sounds of the footsteps to determine how many people came into the room. '*That sound like eight different footsteps. Four people just came in.*' Lil Kilo thought as the room got back quiet for a second. "Quitarse los ojos vendados!" They all heard a voice say in Spanish and immediately after heard footsteps walking towards them then felt the blindfolds being lifted from their eyes. Blinking his eye lids trying to let his pupils adjust to the light in the room Lil Kilo looked to his side and seen his niggas tied up beside him and already knew what this was about. *'Those cops wasn't Mexicans they were Puerto Ricans. That whole thing was a set up!'* Lil Kilo thought looking up at the Puerto Rican standing in front of them who he assumed was the head huncho they were planning on tying up. Sitting next to Lil Kilo was Lil Fresh who just shook his head because he already knew what was going on. Lil Slim on the other hand knew exactly what was going on as well but was trying to figure out if Loreli set them up. *'She couldn't have tho because she don't even know we did it.'* Lil Slim thought trying to be rational about the situation. The Puerto Rican that they all figured was Loreli's uncle said something else in Spanish and the three henchmen that were standing in the room with them left. "Now." The Puerto Rican said taking a step towards Lil Kilo, Lil Fresh and Lil Slim then introduced himself. "I'm Pedro." The Puerto Rican said looking them all in the eyes. "I'm pretty sure you know why you're here under these conditions." Pedro told them then bent down to retie his seven thousand dollar Ferragamo dress shoe that he had hand stitched while he was in Italy that wasn't even untied. *'This some shit a nigga see in a gangsta movie.'* Lil Fresh thought. *'This nigga just untied his shoe just to tie it back.'* "But if you don't know why you're here under these conditions…" Pedro said then stopped and fixed his cuff link. "It's because you had my sister killed." Pedro said then paused again to let what he just said sink in. "I know exactly who you are and I'm pretty sure you know by now who I am. You killed my sister because you knew that would get me here and you thought that you would have the chance to kill me. Am I right?" Pedro asked now pacing slowly back and forth in front of them with his hands behind his back. "And the main reason behind it all is because I killed your da…" Pedro was about to say. "No. Let me correct that. They killed themselves." Pedro said. Pedro could see the anger start to rise in all three of them from the look in their eyes so he explained to them exactly how it all started and ended. Pedro told them all that he could remember. "My brother told your father Kilo that the only way out was death before any kind of business was conducted." Pedro said pointing at Lil Kilo then told them about the successful run he had with their daddies. "I've never in my life met a group of men like them. They were loyal and stuck together. I loved them so seeing them move up in the game is something that I made sure I did. But as time passed, I began to see it in your daddy's face." Pedro paused while looking at Lil Slim thinking about his daddy. "I seen it in Slim's face that he was getting tired of the game." Pedro said looking off towards the window. "But they knew too much to let them walk away. And as bad as I wanted to let them, I couldn't. I must follow the code of conduct or my life will be taken as well my friend. There was nothing I could do." Pedro said then got quiet again. "Now." Pedro said again. "I've told you everything my friend. I've even told you why you were here. So now my friend I'm going to *show* you something then *tell* you one more thing." Pedro told them then yelled something in Spanish and one of his henchmen came walking in holding a large manila envelope and handed it to Pedro then turned and left the room. After the door was shut Pedro opened the large manila envelope and showed them pictures of their mothers, where they lived and where they worked. He even showed them what kind of cars they drove. "Like I said my friend I know everything. I have men outside of each one of those ladies house ready to kidnap and kill as we speak. All it takes is one phone call." Pedro's whole attitude changed instantly and the evilness could be hear in his voice as he showed them the monster that he could be by having their mothers killed if he wanted them killed. "But that all can be avoided with the consent from each of you." Pedro said now sounding like he was sounding when he was telling them stories about their daddy. Pedro said something else in Spanish and the same henchmen came back into the room and grabbed the manila envelope and left out the room again. *'This nigga mean bizniz.'* Lil Fresh thought. *'Fuck he mean this shit can be avoided with a consent?'* Lil Kilo thought trying to figure out what it was that Pedro wanted them to agree to. Lil Slim knew exactly what he was getting at. "I know you must be wondering what kind of consentient you must agree to in order to save not only your mother's life but yours as well..?" Pedro said putting his hands behind his back again. "Am I right my friend...?" Pedro asked them like they could say something. Everything became tensed in the room while they all waited to see what Pedro was about to say. "Well, that consentient is..." Pedro said then paused again to look each of them in the eyes coldly to let them know that he was going to stand on his next words. "Either the three of you join the Cartel and pick up where your daddy left off or you and the rest of your family will join them..."

To Be Continued